SO SURE OF DEATH

Also by Dana Stabenow

The Liam Campbell Series

Fire and Ice

The Kate Shugak Series

A Cold Day for Murder
A Fatal Thaw
Dead in the Water
A Cold-Blooded Business
Play with Fire
Blood Will Tell
Killing Grounds
Breakup
Hunter's Moon

The Star Svensdotter Series

Second Star
A Handful of Stars
Red Planet Run

DANA STABENOW

SO SURE OF DEATH

A LIAM CAMPBELL MYSTERY

A DUTTON BOOK

DUTTON
Published by the Penguin Group
Penguin Putnam Inc., 375 Hudson Street, New York, New York 10014, U.S.A.
Penguin Books Ltd, 27 Wrights Lane, London W8 5TZ, England
Penguin Books Australia Ltd, Ringwood, Victoria, Australia
Penguin Books Canada Ltd, 10 Alcorn Avenue, Toronto, Ontario, Canada M4V 3B2
Penguin Books (N.Z.) Ltd, 182–190 Wairau Road, Auckland 10, New Zealand

Penguin Books Ltd, Registered Offices: Harmondsworth, Middlesex, England

First published by Dutton, a member of Penguin Putnam Inc.

First Printing, October, 1999
10 9 8 7 6 5 4 3 2 1

 REGISTERED TRADEMARK—MARCA REGISTRADA

LIBRARY OF CONGRESS CATALOGING-IN-PUBLICATION DATA
Stabenow, Dana.
   So sure of death : a Liam Campbell mystery / Dana Stabenow.
     p. cm.
   ISBN 0-525-94519-9 (alk. paper)
   I. Title.
   PS3569.T1249S6 1999
   813'.54—dc21   99-25121
                                    CIP

Printed in the United States of America
Set in Cochin
Designed by Leonard Telesca

PUBLISHER'S NOTE
This novel is a work of fiction. Names, characters, places, and incidents either are the products of the author's imagination or are used fictitiously, and any resemblance to actual persons, living or dead, business establishments, events, or locales is entirely coincidental.

For
Don "Slim" Stabenow
1927–1998
Home is the sailor, home from the sea
And the hunter, home from the hill.

SO SURE OF DEATH

ONE

"Now, there is the sound of someone not flying his own plane."

"Shut up and breathe."

Wyanet Chouinard sank obediently, into a modified Horse Stance as the float plane roared overhead. She was a grown woman, the owner and proprietor of her own air taxi service and the mother of a soon-to-be-adopted son. She didn't have to take orders from anyone, but she would from this one old man.

The old man was Moses Alakuyak, short, thick through the chest and shoulders, with his Yupik mother's brown skin and flat cheekbones and hints of his unknown Anglo father in his height, in the high bridge of his nose, the roundness of his eyes, the suppressed curl and color of his hair. Some called him a shaman. Some called him a drunk. On occasion, he was both, and neither.

This morning he was a teacher of tai chi, a sifu, and he demanded his student's full attention and submission. He got it, too, the little despot, Wy thought without rancor. He was standing to her left and a step behind. She could feel his eyes on her, checking the level of her hands, the depth of the cup of her palms, the tilt of her chin, the angle behind her bent knees, the straightness of her spine, the focus of her eyes.

"Lower," he said. "How'n hell you supposed to strengthen your thigh muscles for the real work if you don't push them in Horse Stance?"

She made a silent and anatomically impossible suggestion as to where he could put his Horse Stance, and bent her knees, which after ten minutes were starting to tremble, to a deeper angle. Her center of gravity seemed off, and she swayed back an inch or so. There. She was supposed to feel the balls and heels of her feet rooted to the earth, the crown of her head suspended from a string. Root from below, suspend from above. Her breathing deepened. Her eyelids lowered, her gaze unfocused on the horizon.

The sneaky little son of a bitch waited until she was completely engrossed in the first position of the Yang style of tai chi chuan before he brought out the big gun. "How long you gonna wait before you talk to Liam again?"

She couldn't control the start his words gave her, but she could—and did—bite down on her verbal response. She said nothing, trying to recapture the peace of mind that had been hers only moments before.

"It's going on three months, Wy," Moses said. He stood upright and walked around to face her. "Too stubborn, is that it? Too damn proud to make the first move?"

She stayed in position, staring straight ahead as if she could bore through his skull with her eyes. If only.

He waited. He was good at it. It was six a.m. on a sunny Sunday morning in July. The birds were singing or honking or chirping or croaking. At the foot of the cliff the massive Nushagak River moved by with stately unconcern. Wy had a six-week contract to fly supplies into an archaeological dig ten miles west of Chinook Air Force Base. Moses had volunteered to take Tim to his fish camp upriver for the silver run, away from the rough crowd of boys he had fallen in with during the school year. He'd learn to run a fish wheel, salt eggs, fillet and smoke salmon and, she hoped, realize what a rush it was to earn money of his own. Best of all, he'd be out of the reach of his birth mother, who was prone to fly in from Ualik and, after a night at the bars, shove her way into Wy's house and demand Tim's return, even if the last time he'd been in her custody he'd wound up in the hospital, broken, bruised and bleeding.

All in all, the next month looked positively rosy, especially when she compared it to the previous three years. She was marginally solvent, content in her work and her family, and if the lawyer handling Tim's adoption called a little too frequently for more money, it was summertime and the flying was frantic. She could hear the cash register ringing on every takeoff and the cash drawer sliding out on every landing.

So what if it was three months since she'd spoken to Liam Campbell? There were other fish in the sea, and in particular, there were a whole hell of a lot of other fish in Bristol Bay, with and without fins. The small voice that pointed out that she had allowed only Liam to swim up her stream and spawn could and would be ignored. She was content. She used the word like a mantra. She didn't need anything more—or anyone else—to complicate her life.

Wy became aware that her teeth were clenched so hard that her jaw ached, and made a conscious effort to relax.

Moses, naturally, persisted in attempting to suck the well-being right out of her. "You want him. He wants you." Her sifu snorted. "And it sure as hell ain't like you're getting it anywhere else."

"I have Tim to consider." Her voice had a pronounced edge to it.

Moses pounced. "Give your menfolks a tad more credit than that, Wy. Liam's a grown man, and he had a son of his own. He knows how to handle kids. And as for Tim, hell, having a man—the same man—around on a regular basis would be a new experience for him. Would teach him all men don't get drunk and hit. A good thing for him to learn, I'd've thought. Of course, that's just me."

Wy felt her teeth clamp together again. "I didn't mean it that way."

"Oh, really? How did you mean it, exactly?"

Her neck got warm. "I meant that I have to look good to the adoption board. They look at your lifestyle, at your habits."

"Ah." Moses gave a judicious nod. "I see. So the adoption board won't let kids go to prospective parents who have the audacity to have healthy, normal lives of their own."

The warmth seeped from her neck up into her cheeks.

Moses' eyebrows, thick and black, rose into interrogatory points. "Anything to say about that? Besides 'I'm sorry for trying to bullshit you, Sifu'?"

She hadn't.

"Good," he said briskly. "On your feet."

She rose shakily to her full height, five feet eight inches; five inches taller than Moses, not that it ever seemed like that much of an advantage. Her dark blond hair, streaked with gold by the summer sun, had come loose from its ponytail. Thankful to have something to do with her hands, she made a business out of tying it up again. That done, there was nowhere to run. She blotted her forehead on her sleeve and sought refuge in work. "I've got an early morning flight, I'd better get going."

"You said some harsh things to each other in May," Moses said to her retreating back. "Hurtful things. Especially you."

That did it. She spun around, her face furious with anger, shame and guilt. "I handed him my heart and he ate it for lunch. I am not on the dinner menu!"

Pleased with what she felt was a splendid exit line, she turned to march up the stairs and into her house.

From behind her she heard Moses' voice, acerbic and irascible as always. "How about dessert?"

The slam of the door was his answer.

The old man sighed and shook his head. "Youth is wasted on the young."

He waited for the voices to kick in. For a change, they didn't. Mostly they were insistent, forceful, regular spiritual bulldozers, determined to make him a legend in his own time.

He stepped to the edge of the cliff and looked at the beach below, strewn with boulders and tree trunks, the occasional fifty-five-gallon drum, the odd Styrofoam cooler. It wasn't that far down, but far enough. He could shut the voices up for good. That option had always been open to him, from the time he first heard them when he was twelve and they made him tell his mother that his father was going to kill her. She didn't listen, of course, no one ever did, but that didn't make the voices let up any.

They seldom told him anything straight out, though, and they had a marked tendency to be both insistent and peremptory. Sometimes he wondered if, in seventy-eight years of a very full life, he had perhaps acquired enough wisdom to make his own judgments, his own rulings, his own estimates of what kind of trouble his extended family, stretching from Newenham to Nome, needed his help to get out of.

Not that anyone ever looked happy when they saw him coming. Foresight, the open eye that looked inward to the future, was more of a curse than a blessing. Uilililik, the Little Hairy Man who snatched up children and took them away, never to be seen again, was more welcome in the villages than he was.

He thought of Cassandra, and sighed again. Doomed forever to tell the truth, and equally doomed forever to be disbelieved. She'd died young. Lucky for her. He stepped back from the edge of the cliff, from the fifty-foot drop to the vast expanse of southward-moving water. It wasn't the first time. It wouldn't be the last.

As he walked around the old but well-maintained house set twenty-five feet from the cliff's edge, he thought about the float plane on a short final for the elongated, freshwater lake that served as Newenham's seaplane base. Wy had been right; that had definitely been someone not flying their own plane. There was no need to be at full RPMs on final; it didn't do anything but make a lot of noise and move up the time for an overhaul. Hell, there was no need to be at full RPMs after takeoff, or at least not for long. Once the plane was in the air the pilot should back off on the throttle and the prop pitch. If he didn't, the mini-sonic booms generated by the tip of the prop exceeding the speed of sound were enough to rattle windowpanes for a mile in every direction. The sound was a dead giveaway that the guy or the gal on the yoke didn't have to pay to fix his or her own engine. Or had enough money not to care about maintenance costs.

But this pilot—ah, now, this pilot. Moses smacked his lips and grinned. There had been a gold shield on the pilot-side door, bright with gilt. Wyanet Chouinard might fancy herself content with her life, but she was about to receive a first-class wake-up call. Good.

Meanwhile, he squinted at the sun. Seven-thirty, he estimated, give or take five minutes. "About time for a beer."

He might not be able to drown the voices, but he could and would drown them out, at least for a time.

He heard Charlie crying and sat up to go to him. A solid object whacked him in the forehead. "Ouch! Shit!"

Liam Campbell sat in the narrow bunk, rubbing his head. While his vision cleared, he remembered that he was still sleeping on board a twenty-eight-foot Bristol Bay gillnetter that had seen better decades. Since moving onto the *Dawn P,* he had begun to think longingly of his office chair, which had served as his bed for the first month of his posting to Newenham, in spite of the fact that the chair had a tendency to roll out from under him at three in the morning. At least his office had a higher ceiling than the low bulkhead on this frigging boat. And it didn't smell like an old, wet wool sock.

The pain in his forehead faded and he remembered what had woken him: the sound of his dead son's tears. Before the sense of loss could take hold and pull him under, as it had too many times before during in the last two years, he swung his feet to the floor, and swore again when he splashed down into a half inch of water. His office didn't need its bilge pumped out every morning, either.

This was all Wy Chouinard's fault. He wasn't sure why, but if he gave himself some time he was sure he could come up with three or four excellent reasons.

He struggled into sweats that felt clammy against his skin and stamped up to the harbormaster's office, where the public shower was, for a change, empty. He stood a long time under hot water, and felt marginally better when he came out. Shaved and with his uniform on, he felt almost human again. He checked the knot of his tie, smoothed the line of his left lapel and stepped back for a critical survey of as much of him as he could see in the square little mirror hung over the sink.

The uniform was barely three months old, and tailor-made back in Anchorage. He would have hotly denied that he liked what the uniform did for his looks, but he put it on and his shoulders straightened, his spine stiffened and his chin went up. He'd wanted to be an Alaska state trooper from the time one had visited his fifth-grade class at Chugach Elementary, and nothing that had happened to him since, not even the deaths in Denali Park, had changed the feeling of pride he took in donning the uniform. It was fabric, that was all, a mixture of cotton and wool and synthetic fibers, a slack bundle of blue and gold on the hanger; but on him, it was a tacit investment in the might and majesty of the law.

He plucked a piece of lint from the bill of his cap, pulled it on so that the bill was at precisely the right angle over his eyes and emerged onto the dock to come face-to-face with Jimmy Barnes, the Newenham harbormaster.

Most days, Jimmy looked as if he should have been wearing a red suit with big black boots, with a white beard down to his waist. This morning, his usually rosy round cheeks were pale. Liam's hand dropped instinctively to the polished butt of the nine-millimeter Smith and Wesson automatic holstered on his right hip. "What's the matter, Jimmy?"

"I got an emergency call. A boat was found adrift off the coast about halfway between here and Togiak." He swallowed hard, as if convincing his stomach contents to stay where they were. "Crew of seven. All dead."

"Seven?"

Jimmy nodded. "Seven."

Christ. Liam absorbed this in silence. "Who found it?"

"The Jacobsons on the *Mary J* were drifting just outside of Metervik Bay. They saw the *Marybethia* come out of Kulukak on the tide. They didn't think anything of it until it got closer. Larry said you could see she wasn't under power, and then when they got closer you could see the burn marks on the cabin. She was low in the water, too."

"Burn marks? It had been on fire?"

Jimmy nodded, looking sick, and Liam understood why. On a boat, there was nothing worse than a fire. On a boat in Alaskan waters, which were an average temperature of forty degrees and where hypothermia set in after two minutes' immersion, it was especially deadly. Nowhere to run, no place to hide. "Didn't they have a skiff, or a life raft?"

Jimmy nodded. "Both. The skiff was tied off to the stern, and the raft hadn't been popped. Maybe the fire burned too fast. Maybe they were all asleep, and died of smoke inhalation."

"Where is the boat now?"

"Larry and his dad towed it into Kulukak Bay. It's tied up to a slip in the small boat harbor."

"Can you fly in? Is there a strip?"

Jimmy nodded. "A long one. There's a road to a gold mine a couple of miles inland. They fly supplies into Kulukak strip on a Herc at least once a week."

"Okay. Thanks, Jimmy." Liam pulled the billed cap with the Alaska State Troopers insignia on the brim low over his eyes and headed for the line of vehicles parked between the two docks leading down into the boat harbor. The white Blazer with the same insignia on the door as his cap was midway down the row.

He didn't start the engine at once. What would be the best way to approach her? It didn't have to be personal; he was a state trooper, she was a pilot, there was a case, he needed a ride, the state paid top dollar. Pretty simple.

Except that nothing was simple when it came to Wyanet Chouinard. Perhaps it would be best to keep things formal. A phone call from his office, instead of a knock on her door. A door that could be slammed in his face. Of course, she could hang up on him, too.

He drove to the post, a small, neat building with a parking lot out back enclosed by a twelve-foot chain-link fence. When he had arrived in Newenham that spring the lot had held a sedan, a pickup and a dump truck. The Cadillac Seville had been sold at auction for restitution of a fine imposed on its drug-dealing owner, and the International pickup had been ransomed by an angry fisherman who had thought parking in a handicapped zone was his god-given right. Liam still hadn't been able to find out who the dump truck belonged to, or why it had been impounded. It had since been joined by a gray Ford Ranger pickup with 103,000 miles on it, the vehicle of one Gust Toyukak, who had drunk and driven one too many times. License and truck both had been deemed forfeit by the local magistrate. The pickup would be sold at auction later that year.

He walked up the steps and opened the door.

There was someone sleeping in his chair. Shades of Goldilocks, although this Goldilocks was older and a brunette. The chair was tipped back and her feet were crossed on his desk. She was in uniform, dark blue pants with gold stripes down the side seams, long-sleeved lighter blue shirt with dark blue pocket flaps, dark blue tie. If he was not mistaken, the uniform of his own service.

He stepped inside and let the door shut, loudly. The woman sat up with a jerk, took Liam in with one glance and popped to attention. "Trooper Diana Prince, reporting for duty, sir."

She was almost as tall as Liam was, at least six-one, and that before her boot heels. With her boot heels she looked him straight in the eye. Everything else was height-weight proportionate, in spades. Her eyes were a clear gray and thickly lashed, her black curls were cropped short and her pale skin looked susceptible to sunburn. There was a set of suitcases stacked near the door, maroon leather, bulging at the sides.

"I'm sorry, sir, I overnighted in Lake Clark on the way down from Anchorage and left pretty early this morning. I guess I was tired when I got in."

"How'd you get in the door?"

"Mamie at dispatch has a key. Sir."

"Hold the sirs, I'm a trooper just like you," Liam said.

Maybe now. She didn't say the words out loud, but they hovered in the air regardless. She knew his history, all right.

Just as well. Better she should know the story going in, how Liam had been busted down from sergeant to trooper because five people had frozen to death in Denali Park on his watch. He hadn't been the trooper who had made the decision not to check out the call, but the two troopers who had worked directly under his supervision had, and someone's head had to roll to satisfy the community's not altogether unjustified cries for blood. So Liam had been broken in rank and transferred in disgrace to Newenham, a town of two thousand on the southwestern edge of the Alaskan coast. The next landmass over was Siberia, and Liam was well aware of the inference to be drawn.

It had taken thirty-six hours for that family to die, and for the troopers not to respond to repeated calls reporting their disappearance. It had not been the Alaska State Troopers' finest hour, and Liam felt very much on probation in his new posting. It didn't help that the dead were Natives, and that a large portion of the population of Newenham and its environs was also Native.

All this Trooper Diana Prince would know, and probably

more. It seemed to Liam as if the last two years of his life had
been lived largely on the front pages of every daily newspaper in
the state; the automobile accident, Jenny's coma, Charlie's death,
the trial, the drunk driver's second arrest by none other than the
surviving member of the family, Liam himself. The deaths in Denali were the nadir of three horrible years, all of which made for
fine reading in the Sunday papers, oh yes indeed.

He pulled himself together. "John Barton brief you on the
post?"

"Yes, sir."

"It's Liam. Call me Trooper Campbell in front of civilians."

"All right, s— Liam. I'm Diana."

She smiled, and it was a revelation, a broad, thousand-watt
beam that lit her eyes and transformed her face into that of a little girl's—enthusiastic, energetic, optimistic, all illusions intact
and trumpeting a touching allegiance to truth, justice and the
American way. She probably still believed in honor. She was un-
doubtedly willing to lay down her life for duty. "When did you
graduate from the academy?" Liam said.

"Last year," Diana Prince said promptly.

How the hell did you get a seven-step posting? Liam wondered, and knew without having to ask. Newenham was a Bush
posting, which meant troopers assigned to it received a seven-
step pay increase in recognition of the fact that they were living
and working in the back of beyond. Because of the high pay, and
because retirement was calculated on the last years you worked,
these posts were competed for fiercely by troopers with enough
seniority to make it stick.

Newenham was an exception. The previous first sergeant assigned to the post had publicly screwed up a very high profile
case, and then capped his activities in the area by impregnating
the trooper also assigned there. He should have been removed
from his posting immediately; that he was not was due to fa-
voritism within the good-old-boy trooper hierarchy. Corcoran
had lasted ten years in Newenham, to the outrage of the community and the detriment of the troopers. By the time he left, the
sour smell of the posting was evident as far away as Juneau.

At minimum staffing, a post this size should have had a first sergeant and two troopers assigned to it. In the three months since Liam's arrival, Liam had been it.

No, Newenham was not the usual seven-step plum. Nobody wanted to take it on. The more superstitious among the force might even have said it was bad luck to be posted there. His boss, Lieutenant John Dillinger Barton, supervisor of Section E and Liam's boss both in Glenallen and Newenham, had sent Liam to Newenham for two reasons: one, to tuck him safely out of sight until the fallout from the Denali debacle had deteriorated to a less toxic level, and two, in John's words, "to take the fucking hoodoo off that posting."

And now here was Trooper Diana Prince, John's latest exorcist, all fresh-faced and newly minted and ready to go out and be a hero. Liam made a mental resolve to go through any doors second. "How'd you get here?"

"I flew."

"Commercial?"

She shook her head. "I brought in one of the new Cessnas."

His gaze sharpened. "Floats or wheels?"

"Floats. The gear's coming on Alaska Airlines."

Shit, Liam thought. No need to call Wy now. A couple of hours alone in a plane in the middle of nowhere promoted personal intercourse. A flight to—where had it been? that murder-suicide in Dot Lake?—was how they had first met. "Good," he said, tearing himself from that memory as well. He resettled his cap on his head and sternly quelled the rumble of queasiness that always precipitated his reluctant rise to any altitude above sea level. "Let's go."

"Where?" she said, following him out the door.

"Kulukak."

"What's there?"

"Bodies."

TWO

Chinook Air Force Base was forty miles south of Newenham. It was a small base that had no defensible reason for existence after the invention of the ICBM and, later, the fall of the Berlin Wall, other than as a demonstration of the personal power in Congress of the senior senator from Alaska. The senior senator had outlasted just about everyone else in that august body with the exception of Strom Thurmond, and so by a process of attrition had in the fullness of time procured for himself the chair of the Senate Appropriations Committee. It was a position uniquely qualified to throw pork in Alaska's direction and this the senior senator did with an enthusiasm unequaled since Huey Long brought home the bacon for Louisiana. It made the senior senator immensely popular with his constituents and guaranteed his reelection until such time as he chose to retire, or until he killed himself surfing in Hawaii, which was his main hobby, after politics. His tan looked great on television, too.

The archaeological dig sat ten miles west of the base, from which the sound of F-15s doing touch-and-goes was faint but audible, an intrusion of modern noise into a prehistoric ruin. Evidence had been found at Tulukaruk of human habitation going back two thousand years. The old ones had known what they were doing, Wy thought as she circled for a landing; the settlement had been built on a confluence of two rivers and three streams, all prime salmon waters. The rivers were the Snake and the Weary, the streams the Kayaktak, the Amakayak and the Aluyak, or King Salmon Stream, Humpy Stream and Dog

Stream, the kinds of salmon that ran up each stream and accounted for the settlement being built there in the first place.

The runs were still plentiful enough that silver backs of salmon gleamed up through the water as the Super Cub circled overhead. They hovered in groups of three to a dozen, shoulder to shoulder, noses pointing determinedly upstream. Wy wondered why the villagers had ever left.

But left they had, some three hundred years before, according to Professor Desmond X. McLynn, Ph.D., University of Arizona 1969, archaeologist, and teacher at the University of Alaska, Fairbanks. He could have hauled a four-wheeler to the Air Force base and driven to the site, he could have hired a skiff down the coast and up the river, but for reasons best known to Professor Desmond X. McLynn, Ph.D. and archaeologist, he chose to fly. The site's airstrip was makeshift at best and liberally adorned with boulders and hummocks. Although Wy's Cub was equipped with tundra tires, the bluff upon which the village had perched so many years ago stretched only eleven hundred feet in length before it dropped forty-five precipitous feet straight down into the Snake. The Snake, a wide river that slithered southeast in a series of lazy S-curves, had over the years swallowed its share of boats, planes and snow machines, along with their drivers. The prospect of immersion made for a brisk few seconds during critical periods of flight, such as landing and takeoff.

Wy lined the Cub up on final. The Cub hit a thermal and the plane bucked, only slightly, but enough for Professor Desmond X. McLynn's hands to slap down on the back of her seat. "What's wrong?"

The Cub's wheels touched down in what would have been a runway paint job if there had been any paint, or any true runway, for that matter. Professor Desmond X. McLynn's rapid respiration could be heard over the sound of the headset. Wy didn't much care for the pompous little ass, but it served no purpose to scare him to death and she kicked the rudder over as soon as ground speed allowed, bringing the Cub around to halt a hundred feet short of the abyss.

The engine died and she folded back the door and got out to assist her passenger. His face was pale and his watery blue eyes showed a rim of white all the way around their irises. "Here we are, sir," she said cheerfully.

McLynn was a fussy little man in his fifties who acted the age of most of the artifacts he dug up. His face was screwed into a perpetual frown of dissatisfaction, as if upon assembling the pieces to the puzzles of the past, the one essential fragment upon which the whole picture would be built had fallen out of the box and was lost forever. His conversations with Wy over the last month of flights in and out of the dig had consisted of one long whine: why did they have to fly such a small plane, why wasn't there a proper runway, why couldn't he have electricity on site, why couldn't he have fresh milk every day? Fresh milk wasn't available in Newenham every day, let alone Tulukaruk. Wy knew this because she had a son who could flatfoot a quart in one gulp.

McLynn recovered enough to take his bag and stagger off to a large olive-green tent. It was made of heavy canvas and was pitched twenty feet from the edge of the cliff. The door flaps were closed and fastened against the stiffening breeze. He must really feel sick, because he usually headed straight to the dig, which consisted of two twelve-foot-square excavations, covered with another canvas tent the twin of the first. The breeze at the top of the bluff was brisk and as McLynn untied the flap of the first tent the wind pulled it out of his hands. The flap ties on the second tent held, although its olive-green sides billowed concave and convex with sharp *pops*. It sounded a little like a cap gun going off.

Wy began unloading McLynn's supplies. Said supplies consisted of, among other essentials, four loaves of Wonder bread, a case each of Spam, shredded wheat, Carnation instant milk, baked beans, Nutter-Butter cookies, and enough Sterno to power one of the C-130s over at Chinook for a search-and-rescue mission to Round Island. The dig sat on one of the best fishing rivers south of the Wood River Mountains, in the middle of one of the best berry-picking areas on the Bay. Wy would have thought a dip net and a basket would have satisfied all McLynn's culinary requirements, but it wasn't her camp.

The back of the Cub was empty and the pile of boxes waist-high when she stopped to stretch and admire the view. It was spectacular. The Snake, its water shining like silver scales in the sun, curled and coiled back on itself, a convoluted journey from source, One Lake, to outflow, Bristol Bay. Bristol Bay in turn stretched two hundred miles between Port Molar on the Alaska Peninsula to Cape Newenham on the mainland. She stood on the Nushagak Peninsula, a southwesterly thumb of land that hitched a ride on weather originating from the vast blue expanse of water that stretched west of the Aleutian Peninsula to the Bering Strait.

A region one fifth the size of Texas, its winds blew hell for leather across Bristol Bay out of the northeast from October on, and then in March turned around and blew from the southwest for the next six months. It made for interesting air time. Wy flew daily over the remains of planes whose pilots had not paid proper respect to Bristol Bay's weather. What really gave her the creeps were the wrecks she couldn't see, the planes and boats lying at river and sea bottom, slowly silting over, providing housing for anything with a shell or a fin that cared to move in. Wy, like many of her Alaskan generation, couldn't swim. Not that it would matter, as the water was too cold to survive in for long. "There are old pilots and there are bold pilots," Bob DeCreft had declaimed once, "but there are no old, bold pilots." She also remembered him saying that "any landing you walk away from is a good landing," but Wy had always found it more prudent to stay in the air until you had a runway in front of you.

Bristol Bay's topography ran anywhere from tundra that often seemed to lie lower than sea level to the five-thousand-foot peak of Mount Oratia. Keep going three hundred miles farther north and fifteen thousand more feet up and you'd find Denali, the highest mountain in North America. In between lay icy glaciers, narrow, windy passes, grassy plateaus, heavily wooded bays, thousands of springs, brooks, creeks, streams, rills and rivers, lakes that ranged from shallow ponds to narrow fjords, sandy, soggy, silty river deltas and hundreds of miles of beaches. A cartographer's wet dream. The only stop between Newenham and the Kamchatka Peninsula of Siberia was the Pribilof Islands. The Pribilofs, where German tourists made Kodak moments of the seal harvest, horrifying Europeans and infuriating the islanders.

Wy grinned to herself. A late and not very lamented one-term governor of the state had proclaimed, and on prime time, too, that nature simply could not be allowed to run wild. On that, if nothing else, the people of the Pribilofs agreed with him. The people of the European Community did not, but then they didn't vote in Alaska.

A teeming marine life, including everything from herring to walruses to gray whales, had once provided for the support and maintenance of one of the healthiest and most stable populations of indigenous human inhabitants anywhere in the world. Their modern descendants, the Yupik, still fished the same rivers, hunted the same moose and caribou and walrus and duck and geese, picked the same berries as their ancestors had. The only difference was that present-day Yupik hunted from skiffs with outboard engines instead of kayaks, and four-wheelers and snow machines instead of dog sleds, and much of the time they did it commercially, for sale and not for subsistence. In a good year, Bristol Bay contributed as much as sixteen percent of the world's catch of red salmon.

In bad years, such as last year, they could barely feed themselves, something that heated up talks for rural preference for subsistence every year in Juneau.

Wy raised her face to the sun and drew in a breath of pure enjoyment. There was something for everyone in Bristol Bay. You could fish salmon, sport or commercial or subsistence, you could hunt caribou or moose or bear, you could run a trapline in winter, you could pick blueberries and salmonberries in summer, you could beachcomb for glass floats and walrus tusks—you could, if you chose, simply sit on your butt and admire the scenery. Most of the people who lived in the Bay could not afford that luxury, but thousands of tourists could and did, willingly. If they pulled in a fifty-pound king while they were at it, or took down a caribou with a double shovel rack, so much the better. They'd go home and tell their friends, who would fill Wy's planes next summer.

"Ms. Chouinard!"

Professor Desmond X. McLynn was not in the business of admiring views. Professor Desmond X. McLynn reserved his regard for artifacts of a pre-Columbian nature, preferably in a precarious state of ossified preservation, which left more room for speculation and the positing of new theories, properly attributed to himself, on the course of anthropological and social development of *Homo sapiens* in this godforsaken corner of the world. "I'm coming," she called, and turned to pile a case of Velveeta on a case of Spam. She shuddered a little as she did so, but then she didn't have to eat it, just carry it. She thought of her lawyer, Harold Abood, J.D., and her legal bill the size of which was beginning to resemble interest on the nation's long-term debt, and lugged the boxes to the campsite. Twenty feet away, a ground squirrel chittered at her angrily. There was a whoosh of wings and a bald eagle swooped down and the squirrel was airborne. Wy paused, watching as the eagle gained altitude, heading for a high bluff inland, crowned by a stand of dead white spruce, bark peeled down to a white, hard surface. Squinting, she made out the mess of twigs and sticks crammed into the fork of a branch, and imagined that she saw three heads peering over the side, hungry eyes watching lunch approach, curved beaks open in anticipation.

"Ms. Chouinard!"

She sighed to herself and plodded forward again. McLynn was wearing a displeased expression beneath a sheepskin-lined leather cap with the flaps hanging down over his ears. They bounced and brushed his shoulders when he talked, and together with the hanging pouches beneath his eyes made him look like an irritable bloodhound. "Where is Mr. Nelson?" he said severely.

"I don't know," she said, determined to maintain her cheerfulness. "I haven't been back here since I picked you up on Friday." She looked around. The sun glinted off the corrugated roofs of the Air Force base, ten miles away west-southeast. It was the nearest settlement, if Don Nelson had decided he needed company over the weekend and set out on foot. The journey would have been soggy in places, but if you had boots on, it wouldn't be bad. Maybe three hours to get there, four if you were slow.

Don Nelson wasn't slow. A thin, energetic young man with pale hair shaved into a vee in back, a long, inquisitive nose and bright, inquiring eyes, he was McLynn's gofer. He cooked, he cleaned, he washed clothes, he stood watch over the dig on those days McLynn was torn unwillingly from the site of this future

American Ardèche. He'd been digging the last time Wy saw him, covered in mud and still young enough to enjoy it. He'd grinned up at her from one of the enclosed ditches, skin streaked with dirt and sweat, showing off his developing pecs in a tank top. "Dig, dig, dig with a shovel and a pick."

She had laughed, but McLynn had heard him. "What do you mean, a shovel? I told you, no shovels, no tools at this level except for a trowel and a brush!"

Nelson smothered his grin. "Just a joke, Professor McLynn."

"Not a funny one," McLynn had said.

Nelson had winked at her as she was turning away, and she had been conscious of his eyes on her as she walked to the plane. It made her feel good, even if she did catch herself wishing Liam Campbell had been there to see that other men were still attracted to her. But he hadn't been there, and except for fleeting glimpses as he was coming into the grocery store and she was going rapidly out the other door, she hadn't seen him in months. Which was what she wanted.

She'd heard rumors that he'd rented a boat to live on while he waited for a house to come open. Good luck, she thought; housing everywhere in rural Alaska was tight, and especially so in Newenham, where commercial fishermen made enough money to have homes both here and Outside, and could afford to let them sit empty over the winter. Most building supplies had to be barged in, putting the price of new housing out of most people's reach and putting existing housing at a premium that did the same, no matter how old or run-down it was. Her house had come with the air taxi business she had bought; a good thing, since she had acquired a twelve-year-old son immediately afterward.

"Well, then, where is he?" McLynn demanded, bringing her back to the present.

"I said I don't know," Wy said, a little less patiently. Good money or not, it wasn't her job to keep track of McLynn's employees. "I don't know where Mr. Nelson went. Maybe he walked over to the base and hitched a ride into town."

Chinook Air Force Base was set midway between the Snake and the Igushik Rivers. It was a broad, flat, relatively dry acreage, with access to a large bed of gravel deposited over a geologic period of time at the mouth of one of the Igushik's tributaries, perfect for base fill for runways. Chinook had two, one running northeast-southwest to take year-round advantage of the prevailing winds, and a second, northwest-southeast, to put the contractor's kids through college. Why they hadn't just run a second alongside the first was beyond Wy. Probably made too much sense for government.

Like most Alaskans, and in the Bush it was almost unanimous, the only thing lower than Wy's opinion of the federal government was her opinion of the state government. Although, if she forced herself to be fair, most of the airmen who made their way to town were, on the whole, fairly decent guys, if unrelentingly horny. Most of them were very young and a long way from home, and Newenham didn't provide much relief. The town had a base population of two thousand, the majority of which was male, and most of its female members were snapped up the day after they graduated from high school, if not before. There was one woman with seven children and no job whose rent, it was generally acknowledged, was paid by frequent contributions from the military. Other than that, and spite dates — when local couples broke up, the girls had something to prove and the occasional airman benefitted thereby — opportunities for romance in Newenham were pretty slim. So far as Wy knew, Nelson hadn't hooked up with any of the local girls, so why would he bother going into town? She glanced at Professor McLynn's red and irritated face, and thought he might be risking his job as well.

She shrugged it off. Hope springs eternal in the red-blooded American male. Maybe he had just gone to the base. Maybe he was going to enlist, to get away from McLynn. She carried the boxes into the camp tent and set them down on the table with a thump, then stretched, unconsciously seeking out three-point positions for both feet and settling for just a moment into a modified horse stance. As always, it felt as if her spine were hanging suspended in space, with no weight pulling it down and no muscles pulling it up.

The table was a folding one, four feet long, metal legs, forty bucks at Costco. It held a two-burner Coleman stove, a dingy blue plastic tub full of unwashed camp dishes, a drainer full of clean ones, and a white plastic jug full of water with a filter attached. Beneath the table, boxes of food were piled in haphazard fashion, partial holes torn in their tops to extract one can of peas or one box of macaroni and cheese at a time.

Whatever else he was, Don Nelson wasn't a professional cook. Wy wondered if McLynn had got him from Job Service in Anchorage, notorious all over the state for sending just-released felons to summer jobs in the Bush. Despite the appeal of that idea, it was more likely that he was a college student earning his tuition. If so, this job was better than sliming salmon any day.

There were two cots against the back wall of the tent with Blazo box nightstands and two deck chairs flanking them. A case of Budweiser and a bottle of José Cuervo Gold sat next to one of the chairs, Wy would bet not McLynn's. The boxes overflowed with papers and journals and magazines and hardcover books, some of which were bound in real leather and some of which looked as if they'd outweigh her son.

Her son. She took a moment to savor the words. Liam's image flashed through her mind, and she booted it out before it took hold, only to have her parents' images take his place: thin, quiet people who saw their duty and did it. Her adoptive parents had never had children of their own, had never told her that they expected her to do anything but graduate from college and become a teacher. She'd done the first and blown the last. They still loved her, though, in their undemonstrative fashion. It was why she still loved them. She owed them a call, too, she thought guiltily. Maybe even a trip into town. They'd met Tim, but they needed more time with him to bond into proper grandparents. She hoped they'd spoil him rotten. Tim could use some spoiling.

Maybe after he came back off the river with Moses, he could have a week in town with his grandparents. And she could follow for a quick visit, put the business on hold long enough to —

"He's not supposed to leave the dig unattended," McLynn said.

Recalled to the present, Wy looked around to see him standing in the open flap of the tent, surveying the interior with a disapproving frown.

Wy didn't see anything so valuable it needed guarding, but she remembered her paycheck before she said so. "Let's take a look around. Maybe he didn't hear the plane."

McLynn followed her out of the tent and across the grass-covered earth to the other tent, twenty-five feet away. The steady southwest wind stopped dead in its tracks for a moment, no more. It was enough for the smell to reach her.

She halted, McLynn bumping into her. "What's the matter?" he said, irritated.

It was unlike anything she'd smelled before, a cross between rotting leaves in the fall and a steak too long on the grill. In spite of the warmth of the day she felt a chill settle over her. "Stay here," she said to McLynn.

"What?" He was indignant. "I most certainly will not, I—"

"Stay here," she repeated in a stronger voice, and walked to the second tent. The smell grew stronger with every step. The breeze came up again as she reached the front flap and she was grateful. The ties resisted her fumbling fingers at first, and then loosened suddenly. The flap fell back, and she stood transfixed, staring at the scene before her.

"Really, Ms. Chouinard, I—" McLynn's words died away as he peered around her shoulder. There was a brief, ghastly pause, and then the sounds of his unsteady footsteps backing up, the thump as his knees hit the ground, the retching sound of him bringing up his breakfast.

Wy felt like joining him.

Like the first tent, this one was olive-green canvas stretched over a metal frame, twenty-five feet on a side. Unlike the first tent, it had no floor, only four sides and a roof to protect the dig from the elements, including the wind, which was why the current steady breeze did not reach inside to cool the air heated by the rising sun, or to dissipate the smell. Wy, desperate to look at anything but what was in front of her, saw that the floor of the tent had been hacked off all the way around just below the seam. The sides were pinned to the ground with metal tent stakes spaced a foot apart. More folding tables lined the tent walls, laden with artifacts recovered from the site set in neat rows, each labeled with date and time and location. A master chart was pinned to one wall, representing the dig and showing the various prior locations of the artifacts and their relation to each other. Coleman lanterns hung from the center pole and all four corners. There was a crude wooden shelf that held various implements, chief among them what looked to Wy like ordinary garden trowels and even more ordinary four-inch paintbrushes. She'd seen McLynn at work with the brushes, one delicate whisk at a time, taking infinite pains to see that no artifact came to harm as it was revealed.

The pits dug into the ground beneath the peak of the tent were neatly sectioned into squares, with string and stakes and tags and numbers identifying each square. Different squares had gone down different levels, some so deep that various layers of soil could be distinguished, some so shallow they looked as if all you had to do was scatter some seed and in a year it would look the same as the rest of the bluff. The deeper the level, the more strata were revealed, a geologic calendar of events. There was even a thin line of volcanic ash, which Don Nelson had told her was from an eruption on the Aleutian Peninsula back when her Yupik ancestors were hunting woolly mammoths with rocks and spears. He'd had a twinkle in his eye as he related these facts, though.

There was no twinkle in his eyes today. He lay sprawled on his back, staring at the green canvas ceiling. His right leg had fallen into one of the ditches, disturbing the string and stakes and tags. There was a pool of something beneath his head and neck, dried brown and sticky-looking.

Something protruded from his mouth. It looked like the hilt of a knife. She blinked at it, trying to focus. It was a homemade knife, she thought numbly, carved from antler, or maybe bone. She couldn't bring herself to look more closely to determine which.

The sight and the smell suddenly became too much to be borne and she stumbled outside and a few steps beyond McLynn, bending forward, hands on her thighs, drawing in great gulps of air.

A few minutes or an hour later, she heard McLynn getting to his feet. Making a great effort, she stood upright and turned to face him.

His face had regained its usual choleric color, and he looked furious. "You know what this means, don't you?"

She knew what it meant, all right.

"It means we'll have to suspend the dig! Years of planning and preparation, years of begging for grants, all lost! Policemen and reporters scrambling around, disturbing the site, who knows what will be destroyed! It means we've lost this summer's work!"

She stared at him, incapable as yet of speech, and the sight seemed to enrage him still further. "It means—" he bellowed, "it means that I'm fucked, is what it means!"

Wy suffered her own realization. No. That wasn't what this meant.

Or it wasn't all it meant.

It meant she was going to have to call Liam.

THREE

Once you have smelled the odor of burned flesh, there is no mistaking it for any other. Liam had once had a case in which the perp had killed his wife, wrapped her in Saran Wrap, put her under their trailer and over the next three months doused her body with Clorox whenever the smell interfered with *Monday Night Football.* Clorox might be hell on wine stains on linen napkins, but it didn't do much to hide the smell of decay; a neighbor had reported it and the smell had led the responding officers directly to the body. All this time the guy had been sleeping in this same trailer, eating in it, showering in it, sitting on his ass and scratching it in his trailer. He had to have been among the olfactorily challenged, a new minority group invented on the spot by the crime scene techs.

Still, that smell wasn't as bad as this one. He heard a sound next to him and turned to see Trooper Prince's pale face going even paler. He didn't bother asking if she was okay. She had to be.

So did he. He took a shallow breath, stiffened his spine and opened the door to the smoke-stained cabin.

It looked like one of the rings of hell in Dante's *Inferno.* It seemed as if there were charred bodies everywhere he looked, on the floor, fallen forward across the galley table, at least one under it.

He pulled his head out and took a deep gulp of air. "Go get the body bags," he told Prince.

Her head snapped up and color returned to her face with a rush. "I'm fine, sir, I—"

"I know you are," he said. "We still need the bags."

She hesitated. He pulled a pair of rubber gloves from a pocket, pausing to raise an eyebrow in her direction that said clearly, *And you were waiting around for—what, exactly?* She turned and stepped to the float, her boot heels echoing against the metal grating. The set of her shoulders looked stiff, as if she were holding them straight by sheer effort of will.

Liam took two steps and leaned one hand against the mast, unmindful of the soot smearing his palm.

He'd been a trooper for almost twelve years now, and he had seen his share of carnage. There was the time Norman Murdy shot five people at a holiday camp on the Tonsina River, and then shot a trooper pursuing him in a helicopter. Ray Doucet had ambushed a husband and wife goldpanning on the Telaquana, had shot the husband and raped and murdered the wife. Billy Svenson had taken his father's AK-47 to Tok Middle School for a show-and-tell that resulted in the death of two students, one teacher and the principal and the wounding of nine others.

He had responded to all of those scenes and more, and contrary to popular belief, the emotions inflicted on the people who saw such things first did not, over time, diminish in any way, shape or form. Time numbed your reactions, allowing you to pretend something like composure, but the horror was always there, and the disbelief, and the shock. It still amazed Liam to see how much blood there was in the human body. He opened his eyes and looked around him.

Kulukak was a small village of two hundred, mostly Yupik souls. It sat on the northwest side of Kulukak Bay, a circle of water eight miles across and ten miles north to south, enclosed by rolling hills and thick green vegetation that reminded Liam of Puget Sound without Seattle. It was calm and still, not a ripple marring the surface of the bay, each hill and tree and rock and narrow beach represented on that surface with mirrorlike fidelity. A low-lying mist clung to the tops of the trees, which reflection gave the scene an eerie black and white look, and a still, moody, almost sullen air.

There was no road to Kulukak, and the bay froze over in winter, so the only means of year-round transportation in and out was by air. As an indication of its importance to the life of the village, a gravel airstrip had been carved out of the center of the tiny settlement. There was an orange wind sock on a pole stuck in the ground at one end, today hanging limp, inert. On the other side of the strip was a hangar, and inside it a road grader equipped with a twelve-foot blade.

A few of the homes were built of aged logs, the rest of prefabricated materials shipped up from Outside in a kit, green and blue and cream siding beneath shallow-pitched corrugated metal roofs. A big building set apart from the others on a small hill behind the village had dark blue siding and the American and Alaskan flags hanging out front. Probably the school. The building was too big for a post office in a village this size. The Postal Service probably contracted out to one of the locals, who would run the post office out of his or her living room, as was the practice in the smaller Bush villages.

The boat harbor was a quarter the size of Newenham's, with one dock extending from the narrow strip of gravel and sand that formed Kulukak's waterfront, one gangway descending from the dock and slips enough for forty boats, most of them occupied today. The boat he was on was tied up to the slip farthest from the dock, the closest boat moored three spaces distant. The rest of the fleet seemed to be pressing against the sides of the harbor, keeping as far as they could get from the *Marybethia.*

He realized he was stalling. A soft croak came from above and behind him. He whipped around and beheld a raven sitting on top of one of the light poles illuminating the boat slips. "What the hell?" Liam said involuntarily. "What are you doing here?"

The raven cocked his gleaming black head. His black beady eyes met Liam's, unblinking, as he let loose with a stream of even softer *kuk-kuk-kuk*s.

There was a stir behind him and a few muttered phrases. He dropped his hand from the mast and stood erect. It couldn't be. Newenham was fifty miles to the northwest; there was no way that this was the same raven that had been haunting his steps since his arrival at his new posting. He turned his back on the shiny black incubus and tried not to flinch when a long, derisive caw came from the top of the light pole.

Five men were standing on the slip, waiting, and he turned to meet their eyes, one at a time. All of them bore traces of at least a partial Yupik heritage—one had the high, flat cheekbones, another the thick, straight ebony hair, a third the narrow, tilted eyes. Four of them had the seamed faces of elders, age lending them at least the illusion of wisdom and authority. The fifth was younger, a short, thickset man in his mid-forties with steady dark eyes. He didn't look friendly. The other four looked, not unfriendly, exactly, but more like they were reserving judgment.

Liam doffed his cap and bent his head as a gesture of respect to the authority of the elders. "My name is Liam Campbell, of the Alaska State Troopers, Newenham post." He waited. It never helped to rush anything in the Bay, and it was offensive to the Natives besides, who had made a pretty good living for thousands of years by waiting: waiting for the fish to come up the river, waiting for the caribou to come down out of the mountains, waiting for the bears to wake up in the spring, waiting for the berries to ripen in the fall. Patience wasn't just a virtue for the people of the Bay, it was a way of life. Liam, as new as he was to his posting, knew that much.

The younger man said, his voice curt, "Walter Larsgaard. I'm the council chief. This is the council."

He didn't introduce them. Liam forced the issue, stepping down to the slip and extending his hand to each man in turn. "Willie Kashatok." "Robert Halstensen." "Mike Ekwok." "Carl Andrew." They spoke English easily, albeit with the guttural inflection and heavy rhythm common to those whose first language was Yupik.

"How do you do," Liam said gravely. "In any other circumstances, I'd be glad to meet you. This . . ."—he gestured behind him—"this is awful."

This frank acceptance of the horror of the situation and the open way in which he shared it caused a perceptible relaxation among the four older men, who exchanged glances and looked back at Liam, still watchful but less on guard. One of them—Ekwok, he thought—even went so far as to give an approving nod, and mutter something to the man standing next to him—Halstensen?—that sounded like, "Tookalook," which probably wasn't anything close to what it was. Yupik was all *k*'s and *t*'s and pretty much all of it sounded like "tookalook" to Liam's Anglo ears. The two old men looked from Liam to the raven on the light pole and back again, and said no more.

Larsgaard alone showed no sign, of approval, or anything else. He waited, silent and wary. His straight black hair fell across his forehead and shadowed his eyes, so that Liam couldn't get a read on what he was thinking.

"Who owned this boat?" Liam said. "I see that her home port is registered here." He pointed at the stern, *Marybethia,* and below that *Kulukak, Alaska,* in no-nonsense lettering, spare, neat, easy to read, no unnecessary serifs or flourishes. Some of the names painted on the sides of boats were so elaborately curliqued they were next to impossible to decipher. This boat even had the state registration number lettered on the bow beneath the name, something you almost never saw on anything bigger than a skiff.

"David Malone," Larsgaard said, after a pause just short of inviting a repeat of the question. "And yes, the Malones live here."

Or did, his eyes said.

"Who does he fish with?" Liam said, thinking of the number of bodies he had seen littering the galley.

"His family," one of the elders—Andrew or Ekwok—said.

Liam's heart sank. "His whole family?"

The elder nodded. It was Ekwok, the shortest and fattest member of the group. He had round black eyes set in a round brown face, and he peered up at Liam with all the curiosity of a five-year-old child meeting his kindergarten teacher for the first time. At six-three, Liam felt like a clumsy giant, and repressed an impulse to squat down so he could meet Ekwok at his own eye level. "The first thing you do upon arrival at a crime scene is to establish an air of authority," his instructor had told him at the academy. "You are the law on two legs. Let people know that up front and don't ever let them forget it." Somehow Liam felt that squatting on his haunches would be counter to that directive.

"His wife, his brother, his two children," Ekwok said.

"And two deckhands," a second elder—Kashatok?—volunteered. "*Gussuks.*"

"They were all *guʃʃukʃ*," Ekwok said with an impatient look. "So what? They were our neighbors."

Everyone looked at Larsgaard, as if expecting him to contradict them, and then studiously away again. The raven mocked them from the top of the light pole. "Oh shut up," Liam said without thinking. The older men looked up at the raven, back at Liam, down at their feet, almost as if—what? Liam thought. As if what? They looked respectful and wary at the same time, on the alert, ready for action. It was very odd. It also wasn't anything he had time for.

"Do you want to see the Malones' house?" Larsgaard said, still without emotion.

"Yes," Liam said. "Later, after . . ." He waved a hand at the boat. They understood.

Ekwok's cherubic face hardened into purposeful lines. "Do you want help, moving them out?"

Liam forced a smile. "Thank you. We'll get them out on deck. Afterward, we could use help in getting them to the plane." He nodded at the Cessna, its floats run up on the wooden skid fastened to the end of the slip closest to the mouth of the harbor. Prince was closing the door, a bundle of heavy black plastic under one arm. She came toward them, long legs eating up the distance. They all turned to look. *Guʃʃuk* though she was, Diana Prince was worth a look. She was, Liam thought, surveying her critically over the heads of the other five men, one of the few women he'd met who looked good in a uniform. He knew a mild urge to rip it off her, and glanced at the faces of the other men to see if they shared in the impulse. Impassive expressions or no, he was pretty sure they did.

If she was unnerved by the steady, unwinking regard of six pairs of male eyes, she didn't show it. She looked controlled and very much in command. She halted in front of them. "Gentlemen," she said crisply, looking each one of them straight in the eye, one at a time.

Liam groaned to himself. "We have to bag the bodies," he told the council, unable to dull the harsh effect of the words. "We also have to take pictures and notes of the scene. It'll be a while before we can move the bodies to the plane, and after that I'd like to see the Malones' house and talk to their neighbors. If you could come back in a couple of hours?"

He got a curt nod from Larsgaard and another grave bow from Ekwok and Andrew. The five men turned and moved off in a group. Liam watched them go, noticing they were not speaking to each other as they went.

He turned to Prince. "It's best not to look village elders in this part of the state directly in the eye."

She thought it over. "Because I'm a woman?"

"Mostly. Plus you're a trooper, an employee of the state government. People in general don't like cops, and people in the Bush don't like the state."

"A double whammy."

"Yes. It behooves us to walk very softly." He didn't say anything about a big stick.

"I'll remember." Prince handed him a white cloth mask.

"Thanks," he said, although he doubted anything less than a rebreather would help. He doffed cap and jacket, hoping to keep them free of the smell, put on the mask and the pair of rubber gloves and reopened the door to hell.

Ninety minutes later they had seven body bags out of the *Marybethia*. Between the two of them, they managed to carry the bags one at a time to the Cessna and stack them inside without calling for extra help. The bodies had been so badly charred that identification was impossible, but the two smaller ones were obviously children and one of the bigger ones was equally obviously a woman.

"Why did you become a trooper?" Wy had asked him, so long ago now, three years and change. It had taken him a few moments to come up with an adequate response. "Because I like rules," he had said finally. "I like order. We're animals, Wy, plain and simple, even the best of us, and we need rules so we can live with each other. Sometimes somebody breaks the rules, and that's where I come in."

He could have added that his job let him wear a uniform not of his father's service, in itself a big draw, but he didn't. He didn't talk much about his father to anyone.

"Did you see it?" Prince asked, letting her mask dangle from one ear. Her face was pale but her eyes were bright as she stripped the gloves from her hands.

The game's afoot, Liam thought, looking at her. It was the moment every law officer waited for, when the disgust and dismay of the crime scene had receded and the thrill of the chase began. "I saw it," he said, making an effort to shake off his revulsion. Later he, too, would be outraged, filled with a white-hot determination to bring the perpetrator or perpetrators to justice, but for the moment he was just trying to keep from vomiting.

The fresh air helped some, and he breathed deeply, fixing his eyes on the green, rolling hills of the shore, hidden and then revealed and then hidden again beneath the bank of drifting mist. The world was still there, and it was not all of it a charnel house, a stage for the perpetual reenactment of man's inhumanity to man. If you keep saying that to yourself, he thought, one day you might even come to believe it.

"A depression in the left temple of one of the male victims," she said.

"Looked like a bullet hole to me," he said. "I smelled the gas, too, although that doesn't prove anything on a boat." He thought of the faint gas smell he woke up to every morning on the *Dawn P.* "But we won't know for sure until we get the results back from the M.E., and that'll take a day or two, and that's after the bodies get there. In the meantime—"

She all but went on point, quivering with eagerness to be on the scent. "In the meantime, we question the family—"

"Doesn't look like there are any left to question."

"—the villagers—"

"Beginning with the council. They're bound to know everything there is to know. Always assuming they'll talk to us."

"—and start gathering evidence."

He almost smiled, but the effort proved too great and he abandoned it. "First things first. You take the bodies back to Newenham."

She opened her mouth to protest and he said, "The bodies are our first evidence. We can't allow them to decay any further. And you're the only pilot around here with the only plane I see."

She couldn't argue with that, and closed her mouth again, disappointment clear on her face.

"You're sure you can make it in one trip?"

Her nod was confident. "Not a problem. Not enough weight to overgross the plane."

"Okay, get them to Newenham and on the next available flight to Anchorage. Call the M.E.'s office—the number's on the Rolodex on my desk—and tell them they are on their way. Tell Brillo Pad we need results as fast as he can get them to us."

"Brillo Pad?"

"Dr. Hans Brilleaux, the M.E."

"Brillo Pad?"

"Have you ever seen his hair?"

"I've never met the man."

"Wait until you do. Anyway, tell him I said to giddyap."

"And then?"

"If nothing has blown up back at the post, come get me. If you can't"—he took a deep breath— "call Wy Chouinard at Nushagak Air Taxi and tell her to come get me. We've got a contract with them."

She nodded, and looked perilously close to saluting. "Get a move on," he said, before she could.

She stuffed her notebook back in her pocket, picked up her jacket and hat and marched off, passing Mike Ekwok on her way. She slowed and half turned, catching Liam's eye. He shook his head and waved her on. He waited until Ekwok reached the side of the boat. "Mr. Ekwok," he said, touching the brim of his hat.

"Trooper," Ekwok said, equally grave. He looked up at the raven, still perched on his light pole, his deep black feathers outlined against torn wisps of white mist. Liam wondered when Sam Spade was going to wander in out of the fog.

The Cessna's engine coughed into life and taxied out of the harbor. Liam heard the engine roar and watched it rise into the air and disappear into the fog. All was quiet again. There was nothing quite like the hush of an Alaskan Bush community. An occasional airplane, a truck with no roads on which to get above third gear, a boat engine turning over, seagulls squawking, ravens talking, and the rest was silence. Except for the odd rifle shot, and Liam saw again the round depression in the blackened temple of one of the bodies on board the plane speeding toward Newenham.

"Mr. Campbell," Ekwok said, "I know—"

"Could you hang on just a second, Mr. Ekwok?" Liam said. He turned to look toward the *Mary J*, moored to the third slip over from the *Marybethia*, and beckoned. Larry, legs dangling in the hold as he spliced an eye into the end of a line, nodded acknowledgment. "Dad! I'm going next door for a minute." There was a muffled assent from inside the *Mary J*'s cabin and for a moment Liam saw Darrell's face pressed whitely against the porthole. The *Mary J* was a white, thirty-two-foot Bristol Bay gillnetter with a hot pink trim line, fancy lettering in matching pink spelling out her name on both sides of the bow and across the stern. Her home port, Newenham, was listed on the stern, too, also in pink. Darrell's wife had insisted on the trim being that particular shade of pink, right before she kicked Darrell out and took up with a seiner from Togiak.

Larry, Darrell and Mary's only son, was a taller, fitter edition of his father, with more hair and a nose less bulbous in shape and less red in color. Like his father, Larry did his share of drinking, in tandem with lifelong friend Kelly "Mac" McCormick, but Mac had gotten out of the hospital just in time to go to jail for shooting up the Newenham Post Office, which charge he had not contested in exchange for a shortened sentence. Fortunately, he hadn't put holes into anything except a couple of windows, and also fortunately, at the time of his sentencing the postmaster was in the middle of resigning and had no time to testify against him. Mac would be out in six months, and in the meantime, his incarceration did Larry's liver no harm.

"Larry," Liam said, nodding. The people in Liam's world were divided into those he had arrested and those he hadn't. The former he addressed by their first names, the latter by their surnames. Sometimes the former worked their way back up to being mistered. More often they did not.

Larry Jacobson was still on probation, and he knew it. "Trooper Campbell," he said formally. "Are we done here?

There's an opener in Togiak tomorrow and we need to take on fuel."

"Sure," Liam said. "I'll be in touch if I have any more questions. Anything else you can think of to tell me? Anything you saw, no matter how trivial, could be important."

Larry shrugged. Liam was glad to see that while maintaining his decorous manner Larry was neither defensive nor hostile; he'd apparently come to terms with the events of the previous May, and with Liam's part in them, and had moved on. "Not much else to tell. We saw her drifting and went after her. There'd been a fire, we saw that right off. The plugs had been pulled, and she was about half down in the water. If the drains hadn't plugged up with fish guts she probably would have gone right down to the bottom. Lucky."

Liam could have thought of other adjectives to describe the fortunes of the crew of the *Marybethia*, but he held his peace.

"Anyway, the bilge turned over first thing. After that, we took her in tow and brought her into Kulukak. No luck this period, anyway," he added parenthetically, leaving Liam to understand that if the *Mary J* had been fortunate enough to fish her limit, they would have been well on their way to the cannery, and the *Marybethia* abandoned to her fate.

"Did you go inside?"

"No. I got as far as opening the door. I could see the bodies from where I stood. I didn't want anything to do with them." He shifted a wad of chaw from one cheek to the other and spat over the side. "Death at sea is bad luck."

Violent death is bad luck anywhere, Liam thought. "You see any other boats in the area?"

Larry shook his head again. "Not by then; most everybody had headed back in after the closing. It's a little run thereabouts anyway, we don't usually fish it, but this time Dad had a wild hair there might be some late reds hanging off the point. Wasn't, though." He seemed more resigned to their bad luck than bitter about it.

"Go ahead, then. And good fishing."

"Thanks. Dad's smelling an early run of silvers. Price is always higher on the first run." He strode back to his boat. Darrell, who had been watching from the deck, started the engine, and Larry had just enough time to release the bow and stern lines and jump on board before the gillnetter pulled away from the slip and increased to a slow, no-wake speed.

As they pulled alongside, Larry cut power and let the *Mary J* drift. "There was a skiff last night," he called. "About ten o'clock, coming out from the village, going toward the head of the bay. One person in it. Dad saw him."

"Did he recognize him?"

Larry consulted with Darrell, and shook his head.

"Did he recognize the skiff?"

More consultation. "Big New England dory, Dad says. Guy was standing up, rowing forward." Larry shrugged. "Dad says that's all."

"Okay, Larry," Liam said. "Thanks," he added, and meant it. Eliciting information was hard enough. Volunteers were always welcome. Always supposing the dory wasn't a figment of an alcohol-induced imagination, always a possibility with Jacobson *père et fils*.

The *Mary J* headed straight for the mouth of the harbor, a narrow channel between two arms of steeply piled rock. She made the entrance and picked up speed. Soon all he could see was the masthead.

"Mr. Campbell."

Liam started and turned to Ekwok. "I'm very sorry to have kept you waiting, sir. What was it you wanted to say?"

"I know who did this," Ekwok said, with a jerk of his head toward the *Marybethia*. "I know who killed them."

FOUR

The white Blazer with the shield on the door was parked right in front of the post, and any hope Wy had had of just leaving a note (*Liam, Dig gofer stabbed, body at X longitude, Y latitude, Wy*) died aborning. She raised her chin, climbed the steps, opened the door and halted in her tracks.

There was a trooper on the phone behind the desk, but it wasn't the trooper she was expecting.

"Thank you," the trooper said. "We'll be waiting for your call." She hung up the phone and looked at Wy. "Yes?"

"Who are you?"

"I'm Diana Prince of the Alaska State Troopers. Who are you?"

"Wyanet Chouinard. What are you doing here?"

The trooper looked amused. "I work here. More to the point, what are you doing here?"

"What do you mean, you work here?" Wy knew a sick feeling in the pit of her stomach. "Where's Liam?"

Up with the eyebrow again, as if to say, Liam, is it? "Trooper Campbell is away on a case. How can I help you?"

The sick feeling eased. "He still works here, then?"

"Last time I looked."

"He's still assigned to Newenham?"

"He is still assigned to Newenham," the trooper affirmed gravely. "Now, how may I help you, Ms. Chouinard?"

"Call me Wy," Wy said automatically.

Mercifully, Trooper Prince did not as automatically respond

with Why not? Instead, she said, for the third time, "How may I help you?"

Her manner was so indulgent that Wy bristled. "I found a body." She was pleased when the trooper sat up straight in Liam's chair.

"You found a body?"

"Yes."

"Where?"

"On an archaeological dig about fifty miles south of here. Ten miles more or less west of Chinook Air Force Base."

The trooper stood up and went to the map of Bristol Bay tacked to the wall. "Show me." Wy showed her. "There's a strip there?"

"Not a strip, exactly. More like a flat piece of ground just long enough for a Super Cub to roll out before it falls into the river. I own and operate the—"

"Nushagak Air Taxi Service," Prince said.

Wy turned from the map. "Yes. How did you know?"

"Trooper Campbell may have mentioned it."

"Oh. I see. Of course. Ah." What had she been saying? "Right. I'm on a three-month contract to the state to fly the people working on the dig in and out."

"And this morning?"

"And this morning I was flying the archaeologist—"

"One moment, please." The trooper produced a notebook and a pencil. "Go ahead."

"His name is McLynn, Desmond X. McLynn, and I was flying him to work this morning. We landed and found the body of his gofer, Don Nelson." Wy hesitated. "Uh, it didn't—it wasn't—I don't think—oh hell." She expelled an impatient breath. "He didn't just die," she said bluntly. "He was killed."

As if a switch had been thrown, the indulgent air vanished and the trooper went on alert. Wy could almost hear the howl of the bloodhounds. She'd seen the same expression on Liam's face too many times to mistake it now.

Prince said, "What makes you say that?"

Wy remembered Nelson's body and repressed a roll of nausea. "Well, the handle of the knife sticking out of his mouth was my first clue."

"I see." The trooper seemed to sniff the air. "Where is Professor McLynn now?"

"At Bill's. He wouldn't stay at the site, so I dropped him off on the way into town from the airport."

"Bill's?"

"Bill's Bar and Grill," Wy elaborated.

"This McLynn a drinker?"

"He is today," Wy said, her mouth a grim line. "I would be, too, if I didn't have to fly."

The trooper reached for her cap. "I'll follow you there."

Bill's Bar and Grill was a squat, square building with a shallow-peaked roof of corrugated metal and green vinyl siding. Windows basked in the neon light of a dozen beer signs, and worn wooden stairs led up to double doors.

Inside, the building was divided, the bar in front and the kitchen in back. They were separated by a wall with a pass-through window through which wafted the tantalizing smell of beef burned to the proper degree of char and the occasional bellow, "Order up!" A bar with a black Naugahyde elbow pad ran the length of the front room on the left, booths and a jukebox were on the right, a small stage and an even smaller dance floor in the back. A hardy indoor-outdoor carpet of indeterminate color suffered beer spills and cigarette ashes with equal indifference, and the walls were arrayed in dark wood paneling and still more neon beer signs. The rafters were exposed, sort of, because every available inch had been stapled with business cards, men's shorts and women's bras, Japanese glass fishing floats, a moose rack that looked wide enough to challenge the current record holder in *Boone & Crockett*, a length of baleen, the cork line off a drift net and the inevitable and innumerable square foil packets of Trojans.

It was also, on this early afternoon in late July, almost empty, but for a woman standing behind the bar polishing a glass, a man seated opposite her and another man standing next to him. The standing man was tall, dark and in uniform.

"Liam!" Wy said involuntarily, and started forward.

"Sir?" Trooper Prince said. "How did you get here?"

The man turned his head toward them, bringing it full into the light from one of the windows. Wy halted. So did Prince.

He was tall, broad-shouldered and long-legged, with thick dark hair going a distinguished gray at the temples and blue eyes deepset in a brown face. His nose was high-bridged and arrogant, his mouth ready for an easy, sexy grin and his jaw square and obstinate, but despite these uncanny similarities he was not Liam Campbell. On closer inspection Wy realized that his uniform was not the blue of the Alaska State Troopers, either, it was the blue of the United States Air Force.

"I'm sorry," he said with crisp courtesy, "I'm afraid you've mistaken me for my son." He smiled, first at Wy, then over her shoulder at Trooper Prince, and in a heartbeat Wy understood where Liam got all his charm. "I'm Charles Campbell." He smiled again. "I don't seem to be able to find my son, in fact."

"He's out of town, Colonel," Wy said. He gave her a sharp look, wanting to know how a civilian, and a female civilian at that, knew his rank. "I . . . know your son," she said lamely. There was a comprehensive snort from the man seated at the bar. Campbell glanced down at him, and Moses Alakuyak's bright brown eyes met his with distinct challenge.

Wy shot the shaman a fierce look, and the woman behind the bar put her hand over his, in restraint or encouragement, Wy couldn't tell which, but then Bill was like that. "Liam speaks of you often," she told Campbell. That was a lie, but it was the best she could come up with on the spot. Another snort from Moses told her what he thought of that.

"I flew Trooper Campbell out to Kulukak this morning, sir," Prince said, stepping into the breach. "It is a coastal village about fifty miles southwest of here. He is working on an investigation."

Campbell looked interested. "You're a pilot."

"Yes, sir."

He smiled again. "As am I. We have something in common, then."

Prince eyed the eagles on his collar and the wings on his breast and said in a voice gone very dry, "So we do. Excuse me, sir, I'm here to talk to someone." She looked around.

Wy pointed at a booth, where McLynn sat with a glass

clutched in one hand, scribbling furiously in a notebook. Prince walked to the booth. "Mr. McLynn?"

"It's Professor McLynn, or Doctor, if you prefer," he said without looking up.

"I'm Diana Prince with the Alaska State Troopers," she said. "I'm flying out to your dig immediately. I'd like you to accompany me."

He closed his eyes and shuddered. "Is that really necessary?"

"It would be very helpful," she said mildly.

He opened his eyes and tossed off the last of his drink. "Fine. Whatever. Let's get it over with."

He snapped his notebook closed and rose to his feet, to level an admonitory finger at Prince. "I don't want anything there disturbed, do you understand? I've been working that dig for nearly twenty years. It is an archaeological site containing one-of-a-kind artifacts chronicling the existence of a small band of people that, when presented in its proper context, will rewrite the prehistory of this area." He glared up at the trooper. "My research must not be interfered with."

Trooper Prince didn't raise her voice. "I quite understand, sir, but the area is, unfortunately, also the scene of a crime. Our investigation will intrude as little as possible into your workspace, but it must begin immediately."

Basically, Wy thought with admiration, she outpompoused him. Defeated but grumbling, McLynn followed Prince back to the bar. "I understand that your air taxi service is on contract to the troopers," Prince said to Wy.

Wy groaned inwardly, but the thought of Harold Abood, Esquire, J.D., made her reply, "Yes."

"And that you know where Kulukak is."

Wy nodded.

"In that case, I'd like to charter your services to go pick up Trooper Campbell."

Colonel Campbell looked at Wy. "You're a pilot, too?"

"Place is just lousy with pilots," Bill observed from behind the bar. She was a short woman with eyes the translucent blue glacier ice goes only on a cloudy day, and silver hair swept straight back from her face to her shoulders in a thick, shining fall. Her

T-shirt read "Laissez le bon temps roulez—Mardi Gras," not easy to read unobtrusively because of how well she filled it out. Like Moses, her expression was one of not quite malicious glee.

"Yes, sir," Wy said to Campbell, "I'm a pilot, too."

"In what capacity?"

"I own and operate the Nushagak Air Taxi Service." She said it proudly, because she was proud of it.

"Really." He seemed amused, and she bristled. He saw her reaction and grinned, and again she was put forcibly in mind of his son. "Well, then, we have something in common, too."

Not hardly, she thought, remembering Liam's occasional tales of his father going head to head with Soviet Backfire bombers in the skies over the Bering Strait, back before the Berlin Wall had fallen and taken the Cold War down with it. "Marginally," she said. "I fly a Piper Super Cub. You fly an F-14."

"An F-16C, actually," he said.

"And a Cessna 180," she said.

"Pilots," Moses said to Bill. "Jesus. Even when they don't have cocks, they're comparing sizes."

Campbell said, "I take it you'll be bringing my son back from, er, Kulukak?"

"Yes."

"What time you think you'll get in?"

Wy looked at her watch. "I should get out of here in less than an hour. It's eleven o'clock, say I'm in the air by noon. I should make Kulukak well before one. If Liam's ready to go, we should be back here by, oh, say two-thirty to be safe. I don't know what he's got left to do on the ground."

"All right. Tell Liam I'm here, would you? Liam hates surprises." He donned his cap and smiled again, and this time she saw that his charm was more practiced than Liam's, and more conscious of effect. "I'm at the BOQ on base. I'll be expecting his call. Nice meeting you folks," he said to Bill and Moses. He nodded to Prince and left the bar.

"Whew," Bill breathed as the door swung closed behind him, and pretended to fan herself.

Moses growled something and hooked a hand around her neck to pull her forward. The passionate, carnal kiss then exchanged was enough to make Prince blink and McLynn's jaw drop. Wy was more used to it, but she still felt the temperature of the room go up a couple of degrees. She rolled her eyes, tried not to feel jealous and walked outside, followed by Prince and McLynn on self-conscious tiptoe.

Prince said, "I assume you're taking your Cessna to Kulukak."

"Yes."

"Am I correct in assuming I can't fly a Cessna on floats into the dig?"

"Yes. A Cub's the only aircraft other than a helicopter that'll make it in and out of that strip. It's not even a strip, really, we just moved some rocks and pulled some bushes."

"I see. Do you charter your aircraft?"

"Yes," Wy said, masking a flinch.

"Then I'll need to charter your Cub to fly out to the dig."

"Tulukaruk," Wy said. "That's the name of it. Look, I don't mean to—I mean—well—hell. It's a very short, very rough strip, with a forty-five-foot drop to a river at one end. How many hours you got on a Cub?"

Prince's smile was smug. "Three hundred and four. I've been flying since I was thirteen, and I've done hundreds of Bush landings, Ms. Chouinard. Besides," she added, serious now, "you're insured, aren't you?"

Smart-ass, Wy thought. She sighed and gave in to the inevitable. "You'll need a map. Follow me out to the airport."

"And when we all get back to town, I'll want to talk to you again, take a formal statement."

"Not a problem," Wy said, heading for her truck. "You know where I work, and I'm not going anywhere."

Except to Kulukak to pick up Liam, she thought as she started the truck. She felt her heart skip a beat. She hadn't seen him to speak to in almost three months, and now they were going to spend a minimum of forty-five minutes shoulder to shoulder.

Unwillingly, she remembered the first days of their acquaintance, when she in her innocence had thought they were just friends. The hours spent in the air on their way between Glennallen and various crime scenes, the grisly prospects before them muted by the pleasure they took in each other's company. They had never seemed to stop talking, she remembered painfully: books, music, politics, religion, art, people they both knew, places they'd both been, experiences they'd shared separately.

Oh, they had been such fine, fine days in the air, that summer that now seemed so long ago and so far away.

It was when they had stopped talking that they got into trouble.

She slammed the truck into gear and headed for the airport. The white Blazer with the gold shield on the side fell in behind her like a ghostly shadow.

FIVE

When Liam didn't respond, Ekwok repeated in a louder voice, "I know who did this."

The raven erupted with a staccato *"Kuk-kuk-kuk-kra-kuk"* that sounded eerily like the cadence of Ekwok's own speech patterns. Ekwok looked up with an apprehensive expression. His eyes hardened and he said for the third time, "I know who did this."

Liam wished with all his heart that just once it could be that easy. Well, hell, maybe it could be. "And who might that be, Mr. Ekwok?" he said, pulling out his notebook.

"That David Malone, he fired a guy last year. A deckhand. He wouldn't even give him a ride from Seattle when he brought the *Marybethia* north. This deckhand, he was angry. He said he would kill Malone."

Ekwok shut up, his expression suggesting that he had said all he had to say. His attitude clearly indicated that he had solved all Liam's problems and that he, Liam, should go away now and attend to them.

Quoth the raven, *"Kwark, click, click."*

"Will you knock it off?" Liam said.

"Knock what off?" Ekwok said.

"I'm sorry, Mr. Ekwok, I meant him." Liam jerked a thumb over his shoulder.

Ekwok examined him with an expression on his face that was impossible to read. "You talk to the raven?"

Liam pulled himself together. "No. No, of course not." Pen

poised, he said, "Do you know the name of the deckhand that Malone fired?"

Ekwok shook his head. "No."

"Do you know someone who might?"

"Walter will know. Walter hired him last summer, after Malone fired him."

Had he indeed. "Could you take me to Mr. Larsgaard's house, Mr. Ekwok? I'd like to ask him a few questions."

Walter Larsgaard and the rest of the village council were at Larsgaard's house, sitting around a kitchen table, drinking coffee. As one honor-bound, Walter Larsgaard offered Liam a mug. Liam accepted. It was hot and strong enough to melt the enamel right off his teeth.

They waited politely until he had taken a few sips, and he used the time to look at his surroundings. The kitchen was small but clean, wooden cupboards that went right up to the ceiling painted a white enamel that was beginning to chip down to the original lime-green coat, an old but well-scrubbed gas stove, a Frigidaire refrigerator with a bad-tempered mutter that sounded pre–World War II. The sink was stainless steel with a high arching faucet—high enough to clean salmon under—and the linoleum on the floor had been scoured so often and so well that the blue and white floral pattern was beginning to wear off. The kitchen table was rectangular, with a Formica top and steel legs. The chairs matched. A half-eaten loaf of Wonder bread and a one-pound can of Darigold butter sat on the table, with a box of Lipton tea bags and a jar of homemade jam.

Clear glass canisters with sealed lids lined up against the wall: flour, white sugar, brown sugar, coffee. On one side of the room a window looked over the harbor, and on the other side of the room a magnificent walrus head had been hung on the wall, tusks gleaming with that inner light that only ivory has. One of the tusks was broken off in a painfully jagged point about twelve inches down, the other stretched its full length. Eighteen inches? More like twenty, Liam thought.

Some trick of the light made the hollow eyes of the skull seem to flicker, as if something were staring back at him. He could almost see the walrus raise its lip at him, raise its head and rear back to display those tusks in attack. He raised his mug in its direction, half in salute, half to point. "That's a great head."

"Walter's father did it," Ekwok volunteered. "Don't know why he bothered to mount one with a broken tusk. Plenty out there with both intact."

"It was his first," Walter Larsgaard said, with an almost imperceptible softening of his stern expression. "When he was a boy, we could hunt *asveq*."

"*Asveq*," the rest of them echoed.

"Walrus," Ekwok volunteered when he saw Liam's questioning look. "*Asveq* is Yupik for walrus. He's a carver, is Old Walter. The best in the village. Walter, you ought to let the sheriff see your dad's workshop. He's got some—"

"He's sleeping," Larsgaard said, his face closing up again.

Well. End of subject, obviously. Liam took another sip of coffee. As if it were a signal, Ekwok said, "I told him about the deckhand."

Larsgaard's lips tightened.

"First things first," Liam said, setting the mug down and reaching for his notebook. "Can you tell me who all was on board the *Marybethia*?"

There was an exchange of glances, a shuffling of feet. Kashatok spoke up in a high, thin voice with a precise diction that was almost British in inflection. "David and Molly Malone. David Malone's brother, Jonathan. Their daughter, Kerry. Their son, Michael."

"There were two others, we think adult males," Liam said. "Deckhands?"

There was a universal shrug. "He hired them from Outside," Ekwok said. "Anacortes, or Port Angeles, or Bellingham, maybe."

"Maybe we find their names at Malone's house," Andrew volunteered.

Liam looked down at his pad and doodled. "Mr. Ekwok tells me that Mr. Malone had a problem with a deckhand he hired last summer."

There was a brief silence.

He looked up to meet Larsgaard's eyes. "He also says, Mr. Larsgaard, that you hired this deckhand after Mr. Malone fired him."

There was another brief silence. Larsgaard gave a curt nod. "I did."

"I'll need his name."

For a moment he thought Larsgaard would refuse. The other man had yet to meet his eyes straight on.

Liam was familiar with the attitude, almost, in a perverse way, comfortable with it. To many if not most of the tribal chiefs in Bush Alaska, Liam was a necessary evil to be dealt with civilly but not cordially and certainly never socially. It was one of the things you put up with if you worked for the state of Alaska in the Bush, along with being on call for every disturbance, civil and criminal, that the local police couldn't or wouldn't deal with, along with being confused for a federal agent and held responsible for every ill visited upon mankind by the IRS. It was why a Bush trooper got step increases to his salary, one for every posting farther away from the population centers of the state, where the majority of the population was white and only distrusted you for your uniform and not the color of your skin.

"You were the trooper from Denali," Halstensen said suddenly.

Liam willed himself not to flush, and failed. "Yes."

"Those people died."

Because the troopers working for him were asleep at the switch. No, he thought. Because they hadn't been properly supervised. Because, no matter what shape his personal life was in, a trooper was never off the job. Because when he was, people died. In this case, five people. "Yes," he said baldly.

"Athabascans," Halstensen said.

Liam inclined his head. The temperature in the room cooled noticeably. He made no apologies and attempted no explanations, although he had to grit his teeth to hold back the words.

There was a moment of strained silence, broken when Larsgaard rose to his feet and left the room. There was a murmur of voices, Larsgaard's and another male voice, lighter and more tentative in tone, suggesting age. The voice rose. As always, the Yupik words were incomprehensible to Liam, but the distress in this voice was plain to the ear. Larsgaard's voice, lower, furious, cut him off. In the silence that followed, Ekwok looked at Kashatok. Kashatok stared straight ahead and drank coffee. Andrew and Halstensen buttered slices of bread, spread them with jam and ate them. Safer with your mouth full, Liam thought. Can't say anything then.

Larsgaard returned to the kitchen with a slip of paper, which he handed to Liam. Small, neat block printing spelled out the name Max Bayless, followed by a Seattle address and phone number. "Thank you, Mr. Larsgaard," Liam said, folding and pocketing the slip.

There was a rustle of movement and Liam looked around to see a sixth man enter the room. His was an old face, older even than the others sitting around the table. The once healthy brown of his skin had faded to a pale ocher, the whites of his eyes were yellowed, his movements stiff and slow. His hair was still black, but thinning noticeably.

Liam identified him instantly as Larsgaard's father; the stubborn chin, the snub nose, the high, flat cheekbones, the shape and set of their shoulders were all too similar to make their relationship anything less close. They could have been brothers but for the elder Larsgaard's stoop and the sea of soft folds and wrinkles that engulfed his eyes and mouth, the marks of time passing that had yet to grace the face of his son.

"Dad," Larsgaard said, confirming Liam's guess, and, coincidentally, alerting the company to the fact that he was annoyed with his father.

Dad poured himself a cup of coffee and waited. Larsgaard's lips thinned and he pulled his chair out for his father to sit down. The elder Larsgaard settled in and cupped his mug in gnarled hands, breathing in the steam rising gently from the coffee's surface.

"This is the trooper from Newenham, Dad," Larsgaard said reluctantly. "This is my father, Mr. Campbell. Walter Larsgaard Senior."

"It's nice to meet you, Mr. Larsgaard," Liam said.

Old Walter nodded acknowledgment without meeting Liam's eyes.

It was impossible to miss the air of strain between the senior and junior members of the family, but everyone pretended not to notice. The generation gap was alive and well in Kulukak, Liam decided, and said, "Mr. Larsgaard, why did Mr. Malone fire Max Bayless?"

"He didn't say."

"Was Mr. Bayless angry at Mr. Malone for firing him?"

Larsgaard shrugged. "He shot off his mouth some. I didn't take any of it seriously."

"What did he say?" Their eyes met and Liam added, "Specifically?"

Larsgaard's lips tightened in what was becoming a familiar expression. "He said Malone was a jealous old fool."

Interesting. "Mrs. Malone was a member of the crew, wasn't she?"

"Yes, but . . ."

"Yes, but what?"

There was a long pause. "Yes," Larsgaard said finally, "she was a member of the crew."

Liam remembered the fifty feet of the *Marybethia*, damaged now by smoke and flame and salt water. She'd been a big boat in her time, but not big enough to hide the kind of activities Liam was thinking of from other members of the crew. Still, love will find a way. This, not unnaturally, made him think of Wy, and he cleared his throat. "Did you find Mr. Bayless to be a satisfactory employee, Mr. Larsgaard?"

"Yes."

"He got to work on time, knew what he was doing, did his share?"

"Yes."

"Did you hire him again this summer?"

"No."

"Did he go back to work for the Malones?"

"No."

"Did he get a job on another boat?"

"I don't know."

Andrew and Ekwok exchanged sideways glances.

Fine, Liam thought. He looked at the rest of the council for a thoughtful minute. None of them met his eyes, none had offered any additional information. Old Walter sipped his coffee and continued to look at and say nothing.

All right. Let them think Liam was done with his questions. He would return, perhaps tomorrow morning, when they had become used to his absence, when they had let down their guard a little, and ask more. "Could I see the Malones' house now, please?"

The Malone house was a sprawling affair that had its origins in a one-room log cabin. The logs still formed part of the exterior wall, the southeast corner facing the dirt road that ran north of Kulukak and dead-ended fifty feet beyond the house. Over the years it had acquired a second story and a cedar deck built over a dry dock that looked big enough to accommodate a boat the size of a state ferry. The front half of the house was built on pilings set into the ebb and flow of the tide, the back half rested its haunches on the steep, rocky shore, as if preparing to spring into the water at the first dangle of bait. The unpainted wooden clapboards had faded to gray and the roof needed new shingles, but otherwise it was a house that proclaimed the affluence of its owner in no uncertain terms.

"Mr. Malone was a successful fisherman, I take it," Liam said, one hand on the doorknob.

"Yes," Larsgaard Junior replied.

There was something even in that single, flat syllable that made Liam look around. "Beat you out for high boat a couple of times, did he?"

There was no answering smile on Larsgaard's face. "A couple of times," he agreed in a level voice.

Liam turned the knob. The door opened. "Not locked," he said.

"Nobody locks their doors in Kulukak," Larsgaard said. "It's why most of us live here."

"Nice to know your neighbors," Liam agreed, and stepped inside.

There were four bedrooms, furnished well but not luxuriously, three bathrooms, an office with a computer, a printer, filing cabinets, a fax and a copy machine, a living room with a rock fireplace that had an unfinished jade hearth, a family room with a large-screen television and a bookcase full of videotapes, a Jenn-Air grill in the kitchen that Liam immediately coveted—hell, he thought with a pang, remembering his sloshy awakening that morning, he coveted the whole house—a breakfast nook and a dining room. The artwork was Alaskan, bought with an eye more toward investment than aesthetic value. Each painting, suitably framed, hung directly in the center of each wall—a Machetanz oil of a polar bear in the living room, a Birdsall triptych of Denali in the dining room, a Stonington watercolor of Child's Glacier in the family room. Even the family pictures had been winnowed down and confined to a couple of picture ledges, one in the office, one in the master bedroom.

It was all very neat, very clean. The spice cupboard had no dried parsley spilled on its shelves, all the clothes in the four bedrooms were hung neatly in closets, the washer and dryer in the downstairs half bath stood empty, waiting expectantly for the next load.

"She was a good housekeeper, that Mrs. Malone," Ekwok said.

Larsgaard Junior turned abruptly and walked out of the house.

David Malone had been as orderly in business as his wife had been in keeping house; Liam found the names and address of this summer's deckhands in a file marked "Personnel." Jason Knudson, eighteen, of Bellingham, Washington. Wayne Cullen, nineteen, also of Bellingham. He made a note of their names and addresses. Malone had gone so far as to note down next of kin, a sensible precaution in a business where life expectancy was so problematic that the people who wrote actuarial tables for insurance companies couldn't find a place low enough on their graphs for Alaskan fishermen.

Liam closed the top drawer of the filing cabinet and opened the bottom one, where he found retired files of previous employees, including Max Bayless. Max Bayless was twenty-seven, from Anacortes, Washington. Home address, telephone number and next of kin were noted, along with wages paid and taxes deducted. No reason was given for his termination, but Liam noted that his final check had been drawn on June 20 of the previous year, well before the red season got into full swing on the Bay.

He switched on Malone's computer. The screen requested a password. Without hesitation, Liam typed in "Molly" and with a beep, a click and a whirr, Windows 98 loaded and icons filled the screen. It looked like the kids had spent a lot of time on Dad's computer, playing Sim City, Tetris and Solitaire.

One of the few nongame icons to pop up was Quicken. He clicked on it and a list of accounts appeared, including a checking account with sixty-five hundred dollars in it, two credit card accounts, both zeroed out by the most recent monthly payment, a self-employment retirement account in both David's and Molly's names worth a quarter of million after taxes and a savings account holding over one hundred thousand dollars in cash.

David Malone has been a very successful fisherman indeed.

There was an email icon; Liam clicked on it and was requested to provide a password. "Kerry" didn't work; "Michael" did. Liam shook his head, and clicked on inbox. Wasn't much in it, or in the outbox, or in the trashbox. Kerry had a pen pal in Las Vegas, New Mexico, David had written the Social Security Administration to ask for an updated Personal Earnings and Benefit Estimate Statement, probably to ensure a hard copy of his earnings before the Y2K bug ate their hard drive, Michael had ordered new sneakers from Nike Town, and Molly wasn't represented.

IRS paperwork going back ten years filled a second two-drawer filing cabinet. So far as Liam could tell, Malone had never been audited. There was a copy of a will that divided everything into thirds, with the children's portions held in trust with Molly and Jonathan as trustees. No provision had been made for the simultaneous death of everyone named in the will. Molly Malone's given name had been Marybethia. Liam made a note of the lawyer's name and Anchorage address. It was a considerable estate. It would be interesting to discover who benefited.

He sat for a moment, thinking. On an impulse he pushed back the chair to go upstairs and into the master bedroom.

The picture ledges on the wall opposite the bed held fourteen three-by-five prints, their wooden frames painted in bright primary colors and arranged like a prism in two rows of red, orange, yellow, green, blue, indigo, violet. There were two baby pictures, newborns with red, squinched-up faces and no hair, and the only way Liam could tell them apart was by the color of the blankets they were wrapped in. He remembered his first sight of Charlie, rosy and wrinkled and irate at being thrust from a warm, safe world into the glaring lights of the delivery room at Providence Hospital in Anchorage.

The pictures featured the two children, alone or with one or the other of their parents. The eldest was the girl, Kerry, redheaded and freckle-faced and gap-toothed childhood growing into an auburn-haired adolescent with a thrust-out lower lip she obviously thought gave her mouth a sultry curl, but which only made her look like a ten-year-old who'd been told to go turn off the television and do her homework. Her cheeks were round and full, her chin soft, her nose a snub, her eyes a wide, innocent blue. Although there was no real physical similarity, she reminded Liam of early pictures of Marilyn Monroe, without the jaded knowledge that being Marilyn Monroe brought with it. If she'd survived, the young Malone girl might have lived into the promise of that pout.

The youngest, Michael, had dark hair and eyes and an almost grave expression. He looked straight at the camera, a questioning lift to one dark brow. It seemed to Liam that he should be wearing glasses, or at the very least have Albert Einstein's afro, some outward, manifest indication of the intelligence contained behind that broad brow, some hint of the determination indicated by that strong chin.

How could those two tiny scraps of humanity, brother and sister, both sprung from the same seed, nurtured in the same womb, have grown into two such different creatures? And then of course he thought of Wy, Wy with her Yupik grandparent and her blond hair. No matter what Mr. Kaufman had taught him in sixth-grade science, Mendel's beans made even less sense to him now than they had then.

There was a flushed and excited Kerry in a cheerleader outfit (the Kulukak Kings, green and silver); Michael with a basketball; Kerry with one eye heavily mascaraed and the other eye not, trying to force the bathroom door closed; Michael, a grin splitting his face, standing in front of a blue Super Cub and displaying a hacked-off shirttail, the mark of a successful solo. There was one picture of both children on the deck of the *Marybethia* in jeans and sweatshirts and hip boots and monkey gloves, up to their knees in salmon, looking sweaty and tired and jubilant all at once.

He came to the last picture on the second ledge, which included both parents and both children in the stern of a sailboat surrounded by blue, blue water. He picked it up and moved to a window, holding it up to the light. An island was in the background, and the tanned leg of someone he presumed was the skipper in the foreground. Molly, Kerry, Michael and David sat in a row against the starboard rail. All their feet were tangled together in the middle of the picture, the mystery ankle on top of Molly Malone's, Molly's on top of her daughter's, her daughter's on top of David's, David's on top of his son's. David was smiling at the camera, a quiet smile from a contained face of regular features, nothing too excessive or exuberant, a face that gave very little away. Liam could see his daughter in his eyes, his son in his chin.

Molly, on the other hand, nearly sizzled with life: vital, vibrant, glowing with energy and enthusiasm. Blond curls exploded in ringlets past her shoulders, just begging for a man's hands to get tangled up in them. Bright blue eyes laughed straight at the camera, her daughter's pout made provocative reality on her full, red-lipped mouth, and she was so lush in flesh that she seemed about to spill out of her fire-engine-red halter top and shorts. She radiated sexuality, a delicious, visceral sexuality that demanded recognition, adulation and especially satisfaction.

Every male instinct in Liam sat up to attention. "Christ," he said involuntarily.

"She was a looker, all right," a voice agreed, and Liam jumped and looked around to see Carl Andrew standing next to him, regarding the picture with appreciation. "A man'd have to hustle to keep up with that." He grinned. "But it'd sure be fun trying."

"And how," Liam said, the trooper momentarily subverted by the man, and forgetting for the moment the necessity of establishing his air of authority. He pulled himself together and broke open the frame. On the back of the picture sprawling handwriting said, "Me, Kerry, Michael, David on board the *Scotch Mist* en route between Lanai and Maui. That's Skipper Chris Novak's knee. March, 1998."

From fishing boat to sailboat. A busman's holiday. The Malones, it would seem, never liked to get very far from the water. Liam looked at the reverse side again for a moment before slipping it between the pages of his notebook.

"What, you need a pinup or something?" Andrew said, offended.

"I'll need pictures of all the deceased," Liam said, setting the pieces of the frame down on the nightstand. "Sometimes a picture is all it takes to trigger someone's memory of events." He paused. "What was the brother's name? Jonathan, that's it. He worked as a deckhand on the *Marybethia*, and he lived here, right? Wonder why he didn't go to Hawaii with them."

Andrew snorted. "He probably went to Vegas instead."

Liam went downstairs. The rest of the council was standing around the living room, unwilling to make themselves too comfortable in a house where there was no host to ask them to sit down. "If the kids dead, who get the house?" Halstensen was saying. He had his back to Liam, and continued, "Damn fine house, this. Good house for big family. When you get married up, Walter, *gatcha*, you should buy this house."

Something in Larsgaard Junior's expression must have warned him, because he turned and saw Liam standing in the doorway. He didn't look embarrassed at being caught in a premature division of the spoils, he merely shut up in the presence of a *gussuk*, and a state *gussuk* at that. Liam didn't hold it against him, either the silence in the presence of the enemy or his practical disposition of the belongings of the dead. Housing, as he knew only too well, was a commodity in short supply, and this house, once the formalities were out of the way, wouldn't be on the market for longer than it took to accept an offer. Liam wished he could make one, and for a moment actually toyed with the idea.

But that would have meant a twice-daily flying commute. He shuddered. No. It was bad enough that his job entailed responding by air to villages as far away as New Stoy and Togiak. He didn't need to add to his air time.

He directed his attention from that ghastly prospect to the matter at hand. "What time was the fishing period in Kulukak yesterday?"

"Six to six," Ekwok said. "The tide was low at four-thirty, so everybody dropped their nets right at six."

"Were you all out there?"

"Yes. We all fish this period."

"You each have your own boat?" Nods all around. "So, you were all in the Kulukak at six a.m. on yesterday, Monday morning. Did you see the *Marybethia*? You did. Had her nets in the water, did she? Did she fish the whole period?"

Ekwok scratched his chin and looked at the other men. "Well, it's not like we were keeping track, but yeah, I guess she was there the whole time."

"I saw her at three o'clock," Kashatok said. "She was pulling away from the tender just before I pulled alongside. Molly, Jonathan and the kids were on deck, working on the gear along with those two deckhands. David was on the bridge, at the wheel."

"They set out next to me," Andrew volunteered. "A little bit before four."

"Anybody see them after that?" They exchanged glances, shrugged. "Okay. Can you give me some idea of who else was fishing in the bay yesterday?"

Halstensen spoke up for the second time. "Ask the tender. They'll have fish tickets, a tender summary. They'll have the names of all the boats that delivered to them."

"What's the name of the tender?"

"The *Arctic Wind*."

"Where do they take their fish?"

"Seafood North. In Newenham."

At least he wouldn't have to fly to Togiak, which was even farther west down the coast than Kulukak. "Great, thanks. Now, did anyone see the *Marybethia* after the period was over?"

A general shaking of heads.

"Did you all come back to town after six o'clock?"

"Yes."

"And you didn't see the *Marybethia* follow you in, or tie up in the harbor?"

"No," said Ekwok. "That don't mean nothing, though. There's fifty boats call our harbor home port."

Liam frowned. "Fifty boats?"

Ekwok waved an understanding hand. "Their owners don't all live here. Some live in Togiak, some in Newenham, some come up from Outside."

"They leave their boats here year-round?"

Carl Andrew shook his head. "Most of them are put into dry dock in Togiak or Newenham over the winter."

"Malone kept his here, I suppose." Ekwok nodded, and Liam walked through the living room and opened the door to step out on the deck. He leaned over the railing. The tide was in, but the water was clear and he could see the timbers supporting the dry dock. He looked up. Kulukak village was hidden behind a small point of land, a rocky outcropping with spruce clustered thickly on top. He could see the rock wall of the breakwater surrounding the small boat harbor, and what he thought might be the roof of the school.

Fifty boats, with fifty crews. He thought of the Jacobsons, even now heading for an opener in Togiak. Potential witnesses were going to be scattered across hundreds of square miles of open water, and he didn't even have the consolation of knowing they'd all go back to the same home port after the summer was over. "Fifty boats?" he said, hoping against hope that he'd heard wrong.

"Fifty," Ekwok said with what Liam considered to be entirely unnecessary cheerfulness. "Course, that doesn't count the skiffs. Bunch of people fish subsistence from skiffs."

The buzz of a small plane interrupted Liam's gloom, and he looked up to see a blue and white Cessna with the tail numbers "68 Kilo" on the fuselage lining up for a final approach to the airstrip. His heart skipped a beat, and he made rather a production out of folding up his notebook and stowing it away. "Gentlemen, I think my ride is here. Could someone show me the way to the airstrip?"

SIX

Summertime in the Bush smelled like Off. Well, Off and salmon. Wy smelled of both, but she smelled most strongly of herself, a scent somewhere between lilac and lemon peel, half sweet, half tart, part seduction, part challenge. Liam strapped himself into the shotgun seat of the Cessna and concentrated on that smell. It was easier than thinking about hanging his ass out over a two-thousand-foot precipice for the next hour.

Liam hated to fly. He was, in fact, terrified every time he got into a plane, Super Cub or 737, single or twin, floats or wheels. It simply wasn't natural to trust your existence to two wings and the lifting properties of something as ephemeral as air. You couldn't even *see* air, as he had pointed out to Wy on innumerable occasions when she had tried to alleviate his fear with a technical explanation of the theory of aerodynamics. After a while she'd given up, and Liam continued to sweat his way through more hours in the air than many private pilots. That he had the courage to force himself into the air in spite of his fear was a tribute to his strength of character, not anything his father had ever acknowledged, but then his father, the jet jockey, had never managed to mask his disappointment that his son had not followed him into the Air Force and the elite ranks of zoomies.

However, it didn't matter what Colonel Charles Bradley Campbell thought, because Colonel Charles Bradley Campbell was safely assigned to flight training at a naval base in Florida, over a thousand miles away, about as far as you could get and still be in America, hooray. Liam, a grown man, an Alaska state trooper for eleven years, the holder of a B.A. in criminal justice and an M.S. in counseling psychiatry, the investigating officer on the Houston serial killings and the Cyndi Gordon murder, both high-profile cases resulting in convictions celebrated in headlines as far away as Boston and the latter now an illustration in the textbook of a dozen police academies nationwide, this man had no need of paternal approval.

In the meantime, he stared straight ahead through the windshield, eyes fixed on the distant horizon, and concentrated on slow, deep breaths. His concentration was not what it should have been, given that he was sitting next to Wy, the closest he'd been to her in three months. Her hands were strong and capable on the yoke, her feet quick and deft on the rudders. Her dark blond hair was bound into a loose French braid, her jeans and plaid shirt clean and neat. A blue billed cap advertising Chevron fuel topped the ensemble. A headset with a voice-activated microphone was strapped on over the cap, and sunglasses in gold aviator frames hid her eyes. The ultimate in Bush chic.

She reached up and unhooked a second headset. "Put it on."

He put it on.

She taxied to the end of the runway and turned, adjusted the flaps, pushed in the throttle, pulled back on the yoke and they were airborne. Liam helped her, holding 68 Kilo up in the air by white-knuckled hands wrapped around the edge of his seat.

Not by word or deed did Wy betray how very awkward she must be feeling. A fair man, Liam figured she had to be at least as uncomfortable and tongue-tied as he was. "Your new trooper sent me out to pick you up," she had said briefly when she climbed out of the plane.

"Why didn't she come herself?"

"You've got yourself another murder."

"What!"

She nodded, holding the door for him, all business. "I'm supposed to get you back ASAP."

"Who? And where?"

"Don Nelson. He's been working for Professor McLynn at that archaeological dig on the Snake River."

He thought for a moment. "Yeah, an old Yupik village site or something. Some archaeologist has been digging up things there, right? About ten miles west of the base?"

She nodded, still brisk, waiting for him to get the hell on the plane.

"Who found—what was his name? Nelson?"

There was a brief hesitation. "I'm on contract to the state to support McLynn's project. We flew out this morning. That's when we found him."

"Son of a bitch," was all he could think of to say.

Her eyes met his for the first time, with the merest trace of perceptible humor. "My sentiments exactly."

He had turned to Ekwok, standing pretty much at attention at Liam's elbow. "I left the boat taped off. I'd appreciate it if you'd make sure that no one goes on board."

Ekwok glowed. "You mean I'm your deputy? Like John Wayne and Dean Martin?"

"Close enough," Liam said.

The climb to two thousand feet took maybe ten minutes, followed by the comparative bliss of level flight. The fog dissipated as soon as they were out of Kulukak Bay, and the sun chased cumulus clouds around the horizon. Liam's stomach took another five minutes to settle, at which time Wy's scent came back with a vengeance, teasing his nostrils, reminding him of the last time he'd seen her, and before, the last time he'd slept with her, that rough, hurried coupling in the front seat of her truck, the memory of which alone had been enough to let him live on hope for the last three months. It wasn't going to stay enough for much longer.

Maybe it was being in the air, maybe it was being in the air with her, but he found his body reacting to that memory. He shifted his legs, hoping she wouldn't notice, and then saw her wipe her palms down the legs of her jeans, changing hands on the yoke in a manner too studied to remain unobserved. A rush of heat suffused his body and pooled in his groin. "Wy," he said.

"We'll be there in forty-five minutes, relax," she said.

He looked at the back of that obdurate head, and a wonderfully welcome burst of anger washed away every other feeling he had, including fear of flying. He grabbed her braid and pulled her head around. "Set her down," he said.

"What?"

"Set her down!" he roared, and shoved the yoke forward with his right hand.

The Cessna took a nosedive.

"You son of a bitch!" She grabbed the yoke. "All right, you want down, you get down!"

The Cessna went into a shallow spiral, down, down, down, and Liam felt all the blood rise from his groin to pool just beneath the top of his skull. His lungs stopped working at fifteen hundred feet, his heart at a thousand, his sphincter muscle at five hundred. The needle on the altitude gauge backed off until the number one, one hundred feet, and Liam risked a look out his window to see the gear about to skim the tops of trees, growing ever larger in his terror-stricken eyes. "Wy!"

Her face was tight but she said coolly enough, "You're paying the freight. You wanted down, you get down," and in the next second the trees ended and a gravel runway appeared. The Cessna set down on a surface that was more root than rock and bounced to a lurching halt. Wy slammed her headset into its cradle and baled out to march up and down, swearing at him, swearing at herself, swearing at the strip, just generally laying a pretty good curse on life, the universe and everything.

Liam waited for his heart and lungs to resume normal function and his stomach to settle, and climbed out on shaky legs.

Wy wheeled around and poked him in the chest with a furious finger. "Of all the goddamn dumb things for you to do, that took the cake! You want to land, we can land, but I'll do it! You want to talk, we can talk, but on my terms! Don't you pull something like that in one of my planes ever again, do you hear?"

"I hear," Liam said, a bit light-headed and very glad to be back on terra firma. The strip, made of gravel and sand, seemed to be in the middle of nowhere, with no reason for its existence, a not unheard of occurrence in the Bush. The rustle of the black cottonwood and the balsam poplar in the gentle breeze, the tumble of water down a creek, the distant cry of an eagle were all that broke the silence. "What is this place?"

"Some oil company built it to drill a test well for natural gas," she said curtly, still steaming.

"Was there any?"

"No."

"Wy," he said.

Her head snapped up, but whatever she'd been about to say died on her lips when she met his eyes.

"I think three months is enough," he said. "You were angry. So was I. We said some things we shouldn't have. It hasn't changed how I feel about you." His smile was brief and painful. "Sometimes I wish it had. Sometimes I think you're more trouble than you're worth, Chouinard."

"You should talk," she replied automatically, but her hackles went down. She pulled off her cap and shook back her braid. There was a downed tree to one side of the runway and she walked over to sit on it.

He walked over to sit next to her, carefully maintaining a discreet distance. He wanted her right down to his fingernails, but the words were important, and came first. Before him, he thought with a inward grin, and almost laughed out loud.

"What?" she said, eyes on the cap she was pulling through her fingers. "What was so all-fired important you had to nearly wreck my plane to tell me?"

All impulse to laugh faded, and he sorted through what he'd been planning to say for three months, if not quite in this fashion or in this setting.

"You live awhile," he said slowly, feeling his way. He wanted to get this right. He wasn't as confident as he used to be of his ability to do that, not anymore. There were a lot of things he wasn't as sure of as he used to be. "You live awhile," he repeated, "and you gain some knowledge, and you hope a little wisdom, and you build this picture of yourself. You have sense, and integrity. You know what you will do, and what you won't. You draw a line, a line you know you won't cross, because you're a better person than that."

He glanced at her. She was staring hard at the opposite side of the runway.

"And then something happens, something you never expected, something you never imagined, and you find yourself doing something you never thought you'd do. You cross that uncrossable line, and that picture you had of yourself shatters. If you ever want to be sane again, you have to pick up the pieces and try to put the picture back together. But now it's flawed, cracked, out of focus. It'll never be the same."

He stopped, unable for a moment to go on.

"I know." Her voice was soft. "I know everything that you're saying. I know because I went through the same thing. But there is more to it than that."

He turned to look at her. "What?"

"I could have lived with the loss of my integrity, Liam," she said. "I could even have lived with the loss of your love. But I missed my friend."

He closed his eyes briefly.

"My integrity was gone, that picture of myself was gone, my lover was gone. And my friend was gone. We were friends first, Liam. I knew you were married. I knew about Charlie. Left to myself, I wouldn't have pushed it beyond friendship, not ever, no matter how much I was attracted to you. I don't do that! I've never done that, ever."

"And I did," he said, his voice wooden.

"Yes," she said. "You did. But I let you. I'm not blaming it all on you. We did it together. That's part of it, too. I'm not a home-wrecker." She paused, and added painfully, "And then I was one."

There was silence for a few moments. Liam could think of nothing to say.

A raven croaked somewhere off in the treetops. Liam looked up, but couldn't see him.

"I've got a puritan streak a mile wide, Liam. No matter how much I hated the waste of what we could have given each other, of what we could have been, of what together we could have given others, there was a little voice inside that said we did the right thing. You belonged with Jenny and Charlie, and I had no business, no right to try to tempt you away from them." She faced Liam squarely. "You said the words, Liam. For better or worse, for richer or poorer, in sickness or in health, so long as you both shall live. Till death do you part." She shook her head. "Nobody ever thinks about what those words really mean when they say them."

"Maybe not nobody," Liam said. "But damn few."

She nodded. "Damn few," she echoed.

"And not me."

"No," she said softly.

There was a short silence as they listened to the creek chuckle beyond the trees. "Jenny's dead," Liam said.

"I know. Moses told me. I'm sorry." She turned to meet his eyes. "I mean that, Liam. From everything you told me, I think Jenny and I could have been friends." She swallowed, and added in a painful whisper, "And I know you loved her. Maybe not like . . . Well. I know you loved her. Loved them."

"Yes." He thought of little baby Charlie, all cherub cheeks and lion's roar, and grieved again.

There was another silence. "What now?" Liam said at last.

She didn't look at him. "You'll notice I've never said those words. So long as you both shall live."

"I've noticed," he said, a little grimly. "And I have, and I didn't keep them."

"That's not where I was headed, Liam," she said, a little impatiently. "God, let's just set aside the blame for one minute, okay? We both made mistakes, big, fat, juicy ones, all right?" She turned to look at him, eyes level and serious. The sun sidled out from behind a cloud and turned her hair into a gleaming helmet of dark gold. "You asked me to marry you, remember?"

"I remember."

"You had no right to, and I had no right to listen. But you asked."

"You didn't answer."

"No. I didn't."

"Why?"

"Because however much I loved you, I wasn't sure I could say those words and mean them," she said simply.

It hurt, more than he would have expected it to. It took him a moment to form a reply. "And now?"

"And now?" She turned away from him. "I don't know, Liam."

His heart seemed to stop beating. "Don't you love me enough?"

Moments crept by. "I don't know," she said at last. "I want you, you know that."

"I know that. It's not enough."

"No."

He was angry suddenly. "Goddamn it, Wy. I've waited long enough. I want an answer."

"I'm not ready to give you one," she said levelly.

"Fine." He got to his feet and dusted off his pants. "Let me know when you are. I may or may not be around. No promises."

"Liam—"

"No." He cut off her words with a chopping motion, and fixed her with a piercing stare. "Just so you know, I'm not looking for one meal. I'm in the market for a lifetime supply of grub."

An involuntary laugh escaped her lips. "Liam—"

"No," he said, furious now, with her amusement and his own inability to put his feelings into words that would be taken seriously. "We've said all there is to say." He reached down a hand and hauled her to her feet. "Think about this, too, while you're thinking things over." He kissed her then, roughly, angrily, cupping his hands over her ass and grinding against her. She melted into him and his touch gentled without him realizing it.

That's all it took, all it had ever taken. His hands slid up and there was nothing but the taste of her mouth, nothing but the feel of her breasts against his palms, nothing but the sound of her breath coming in short, hard pants, of the little moans she gave as she strained against him. He felt the earth come up against his back with a solid thump. The material between his hand and her skin was suddenly intolerable and he ripped the front of her shirt open and shoved her bra up and took her nipple into his mouth. He wasn't gentle but she didn't want gentleness, tea.ing at the front of his jeans and thrusting her hand down the front of his shorts. "Oh," she said, when he filled her hand. "Liam, please." She knotted a fist in his hair and pulled his mouth from her breast. She bit his lower lip, and pulled one of his hands down between her legs, pushing up against it. "Liam, please!"

Her face was flushed, her eyes wild, and every instinct he had screamed yes. It would be fast and furious, hot and supremely satisfying, it would fulfill every dream he'd had in the last three months, hell, in the last three years. The heat came off her in waves, scorching him. She shoved him down and straddled his body, and it was his turn, eyes closed. "Wy . . ." He felt her hands tugging at his jeans and heard something halfway between a growl and a groan rip out of his throat.

"Shut up. Just shut up and let me— Jesus, Liam." Her hand closed around him and she leaned down.

He felt her breath on his skin and nearly came right then. "Wait," he said. "Wy, wait."

"What?" She sounded dazed.

He took her upper arms in his hands and sat up, sliding out from under her.

"Liam?"

He climbed to his feet, turning his back to fasten his fly. It wasn't easy, and it didn't help that his blurred vision couldn't seem to find the zipper tab, and when it did, that his fingers couldn't seem to hold on to it.

Behind him he heard the rustle of clothing, and knew she was putting herself back together, too. He took a couple of deep, steadying breaths. When his vision cleared the first thing he saw was his cap lying on the ground where she had thrown it after pulling it off. He swept it up and turned to face her.

The pulse was beating in her throat, hard enough to cause her collar to flutter. She was trembling, and she wouldn't look at him, fussing instead with one of the buttons on her shirt.

It would have been so easy to have taken each other then and there, on the rocks of the riverbank. He remembered in detail the clasp of her warm, wet flesh, the sound of the hitch in her breath, the salt taste of her tears, the smell of her sweat and that elusive, sweet-tart fragrance that was all her own. The way she arched up when she came, the surprise and pleasure in her voice when she cried out. And he remembered what it was like to kiss and touch and talk his way through a night with her, to come into her, to come inside her.

But one night was not what he wanted. One quick rutting on the deserted bank of a river was not what he wanted. Before, he had settled. Now, he wanted more, more than a hasty coupling in the front seat of her truck, or on the side of a deserted airstrip.

She finally finished with her shirt, but she still wouldn't look at him. She turned and took a step toward the plane. He caught her arm and pulled her to a halt.

She didn't try to pull away. He could feel the faint tremor in her body. "Why?" she said, her voice husky. "Why, Liam?"

Liam took a deep breath and expelled it. He pulled off his cap again and ran his hand through his hair, trying to choose the right words. "Because this isn't all I want," he said at last. "I want it, mind." He tried to smile. "Pretty hard to hide that." His smile faded. "But it isn't all I want."

Her voice was almost inaudible when she spoke. "What if it's all I want?"

He set his teeth and took his time resettling his cap on his head. "I'm a domesticated man, Wy. Okay"—he held up one hand—"maybe I wasn't always. I had my share of fun. But I liked being married. I liked waking up in the same bed every morning. I liked coming home to the same house every night." He hesitated. "I loved being a father."

He met her eyes straight on. "I want it all, Wy. All or nothing. Marriage, kids, starting with Tim, so long as we both shall live. For better or for worse. For richer or for poorer. Till death do us part. I know what the words mean now, Wy. Take it or leave it."

And then, with as much dignity as a man with an erection straining at the front of his jeans can muster, he turned and limped to the plane.

When they rolled to a halt in Newenham, he said, "You said Prince went out to the dig in your Cub?"

She nodded.

"You can't get a Cessna in there, can you?"

She shook her head.

"Can you scare up another Cub?"

She nodded again.

"Okay, I have to make a few phone calls. I'll meet you back here in about an hour?"

She nodded.

Fine. "Okay, see you then."

He walked away, cursing himself for ten different kinds of fool.

"Oh come on," Moses was shouting over the noise of the smoky bar, crowded with fishermen getting an early start on the evening. "There was nothing noble or tragic in that kid's death. This country has the potential to kill me six different ways before I get up every morning, but at least I know what I'm up against."

He drained his bottle and smacked it down on the counter and fixed the poor unfortunate who had incited his wrath that afternoon with a beady and, Liam noticed for the first time, very ravenlike eye. "This kid gets some half-assed idea, probably from Thoreau, who hasn't gotten half the kicking around he deserved, to wander out into the woods and live off the land. He has no survival skills, no woodcraft and he starves to death."

"Still—"

"He was on a road, for crissake!" Moses bellowed. "He even had a goddamn abandoned trailer for shelter! All he had to do was step outside and turn right and he could have hitched a ride to the nearest burger!"

Bill brought him another Rainier and he snatched it from her hand and took a long, steady swallow that drained half the bottle. "Frankly," he said, after a long, loud burp, "I'm grateful he died before he could lower the I.Q. level of the gene pool by procreating. I'm just sorry he left a diary so that yo-yo could write a book about him and inflict it on the reading public." Moses drained the other half of the bottle with another long swallow that everyone hoped would cool his choler. It didn't. "Make a hero out of him, you want to. In my book, he was just a dumb kid who literally didn't know enough to come in out of the cold."

He surveyed the bar in search of someone to disagree. Prudently, no one did so. Not only an elder, not only a shaman, not only a government-certified, Grade-A Alaskan Old Fart, Moses was a man it was unwise to cross when he got himself on the outside of a few beers. From the level of belligerence Liam could read in his attitude, it was evident that Moses had started drinking early this morning.

The shaman turned and caught sight of Liam. "Our man in Newenham! You didn't do form this morning."

Liam looked and felt guilty. "I'll do it tonight, Sifu."

"No, you won't, you'll be visiting with your dad."

Liam froze in midstride. "Excuse me?"

"Your dad, he's here, he wants to see you," Moses said. He surveyed Liam with eyes as shrewd as they were bloodshot. "You can run away to Newenham, but you're still in the world, boy. Didn't you know?"

Liam looked at Bill, who had her arms crossed on the bar. "Say it isn't so."

Bill nodded.

Liam realized he still had one foot in the air, and put it down. "My father is in town?"

"What, celibacy starting to affect your hearing now?" Moses roared. Heads swiveled in their direction from all around the bar, and Bill couldn't hide a grin.

"Let me get this straight," Liam said with determined deliberation. "My father, Air Force Colonel Charles B. Campbell, is in Newenham?"

A loud snort was all he got from Moses. "Afraid so, Liam," Bill said, trying for sympathetic and missing by a mile. The jukebox shifted CDs and Jimmy Buffett started singing about flying the shuttle somewhere over China, which was where Liam wished he was right now. It was a measure of his dismay that he could contemplate a trip on board anything with wings as an escape.

He pulled at a collar grown suddenly too tight. "Did he say where he was staying?"

"He said he'd be out at the base," Bill said. "BOQ."

"Thank you for passing on the message," Liam said, taking refuge in professional dignity. Establishing his air of authority, that's what he was doing. "I need to talk to you for a minute, Bill. It's business. Can we go into your office?"

Bill's gaze sharpened. "Sure."

He followed her through the kitchen, where a thickset Yupik woman in stained whites slapped thick patties of beef on a smoking grill and hounded a thin young man who looked enough like her to be her son to simultaneously take out the garbage, slice more onions, open more buns and wash more dishes. "Hey, Dottie," Bill said. "Keep 'em coming, we got a hungry crowd out there."

"And while you're at it, get some more hamburger out of the freezer!" Dottie said.

Bill's office was a cramped room next to the back door, with a desk, two chairs and a filing cabinet. The phone was ringing as they walked in. Bill pulled the jack out of the wall and the ring-ing stopped. She sat in the chair behind the desk and waved Liam into the other. "What's up?"

Liam told her about his morning, from the time Jimmy Barnes had given him the message until his landing half an hour ago at Newenham airport. He told her everything, with the exception of the impromptu stop on the deserted airstrip, because there were some things even the Newenham magistrate in all her judicial au-thority didn't need to know.

Bill listened, leaning back in her chair, hands clasped behind her head, a remote look on her face, breasts doing nice things to the front of her T-shirt. The woman was sixty if she was a day, and proof positive if anybody needed it that sex appeal did not end with menopause. When he was done, she said, "David and Molly Malone, and David's brother, Jonathan, and their kids, and their deckhands." She met his eyes. "Must have been tough to take."

Those endless moments breathing fetid air and wrestling charred flesh into body bags rolled back over him in an instant. "Tough enough," he said, his voice clipped.

She understood and accepted his refusal of sympathy. "And you're sure it's murder."

"One of the men was shot," Liam said flatly.

"You could tell that even though the bodies were burned?"

"I'm figuring the bodies were burned to hide that fact, and that the M.E. will find that they'd all been shot."

"The fire didn't do the job, though."

"No. That's when I figure whoever did it pulled the plugs on the boat."

"Hoping she'd sink."

"Yes. The bodies are on their way to Anchorage."

Bill took a deep breath and her breasts strained the words on her T-shirt all out of alignment. Liam looked over her head and thought of other things. For a woman who professed to be older and longer in Newenham than anyone else, Bill packed a punch as powerful as Molly Malone's picture. The stopover with Wy wasn't helping him maintain the fabled Trooper Campbell cool, either. "Did you know the Malones?"

Bill shook her head. "Not well. Oh, I cashed a couple of checks for David after bank hours. None of them bounced."

"What was his reputation?"

She considered. "I remember one time Harry Hart said Malone reneged on paying for a skiff Harry built for him. But I don't believe a tenth of what Harry says."

"Any romantic interests outside his marriage?"

"Not that I know of."

Not much to go on, but he'd started other cases with less. "Anything else?"

She grinned, displaying the merest hint of dimples and a set of white, even teeth. "Well, one time his daughter was in town on a school trip and her and a couple of her friends got all lipsticked up and tried to pass for drinking age. I ran them out, of course. I don't think I ever met the boy."

"How about Molly?"

"She never came in here. Never saw her anywhere else." She paused. "Heard plenty, though."

"What was said? And who said it?" Pretty much everyone came into Bill's place sooner or later. In her position as magistrate, she was on a first-name basis with every offender against the public peace, repeat or first-timer. In her self-styled role as the Elder of Newenham, she'd been in the area long enough to know where all the bodies were buried. Liam was no fool; in the past three months, Bill had become his central data bank.

"Mostly men coming in off the grounds, who'd been delivering fish to the cannery or been tied up to the processor at the same time as the *Marybethia*. They'd come in looking poleaxed and very, very needy. Usually they'd hook up with the first available woman and head for the nearest pair of sheets. She must have packed one hell of a punch, that Molly Malone."

Liam pulled out the picture of the Malones on the sailboat and handed it over. Bill studied it, lips pursed, and handed it back. "I see. I thought so. One hell of a punch. Must have been even stronger in person."

"Yeah." Liam looked again before pocketing the picture again. "Have to wonder if she saved it all for her husband."

"I didn't hear otherwise, I just heard a lot of wishing she did."
She paused. "You got any idea who killed them?"

Liam shook his head. "Not so far. Something going on with the
tribal chief out at Kulukak. I asked a few questions, I'm letting
him stew for now." He sighed. "The boat was adrift, looked like
it had been overnight. They'd been fishing, everybody agreed on
that because everybody else was out on the water, too. Nobody
saw them come home, so it probably happened out there. Could
have been any one of fifty fishers. Darrell Jacobson says he saw
a skiff leave Kulukak harbor about ten o'clock last night. Didn't
recognize who was driving it."

"Great. What now?"

"I called the Malones' lawyer from the post. Next of kin is
David's sister in Anacortes. He's calling her, and he'll call me
back. A tender was picking up fish during the period."

"Which one?"

"The *Arctic Wind*."

Bill nodded. "Seafood North. Right here in town."

"Yeah. I'm going to want to check all the *Arctic Wind*'s fish tickets for yesterday's period in Kulukak, get a list of the boats that
delivered. If Seafood North is reluctant—"

"Not a problem," Bill said, waving a dismissive hand. "I'll slap
a warrant on Virgil Ballard so fast it'll drop his socks."

In the absence of a judge, Liam relied on the magistrate to
back him up, and truth be told, Bill was more than delighted to
oblige. On occasion she had even been known to take the law
into her own hands, the most recent incident having been a man
apprehended by the local police in the act of beating his wife.
Drunk, disorderly and abusive, he'd made the mistake of hitting
the arresting officer.

The Newenham Police Department was understaffed, under-
funded and underestimated, although Liam could only judge by
reputation, as he had yet to meet any of them. The chief of police had resigned six months before under suspicion of embezzlement of public funds; in that same six months two officers
had been accepted into the state police academy, leaving the re-
maining two officers overworked, overburdened and overwhelmed. During the past three months the two of them had

either been in the middle of an armed conflict or sleeping under guard of wives armed with shotguns whenever Liam had tried to contact them.

All he knew for sure was that this particular officer had greeted this particular perpetrator's assault with such enthusiasm that the alleged perpetrator had been wheeled into the magistrate's hearing on local EMT Joe Gould's gurney. Bill had greeted his arrival with enthusiasm, deputized Moses to pull the public defender off his fishing boat and empaneled twelve people from the bar who had taken forty-five minutes to find the perp guilty of assault in three different degrees (he'd backhanded his eight-year-old son on the way to his wife). Bill thanked the jury for their service, dismissed them and sentenced the new felon to six months in jail then and there. As a magistrate Bill had no business trying anything but misdemeanors, but that didn't stop her. She didn't hold much with jury trials anyway, deeming them a waste of honest, hardworking citizens' time. "People got to work," she told Liam indignantly when he tried, delicately, to show her the error of her ways.

Liam hoped mightily that their district was never subject to review by the state Department of Justice, and that they never got a better public defender than the one they had now. Any case arising from judicial misconduct in Bill's court was bound to go all the way to the Supreme Court.

On the other hand, it was a Rehnquist court. Comforted, he said, "Thanks. I appreciate the help."

"No problem. You heading back over there now?"

Liam shook his head. "I've got another problem out at that village site that this university guy is digging up."

"I heard. McLynn was in the bar, trying to drink away the memory. Your new trooper came in after him." Bill raised an eyebrow.

"She's not my new trooper, she's the trooper newly assigned to Newenham."

The eyebrow stayed up. "Funny, I got the distinct impression she was working for you."

Liam took a deep breath. "I suppose she was here the same time as my father?"

Bill nodded, smile fading when she saw Liam's expression. "Did he say what he wanted?"

Bill looked at him for a moment. "He's your father, Liam. He doesn't need a reason to see you."

Wanna bet? Liam thought. "Okay, I'm headed back to the airport. Wy's flying me into the village site where she and this guy found the body. See what Prince has dug up. So to speak."

She winced and followed him into the kitchen. "Have you had lunch?"

A loud sizzling sound as raw potatoes hit boiling grease was echoed by the growl of his stomach. Suddenly he realized he'd flown a hundred miles on no breakfast, and that fear of flying burned calories better than the Boston Marathon.

"Wy, either, I suppose." He didn't have to say a word. "Dottie! Two burgers and fries, one to go, for the trooper!"

Dottie's expression didn't change. "I told you to peel some more potatoes, Paul! Get to it!"

Paul got to it.

SEVEN

The borrowed Super Cub, a two-seater with more wing than fuselage, looked familiar. "Didn't we spot herring in this puppy three months ago?" he wondered out loud.

Without answering, Wy pushed the pilot's seat forward on its tracks. Liam wedged himself into the seat behind, disposing his long legs in the limited space as best he could. "You sure the dentist from Anchorage isn't going to show up on the next Alaska Airlines jet and want to go fishing?"

"You want to get to the dig or not?" she demanded.

"I want to get to the dig," Liam said meekly.

"Fine." Wy climbed into the front seat and pulled it forward, which helped. This craft had no matching headsets, and Liam watched as she fastened the fold-up door and started the engine. Her fat braid hung down the back of her seat, curls escaping around her hairline and from every plait. She wore her hair long, she had told him, because it was easier to care for. Wash-and-wear hair, she had said, laughing at his intent expression as he used a blow-dryer to tame his own thick pelt.

He tried not to remember what her hair looked like loose on a pillow, a mass of blond-brown curls that wrapped around his fingers with a life all their own. He was still trying when they took off, so that he barely noticed when they became airborne, one good use his obsession with her served.

He approved of the thought the old ones had put into siting Tulukaruk, on a bluff where what looked like half a dozen streams joined before heading southeast into the Bay. Easy to defend, and an escape route if defense proved inadequate. Food and water plenty to hand, in the form of those selfsame creeks and the salmon that swam up them to spawn. The Natives were still waiting for them, at sites like this one, all over the Bay and the Delta. The fish fed their families and their dog teams. When the dog team was replaced by the snow machine, fish sold to Outside processors paid for their gasoline.

The last two years hadn't been good ones. Some people said it was the trawlers, the ones with nets a mile long, dragging the bottom of the north Pacific Ocean and hauling up every species, endangered or not, in its way to the surface. Some said it was El Niño, causing an increase in the ambient temperature of the Gulf of Alaska and moving new species north, as witnessed by the tuna caught off Kodiak Island for the first time last summer. Some said it was nature, and the cycle of life. No one really knew.

Some fishermen were selling up and moving Outside. Others were taking odd jobs, working construction in Anchorage or Prudhoe Bay, enrolling in computer classes, doing anything to maintain their families until the next big run came in.

As they approached the bluff and the remains of the tiny settlement, Liam wondered why its inhabitants had left. Had the salmon deserted them, too? Or had they been chased off by another, bigger, stronger clan who wanted the site for their own? Had the *gussuk* brought annihilation in the form of measles or influenza? He remembered reading in Alaska history class about the great flu epidemic of 1919, as terrible in Alaska as it was worldwide, how it had wiped out entire villages.

He saw Wy's cub, 78 Zulu, on the ground at one end of the bluff, and nearly swallowed his tongue. "We're going to land there?" he managed to croak.

She ignored him. They circled once over the camp and what Liam saw made him forget his fear for the second time. "Hey!"

"I see her!" Wy yelled over the sound of the engine. She banked to line up with the edge of the bluff and throttled back so far Liam thought the engine had died. They touched down lightly and rolled to a halt. Liam was out of the plane the instant it stopped moving and his longs legs ate up the ground between the bluff and the tents in seconds.

He knelt next to Prince, who was lying on her back, half in and half out of one of the tents, her hat a few feet away. "Prince? Diana?" He felt her throat for a pulse, and was infinitely relieved when it thudded against his fingertips.

Wy went past him and bent over the man.

"Is he alive?"

"Yes."

Prince's eyes opened. "Whozzit?"

"It's Liam Campbell, Diana, and Wy Chouinard. You're at the village site with . . . ah . . ." He looked at Wy for help.

"Professor McLynn," she said, and helped McLynn, groaning, to a sitting position. The left shoulder of his khaki shirt was stained with blood, which did not obscure the neat hole through his sleeve.

Prince sat up on her own. Her hand went to her head and she groaned. "Damn. I have got the worst headache."

She reached up. Liam caught her hand. "Let me look."

The hat and her thick hair had cushioned most of the blow, but there was a goose egg, swollen and tender, swelling her scalp. "Somebody clobbered you a good one." He sat back on his heels. "What happened? Can you remember?" Head injury was frequently associated with short-term memory loss; he hoped that was not the case here.

He watched her struggle to regain some kind of composure. "I don't know. Wait a minute." She closed her eyes briefly, opened them again. "There was a four-wheeler. When we landed."

"Where?"

She pointed with a shaking finger, and he got up and walked around the tent. There were fresh tracks, but no four-wheeler. He returned to Prince. "How long ago?"

She looked at the no-nonsense watch with the large round face and the big numbers strapped to her left wrist. "I don't . . . Fifteen minutes. Thirty. Maybe an hour? We were late getting off from Newenham, I had to preflight the Cub." Prince sighed, looking suddenly tired, and closed her eyes. "We saw the four-wheeler from the air. He was hiding inside the tent. He clobbered me with something, I don't know what. Felt like a sledgehammer. That's all I remember."

There wasn't any point in asking her if she recognized the guy;

she was too new to the area. McLynn might have, though. "Mr. McLynn?"

The man's voice was faint but definite. "Professor McLynn."

"Professor McLynn, did you see who shot you?" McLynn muttered something inaudible. "I beg your pardon?"

McLynn opened his eyes and shouted, "Miserable grave robber!"

"Did you see who it was, sir? Did you recognize him?"

Wy pressed him forward to glance down at his back, and he gave an involuntary, pain-filled groan.

"Wy? How's he look?"

She was shaken but her voice was firm. "He's only creased. He can make a fist. He's not bleeding much anymore. His skin is clammy and his pulse is fast but steady."

"You have a first-aid kit in the plane?" She nodded, and got it. Between them, they patched McLynn's shoulder and Prince's head. Liam closed the kit and stood up. "Wy?"

She looked up from helping McLynn to a seat on a log. "What?"

"Get in the air and start circling the area. Look for a four-wheeler heading away from here. Don't try to stop them, just figure out where they're going."

Prince got up and moved forward slowly. "It's all right. I can secure the scene. Go with her, sir."

He gave her a sharp glance. "Are you sure?"

"I'll be all right. I'll secure the scene."

For the fifth time that day Liam got into an airplane. This time his rage eclipsed his fear of flying, and he waited almost impatiently for Wy to climb into the front seat and start the engine.

Diana Prince was an Alaska state trooper. Nobody, nowhere, nohow assaulted an Alaska state trooper and got away with it. Liam wanted this perp's scalp, and he wanted to be the one personally to take it. "Come on," he barked. "Let's get the lead out."

Wy let down the flaps and pushed in the throttle and the Cub shot off the edge of the bluff, dropped a little and then grabbed for air and soared. "Don't get too high," Liam yelled. "Make a circle close in first. Then move out, a little at a time. I don't want to miss anything."

She nodded and banked left. Liam set his teeth and held on to his seat and stared out the left window. The area beneath them unfolded like an uneven patchwork quilt made of silver and green. Sections of river, flashes of streams, glints of lakes alternated with stands of cottonwood, poplar, aspen, birch and evergreen. Diamond willow bordered swamp, swamp edged lakes, lakes flowed into streams and rivers, and, "There!" In a move reminiscent of their experiences herring-spotting the previous spring, Liam hit Wy on the shoulder and pointed. "Right there!"

A four-wheeler trundled over the top of a rise in front of them. Wy dropped down to a hundred feet and roared right over the top of it. The driver cast a white-faced look over his shoulder and gunned the motor.

"Do you know him?" Liam yelled. Wy shook her head. "Go around again!"

She nodded to show she'd heard, and banked left to make a wide circle around the man on the fleeing four-wheeler.

Liam unsnapped his holster and pulled his weapon with his right hand. With his left he reached for the fastening on the door, folding the top half up until it latched against the underside of the left wing. Below, brush and trees and ponds and streams slid past at an unhealthy rate of speed.

Wy's head jerked around, even as they regained level flight. "What the hell are you doing, Campbell?"

"Find me a lake in front of him. Drop down as low as you can without landing and throttle back as far as you can without stalling!"

"Liam—"

"Just do it!"

She twisted her head enough to see his weapon, a nine-millimeter automatic, now stuffed into a gallon-size freezer Ziploc bag he'd pulled from the box of essentials she kept in back of the passenger seat, including a roll of duct tape, which he used to tape the bagged pistol to his right hand. With his left hand he folded down the bottom half of the door. Wind and the noise of the engine howled through the plane.

"No!" Wy shouted. "Liam, you can't! Don't—"

"You're working for me, Chouinard! Find me that goddamn lake or I'll jump right here!"

Her hands moved and the Cub took a nosedive, this time the throttle going back so far he thought for a fleeting moment she'd cut fuel entirely. They dropped to fifty feet above the deck, drifting above the ground like a kite.

Liam was terrified and furious and grimly determined. If all they did was follow, either the four-wheeler or the Cub would run out of gas. If it was the four-wheeler, the Cub still had no place to land nearby and the driver could disappear into the brush. If it was the Cub, the four-wheeler could make its escape while they were refueling in Newenham. A man was dead and two people had been assaulted, and Liam simply couldn't take the chance that the man on the four-wheeler, at the very least a material witness and at most the perpetrator himself, would get away.

He tossed his hat behind his seat, grabbed with his left hand for the handhold on the interior fuselage above Wy's head and twisted around to extend his left foot between the edge of the fuselage and Wy's seat, over the side, feeling for the tiny, treaded step bolted to the strut. He couldn't find it at first, and the bottom dropped out of his stomach. He forced himself to look down, spot the step and guide his toe to it.

A quick look at Wy showed him a pulse thudding at the side of her neck, her lips pulled into a snarl. Her hands were clenched on the yoke, and her eyes glanced from the dials on the control panel to the terrain below like someone watching a tennis match. His body weight hanging off the left side of the plane threw the trim out of kilter, and the muscles of her wrists stood out in an effort to hold the Cub to its slow turn.

She glanced in his direction and saw him looking at her. She unclamped her jaw long enough to shout over the sound of the wind roaring through the cabin, "If the fall doesn't kill you, Campbell, I will! Lake coming up! I'll count down from five! Jump on my mark!"

He nodded, all the response he was capable of, and settled his right foot on the edge of the fuselage where the door folded down. His left hand gripped the handhold like grim death and his right, awkwardly because of the pistol taped to it, grasped the edge of the door opening.

"When you jump, don't just fall, push yourself away! I'll bank right! Do you understand?"

He nodded.

She trimmed the plane, adjusted the throttle, checked their airspeed, ran a swift calculation for drift. "All right! Five!"

His fingers tightened.

"Four!"

The plane hit a bump and his right hand jerked free. The right side of his body swayed away from the fuselage, his hand flailing wildly for a grip, his body throwing the aircraft even further out of trim because of the wind resistance. Wy cursed and banked a short, hard right, and Liam fell forward, grasping at the door-frame. He'd just gotten hold of it again when his right foot slid off the edge. The entire weight of his body was supported between his left hand on the handhold and his left foot on the strut step.

The plane, mercifully, leveled out. "Three!"

The four-wheeler passed beneath them, the driver a transitory impression of black hair and faded blue plaid, hunched over the handlebars, driving desperately toward an escape that just wasn't in the cards.

"Two!"

Liam looked over his shoulder and wished he hadn't. They were skimming maybe twenty feet above the surface now. A clump of white spruce jumped out in front of them and Wy swore, and the Cub hopped up and over like a startled rabbit. Even at their reduced pace their airspeed felt entirely too fast for comfort, and like warp nine for someone about to jump.

"One!"

Liam summoned up every ounce of courage he had and tightened muscles he didn't even know existed. A flash of silver glinted ahead.

"MARK!"

He closed his eyes and pushed, the hand with the gun in it knocking awkwardly against the side of the plane. The Cub fell away from him as if slapped aside by his thrust alone, and he had just enough time to hear the roar of the engine as Wy shoved the throttle all the way in.

She'd brought the Cub so low he didn't have time to curl into a protective ball, and his back hit the water with a loud *smack!* He froze, more at the shock of impact than at the temperature of the water, which seemed almost lukewarm compared to his imagining. The reason became clear when he brought his legs down and touched bottom almost immediately. Shallow waters, even shallow waters in Alaska, had warmed up by the third week of July.

He stood up and his head broke water. The lake came to his chest. An explosion of sound he momentarily mistook for the Cub crashing came from the opposite end of the lake, and he turned to see a terror-stricken moose crash through the brush and vanish into the undergrowth.

His hearing was a little watery. He slapped the sides of his head to clear his ears, and was rewarded by the irritated buzzing of the Cub. He looked around and found it making a tight circle in the air just over a knoll to his right. He waved reassurance, and the Cub waggled its wings and pulled out of the circle to head back in the direction from which they had come, an arrow pointing his way.

Liam took a step forward and found the bottom of the little lake, barely a hundred feet across, rich with mud and rotting vegetation that clung lovingly to his feet. He slogged out eventually. The edge of the lake was not an improvement, a soggy marsh interspersed with pools of water and grassy hillocks.

He plodded grimly on until he reached the top of the knoll Wy had buzzed, where the ground was comparatively drier. The sound of the plane was nearer now, as was the sound of the four-wheeler, and his head cleared the top of the fifty-foot summit to see the Cub make a very low pass over the four-wheeler, only missing the driver's head with the gear by inches. The four-wheeler swerved and almost overturned and then straightened at the last possible moment.

The Cub came back for another pass, and this time, by god, she clipped him, the gear catching one of the handlebars with a thump. This time it was the Cub that wobbled off.

"Wy!" Liam roared, angry and terrified. "Goddamn it, be careful!"

Wy steadied the Cub, banked right and came back for a third pass. The driver of the four-wheeler pressed his chest to the gas tank and opened the throttle up as far as it would go. It hurtled up the slope of the knoll Liam was standing on and directly at him.

"Christ!" Liam yelped, and leapt to one side.

The man at the controls opened his eyes, saw Liam, let out a terrified yell and tried to swerve, but it was too late. Man and machine missed Liam with a foot to spare, and flew over the top of the knoll. They parted company about halfway down and crashed separately into the other side. Liam regained his feet and took the hill back down in giant steps, reaching the man as he got to all fours, shaking his head.

"Halt!" Liam said, and pointed his nine-millimeter.

The pistol was still in its Ziploc bag, still duct-taped to his hand. The man, revealed to be young and Yupik, looked at the gun, looked at Liam and got to his feet to run.

Liam had had just about enough of jumping out of planes and out of the way of oncoming four-wheelers, and he wasn't about to go haring after someone through the Alaskan Bush, especially in July. The mosquitoes had already formed a fierce cloud around his head. He felt for the trigger and fired a round skyward through the plastic. The resulting boom echoed for miles. "You run, by god, I'll shoot your ass off," he said, and he meant it.

The young man surrendered.

It was a full fifty-two minutes before the four-wheeler rumbled up the slope and onto the surface of the Tulukaruk bluff. Liam was driving. The previous driver was sitting behind, cuffed to the freight rack over the rear wheels. He was a chunky man who looked like he was in his early thirties, with golden skin scarred with acne, shoulder-length black hair that would have been beautiful if it had been washed anytime in the past month, and black button eyes that seemed unable to focus properly. He had a wispy mustache that made him look like a youthful, Yupik version of Wyatt Earp.

Liam was carrying a rifle in the crook of one arm, steering with the other. His brand-new uniform was damp and mud-streaked, there were strands of goose grass adorning his person and he had at least a dozen welts on his face and neck from mosquito bites, but he was at peace with his world.

That lasted as long as it took for him to pull the four-wheeler to a halt in front of the service tent. He dismounted, and Wy took three steps forward, made a fist and hit him in the gut with all the not inconsiderable force in her five-foot-eight-inch, 135-pound frame.

"Oof!" With a look of astonishment, Liam backed up a step and sat down hard on the four-wheeler seat he had just vacated.

"Hey," Prince said, eyes blinking open. She was sitting on a deck chair retrieved from inside the tent, one hand holding her head up. McLynn, his arm bound, appeared to be dozing in his chair.

"You suicidal son of a bitch!" Wy said, eyes blazing. "That is the last time you go up in a plane with me, I don't care how much the frigging state is paying! You could have been hurt! You could have been *killed*!" She wound up and hit him again, this time her clenched fist hitting him flush on the nose, and he was so befuddled he went backward ass over teakettle to fall heavily on the opposite side of the four-wheeler.

"Hey," the man cuffed to the back of the four-wheeler said, "fight!" He peered around himself with shortsighted eyes.

Prince rose to her feet, shaky but determined. "All right, that's enough." She managed to grab hold of one of Wy's arms.

Wy, unheeding, continued to shout, the volume steadily increasing. "You've got a death wish, fine, throw yourself off the deck of that derelict you're sleeping on! Jump in front of a truck! Get yourself shot by some drunk in a bar, I don't care!"

Liam raised himself to his knees. He gulped in a welcome breath of air and felt his belly. It was sore but it was still there. He tried hard to keep the grin from spreading across his face, and failed. "And to think I wasn't sure you cared."

It only fanned the flames. "You miserable prick!" She actually came around the four-wheeler and pulled back her foot to kick him, and was thwarted only when Prince caught both her arms this time.

"All right," Prince said, probably as sternly as she could with her head beating like a tomtom. "That's enough."

Wy wrestled free and would have clocked her, too, if Liam hadn't managed to get up and catch her fist in one hand. She tried to kick him in the shins then, which he thwarted by catching her foot and holding it in the air. He shook his head at Prince when she made as if to grab Wy from behind. "Stop it, Wy," he said, his firm tone belied by the grin, which had managed to spread all over his face and whose beam could probably be seen from orbit. "You hit her and you're assaulting a police officer." The grin widened impossibly further. "Hit me again, and it's a lover's quarrel."

She was visibly trembling with rage, a thing Liam had read about but never actually seen. "Fine," she said. He had her by her right hand and her left foot, and she had to give a little hop to maintain her balance. Tight-lipped, she said, "Will you please let go of me?"

"Certainly." All the same, he took a cautious step backward before he did. She turned and marched off to the borrowed Cub, parked precariously near the edge of the bluff and bearing all the signs of a hasty exit. She unfastened the cowling and became preoccupied with the engine, which Liam had reason to know was already in perfect shape. Her own Cub was parked more decorously at the opposite end of the makeshift airstrip.

He managed to get his grin under control before he returned to the tent area, and humor vanished as soon as he stepped inside the far tent and saw Don Nelson's body. He crouched next to it, elbows on his knees, hands dangling. Rigor had gone off; the joints were loose. Lividity was fully established. A rough guess would put Nelson's death somewhere in the past two days, sometime over the weekend, probably. Judging from the amount of blood at the scene, he'd been killed where he'd been found. The sooner they got the body to the M.E. to narrow it down, the better. It was hot, probably seventy-five, eighty degrees inside the tent, and even now the corpse was deteriorating. The smell wasn't as bad as it had been on board the *Marybethia,* but it was bad enough, and it would grow if the body was left there much longer, the decay that caused the smell taking precious evidence along with it.

Nelson's mouth was partly open. Liam leaned forward and pulled down gently on the jaw. There appeared to be a hole at the back of Nelson's throat, which would confirm what Wy had told him about Nelson's wound. It was too dark to make out details. He never carried his flashlight in the summertime, damn it.

"Here," Prince said from the tent flap, handing him hers. Of course she would be wearing a full belt.

He thanked her and clicked it on. The light revealed a horizontal and surprisingly neat wound at the back of the throat. He peered beneath the skull and saw the exit wound, partially hidden by lividity and the hair at the base of the skull. It looked as if the weapon had been wider at the entry point and narrower at the exit. Rough marks not unlike that of an open hand planted palm down smudged the skin of Nelson's forehead and eyes.

"Looks like a knife wound, all right," Liam said, getting to his feet. "And then somebody pulled it out."

EIGHT

The owner of the four-wheeler had fallen asleep, his head sunk to his chest at an awkward angle. "You know this man?" Liam asked McLynn.

"No," said McLynn, who looked pale and strained but alert. "Looks like he's from the village."

"A village," Liam said, agreeing, "but which?" He walked over to the four-wheeler and put his hand on the man's shoulder, giving it a gentle shake.

The man woke up with a phlegmy snort. "Whuh? Whazzat?" He blinked at Liam. "Who you?"

"I think that's my question," Liam said. The man looked confused. "Who are you, sir? What is your name?" Start with the easy stuff first, the information they had no reason to lie about.

"Frank," the young man said, willingly enough. He seemed less out of it that he had been when apprehended, although the smell of alcohol that emanated from his breath and clothes was still strong. His voice was low, and, like the Kulukak elders, he had the accent of someone who had grown up speaking Yupik at home and English at school.

"Frank what?" Liam said patiently.

"Frank Petla."

"Where are you from, Frank?"

Frank took time out to remember. "Koliganek."

Koliganek was a Yupik village halfway up the Nushagak River. "What are you doing so far away from home, Frank?" Liam said, perching on the four-wheeler seat, folding his arms and assuming the mien of someone who had all the time in the world to shoot a little breeze. It was after four o'clock, the afternoon sun was warm on their faces and a light wind was keeping the bugs off. His uniform was damp and uncomfortable, but he ignored it. He heard Prince shift restlessly behind him and turned his head to give her a warning look. Her eyes widened, and she subsided. Wy had moved from the borrowed Cub to her own, cowling up, head down in the engine, back turned to the others, the set of her spine a clear indication that he was still being ignored.

"Fishing," Frank said. He could have added, What else? but he didn't. Liam's uniform, damp or not, had finally registered. "You a trooper?"

"Uh-huh," Liam said peaceably.

Frank gave his wrists a futile tug. "You the one got me tied up here?"

"Yeah."

Frank frowned a little, thinking. "You jumped out of a plane."

"Sure did." Although it was something he'd rather not think about.

Frank was impressed. "Jesus, man, you coulda killed yourself."

From the corner of his eye Liam saw Wy's back stiffen. "I had to talk to you, Frank."

"Jesus," Frank said again. "You're worse'n the Mounties."

Liam smiled. "Why, thank you, Frank. I don't think anyone's ever made me a nicer compliment."

Frank's expression indicated that a compliment was not exactly what he'd had in mind. Awareness, and with it truculence, settled over him like fog down a mountain.

Liam did not depart from geniality. "What were you doing up here on the bluff, Frank?"

Frank tried bluster. "I don't know what you're talking about. I wasn't up here, I was minding my own business, riding my four-wheeler around, when you come flying out of the sky. You threatened to shoot my ass off," he remembered suddenly. He became indignant, or pretended to. "Waving that gun around like nobody's business."

"Speaking of waving a gun around—" Prince said hotly.

"Trooper," Liam said. He didn't raise his voice, but she shut up, jaw closing with an audible snap. He smiled at Frank. "I've got this problem, Frank. Maybe you can help me."

Frank eyed him suspiciously but didn't say he wouldn't.

"I've got a couple of people assaulted on this bluff, right here, less than two hours ago, by someone we think drove in on a four-wheeler." He clicked his tongue. "I'm sorry to have to say it, but yours was the only four-wheeler around."

Frank tried bravado. "That don't mean nothing. Hell, everybody's got a four-wheeler in this country." He jerked his head in the direction of the air base. "The goddamn military's got a dozen, they're all over the place looking for stuff that falls off their planes. Not to mention shooting moose they got no right to," he added bitterly.

"You're probably right, Frank," Liam said, nodding. "Still, I have to say we did a pretty thorough search from the air, and yours was the only vehicle we saw anywhere near here."

Frank hunched a shoulder. "Not my problem."

"Probably not," Liam said. He waited.

Frank grew uneasy in the silence. He tugged at the cuffs, and tried whining. "Man, can't you loosen these up? My hands are hurting."

"I'm sorry, Frank," Liam said, shaking his head sadly. "I can't do that."

Frank tried belligerence. "Why not? You got no right to hold me, man, I'm a Native. You got to turn me over to my elders."

"Your elders are about eighty miles northeast of here," Liam said dryly, "and I don't think they're going to want to have anything to do with you anyway. Village elders don't hold with murder any more than the state does, Frank."

Frank tried bluster again. "I don't know what you're talking about, man."

Liam became serious. "I think you do, Frank. I think you know exactly what I'm talking about." He saw the panic in Frank's eyes, and dropped his voice to a confidential level. "Look, Frank, I know how it is, you get a few drinks in you, you get in a fight with your girl, you climb on the four-wheeler and light out. You drive out over the tundra, you wind up here, you don't really know how, and you find a couple of *gussuks* messing with the bones of your ancestors."

"Yeah," Frank said, eyes locked to Liam's. "Messing with my ancestors, man."

"So you lose it. You coldcock one, you let off a couple of rounds at the other, winging him—nice shooting, Frank, by the way."

"Thanks, man," Frank said involuntarily.

"So you did shoot him," Liam said softly.

Frank tried panic. "No! I didn't shoot nobody! I don't even have a gun!"

Liam looked surprised. "You don't? Well, gee, Frank, who does this rifle belong to, then?" He picked up the .30-06 he'd leaned against the left front tire. "You had it when I caught up with you."

"I found it," Frank said. "It was laying on the ground." Inspired, he added, "I almost ran over the top of it with my four-wheeler, man. Somebody must have dropped it."

"Maybe a hunter," Liam suggested.

"Sure," Frank said eagerly. "A hunter."

Liam scratched his chin. "Well, maybe that's so, Frank." He paused, and looked skyward for revelation. "It's a pretty nice rifle, guy what owns it must take pretty good care of it. Doesn't look like it's been laying out too long."

Frank hunched a shoulder.

"What do you think he was hunting?" Liam said.

"What?" Frank said. "Who?"

"The man who lost the rifle," Liam said patiently. "What do you think he was hunting?"

"I dunno," Frank said, bewildered. "Ducks, I guess. Geese? Plenty of those around, this time of year."

"Well, sure," Liam said, warmly congratulatory. "Ducks and geese." He paused, and added reluctantly, "Of course, they aren't in season at the moment. Another month or so to go before you can even buy a duck stamp."

Frank forced a smile. "That don't mean nothing out here."

"No," Liam agreed. "You're surely right about that, Frank."

Frank brightened, until Liam added, "Of course, I don't believe a lot of hunters go after ducks and geese with a thirty-ought-six, now, do they? You'd have to be a mighty fine shot to do that, wouldn't you?"

"I dunno."

"A shotgun would be more likely for someone looking to bring home some birds for the stew pot, now, wouldn't it?"

"I dunno," said poor Frank.

"And I think any hunter worthy of the name takes better care of his firepower than to leave it lie in a swamp somewhere." Liam shook his head disapprovingly. "Lousy thing to do to a fine piece of equipment like this here Winchester."

"It's a Remington," Frank said. "A two-eighty. Oh." He looked wildly around for support and found none.

"It's your rifle, isn't it, Frank?" Liam said sorrowfully.

"I guess so," Frank said, looking ready to burst into tears.

"And you shot this man and hit this trooper with it, didn't you?"

Too late Frank realized what he'd admitted to and tried desperately to backtrack. "I never shot nobody!"

"I can see how it would happen," Liam said, ignoring Frank's outburst to paint a revised scenario. "You're fishing out of Newenham, you're between periods, you borrow a four-wheeler and you come here to visit the village. Maybe your folks come from here, and you've come to pay your respects." Liam folded his hands and did his best to look pious. "But maybe you had a few before you came, and when you got here you found two people poking their noses in where they didn't belong."

"Now, wait just a minute!" McLynn exploded. He was on his feet, and feeling much healthier, if the look of outrage on his face was any indication. "This man was grave-robbing! I got here and he was stuffing all the artifacts that I had excavated over the summer into a bag!" He pointed, triumphant. "That bag right there, tied to the handlebars!"

Liam looked thunderstruck, and slid the drawstring of the dark blue nylon stuff sack from the right handlebar to hold it aloft. Its contents pressed against the sides to cause interesting bulges in the thin fabric. "This bag?"

"That exact bag!" McLynn stood where he was, glaring. "I was going to stop him and he shot me!"

"Frank," Liam said, his heart broken. "This can't be true."

"I didn't shoot anybody," Frank said obstinately.

Liam emptied the contents of the sack on the ground.

McLynn pounced. "There, there's the carvings we found in two-E, probably amulets. This is the needle we found in five-F, and this is the awl we found in six-C."

"And this?" Liam held up what looked very much like a knife carved from a translucent length of bone. It had a short hilt, carved with figures long since worn to little more than faint ridges, and a short, wide, slightly curved blade that came to a sharp point. There was blood on it, dried brown and flaking, but it was something Liam had seen too often to mistake now.

Frank looked frightened. He said nothing.

McLynn hesitated.

"That's a storyknife," Wy said from behind Liam.

He'd known she was there and didn't jump, but Prince and McLynn did. "What's a storyknife?"

Too interested in the artifact to maintain her attitude of frozen fury, she took the knife and held it up. "I've got one of these. Mine's made of ivory. It's much smaller, though. This is beautiful. Look at the carving on the hilt. And it's old, too." She lowered the knife and looked at Prince. "It's a toy used by young Yupik girls. They take their younger siblings down to the riverbank and carve stories into the sand. Teaching stories, mostly, about kids who disobey their parents and are subsequently killed and eaten by monsters."

Prince chuckled. "That'll teach 'em, all right." She winced and put a hand to her head.

"I'm surprised to see one here, though," Wy said. "I thought storyknifing was a custom practiced only on the Delta. North of the Kuskokwim Mountains, anyway."

McLynn came forward and nipped the storyknife out of her hands. "Yes, well, that's all very well, but it is an important part of my research and my paper—"

"That's the knife we saw sticking out of Nelson's mouth when we found the body," Prince said.

"I thought it might be," Liam said, and took the knife from McLynn. He looked at Frank.

"I didn't do it!" Frank said frantically. "I found the sack! It was laying on the ground!"

"Right next to the rifle, I bet," Liam said.

Frank didn't even hear him. "I didn't take nothing! I didn't shoot anybody! I didn't kill nobody! I didn't do anything! I want a lawyer!"

There were six people, one of them dead, and two 2-seater planes, not to mention a pilot with a bump on her head. "Can you fly?" Liam asked Prince.

She managed a nod, although it looked painful.

"No shit, now, Prince," he said sternly. "Are you fit to fly?"

"Yeah, no shit," Wy said, the owner of the plane Prince was about to strap on.

"I can fly," Prince said shortly.

Wy surveyed her with a narrow stare. Prince met it without flinching. "All right," Wy said at last. She really had no other option, not if she wanted the Cub back at its tiedown that evening, and she knew it. She had an early flight the next morning, too, into a strip like this one that the Cessna was too heavy for, and she wasn't sure how many times the dentist from Anchorage was going to let her borrow the other Cub. "What about you?" she said, staring fixedly at a point somewhere above Liam's right shoulder. "We're flying full. How do you get back?"

The afternoon sun glinted off the rooftops of the Air Force base, ten miles to the east, and Liam, unwillingly, was put forcibly in mind of Moses' announcement of Colonel Charles Bradley Campbell's arrival in Newenham, and his request to see his only son and heir. It was a reunion Liam would just as soon take place in private. "You take McLynn back. Prince will take the suspect and the body." To Prince he said, "Take Frank here to the local lockup. Get Wy to show you where. Take the body to Alaska Airlines. Get it out to Anchorage on the next jet. I'll call the M.E." Which crusty old bastard would have a few pithy things to say on the subject of filling up his morgue. "I'll take the four-wheeler over to the base and hitch a ride in from there."

"Oh." Wy hesitated. He was surprised to see a flush rise into her cheeks. "I'm sorry, I forgot to tell you," she said lamely. "Your father—"

"You've seen him?" The words snapped out before he could stop them.

She nodded. "At Bill's, when I took Prince to find Professor McLynn. He was looking for you."

"I heard."

"Oh," she said again. "He told me to tell you he was here, because you didn't like surprises."

"He was right." About that, if about nothing else.

Wy opened her mouth, looked at Prince and McLynn, and closed it again. "Come on, Professor," she told McLynn. "Let's get back to town."

"I need to stay here," he said obstinately. "Somebody has to guard the dig."

Liam sighed, and said, gently but firmly, "You need that shoulder looked at, sir, and as I said before, this is now a crime scene. I have to take some pictures, draw some sketches, do an inventory. You can come back tomorrow."

"You're not staying here overnight, are you?" McLynn demanded. Liam shook his head. "Who's to stop some other cretin"—a pointing finger accused Frank Petla, who cringed away from it—"from coming in and trashing the place? I have weeks of work invested here, Officer, and months, hell, years of research! I have a paper to finish for delivery before the American Archeological Society that will open up an entirely new line of inquiry into the migratory patterns of the indigenous—"

Liam said in a mild voice, "Your work will have to wait at least a day, sir. I'm sorry, but that's the way it is."

Something in that mild tone convinced McLynn to shut up, but he glared impartially at everyone as he was assisted into the back seat of the borrowed Cub. With less care, Liam and Prince jammed Frank Petla into the back of Wy's Cub. Nelson's body had been bagged and stowed beneath Frank's seat. Frank looked down at the plastic-covered head lying beneath his feet and whimpered a little. Everyone ignored him.

Five minutes later Wy was in the air. She banked and made a wide circle around the bluff, watching Prince take off and dropping in directly behind her, her nose on Prince's six like a sheep dog herding one of its flock back to the barn.

Liam fetched camera and sketch pad from his crime scene kit. He wasn't going to knock himself out; he had a prime suspect in the bag, not to mention two superb witnesses to two additional assaults, one a distinguished scholar Liam assumed was a highly respected member of his field, no matter how much the pompous little fart annoyed him personally, and the other, glory of glories, an Alaska state trooper. Juries had a fondness for hard evidence, though, and he set about collecting some for those twelve good and true men and women.

He started in the service tent. One of the tables had been knocked completely over, a second leaned up against a third. Possibly where Prince had fallen when Petla hit her. She could have crawled outside afterward.

He righted the table. Scattered on the floor he found several items Petla had missed. There was a seal-oil lamp fashioned from a hollow stone. A tiny ivory otter, cracked and yellow with age and grimed with dirt, had rolled beneath one of the cots. Caught in the fold of fabric between tent wall and tent floor, he found a single walrus tusk, broken off halfway up its ivory length, which must have given the bull one hell of a toothache. It looked suspiciously white, and suspiciously like it was fresh off the walrus. It reminded him of the walrus head on Larsgaard's kitchen wall. *Asveq.*

There were walrus in the bay, hundreds of them, maybe even thousands, hauling out in the Walrus Islands State Game Sanctuary. The Marine Mammal Protection Act of 1972 provided for their complete and total protection from any and all human predation, until such time as they could be harvested in concert with an "optimum sustainable population keeping in mind the carrying capacity of the habitat." When a walrus got tangled up in a net chasing the same school of reds a fisherman was after, the fisherman in question generally decided that the habitat was carrying its full load of walrus and wouldn't miss one. A lot of walrus washed up on the Bay's beaches, dead of lead poisoning. Most of them had no heads, a little-known—little-known in scientific circles, that is—side effect of lead poisoning.

The Yupik, of course, had been harvesting walrus for the last ten thousand years, eating the flesh, making clothes and snowshoes and sled runners and water bottles and boat hulls from the skin and carving the tusks into masks and dolls and totems of animal figures, like the otter Liam had found.

And storyknives.

Liam was a little hazy on the rules of engagement regarding walrus tusks. Only Alaska Natives could take them, he thought, but they could be sold to non-Natives. Could they be sold simply as a tusk, or a pair of tusks, or did they have to be made into something? He couldn't remember. Charlene Taylor, the fish and game trooper for the district, would know. He'd ask her sometime.

He set the fragment of tusk on the table. Next to one of the cots a Blazo box did duty as nightstand, bookshelf and clothes drawer. One of the books stacked on it was a companion publication to a cultural exhibit, published five years before by the University of Alaska Department of Anthropology. The prologue thanked McLynn for contributing. He leafed through it, stopping when he came to a chapter headed "Aboriginal Life in Southwestern Alaska."

There were illustrations of various artifacts, including bentwood visors, seal-gut tunics, wooden breastplates, spirit masks wonderfully carved and decorated with beads, feathers and shells, and ivory figurines representing salmon, otters, seals, whales. It was illustrative of a rich and varied culture, and deeply interesting to Liam, who as a resident of southwest Alaska for less than three months was a stranger in the strangest land he had ever visited.

He turned the page and halted. The caption read, "Storyknife," and the illustration showed something eerily similar to the ivory knife that had been used to murder Don Nelson. The one in the book was more slender in form, more graceful in curve, with a narrower blade and a softer point, but still the two were recognizable as serving the same purpose. Liam's eyes dropped to the text. The knife in the book, unlike the murder weapon, had been carved of ivory, although the text indicated that they could be carved of bone, wood or antler as well. Tradition held that story-knives were made by uncles for nieces. There wasn't all that much to be known about storyknives, he gathered, as it was a custom that had died out about the same time contact had been made with the first Russian explorers. The curse of a culture with no written language.

He closed the book and looked at the map of Alaska stuck to the near wall of the tent with duct tape. Bristol Bay was south and east of the Yukon-Kuskokwim River Delta, but not so far and not so thin of rivers that the Delta Yupik couldn't have wandered into the Bay. They must have come, and brought their storyknives with them. The method of Don Nelson's murder was all Liam needed for proof.

He opened the book again and saw the owner's name inside the cover. Don Nelson, a street address, Seattle. If found, return postage guaranteed. He closed the book again. If he wasn't mistaken in his Seattle geography, that address was north of the University of Washington. Nelson, who looked young enough to be a graduate student, might have been enrolled at U-Dub. Maybe a call would put Liam in touch with his next of kin.

Not a task he was looking forward to, that he ever looked forward to, the part of the job that any law enforcement officer dreaded. He put the book back and bumped the Blazo box in the process. A small spiral notebook with a bright blue cover dropped from the folds of a white Gap Beefy T-shirt, size medium. He opened it and read a few entries in a b.g, looping hand.

June 28
Found an otter charm, probably off a visor. Man, did the old folks know how to carve! There is more art in an Aleut visor than there is in a '57 Chevy. Says a lot about a people when they could make something so necessary and so functional so beautiful as well.

July 1
A family from Icky came down the river today in skiffs. Looked

like they were going fishing. Said they were descendants of the people who lived on this bluff. Lynny pissed off the father when he said this was now Park Service land and they were trespassing. Daughter sure was pretty. Tried to talk to her but Mom wasn't having any. Maybe I'll look her up, if Lynny ever gives me any time off. Hasn't happened yet.

July 6
Uncovered a storyknife today. Made of bone, old enough for the carving to be worn smooth. Lynny's all torqued because it's too far east.

July 9
There's a dump site of some kind a mile east from camp. Lynny's not interested in anything but what we can find here. Which means what he can find to support his thesis. Academics.

The one-word condemnation made Liam smile. He'd been to graduate school himself. The truth was that Nelson, if he was a graduate student, would eventually have evolved into an academic himself, scrambling to defend his own thesis from the attacks of competitors. The fight for an original thesis was bellicose and bloody, especially since the advent of offset printing. If you wanted tenure, you had to publish. If you wanted to publish, you needed a thesis topic sexy enough to satisfy your committee and attract a publisher. Liam had suffered through his share of required texts, and his opinion was that academic writers who could get through a hundred thousand words without once using the phrase "As we shall see" were deserving of the Nobel Prize in literature, not to mention the grateful adulation of advanced students everywhere. But then, not everyone could be Barbara Tuchman. Liam was still mad at her for dying.

He flipped to the last page of the journal, which was dated the previous Saturday.

July 25
Lynny went to town yesterday, like always. He told me to work on three-C but I poked around the dump site instead. Hate to admit it

but I think it's modern. Feeling sick. Couldn't eat. Don't know how
I could have picked up a bug out here. Lynny must have brought
one back from town.

Poor Nelson. The sick and the dead, he thought irrepressibly. He chastised himself for the irreverence, and pocketed the journal to read through completely later. Frank Petla had seemed familiar with the village site and the surrounding area; perhaps he'd made a habit of dropping in to see what he could scrounge in the way of marketable artifacts. Perhaps that habit had been witnessed by Don Nelson. Perhaps Nelson had noted it down in his journal. The district prosecutor, a short, bellicose redhead of Irish descent who advocated the return of the death penalty, would like that. The jury would positively love it.

He picked through the rest of the detritus, not finding much. There were a lot of tools, and six large three-ring binders labeled "Costumes," "Weapons," "Utensils," "Hunting," "Crafts," "Religion." They were filled with a cramped, deliberate handwriting totally unlike Nelson's sprawling penmanship, by which Liam deduced that they were McLynn's notebooks. They included penciled drawings of various artifacts of such precision and delicacy that Liam reluctantly revised his opinion of McLynn's talents up a notch.

There wasn't much else. Some clothes that smelled as if they hadn't been washed in weeks, some recreational reading featuring such diverse characters as Emma Woodhouse, Richard Sharpe and Job Napoleon Salk. There was a Walkman with a dozen tapes, including the Beastie Boys, Loreena McKennitt, Fastball and the *Titanic* soundtrack. Liam was not impressed, but then under Bill's tutelage he was learning to appreciate Jimmy Buffett. Plowing straight ahead come what may. That's me, Liam thought, the cowboy in the jungle.

He poked around some more, but there wasn't much else to find. He was reluctant to leave, though, and not just because Colonel Charles Bradley Campbell was waiting for him at the other end. Liam had never been on the site of an archaeological dig before and he admitted to some curiosity. All the neat little squares with all their neat little layers being revealed one at a time. There were half a dozen brushes of various sizes and kinds of bristles lying around; Liam realized that the brushes must be what were used to reveal the next layer down, and marveled at the patience the science required. It was probably enormously taxing physically as well: long hours of crouching over a specific section of dirt, moving the bristles patiently back and forth, back and forth. There was a square sieve made of wire mesh in a wooden frame; they must strain the dirt before they tossed it so they didn't miss any pieces, however tiny. Kind of like casework, Liam thought. Only in casework he was the sieve.

It was by now late afternoon, and the sun still beat on the outside of the tent, raising the interior temperature to what felt like ninety degrees. Flies buzzed over the patch of dried blood, but they didn't sound very enthusiastic about it. During the excavation process the flaps would probably have to remain closed to keep the bugs out, so there would be little or no circulation. Liam preferred a job that kept him outside much of the time, even if it meant that he must occasionally suffer the slings and arrows— not to mention the knives and bullets—of outrageous citizenry. But he'd take fresh air with a bullet over crouching in an old grave in a closed tent any day.

He went back outside and drew in a breath of that fresh air. It tasted good. It was a beautiful view, too, he thought, without knowing it joining Wy in her admiration of the fall of ground from in front of the bluff to the river below, the scattering of glittering lakes and streams, the distant surface of the bay gleaming blue in the sun. Yes, the old ones had known what they were doing when they built here. A defensible position, an accessible escape route, food, water and a vista that went on forever. He wondered what they had thought about the edge of the ocean where it vanished over the horizon. Did they fear it? Yearn after it? Was it where they ascended to heaven? Was it where they placed their gods' homes?

He turned and looked at the dig, the two tents, walls flapping in the afternoon breeze. The prospect seemed somehow forlorn, almost lonely, and a fragment of verse from his favorite poet came to his mind, describing another forsaken graveyard nobody visited. So sure of death was this place, too, from which living men shrank, as if denying a place of death denied your own. Liam knew better.

So did Don Nelson, now.

NINE

A mile from the dig he found the dump Nelson had referred to in his journal and, glad to delay the inevitable, stopped the four-wheeler. It was a mound of dirt fifty feet across, and some of it had been there long enough for the grass to sprout. There was even some Alaska cotton, white tufted blooms waving in the breeze, and some dwarf fireweed, although those two hardy plants would probably sprout before the lava cooled off after a volcanic eruption. Over the other, fresher dirt, there were marks of some tracked vehicle, a small bulldozer maybe, or a backhoe. Liam walked all the way around the mound, and found a hole dug in the far side, away from the dig. He wondered if Don Nelson had been digging there. He kicked at the sides of the hole, and the clods came away easily, not yet hardened into place by the passage of time. He didn't see anything but dirt and more dirt, so he climbed back on the four-wheeler.

It took over an hour to get to the Air Force base, and by the end of the journey Liam was heartily sick of trying to keep the four-wheeler upright. There was nothing intrinsically unstable in the design—handlebars, a seat and a freight rack equally balanced over four wheels—but for some reason it threw his balance off. The only time he'd been on the direct path to the base was when he'd been crossing it, and he'd had to get out and push his way through the mud three times, which didn't improve his frame of mind. The knowledge that he was going to face his father for the first time in over three years with a stained uniform and muddy footgear soured his mood even further.

He knew enough to go around the runway, not across it, but they were waiting for him anyway, a Jeep with a couple of M.P.'s in white helmets sitting in front, identical quizzical expressions on their very young faces. Military men always wore the same mustaches: a thin fringe of hair that never quite seemed to fill in. Theirs were brown and blond, and only served to make them look even younger and more government-issue than they already were.

Liam said who he was and what he wanted, and the driver slammed the Jeep in gear and made a wide, flamboyant circle around Liam to lead the way. Liam fell in behind, the four-wheeler marginally more stable now that he was on pavement.

He'd been born on an Air Force base in Germany, and he'd spent most of his formative years on Elmendorf Air Force Base in Anchorage. Here were the same regulation buildings lined up at the same regulation angles, the bunkhouses for the enlisted men, the shops and hangars lining the runways, the command and administrative offices, always the biggest buildings on any base. Everything was made of the same material, too, siding and shingles covered with regulation gray paint, all purchased in bulk by the Department of Defense from the lowest bidder, who was usually one of the larger contributors to reelection campaigns of members of the Senate Armed Services Committee. Squares of regulation-height grass fronted the living quarters and the administration building, and someone had taken the time to comb the banks of the Nushagak River for regulation-size rocks, paint them a regulation white and line them up around the regulated squares of lawn. The benevolent old sun bathed everything in deceptively mellow light, miles of gleaming black tarmac, the runnels of the corrugated tin roofs, the surface of the great river and the Bay beyond.

That selfsame sun positively glittered off the metal wings of the aircraft parked on both sides of the strip, outlining the silver fuselage of the jets, the camouflage patterns of the Hercs and the bright orange paint jobs of the AirSea Rescue units with almost painful clarity. Heavy equipment was lined up like soldiers next to a garage, a tractor with a big silver blade, a road grader with an even bigger blade, a dump truck, a front-end loader, a backhoe and some others Liam didn't recognize. He'd bet the Air Force base's taxiways were clear of snow before the runway in Newenham was.

Liam followed the Jeep along a regulation route and pulled in next to them in front of the regulation Base Officers' Quarters, which naturally had the largest lawn, the nicest view and was the farthest away from those noisy runways. The M.P.'s got out, straightened their regulation uniforms and trod the regulation steps. The second waited for him, regulation door held open.

Liam interrupted his snide inner commentary with a pithy warning to pull up his regulation socks. Okay, he'd affronted his father, a career man, by refusing a similar life in the military, and he'd further annoyed Charles by being afraid to fly, thus condemning himself to a lifetime of not necessarily silent disapproval. That said, Colonel Charles Bradley Campbell was not the entire United States Air Force. Chinook Air Force Base was a pretty little base, neat and tidy, in a beautiful setting, and seemed prepared for action. The men and women stationed here were serving their country for a paltry remuneration and at considerable personal sacrifice, most of them far from homes and families. He brushed futilely at the dirt on his pants, squared his hat, thanked the men in the Jeep with grave courtesy and climbed the stairs, trying not to feel that he had descended from the tumbrel only to ascend to the guillotine.

There was a comfortably furnished sitting room, with chairs and couches and tables and lamps scattered here and there. A writing desk sat in one corner, furnished with notepaper, envelopes and pens. A small refrigerator hummed in another corner. A baseball game played on television, courtesy of the satellite dish on the roof outside. An open window looked toward the river and the opposite bank, a mile away. At night you could probably see the lights of Port of Call, the tiny little village perched at the eastern edge of the river mouth. Every five or six years a winter storm took out more of that sandy bank, and every year those who refused to give up and move into Newenham moved their houses back another ten feet.

The room held only one occupant. Charles Bradley Campbell flicked off the television and rose to his feet. The M.P.'s stiffened into braces and snapped off salutes. "Colonel Campbell? This is Alaska State Trooper Liam Campbell. He says he's looking for you."

Liam's father gave Liam's uniform the once-over and his brows drew together. "I'm not sure I should claim him, boys."

The boys didn't risk a smile.

"Dismissed," Charles told them, and they fell back a step, pivoted and marched out.

"Dad," Liam said.

"Son," Charles said. He held out a hand. Liam took it. His father's grip was warm and strong and didn't linger. "How have you been?"

"Swell," Liam said.

One dark eyebrow went up, but all his father said was, "I was sorry I couldn't make it back in time for the funeral."

"Either of them," Liam heard himself say.

The eyebrow came down. "I called you."

"Yes." Both times.

"I was on duty when Charlie was buried, Liam," Charles said in a level voice. "In the Gulf."

Translation: I was under arms, serving my country in the front lines. Personal considerations must be sacrificed when the fate of the nation hangs in the balance. "I know," Liam said.

"And as for Jenny, it happened so fast. I couldn't have made it back in time."

You fly jets at twice the speed of sound, Liam thought. You couldn't have signed one out for a cross-country check ride, two days there and back again? "I know," he said again. "I'm sorry."

His apology was less than sincere and they both knew it, but it gave them room to move on. "What happened to you?" Charles said, indicating Liam's uniform.

"I fell into a lake."

Charles sat down and waved a hand. Liam brushed at the seat of his pants and sat down opposite him. "How did you do that?"

"I was in pursuit of a suspect."

Charles smiled. "Did you catch him?" Liam nodded. "Good. That's all that matters, then."

Not quite all, Liam thought. "What are you doing in Newenham?"

Charles shrugged and sat back. "The 611th Engineer Squadron is doing a risk assessment study of Chinook Air Force Base, prior to an evaluation as to its continued viability."

Liam fast-forwarded the words through a mental decoder, militaryese to English. "They thinking of closing the base?"

"It's a possibility."

Chinook Air Force Base funneled a lot of cash into the Newenham economy. Combined with the last disastrous fishing season and the one currently in the making, the closing of Chinook might provide the third strike, you're out. It would severely impact Liam's job as well; an economic downturn invariably coincided with an upturn in alcoholic intake, and alcohol already fueled eighty percent of the offenses on his arrest reports. Child abuse, spousal abuse, assault, rape, murder—he could look for increases across the board. "Sometimes I think the fall of the Berlin Wall wasn't entirely a good thing."

"It's not a done deal," Charles said, "or even a sure thing. But with long-range jets and midair refuelings, we can police the North Pacific very efficiently from fewer and more centrally located bases." He shrugged again. "And, as you say, the fall of the Wall hasn't provided an incentive for Congress to continue to pour funds into national defense. The Cold War is over, we won, and it's time to stand down." A lift of his lip told Liam what Charles thought of Congress's take on the situation.

"What will happen to the base?"

"That's what we're working on now. The Air Force is committed to a safe community reuse of its former facilities." Charles sounded as if he were reading from a press release. "The base has a lot of potential. We're reaching out to the local Native association. The state Department of Transportation is interested. It could even be turned into an extension of the University of Alaska, bunkhouses for dormitories, plenty of classroom space in the admin buildings. You could put an aviation school here; you've got runways and hangars and fairly consistent weather. Maybe set up an AirSea Rescue training facility. Or perhaps a fish-processing operation. But like I said, it's not a done deal. I'm here to talk to the base commander and his staff, and to evaluate their operation, see how necessary it is to the Alaska Defense Command."

"They pick you because of your time at Elmendorf?"

"My familiarity with the Alaskan Air Command didn't hurt."

"How long will you be here?"

"I don't know. A week, ten days, maybe." Charles changed the subject. "I met a friend of yours this morning."

In spite of everything he did to prevent it, Liam's shoulders tensed, and Charles's twenty-twenty pilot's vision spotted it right off. "Who was that?" Liam said.

"A local pilot, name of Schwenard."

"Chouinard," Liam said automatically, and cursed himself. Hell. Might as well go the whole route. "Wy Chouinard."

"Ah. What kind of name is Wy?"

"Lakota Sioux. Short for Wyanet. Means beautiful."

"Um." Charles was good at those noncommittal noises that said nothing and meant everything. It was part of Liam's patrimony, and a useful adjunct to his interrogation technique, but he wasn't in the mood to be grateful today. "She mistook me for you at first."

Liam refused to be drawn. "Well, you know how men in uniform all look alike."

Charles laughed, a sound of genuine amusement. "I don't think that was it." He raised his brows, a clear invitation for Liam to confide in him.

Liam thought about what his father would say if he knew that Liam and Wy had had an affair before Jenny's death, and decided to keep his own counsel, although exactly why was beyond him. Why should it matter what Charles thought of him? It wasn't like the older man was around all that much, it wasn't like they had anything in common to begin with, it wasn't as if anything in Liam's life was predicated on the fact of their kinship.

And it wasn't like Liam knew exactly what his relationship with Wy was at present, anyway. He remained silent.

Charles's expectant smile faded, and he said in a flat voice, "I also met the other trooper for the area. An Officer Prince?"

Liam relaxed, just a little. "Yes. She's new. Just arrived today, in fact."

"She's also a pilot, she tells me."

Liam nodded. "The troopers are looking for pilots nowadays."

Yet another conversational pit yawned in front of them. Charles Campbell had done his best to cure Liam, stuffing his ten-year-old son into the cockpit of a Piper Tri-Pacer and talking him through endless takeoffs and landings, but Liam's fear was real, visceral and debilitating to the point of making him physically ill. Charles had persisted with recreational flying trips to Talkeetna and Seldovia and Iliamna, up until Liam was sixteen and reached his full height, six feet three inches, and could look Charles straight in the eye and say, "No."

Liam supposed he should be thankful for Charles's attempts, as they had taught him just how tightly he could hold his sphincter muscles, a habit which proved invaluable when he became a trooper and flying into remote communities became part of the job.

But he wasn't.

Unwisely, Charles said, "Ever thought of trying to learn again yourself?"

"No."

Subject closed. "She's a looker," Charles said. "Your new trooper," he added when he saw Liam's moment of confusion.

With an effort, Liam recalled Prince to mind. "I guess so," he said.

"You guess so?" Charles chuckled. "I know so."

Liam's gaze sharpened. "You're here for a week, ten days tops. Don't."

If anything Charles's smile widened. "She's a grown woman."

What could Liam say? It was true. He got to his feet. "I'd better head back into town."

"What's the rush?" Charles said, rising in turn. "I thought you caught the guy."

"I caught one. I'm working two cases at the moment."

"What's the other?"

"A mass murder in Kulukak."

"A mass murder? How many?"

"Seven."

Charles grimaced. "Ouch. Sounds like a battlefield."

Liam shrugged, the movement an unconsciously perfect copy of his father's, a smooth integration of muscle and bone that made both men look like big, lazy tigers just before they attacked. "Dead is dead," he said, not quite lying and not quite telling the truth, either. "Can I hitch a ride into town?"

Charles's brows went up. "How did you get here?"

"Prince flew the perp I caught back to Newenham. There wasn't room in the plane for all three of us, so I drove his four-wheeler here. It was a shorter drive to the base than it was to town."

"What do you want to do with the four-wheeler?"

"Somebody else can pick it up. I'm not driving it another inch, let alone forty miles."

Another officer passed them as they came out of the building. He saluted Charles and did a double-take at Liam. "Hey, you the guy who jumped out of the plane? Man, are you crazy?"

Charles's head whipped around. The other officer said to him, "You should have seen it, sir. We saw this Cub buzzing around about ten miles west of here, and we started monitoring things through the scope. And then this guy bails out, just bails out and splashes down into a lake." He shook his head, half in admiration.

Liam said shortly, "I don't know what you're talking about," and followed his father to a row of trucks lined up in front of a bull rail; Detroit-issue steeds with government plates and Air Force brands on the doors. Charles climbed into one, Liam took the shotgun seat and as they rolled through the base gates Charles said, "Just how did you apprehend your suspect, Liam?"

"Have you talked to Callahan lately?" Liam said. "Last time I saw him, must have been fifteen years ago. Has the old bastard taken retirement yet?"

And they spent the forty miles of gravel road between Chinook Air Force Base and Newenham talking of old acquaintances from Anchorage and Elmendorf. One thing about Campbell Senior, he could take a hint. If he wanted to.

He dropped Liam in front of the trooper post, came inside ostensibly to check out Liam's office, really to see if Prince was there, which she wasn't, and made a date with Liam for dinner the following evening at Bill's. Liam stood on the porch, watching the truck go around a corner and out of sight. "Wait a minute," he said suddenly. "You're a pilot, not an engineer."

He went back inside and called his father's office in Florida. It was six o'clock Alaska time, which made it ten o'clock Florida time, so there was no answer. Tomorrow, he thought, hanging up the phone.

He tried the number David Malone had had on file for Max Bayless, and got the not-in-service message that began with those three loud and infinitely irritating tones that jarred the phlegm loose in his sinuses. He called Directory Assistance. The phone on the other end rang thirteen times—he counted—and then was answered by a breathless voice that had to rise over the noises of squabbling children in the background to inform him that she had no listing for a Bayless, Max, a Bayless, Maxim, a Bayless, Maximilien, or a Bayless of any kind, for that matter. A dead loss to the state of Alaska of sixty cents.

Prince walked in. "You been to the hospital?" he said.

She nodded. The gesture didn't look as painful as it had a couple of hours before. "I'm okay. They gave me some pain pills if I need them."

"You need them?"

"No," she said firmly, and made her report. She had managed to get Don Nelson's body on the last plane out to Anchorage. Frank Petla was locked up in one of the six cells located behind the local police department's dispatch office, waiting on arraignment. If Liam couldn't talk Frank around his request for a lawyer, he would have to delay further interrogation for either an early return of silvers, which would precipitate an equally early return to town by local public defender Cecilie Lundren from her fish camp up the river, or request a public defender from Anchorage. The way the fishing season wasn't going, it looked like requesting a P.D. from Anchorage would be preferable, although with state cutbacks it would probably be a week before one showed.

There was no longer any pretense in the American judicial system of a swift and speedy trial, Liam thought. So much for the Sixth Amendment.

But the sooner Liam informed Bill Billington of Don Nelson's death and Frank Petla's apprehension, the sooner she could swear out a felony warrant and the better for his chances of a conviction. Liam dearly loved convictions, and he didn't want this one screwed up because he'd violated the doctrine of habeas corpus. Too bad Frank Petla couldn't be tried before Bill. The letter of the law did not worry Bill a great deal, and her trials, conducted at Bill's Bar and Grill with Bill presiding over the bar and before a Greek chorus of bar patrons, most of whom were a little worse for the wear, frequently achieved the level of performance art.

He thought of Teddy Engebretsen, defendant in the first of Bill's trials Liam had witnessed, and grinned involuntarily. "Sorry, Prince. No, go ahead. What else?"

The phone rang as Prince was finishing her report. Liam picked up the receiver and said, "One moment, please," and covered the receiver with his hand. "Have you looked for a place to stay?"

Prince shook her head. "Well, go look. I'd recommend the local hotel. It's expensive but it's clean, and it has hot and cold running water." She started to speak, and he overrode her. "You're off duty, Trooper, as of now. There's a truck in the lockup out back." He fished for the keys in the desk drawer. "Eat, grab some sleep and be back here in the morning ready to fly."

She looked eager. "We'll be going back to Kulukak?" He nodded, and she said, "I'll be here at eight."

"Fine," he said. "I'll be here at ten." He waited until the door closed behind her before saying into receiver, "Alaska State Troopers, Newenham post, Campbell speaking."

The blast from the other end of the line nearly knocked him out of his chair. "What the hell you mean, wait a minute! What the hell kind of way is that for an Alaska state trooper to answer the phone! Supposing somebody was shooting me; was I just supposed to take a number while you got around to talking to me?"

Liam sat back up, crossed his feet on the desk and said, "Well, hey, John. How've you been?"

TEN

"Who the hell cares where I been! What's this I hear about you jumping out of airplanes!"

"News travels fast."

There was a short, electric silence. "Jesus!" Barton spluttered finally. "You mean it's true?"

"Yup," Liam said, and waited.

The explosion was not long in coming. Barton erupted into the phone, called Liam ten kinds of fool, questioned the legitimacy of his ancestors to the fourth generation, libeled his education, condemned his training and subjected his intelligence to a scathing review. He paused for breath, and Liam said sweetly, savoring the moment, "Just doing my duty, John. You know we troopers always get our man."

Another eruption followed, and Liam waited it out, checking the level of paper in the printer tray, rearranging the inbox, the outbox and the to-be-filed box. By the time John ran down the second time, he'd closed two files, one for drunken driving and reckless endangerment on the road between Newenham and the Air Force base, one for sexual assault in the third degree, and had started on a third, embezzlement of funds from the local Native corporation. This last was being closed because there was no point in a prosecution, as no one could be found to testify for or against anyone else, no matter how much money was missing, and the person who had reported it gone had been fired and the person accused of stealing it named to the board of directors.

"Liam!"

The bellow broke his concentration. "John? You still there?"

"Yes, you smug bastard, I am still here." A pause. Almost pleadingly, his boss said, "What the hell were you thinking?"

Liam put down his pen and sat back again. "I was thinking that a guy who maybe killed one person, who actually did shoot another and assault a third—one of our own, I might add—I was thinking this guy was going to get clean away if I didn't do something, and do it fast."

A brief pause. "You're sure this guy did it?"

"The shooting and the assault, yes. I don't have his confession on the stabbing yet, but he was there, he had the murder weapon, he was fleeing the scene. And he was drunk. He looks pretty good to me."

Another pause, while they both thought about what booze did in the Alaskan Bush to keep up the rates of child abuse, rape and murder every month. "There wasn't any other way to apprehend him?"

"No." There might have been, but Liam had been the trooper on the spot, and it had been his decision to make. He wasn't going to back away from it.

Another pause. "All right." A long sigh. "But, Jesus, Liam."

Liam grinned at the calendar on the opposite wall. "Well, John, you know how I hate to fly."

"Fine," Barton said, "then just don't get on them in the first place. You don't have to jump out of them in midair."

He didn't say and Liam didn't mention that if you were a trooper in the Bush, you flew.

Their minds must have been following the same track, because Barton said, "You ever think about learning to fly, Liam?"

"No," Liam said for the second time that day.

"All right, all right," Barton said, "never mind, it was just a suggestion. Who was this guy and what'd he do?"

Liam told him. Barton grunted. "Nice he returned to the scene of the crime."

"You know what they say," Liam said blandly. "That is your standard deviant sociopath's customary behavior."

Barton made a rude suggestion as to what Liam could do with "they say." "What about this boat thing?"

Liam's smile faded. He fished out the picture of the Malones in Hawaii. It was a little waterlogged but Molly's impact was undiminished. "Seven dead; father, mother, two kids, father's brother and two deckhands. Or so I gather, from talking with the locals and going through the father's business records. We'll have to wait for the M.E.'s ID to be sure."

"Why?"

"There'd been a fire."

"They die of smoke inhalation?"

Liam didn't hesitate. "I don't think so."

Barton's voice sharpened. "Why not?"

Liam paused, putting things in order in his mind before he said the words out loud. He hated repeating himself, and he knew Barton hated listening to people repeat themselves. "Let me run it down for you. At approximately nine this morning, a couple of fishers spotted the *Marybethia,* drifting. At first they didn't think anything of it, but then they noticed she didn't have her nets out. When she got closer, they could see what looked like soot and scorch marks and nobody on deck. So they pulled their gear and took a look. Seven bodies and a boat that looked like it had been on fire. The fire was out by the time they got there. So they took her in tow, only she was down so much in the water they took another look around."

Liam could hear the rat-a-tat of a pencil hitting Barton's desk. "And found what?"

"Do you know about drain plugs?"

Barton's chair creaked. "Yeah, the plugs in the stern. Usually rubber or plastic? You pull them when you pull the boat out of the water, to drain it. Also allows for snowmelt to drain when you've got it in dry dock over the winter."

"Right. Well, someone pulled those plugs."

Dead silence. "You don't say."

"I do say. And not while they were in dry dock."

"Interesting."

"Very."

"What else?"

"They towed the *Marybethia* to Kulukak, a little village on Kulukak Bay."

The chair creaked and there was the sound of footsteps. "Where?"

"About forty-some miles east of Togiak."

The sound of a finger tracing a map, mumbled curses. John had trouble distinguishing latitude from longitude. "Okay, got it."

"Then they called me. I flew out with Prince—thanks for telling me she was coming, by the way—and boarded her." Liam took a deep breath and said evenly, "It was a charnel house, John. All bodies burned beyond recognition. You could tell there'd been five adults and two kids by the difference in size, but that was about it." He didn't mention the smell. He was doing his best to forget it.

Footsteps, creak of chair, thump as feet went on the desk, rat-a-tat of pencil. "So what makes you think this was anything more than a boat fire?"

"First, the plugs."

"Yeah, but that happens, sometimes even to the most experienced fisherman. You hear about it all the time. Like the float planes on Lake Hood. Every other fall or so, somebody leaves taking off the floats until it's too late and the floats freeze in the ice. Or in the spring somebody forgets to take off the skis and put on the floats and the lake melts and their plane sinks. It happens. That all you got?"

"No. At least one of the adults was shot in the head."

Creak of chair, thump of feet on the floor as Barton sat straight up. "Are you sure about that?" he said sharply.

"As sure as I can be without confirmation by autopsy. There is a wound in the left temple of one of the adult males that looks exactly like the entry wound of what I'd say was a nine-millimeter bullet."

"Was there an exit wound?"

"I think so, but it's hard to tell for sure. The fire messed that side of him up pretty good."

The pencil tapping resumed. Barton couldn't sit still at gunpoint. "You want me to fly an arson investigator out there?"

"The sooner the better. I had to leave the boat moored in the Kulukak small boat harbor. I've got one of the tribal council members watching it, but the Malones lived in Kulukak."

Liam didn't have to say anything more. "I'll call the fire marshal tonight. He owes me a few. I'll have someone on the way first light tomorrow. When's the earliest flight into Newenham?"

"Nine, I think."

"Okay, probably leaves Anchorage around six-thirty, seven. I'll have somebody on it."

"Thanks."

A pause. "Which came first, pulling the plugs or the fire?"

"Maybe he killed them and pulled the plugs to sink the evidence. Maybe she wouldn't go down and he set her on fire to cover up the evidence. I don't know, John. It's all just speculation at this point. Forensics will tell us more."

"Did you find a gun on board?"

"Yes. A rifle, a thirty-ought-six. Couldn't tell if it had been fired. I sent it in with the bodies."

"I'll call Bob down at the crime lab, make sure he gets right on it. Could be a murder-suicide thing, you know."

"Could be."

"But you don't think so."

"No."

Rat-a-tat, rat-a-tat, rat-a-tat. "How many people fishing in that area yesterday?"

"I don't know for sure. There was a tender taking on fish in Kulukak. The processor they work for operates out of Newenham. I'm going over to their office to talk to the superintendent."

"You must have some kind of estimate on the number of boats in the area."

Liam sighed. "The locals told me upwards of fifty."

Silence.

"What the hell, John," Liam said wryly, "if it was easy, everybody'd be doing it."

"You need help?"

"Not yet. I may. I'll let you know."

"Prince working out all right?"

"She calls me sir."

Barton grunted. "Good. She's working for you."

It was Liam's turn to be quiet.

"Oh hell." Barton blew out a breath. "You're back up to corporal."

Liam waited, trying to sort this out. "I haven't been a trooper for four months."

"Corcoran put the hoodoo on Newenham," Barton said bluntly. Corcoran had been the trooper sergeant in charge previously assigned to Newenham. "No one wants to transfer there. Somebody needs to be boss. You've got the time in. You have management experience. You're it."

"That's why I got a probationer," Liam said. "She's too new to know the difference."

"That's why," Barton said. "She'll be okay with a little seasoning. If it's any comfort to you, she scored in the top three percent of her class."

"It isn't."

"I don't blame you," Barton said, and in an eerie echo of Liam's own first impression, "Just be careful how you go through any doors."

"I plan on it. In the meantime," Liam added, "you better make sure the media doesn't get hold of my promotion. They yelled loud enough when you didn't fire me."

Barton hung up. Liam replaced the phone in its cradle and folded his hands on the desk, studying them with a frown.

In another life, John Dillinger Barton might have lived up to the promise of his first two names, but fortunately for the citizens of the state of Alaska he had been seduced early on into the practice of law enforcement, and rose high and fast through the ranks. At one time, there was nothing that Liam wanted so much as to move as high and as fast, even aspiring to as lofty a goal as colonel in charge of the entire organization.

And now, here it was for the second time, against all odds, against all expectations: preferment. Congratulations, he thought. You're a corporal. Again.

He waited for the surge of pleasure the news had brought the last time. It didn't come, and what was even more odd, he didn't miss it. The affair with Wy and the deaths of his wife and son and of those five people in Denali National Park had changed his perspective. He was still ambitious, but his ambition had been tempered by events. Being a trooper was important, but it wasn't everything.

Right now, today, he had a job he was good at, that he enjoyed, that contributed to the well-being of the community. He had at least the hope of a relationship with a woman he had thought lost to him three years before. He'd made a friend in Bill. He'd been more or less adopted by Moses. He was getting to know the people in his district, from the tiniest village upriver to the most isolated coastal community. He'd even begun to recognize a Yupik word here and there; the *gatcha* he had heard Halstensen use today in the Malones' living room. It was a word with a heavy accent on the second syllable and appeared to be used for exclamatory purposes, as when, coming out of AC, an old Yupik woman had slipped and spilled her groceries. "*Gatcha!*" she had said, clearly annoyed. He tested it out now, trying to imitate the sounds, putting the *g* in the back of his throat and loading it down.

There was a squawk from outside that sounded unnaturally close to a human chuckle. He got up and looked out the window, and a black and beady eye met his with an inquisitive cock of its head.

Even the goddamn ravens seemed to have stamped him with their croaky seal of approval.

He was putting down roots.

Not a man accustomed to introspection, Liam looked inside himself and for the first time in a long time did not despise what he saw.

It was a start.

ELEVEN

Seafood North was a big square building painted a solid sea green. Their logo was a stylized fish head with a diamond-shaped patch of roe behind it, white on blue. It looked as if it had been generated by a computer: neat lines, perfect circles and no artistic value whatsoever. Liam thought of Nelson's remark about Yupik style, and wondered what the logo would have looked like if the company had asked a local to design it.

They were canning, Liam could tell by the thunks of the chink that echoed from within the building, chopping off the salmon heads before passing the bodies down the line to the butchers, who cleaned and gutted them before passing them down to the canners, who stuffed the raw fish into cans before the cans passed through the lidders and then into the pressure cookers.

Prior to his arrival in Newenham, what Liam had known about the science of salmon processing could have been writ large on the back of his badge, but over the past three months he had been at some pains to become familiar with his new posting, and that included the economic force which drove it. As any good beat cop could tell you, when you lived where you worked, when you knew all the players on a first-name basis, you were halfway to the solution of any crime practically before it had been committed.

The office was located in the right-hand corner of the building that fronted the road leading down to the docks. He opened the door and went in.

A young woman sat behind a counter, filling out a form. "Just a minute, please."

A counter stood between Liam and the girl's desk. Behind her were the doors to what looked like two offices, both closed. The walls were lined with the cheap, quarter-inch dark wood paneling that had been the last, chic word in interior decorating in the fifties and sixties, before people had come to their senses and started Sheetrocking. In Alaska the paneling was particularly egregious because of the long hours of darkness during the winter, when you needed all the light in a room that you could get.

The paneling in this room was pockmarked with nail holes and patched with duct tape and maps. There were maps of the Bay area, fishing district by fishing district, the Ugashik, the Egegik, the Naknek, the Kvichak, the Nushagak, the Togiak. There were three different maps of Alaska, one geographical, one political and one divided into the twelve Native regions. There was a map of the North Pacific, with lines drawn between Seattle, Anchorage and Tokyo. There were a scattering of maps that upon closer inspection proved to be published by the Alaska Geographic Society, and variously depicted the Wrangell-St. Elias International Mountain Wilderness, the Aleutian Peninsula, prehistoric Alaska, the Kuskokwim River and Alaska's Native People, Their Villages and Languages.

He stepped to take a closer look at this last one, searching for Tulukaruk, but the only village listed on the thumb was Manokotak. It was a long way from Bristol Bay to the Yukon-Kuskokwim River Delta, too; he hadn't realized quite how far until now. There was a mountain range in between the two, the Ahkluns, that began where the Kuskokwim Mountains left off. Probably one of the reasons there were trees in the Bay and not on the Delta. Like the trees in Kulukak, he thought, although the fog had obscured most of them. He wondered how the old ones had made it over those dividing mountains to settle in the Bay. Probably paddled around. With their storyknives.

The rustle of paper made him turn. The girl was neatening a stack of yellow forms. The lighting was rectangular and fluorescent, with two of four tubes burned out. The only natural light was from the window in the door. The place felt like a cave. The girl at the desk still hadn't looked up. He cleared his throat. "All right," she said sharply. She looked up and saw the uniform. "Oh."

"Hi." Liam removed his cap. "My name is Liam Campbell. Alaska State Troopers."

She got to her feet. "Tanya Bernard." Her hand was warm and a little sweaty, her handshake firm and businesslike.

He smiled. "Hi, Tanya. Is the superintendent in?"

She blinked under the influence of that smile, and looked down at her feet, as if surprised to find herself on them. She pulled herself together. "Certainly. I'll tell him you're here."

She got halfway to the office door on the left-hand side and stopped. "Did you have an appointment?"

Liam shook his head. "No." With a faint air of apology, he admitted, "I'm afraid there has been an incident with one of your fishing boats."

"Which one?"

Liam saw no reason not to tell her; the Bush telegraph being what it was, the news would be all over the state before midnight. "The *Marybethia*."

She paled. "Dave Malone's boat?"

"Yes."

"Is he all right?" She recollected herself. "Molly? The kids?"

"I'm afraid not," he said regretfully, watching with interest as more color washed from her face. "I really can't say any more, Tanya." She remained still, staring at him, and he said gently, "Your boss?"

She recollected herself with a start. "Oh. Right. Just a moment."

She walked back to the office on not quite steady feet. Interesting. She tapped on the door. "Mr. Ballard?" She waited a moment, then opened the door just wide enough to stick her head in.

It was wide enough for Liam to see the feet propped on the desk, and certainly wide enough to hear the crash when the chair tipped over. There were some oaths. Tanya, with a discretion worthy of a personal assistant of many years' experience, slipped inside and closed the door behind her.

A few moments later the door opened, revealing a tall, bald man with a solid beer belly, wearing a rumpled navy blue sports coat over a brown plaid cotton shirt and khaki pants. "Yes?" He stifled a yawn and looked mildly puzzled. "Er, you're a trooper?"

"Yes," Liam said. "I need to talk to you about one of your fishermen. Could we go into your office?"

He went in as Tanya went out. "I'd appreciate it if you would stick around until I can talk to you," he told her.

She met his eyes with perfect composure, armor firmly in place. "Certainly."

Five minutes later the superintendent's bewilderment had given way to sick comprehension. "All dead?"

Liam nodded. "All."

"But . . . how?"

Liam had already told him once, but typically news this bad had to be repeated, and often more than once, to be fully assimilated. "It appears they died of smoke inhalation during a boat fire," he said, which was perfectly true, so far as it went. Someone had certainly gone to great lengths to make it seem so. Anticipating the next question, he added, "In Alaska, violent death, even by misadventure, must be thoroughly investigated. Which is why I'm here, Mr. Ballard."

Liam rearranged himself more comfortably in the hard plastic chair. "The bodies have been transported to Anchorage for autopsy. While we wait for the results, I am reconstructing the last known actions of the victims." He produced his notebook and a pen, and fixed Ballard with a polite, inquiring stare. "It is my understanding that the *Marybethia* delivered to Seafood North. Is that correct?"

Ballard, still numb, nodded.

"It is also my understanding that your tender, the *Arctic Wind*, was taking deliveries in Kulukak Bay yesterday."

Ballard nodded again.

"Did they take delivery anywhere else?"

Ballard pawed through the paperwork on his desk in a haphazard fashion. "I don't think so." He raised his voice. "Tanya!"

The rollers of a chair protested, footsteps sounded, the door behind Liam opened. "Yes, Mr. Ballard?"

"Are you still working on the fish tickets from the *Arctic Wind*?"

"I just finished the tender summary."

"Could you bring them in here, please?"

Tanya hesitated. "Did you want a printout?"

Ballard stifled a curse. "Oh hell, I keep forgetting." To Liam, he said, "I'm used to everything being done by hand, in triplicate, one for us, one for the Fish and Game, one for the Seattle office. With carbons, no less. Unfortunately, we have now moved into the Information Age." To Tanya, he said, "Yes, please, bring a printout."

There was a whir and a click from the outer office, followed by the sound of an ink cartridge going back and forth on a carriage. Ballard shook his head with admiration. "That Tanya, she can make those electronic bastards sit up and beg. I don't know what I'd do without her."

Moments later Tanya was back, carrying a sheaf of flimsy yellow tickets, letter-size, and a spreadsheet, white and legal-size and read sideways.

Ballard indicated the yellow sheets. "Those are our copies of the fish tickets. The originals go to Seattle, one copy to the Fish and Game, the third stays here." He held up the spreadsheet. "This lists all the tickets written by the *Arctic Wind* during the last period in Kulukak."

Liam picked it up and scanned it. "So anyone who was fishing that period who delivered to your tender would be on this list?"

"Well . . ." Ballard said.

Liam looked up. "Well, what?"

"The ones who caught enough fish to deliver are the ones who delivered," Ballard said. "Sometimes, if they get skunked, or maybe only pull a dozen reds, they'll head for home and can them for their own use."

Liam repressed a sigh. "So the boat skippers sign the tickets?"

"Yeah, or one of the deckhands."

The *Marybethia* was on the tender summary list, in the *M*'s under Malone, David A. His name was followed by a series of columns headed with salmon species, "King," "Red," "Coho," "Pink," "Chum." Each of these columns was divided into two, "Number" and "Pounds." The *Marybethia* had delivered one thousand seven hundred and fifty reds, for a total of fourteen thousand pounds. He sifted through the tickets to find the *Mary-bethia*'s. It had been signed by Jason Knudson, with a signature formed of large, almost childish loops. Jason Knudson, 18, of Bellingham, Washington; just another statistic the insurance companies would incorporate into their databases to help them calculate rates for term life policies. Just don't be a fisher, and you'll be eligible, Liam thought.

Jason Knudson, 18, of Bellingham, Washington, no longer had a choice. "Is that a lot of fish?" Liam said.

"It'd be a three-cherry jackpot for anyone else," Ballard said, "but for a twelve-hour period, with a boat the size of the *Mary-bethia*, that big a crew and a skipper of Dave's experience, it's just pretty good. He's—" Ballard halted. "He had done better," he said, sounding out the past tense with doubtful care.

"Fourteen thousand pounds seems like an awfully even number."

Ballard nodded. "It's generated by an average weight. The tenders take an average at the beginning of every period, weighing a batch of whatever's being delivered and dividing by the amount of fish they are weighing. It saves time."

"The fishermen agree to this?"

Ballard gave a short laugh. "Absolutely. Our tender captains always make sure there is someone right there watching." He leaned forward. "There is no one on earth as pigheaded and as ornery as an Alaskan fisherman. You screw with one of them, you screw with them all. He—or she—will never forget and he'll never forgive. He tells his friends, too. If we want their fish, not just this year but next year, we deal fair and square." He leaned back and shook his head, repeating, "Fair and square, or a processor can just pack it in." He ran a hand over his bald head. "The infighting that goes on over the price negotiations is bad enough. This year it's even worse because for the second year in a row the catch is coming in at below half of the projections. In one way, it's good, because when they do catch them, they're getting a good price, so guys like Malone make out okay."

He sighed. "In the obvious way, it's lousy for the guys not like Malone. I've already had some in here wanting to settle up." He saw Liam's eyebrow go up, and explained, "Year-end accounting.

We add up the price of all the groceries and gas they've bought through us, price out their fish tickets, subtract one from the other and hopefully write them a check. This year, they're taking their checks and financing a change of profession."

"It looks like Malone delivered the most fish this period."

Ballard scanned the spreadsheet. "Looks like it. He was high boat a lot." This time, the past tense came more easily to his tongue.

"Would being high boat generate bad feelings among the rest of the fishermen?"

Ballard looked surprised. "Hell no. Look, Officer, you have to understand, as smart as you are, as quick as you are, with the best boat and gear you can buy and the best crew you can hire, a fisherman, any fisherman, can still get skunked. The weather can come up, the fish can be late, you can set in front of the wrong creek, you can snag a deadhead in your net, another boat can run over your cork line, you can get hung up on a sandbar, your impeller can blow out, your engine can blow up. There's fifty ways to fail at fishing in Alaska for every one way to succeed." Ballard looked pleased with this aphorism, and sat back, preening a little.

Liam said nothing.

Awareness dawned. Ballard sat up straight and said sharply, "Why do you ask? Is there something you're not telling me about their deaths?"

Liam put his notebook away. "I'll need that spreadsheet."

Ballard held it out but wouldn't let go. "Is there?"

Liam tugged the document free, folded it into careful squares and pocketed it. "There are questions, but there usually are in deaths of this nature. I really can't say anything more at present." He hoped he sounded just pompous enough to quell further questions, and stood up. "Will most of the fishermen listed on this summary be in Newenham? I might need to talk to some of them."

"There are twenty-two names on that list," Ballard pointed out.

"Yes."

Ballard rose to his feet, his face troubled. "A lot of them are from Outside: Washington, Oregon, California. They're in town for six, eight weeks, however long the fish last. Some of them shack up on shore, some rent rooms, but most stay on board."

"Will Tanya know who does and who doesn't?"

Ballard's expression lightened. "Tanya knows everything."

"Okay if I talk to her?"

Ballard waved a hand. "Sure." He hesitated. "Can you let me know what's going on? I mean, I knew the Malones, I liked them. Dave was a damn fine fisherman, and Molly . . ."

"What about Molly?" Liam said with studied indifference.

"Molly." There was a wealth of meaning in that one word. "You know how some women can rub up against every nerve ending you've got from across the street? Molly was like that. But she was nice, too. Good mother, good homemaker, good deckhand." He paused, and admitted, "I didn't have much use for Jonathan, Dave's brother."

"Why is that?"

"It was pretty obvious that he would have been unemployable by anyone else other than a family member," Ballard replied with heavy irony. "If you get my drift. Whatever trouble he could get into, Jonathan got into. It was like he was keeping score or something."

"Misdemeanor or felony trouble?"

Ballard hesitated. "I don't know that anything ever actually came to trial," he said cautiously. "There were rumors, nothing specific."

He let his eyes wander off, and Liam knew he was lying. Could be Ballard was keeping quiet out of respect for Jonathan's brother. Could be he was close to someone else involved in Jonathan's shenanigans. It was a small town.

Ballard said, "David Malone did come in once and tell us never to let Jonathan pick up any checks David had requested on his account." He paused. "You see that a lot, you know? Good brother, bad brother. It's almost a cliché. I'd liked to have met their father."

"Why?"

"Because it's all about fathers, isn't it?" Ballard said, sounding surprised that he had to explain it. "A man is what his father makes him." As an afterthought, he added, "And his mother, of course."

Liam thought of his mother and managed not to wince. "I like to think a man is what he makes himself."

Ballard's smile was kind. "You're young. You'll learn better."

No more than the next man did Liam enjoy being patronized, however kindly meant. Hand on the doorknob, he said, "Oh, one more thing. Have you ever heard of a deckhand named Max Bayless?"

Ballard's smile vanished and he looked wary. "Yes."

Liam waited, and when Ballard didn't volunteer anything, said, "Well? What have you heard?"

"Just that he's for hire," Ballard said.

He was lying again. "Do you know who he's working for this summer?"

Ballard shook his head, tight-lipped.

Liam could have pushed it, but as with the elders in Kulukak, he believed in letting witnesses stew a little, so long as they weren't a flight risk. "If you do hear who he's working for, would you let me know?"

"Certainly." Ballard came around his desk and held out his hand, bringing the interview to a close. "If I hear anything at all, I'll certainly pass it on."

In the outer office, Liam paused beside Tanya's desk, watching the blur of her fingers as they tapped information into the keyboard and letters and numbers appeared on the screen in front of her. "May I speak with you, Tanya?"

"Of course," she said, her fingers not missing a shift key. "Let me finish this entry and save my work and I'll be right with you."

Liam found a chair and placed it next to her desk. He pulled out the tender summary and unfolded it. He was aware that although he had closed the door to Ballard's office behind him, it was now open a few inches.

The computer hummed and Tanya inserted a floppy into a slot. Something clicked and she replaced the first disk with a second. "I back everything up twice," she said with a bright smile.

"Very wise," Liam said.

"Are the troopers computerized yet?"

"Oh yes," he said. "It's very useful, being connected to other law enforcement agencies around the state, even around the nation."

"You can run but you can't hide?" she said, her archness a bit forced.

He smiled. "Nope. We always get our man."

"Isn't that what they used to say about the Mounties?"

Liam thought of Frank Petla and smiled to himself. "I think they still do."

"There," she said, replacing the disks in a box and putting the box in a drawer of her desk. She folded her hands on her blotter and looked him straight in the eye. "How may I help you—is it Trooper? Officer Campbell?" She smiled again. "Or just plain sir?"

"Officer is fine," Liam said. "Sir makes me feel like my grandfather."

Her smile warmed a trifle, but she was still on edge. He said, holding out the tender summary, "It would be very useful if you could tell me which of these fishermen live on board their boats, and which don't."

She took the summary and began marking names with checkmarks from a red pen. It took about thirty seconds, and when she was done she'd marked all but eight names and provided phone numbers for many of them.

He blinked.

"Hold on," she said, "and I'll get you the contact numbers I have for the rest of them." Her hands stilled when she saw his surprise. She smiled at him, queening it a little in her superior knowledge. "We're in the business of buying fish. Fishermen sell us their fish. If they don't know when the periods are, they won't be fishing, and they won't be selling us fish. When the Fish and Game announce a fishing period in a particular district—say the Kulukak—we have a list of all the fishermen who deliver to us and who have permits to fish that district. We make sure they are aware of the opener, and the only way we can do that is to keep track of their whereabouts."

She paused, very cool, very smooth, from the sweep of her short, fine brown hair to her big brown eyes. Liam felt like someone should applaud.

"Usually we don't have to bother," she added. "The fishermen want to catch fish as much as we want to buy them, and they are standing by their marine radios, waiting to hear. But sometimes, one or two of them have been out for a night on the town and haven't heard. So I call them all, or I send Benny down to their boat. They know to check in with me now."

Liam just bet they did. "Tell me, Tanya, how long have you been doing this job?"

"Three years. I'll only have one more summer here, though. I'm putting myself through the University of Alaska, Fairbanks, and I'm in my senior year."

It might have been Liam's imagination, but it seemed as if she raised her voice, not to any blatant pitch but just a little, just enough to be heard in her boss's office. "I see," he said. "What's your major?"

"Business administration."

Liam couldn't stop the smile from spreading across his face. "A natural choice."

"I thought so," she said, and referred back to the summary. "All the checkmarked names live on their boats. However, some of the guys on the crews have girlfriends in town, so they won't be every night on their boats."

"Mr. Ballard mentioned that."

"I've put the phone numbers of the skippers who maintain apartments in town next to their names. I don't often have to call them, because there is usually always at least one deckhand on board overnight. You know. Standing watch."

"I understand," Liam said gravely, and refolded the summary and pocketed it. "Have you met a deckhand called Max Bayless?"

"I have."

"Do you know which boat he's on this summer?"

She thought. "Not on one of ours, not so far as I know. I think I heard he was working for someone out of Togiak."

Liam looked at the map on the wall in back of her. "That's on the coast southwest of Kulukak, right?"

She rose to her feet in a smooth, economical movement and pointed first at Newenham, then Kulukak, then Togiak, tracing the coast between them with one slender forefinger, calling off the names one at a time.

Great. Yet another plane trip in his future. For some odd reason, the prospect did not terrify him as much as it once would have. Maybe bailing out in midair had burned out his nerve endings. "You sound like you know pretty much everything there is to know about the fishing fleet, Tanya."

Her steady gaze met his, with the merest lift of an eyebrow to indicate acknowledgment. Not susceptible to flattery, Ms. Tanya Bernard. Liam plowed on. "Do you think you could find out which boat Max Bayless is on this summer, and where that boat is at the moment?"

"I think so." She paused. "I could put it out on the schedule in the morning, if you like."

"The schedule?"

"We keep a radio schedule with our tenders every morning at ten."

"No." His voice was abrupt and he saw her eyes widen. He moderated his tone. "I would prefer that my looking for him is not broadcast over the air. Is there another way you can find out?"

"Several, although it'll take longer."

"That's fine. Thank you. Here's the number of the post."

She inclined her head in the same gracious gesture as before, with all the dignity of the queen of England and none of the pretentiousness.

"Have you met Mr. Bayless?"

"A few times."

"Do you know anything about him?"

The brown eyes regarded him steadily. "Such as?"

"Such as a report of a blowup he might have had with David Malone, after Malone fired him from his job on the *Marybethia* last summer."

"I remember. He was angry. He made a lot of threats."

"Such as?"

She hesitated. "Well, he said he was going to kill David. He also said he was going to blow up his boat."

"Did you hear him say this?"

She shook her head. "No. One of the fishermen who was in the harbor was telling me about it when he came in to settle up at the end of the summer. Daniel, Daniel Walker."

He jotted the name down, and the name of Walker's boat, the *Andrea W.* Notebook folded and restowed, he looked at Tanya, her sleek cap of hair, her steady gaze. An intelligent and composed young woman. "Did you know the Malones?"

Her face closed up again. "Yes. David Malone came often to the office, to draw an advance, to get copies of his tickets. And of course he came in every fall to settle up." She swallowed, and said, steadily enough, "Is it true that he is dead?" She saw his look. "I knew something was wrong by the expression on your face. I made a couple of calls. Is he dead?"

"Yes. Along with his wife, his two children, his brother and both deckhands."

She put a hand over her eyes in an involuntary gesture.

Liam took a chance. "Forgive me, Tanya, but did you know Mr. Malone on a personal basis?"

She dropped her hand. "No," she said, with determined composure. "I knew Dave only from the office. Well . . ." She hesitated for a moment. "He did sit with me at Bill's once, when I was having dinner there one evening, he and his brother." The curl of her lip told Liam that Tanya shared Ballard's opinion of Jonathan Malone.

"You liked him."

She met his eyes without flinching. "Yes."

"If he hadn't been married . . . ?"

She took a deep breath, held it, let it out slowly. "Does your investigation require that I answer that question?"

"No," Liam said, conscious of a feeling of shame. "No, Tanya, it doesn't. I'm sorry." He got up to leave.

Her voice stopped him at the door. "If he hadn't already been married when I met him, Mr. Campbell, he would have been shortly thereafter. But he was."

"Did he feel that way, too?"

Again she hesitated. "I think so, yes." Her smile was bleak. "I made sure we never had the opportunity to speak in private."

He nodded. "You were both better people than I was," he said, and went out the door before he had to face the surprise he knew would show on her face.

TWELVE

Wy had dogged Prince from the dig all the way into Newenham, unloaded McLynn and accepted a last-minute charter to Three Lake Lodge for two corn growers from Iowa. They were both blond and blue-eyed, short and stocky and pink-cheeked with excitement. They'd never been to Alaska before, they'd never fished for salmon and, as it turned out, they'd never flown in a small plane, either, as was made manifest when one of them had to throw up into his brand-new hip waders while they were going through Jackknife Pass.

The good news was that he did use the waders, without spattering so much as a drop on the brand-new carpet she'd just installed in the 180, and that they paid in advance in cash. She arranged to pick them up a week later and made the trip home a short one. It had been a long, long day, and she was weary to the bone.

"Tim?" she said, as she walked in the door of the white clapboard house on the bluff of the Nushagak River. "You home?"

"I'm in here."

The kitchen. It figured. Tim spent half his life with his head in the refrigerator.

"What's for dinner?" She closed the door.

"I have to cook again?" he whined, but she heard the smile in his voice.

"It's your turn, I told you that this morning," she said, and then halted in surprise in the kitchen doorway. "Jo!"

The short, stocky woman with the blond, frizzy hair came

around the counter and enveloped Wy in a warm, solid hug. "Hey, girl."

Wy returned the hug with as much energy and enthusiasm as she was capable of on this day, and Jo pulled back. "You're a wreck."

"Gee, thanks, you look great, too."

"I can go away, if you need me to."

Wy made a rude noise. "Like hell. If I can't be mean to you, who can I be mean to?"

Jo's green eyes were shrewd. "Liam?"

Wy looked at Tim, leaning against the kitchen counter, dipping a plain hot dog into a jar of mustard. He was slight and dark, with flat cheekbones and compact frame. His dark eyes were wary and suspicious, and much older than the rest of him. No child of twelve should look out on the world with such distrust.

Tim saw her looking and thought it was at the hot dog. "Just a snack," he said, and with one bite made the rest of it disappear.

"Uh-huh," Wy said. "Is that what we're having for dinner again?"

He drew himself up, offended. "No. We're having something different, like you said you wanted." He stepped back, revealing the culinary riches behind him on the counter. "We're having polish sausage and sauerkraut," he said proudly. He held up an empty package of Alaska Sausage's finest, and pointed at a quart jar of Claussen's Crisp Sauerkraut, also empty.

Wy, who after a year's steady indoctrination knew enough to be grateful that Tim allowed himself to be part of the kitchen crew rotation, said, "Looks good. Do I get anything green along with that?"

He looked doubtful. "Well," he offered, "the sauerkraut used to be cabbage, and cabbage is green." He brightened. "I got ice cream for dessert, though."

"What kind?"

His smile was sly. "Häagen-Dazs. Vanilla."

Wy sighed. "I am so easy."

Jo laughed, and tugged Wy out of the room. "Come on, let's get you cleaned up while Chef Paul here does his thing."

In her bedroom, Wy stripped off her clothes as Jo lounged on the bed. "Still sleeping alone, I see."

Wy stopped, half in and half out of her jeans. "How can you tell?"

Jo made a face. "I'm a reporter. I notice the details. Like a full-size bed in the room of a woman hankering after a king-size-bed guy."

Liam was six-three. Wy tossed her jeans in the hamper and grabbed for the Sea Wolves T-shirt she used for a robe. "I'll be right back."

She used up all the hot water and then some. When she came back into her bedroom Jo had picked up the little embroidered box on Wy's dresser, identical to the one Jo had on hers, both of which had been acquired on the isle of Crete during the European vacation that had been the reward of both sets of parents following a successful graduation from college. "Remember the store where we got these, how the guy behind the counter tried to pick us up?"

"Remember how we let him?" Wy said dryly, stepping into clean underwear.

"Ah yes, the Labyrinth by moonlight," Jo said dreamily. "One of my favorite memories."

"All you saw was stars, girl," Wy retorted, "which is generally what you do see from lying on your back outside at night."

"Slander, calumny and defamation of character," Jo said peacefully. "I'll sue. What's this?"

Wy pushed her head through the neck of her T-shirt and peered over Jo's shoulder. "That? It's my high school class ring. Mr. Strohmeyer told me not to buy one, that I'd probably never wear it again. He was right, as usual."

"Don't you just hate that? What's this?"

Wy looked, and her hands stilled on the zipper of her jeans. "A pair of earrings, what do they look like?"

"They are beautiful. I don't generally like gold nuggets, but these are really nice." Jo held one of the flat, heavy loops up to her ear, admiring the effect in the mirror. "Where'd you get them?"

"A friend," Wy said. She was sure there was no inflection in her voice to give warning, but she felt Jo's eyes boring into the back of her head. Being friends with a reporter could be a pain in the ass. "What are you doing in town, Jo?"

"Liam gave them to you."

A real pain in the ass. "Yes."

Jo put the earring back in the box and the box back on the dresser. She regarded it for a moment, and then turned to look at Wy. Jo had newspaper eyes, a steady, unwinking, patient stare that watched and weighed and waited, waited for the answers to her questions, waited for the truth. You could dodge, evade, equivocate, you could even lie, but those newspaper eyes would wait you out every time.

Joan Dunaway was a reporter for the *News*, and had been one since she and Wy had returned from Europe the year they graduated from the University of Alaska, Fairbanks, Wy with a degree in education and Jo with a degree in journalism. She'd built up a reputation over the years for ferreting out bad behavior on a legislative and bureaucratic level and writing pull-no-punches stories about it. One of the more delightful stories Wy remembered had exposed the invariable habit of the commissioner of the Department of Corrections in hiring longtime friends for jobs tailored to suit their special talents. One of them had been a grocer, Wy recalled. At least the Department of Corrections had made some terrific deals on fresh produce for the four and a half months of the grocer's tenure of office.

Jo's juiciest story to date had concerned the then sitting governor who had vacationed, all expenses paid, in Baja, Bali and Biarritz courtesy of one of the North Slope's major oil producers. The executive responsible had made the grievous error of not recognizing Jo in the bar of the Baranof Hotel. He had compounded this error by picking her up, seducing her and afterward indulging in pillow talk that drew connections between the vacations and a revision of the state's subsurface mineral rights law being debated before the legislature the following day. This not unnaturally wound up on the front page of the *News*. He was a very attractive slimeball, she explained later to Wy, with very blue eyes and an ass as firm and round as a Delicious apple. "I swear to god, I wanted to bite it," she declared, and she was regretful when he and his ass were indicted and later convicted, fined and imprisoned for bribery of a public official. The governor narrowly escaped prison only by payment of a $330,000 fine, but when the legislature changed hands two years later, they vacated the judgment and repaid the fine to him, with interest. "Ah, Alaska," Jo had said fondly when she heard. "Gays can't marry and you have to speak English, but you can legally smoke pot and embezzlers never go hungry. Gotta love it."

And she did, and she wrote about it every day, not only stories of bribery and corruption in the legislature, but stories of how the state worked. She wrote profiles of the weights-and-measures man who checked to see that you got the five gallons of gas you'd paid for, the waitress at Simon and Seafort's who retired after nineteen years on the job, the Alaskan old fart who cut firewood from his lot in Talkeetna and delivered it, one cord at a time, to buyers in Anchorage. She wrote about the people who fixed the potholes and tarred the roofs and shoveled the snow and loaded luggage onto planes, about the gardeners at the Municipal Greenhouse and the clerks at City Hall, about the woman who answered the phone at Victims of Violent Crimes in Juneau and the man who ran the flight service station in Soldotna. She was on a first-name basis with just about everyone in the state, from the man who set the tracks on the cross-country ski trails at Kincaid Park to the ranger who tracked down poachers in the Gates of the Arctic. Some of them loved her. Some of them hated her. None of it stopped her.

And it didn't stop her now. "How's it going? You and Liam?"

"It's not," Wy said, hoping that would be the end of it.

A vain hope. "Why not?"

Wy sighed. All right, then, and maybe it would help if she said the words out loud. "Jo, if he'd left Jenny and Charlie . . ." She stopped. It was incredible how, even now, three years later, she had to force their names out of her mouth. "Wife and child" were generic terms, without personalities, wants, demands. "Jenny and Charlie" were people, people with needs and privileges that superseded hers.

She looked at Jo. Jo looked back with an uncharacteristically solemn expression. "I've got a Puritan streak a mile wide, Jo. What I did was wrong. You don't screw around with someone else's husband, you just don't. And you don't take the attention that rightfully belongs to his child. Children need their fathers."

Her shoulders slumped and she sighed. "If he'd come to me, if we'd married, I would have spent the next fifty years trying to make it up to his son. I would have been oh so considerate and understanding, I would have relinquished my time with Liam so he could spend time with his son, I would have tried to be friends with his wife, no matter how much she hated me, and she was bound to hate me."

"And after a while," Jo said slowly, "you would have come to resent it."

"Probably."

"And to take it out on Liam."

"Probably," Wy repeated.

"And yourself."

"Especially myself." Wy stood up. "So you see, Jo, as much as it hurt, it was the right thing to do."

"Cutting things off, never seeing him or talking to him again."

"Yes."

"Except that now you are."

Wy wandered over to the window and looked out at the fascinating view of her truck and Jo's rental car parked in the driveway. "Yes."

There was a brief silence. Jo looked at the top of Wy's dresser. There was very little clutter: the embroidered box from Greece, a few ivory carvings, one a walrus rearing up with his tusks on display and his fat sides wonderfully wrinkled, another that looked like a little knife, no more than three inches in length, with a curved blade and a mask carved into the hilt. From the right eye of the mask a tiny face looked out, laughing. "You still love him."

"Only because NPR's Scott Simon's never given me a tumble, and that's only because I have not been afforded the opportunity to meet him, swamp him with my extensive personal charm and carry him off to my tent."

Jo had the reporter's indispensable and extremely irritating ability to stick to the point. "Jenny and Charlie are dead."

"I know. Convenient, isn't it?"

"Oh Jesus," Jo said, disgusted. "Martyrdom does not become you, Wy."

Wy turned. "What?"

"You heard me," Jo said, the ruthless gleam back in her newspaper eyes. "You've steeled yourself to make this great sacrifice, you've even managed to round up a child of your own without having to betray the great love of your life—speaking of convenient—"

"Wait just a goddamn minute!" Wy said hotly. "Where do you get off—"

"—and now that the love of your life—we may fairly call him that, I suppose, since you haven't let anyone else within sniffing distance since, other than that wimpy little wing cover salesman—"

"He wasn't a wimp!"

"—now that the love of your life is free, due, I might add, to no fault of your own, so that the two of you can join hands and waltz off into the sunset together, you're so in love with this noble renunciation act of yours that you're willing to do it all over again." Jo shook her head. "Shit happens, Wy. It happened here, and it had absolutely nothing to do with you." She paused, and gave Wy a considering look. "You didn't even wish them dead, did you?"

"What?" Wy said, horrified. "No! Never!"

"God, you were right about that Puritan streak," Jo said, disgusted. "Sometimes I think you're not even human. Saint Wyanet, your strength is as the strength of ten because your heart is pure."

"Fuck you, Dunaway!"

"Backatcha and times two, Chouinard!" Jo stepped up to go nose to nose. In your face was her specialty, and where she scored most of her best stories. "Jenny and Charlie were killed by a drunk driver. Liam is single, and has somehow managed to find you again." Her brows snapped together. "Are you afraid that it wasn't real after all?" she said with sudden suspicion. "Are you afraid that what you could have with Liam won't measure up to what you did have?"

"Oh for crissake," Wy exploded, "don't say 'what we had' like I was Streisand and he was Redford. 'What we had' amounted to twenty-three flights into the Bush, four days in Anchorage and a thousand dollars in phone bills. It wasn't like we ran away to Paris together or something."

Jo's smile was sly. "What?" Wy said, on the defensive. She knew that smile.

"Twenty-three flights, huh?" Jo said smugly. "Pretty specific number. Interesting that you remember it so exactly."

Wy blushed again. The hell with this. She went to the bureau and picked up her hairbrush, yanking it ruthlessly through her shower-tangled curls. "So," she said in an artificially bright voice. "What are you doing in town, anyway?"

Jo weighed Wy's determination to change the subject, found it inflexible, decided she'd said enough and dropped the subject of Liam. For the moment. "Following up on a story."

"Oh yeah? What one?"

"I can't say right now."

Jo's voice was sober, and Wy put down the brush. "Why not?"

Jo saw Wy's expression and made an obvious effort to lighten up. "Because it has to do with government shenanigans at high levels," she said teasingly. "My specialty."

"What, the *News* is looking for another Pulitzer?" Wy said, falling in with the new mood. One reason they'd been friends for as long as they had was because they respected each other's boundaries. Another was that they could get mad at each other, secure in the knowledge that neither was going anywhere, no matter how heated—or personal—the debate became.

Jo shook her head. "I'm on my own on this one. A source contacted me with the story. I'm here to talk to him in person."

Wy's brow creased. "It isn't about the killings, is it?"

"Killings?" Jo's eyes narrowed. "What killings?"

Wy hesitated, but there wasn't any point in not telling her. Like Liam, she was well aware of the efficiency of the Bush telegraph. "Seven people were killed in a boat fire in Kulukak. It might not have been an accident. Not to mention which, I found a—"

"Seven people?" Jo vaulted off the bed. "Jesus! Are you serious?"

"No, Jo, I made it up. Plus I myself just happened to—"

"And not an accident? You mean murdered?"

"Liam thinks so, and by the way, I—"

"Is Liam the investigating officer? Where's your phone? Kitchen, right?" Jo shot out of the room and down the hall, where Wy heard her badgering Tim for the phone. Sighing, she sat on her chaste, full-size bed and put on her socks. One body wasn't much by comparison to seven, she supposed. Still, stumbling across murder victims wasn't something she did on a regular basis. Once every three months was about her average.

She remembered Bob DeCreft, the occupant of the last body she'd stumbled across, and chastised herself, although Bob, the crusty old coot, would have been the first to laugh. She wondered how Laura Nanalook, Bob's daughter, was doing on her own in Anchorage. Well, she hoped. If anyone deserved a break, it was Laura.

Liam. His face rose unbidden before her eyes and she thought of Jo's words. Was it true? Was she so afraid that an actual relationship with Liam would pale in comparison to their affair? She winced away from the idea. She'd never thought of herself as a coward. She flew in Alaska for a living, didn't she? She'd taken on the raising of a twelve-year-old boy with a lot of nasty relatives, hadn't she? She'd returned to Newenham, hadn't she, risking contact with her birth family?

The first time she'd seen Liam he'd been just another uniform. Then, seated next to each other in her plane, on their way to a stabbing northwest of Glenallen, she'd noticed his hands gripping the sides of his seat. His knuckles were white and his face was the same color. Here was this big, tall, strong, good-looking man, an officer of the court, an enforcer of the law. Why did she suddenly feel the need to help him fight his fear? They'd talked about books that day. She'd been reading Barbara Tuchman's *A Distant Mirror* for the second time, and they'd compared notes on the calamitous fourteenth century, arguing Tuchman's comparison of that century to this.

By the time they landed in Mentasta Lake they were old friends. How could anything be that simple? Nothing else ever in her life had been up to then.

She followed Jo into the kitchen, and found her talking rapidly into the phone as Tim set the table. He folded paper napkins and placed them beneath the flatware, a frown of concentration on his face. He performed the simple task the way he did every household chore, as if getting it wrong meant expulsion from Eden. Compared to what Tim had come from, a place where he'd been beaten regularly and the last time nearly to death, her home probably did seem like heaven on earth.

He stepped back from the table and surveyed it, reaching out to move a glass an inch to the left. He turned and saw Wy watching, and a faint color crept up into his cheeks.

She hugged him, ignoring the momentary stiffening in his body. He had yet to become accustomed to casual physical affection. For that matter, she was just now learning it herself, but she was determined that Tim, by the time he was eighteen and ready to go to college, would know how to give and receive a hug, and mean it.

Jo hung up the phone. "Where does Liam live?"

"The last time I checked, he was still sleeping in his office," Wy lied with determined unconcern.

"He's bunking on a boat down at the harbor," Tim volunteered.

Jo pounced. "Which one?"

Tim was startled at the ferocity of Jo's interest. "Uh, er, the *Dawn P,* I think."

Wy stared. "How do you know that?"

She cursed herself for not moderating her tone of voice, because he was immediately defensive. "I remember because it's named after this girl I go to school with." As they spoke, he flushed a deep, vivid red.

Wy gaped, and Jo grinned. "Is she pretty?" Jo said.

Tim hunched a shoulder, and shot Wy a sidelong glance. "She's okay, I guess," he mumbled. The lid on the pot on the stove gave a clatter and with the air of one rescued from the deck of the *Titanic* just before the stern went under he leapt gladly around the counter and pulled it off the burner.

The sausage was a little charred, but Wy liked her sausage crisp. They ate in silence for a few moments. "Who was that on the phone, if it wasn't Liam?" Wy said.

Jo took a bite of sausage and washed it down with a long swallow of Killian's. Jo must have brought some with her, because Wy didn't drink beer. She stole a covert look at Tim. A strand of sauerkraut had latched on to the front of his Nike Town T-shirt; other than that, he looked reassuringly substance-free. Girls to booze in one night, she thought gloomily. Somebody was going to have to talk to Tim about birth control, THE TALK every parent dreaded, and she had a pretty good idea who that someone should be. She remembered THE TALK she'd had with her adoptive parents, two schoolteachers only slightly more uptight than Queen Victoria. Certainly she could do better than that, but she surveyed Tim with disfavor on general principles anyway. Whose bright idea had it been to adopt this kid, again?

"Pete," Jo said, setting the bottle down with a satisfied smack and burping without apology. "My managing editor. He wants me to check out your story. I need to talk to Liam. He didn't answer at the post." To Tim she said, "You know which slip the *Dawn P* is tied up at?"

He shook his head. "There's a map at the head of both ramps. It'll show you."

"You want to walk down with me?"

He brightened. "Sure." He looked at Wy. "Can I, Mom?"

"Why not?"

"Great," Jo said, reaching for the Killian's again. She paused with it halfway to her mouth. "You could come with us."

Wy shook her head. "Not just now. I was going to go down the bluff to the river, see if I could catch us a few late reds or a couple of early silvers. I want to get some in the can before they all get up the river."

Jo waited until Tim's head was turned before mouthing the word, Coward.

Tim groaned. "Salmon sandwiches for school again."

"Just for that, you little ingrate, I'm telling Moses I want ten gallons of blueberries, not five, when he brings you back from fish camp, and guess who gets to pick them?"

Tim groaned again.

"Life's tough all over, kid," Jo said. "Now hurry up and finish, I want to catch up to that trooper."

"Are you writing a story?"

"Sure am," Jo said, rising to carry her plate to the sink.

"What about?" Tim said, following her.

Jo dropped her voice to a deep baritone filled with terrible se-crets. "Murder and mayhem on the high seas, me boy."

"Wow!" he said, brightening. "You mean like pirates?"

Jo paused in the act of putting dishes in the dishwasher. "Maybe," she said slowly. "Maybe, by god. Anything's possible on the Bay."

Before the door closed behind them, Wy heard Tim ask, "Jo, what's an ingrate?"

THIRTEEN

Back at the post, Liam assembled two piles of evidence. One pile consisted of Nelson's notebook, the pencil drawings he'd made of the scene of Nelson's death, the notes he'd made after talking to Frank Petla, Wy, Prince and McLynn. The other pile consisted of the notes he'd taken at Kulukak, the picture of the Malone family sailing in Hawaii, the notes of the conversations with the Kulukak elders, Bill, Tanya and Ballard, the tender summary, the two rolls of film he'd taken of the *Marybethia*. The film would have to go into Anchorage by pouch tomorrow morning for development into trial exhibits. He wouldn't need to see the photographs. The scene was etched on the gray matter of his mind for life.

It was after eight o'clock in the evening. The day was three hours away from sunset. He thought about going over to Wy's. He had this need to see her, to breathe her air, to feel her flesh beneath his hands. It was growing stronger with every day, and half the time when he started going somewhere in the Blazer he'd find himself on the road to her house.

He picked up the local paper and turned to the classifieds. There was an actual house for sale, south of town on the road to Chinook, two bedrooms, one bathroom, a five-acre lot. Neither price nor location was listed. He dialed the number.

The phone rang once. The voice that answered was male and brusque. "Yeah?"

"Hi, my name's Liam Campbell. I was calling about the ad in the paper. The house for sale?"

"What's your driver's license number?"

Liam blinked. "I beg your pardon?"

"What, you don't understand English? I asked you what your driver's license number was. And I don't got all day."

Liam found himself fishing out his wallet. He read the number off, and waited.

"Huh. You born here?"

"Germany."

"Huh. Army brat, I suppose."

"Air Force, actually," Liam said, struggling not to sound apologetic. "We moved to Anchorage that year."

"Huh." The syllable was disparaging.

Liam maintained a hopeful silence. Although it was heresy to admit in Alaska, he kind of liked Anchorage, but he wasn't going to say so if liking Anchorage was going to make the man on the other end of the line deem him an unsuitable candidate to purchase the house.

"Well, you can come over and look at it, but I ain't making no promises. Somebody comes along with a lower number, I give them first consideration."

"Right," Liam said. "Makes perfect sense. I understand completely." He paused. "Okay. No, I don't. Mind telling me why?"

"I guess you really don't understand English, do you? The lower your driver's license number, the longer you been in the state. The longer you been in the state, the more likely you are to stay. If you look like a stayer, you get the house. If you don't, forget it. When you coming over?"

"How about tomorrow morning?" Liam said meekly.

"Can't, I'll be out fishing. Next Monday. Nine a.m. And don't be late."

"Wait! I need directions!"

There was a grunt, and then directions, grudgingly given.

"And what's your name? Sir? Sir?"

The dial tone was his reply. He replaced the receiver, wondered what was going to happen on Monday, remembered waking up on the *Dawn P* this morning and decided that if the house had working plumbing and a good roof, he would take it, no matter what kind of price had been hung on it.

There was one other house listed for sale in the paper, in Manokotak, forty miles west by air, which, according to the ad, needed a lot of work, was ineligible for financing and was available for rent for fifteen hundred a month with an additional month's rent for a security deposit, but only until the owner found a buyer. If it had running hot and cold, Liam might have been interested.

On the other hand, there were three boats for sale, two thirty-two-foot drifters and a fifty-four-foot seiner. One drifter was going for fifty thousand or best offer, one for two hundred thousand if you bought the permit, too, and the seiner for eighty, although the electronics needed replacing.

He folded the paper and put it down. Bristol Bay was looking at a fifty percent bankruptcy rate for fishermen these days, what with the vanishing salmon runs and the rise of farmed salmon everywhere but Alaska, where farmed salmon was outlawed. A lot of people were making career-changing decisions, including sons and daughters whose families had made their livings on the Bay since back before engines were legal and all the Bay drifters operated under sail. It was anybody's guess what would happen next.

It didn't mean the availability of real estate was going up, or its price coming down, though.

His stomach growled. One of Bill's burgers sounded about right, but Bill's Bar and Grill was a public place. You never knew who you might run into there. He decided he was more in the mood for the deli takeout at the NC market, and a cozy evening at home with a couple of fingers of Glenmorangie and a good book.

Even if that home was slowly sinking into the boat harbor, one inexorable inch at a time.

An hour later, he'd settled back with a porcelain mug half full of single-malt scotch and a copy of *Pillar of Fire* by Taylor Branch, a historian who managed to combine scholarship with a talent for writing. Liam liked reading history, and it wasn't often he came across the two skills in the same package. He piled pillows in back of his head and paged through the preface to chapter one.

He always read prefaces and prologues and introductions after he'd read the book. Partly he was impatient to get on with the story, partly he didn't want anything in the book spoiled for him, partly he didn't care how many people the author wanted to thank and partly he just wanted to get on with it.

He got on with it, and the scotch was down by half when he reached page 26 and first mention of Eugene T. "Bull" Connor, police commissioner in Birmingham, Alabama, whose actions in the late fifties and early sixties were still being lived down by police departments all over the nation. Liam had seen videotapes of the Birmingham police using fire hoses and German shepherds to quell demonstrators, most of them black, most of them nonviolent. They hadn't needed quelling, but then that hadn't been the point. Liam thought of Rodney King and wondered when America was going to get it right.

The boat shifted suddenly and he almost rolled out of bed. The rest of his scotch got away from him, which put him in no good mood to answer the knock on the hatch. "Who the hell is it?" he barked.

The door opened, and Trooper Diana Prince ducked her head inside. Her uniform was still immaculate, although she did look tired. Curious, as well. She took in the cramped quarters, the minuscule galley, consisting of two gas burners and a sink the size of a teacup, the marine toilet tucked into an alcove, and with a heroic effort managed not to wrinkle her nose at the dank smell. "Sir."

Liam, dressed for bed in T-shirt and jockey briefs, sat abruptly upright and smacked the same part of his forehead against the same section of bulkhead that he had that morning. "Shit! Son of a bitch! Goddamn it to hell!"

He held his head and swung his legs over the side. "Damn, damn, damn." He stood up, feet squishing in the damp carpet.

"I'm sorry, sir. Are you all right?"

He felt her hand on his arm, and yanked it free. "I'm fine," he said, retreated a step. His heel came down on a church key previously secreted beneath the lip of his bunk. "Ouch!" He hopped into the air, clutching his foot, and whacked his head on the bulkhead again.

"Sir, let me —"

"No!" he roared. "Don't help me, for crissake please don't help me!" Vision blurred, he pawed for his pants, draped over the opposite bunk. Helpfully, she put them into his hands. "Go outside and wait, goddamn it," he growled, and heard the hatch slide open behind him.

"Oh hello," he heard her say, and whirled around on one leg to meet the startled gazes of Jo Dunaway and Tim Gosuk.

His pants legs developed a reluctance to fit over his legs heretofore unknown in their history as his pants. He drew himself up, necessarily stooping some because of the level of the ceiling, and said with awful politeness, "Could you please wait outside while I get some clothes on? Thank you." Without waiting for an answer, he hopped forward on one foot, herding Prince in front of him, and slid the hatch shut in their faces.

A minute later, a scowl on his face that dared any one of them to comment on the prior scene, he reopened the hatch. Very gruff and businesslike, he said to Prince, "Did you have something to report, Trooper?"

"Yes, sir, I did, but it can wait," Prince said from a brace that looked as rigid as the expression on her face.

It couldn't have waited until morning, when he wouldn't be caught with his pants down by Wy's best friend and son? To Jo he said with unbending courtesy, "What can I do for you?"

One thing about Jo, she wasn't afraid to come right to the point. "I heard about the killings on the *Marybethia*."

"How?" Liam waved a hand in his own reply. "Never mind. Doesn't matter. Is this on the record?" She nodded. "All right, get out your recorder." She produced a tiny black Sony. Click. "My name is Trooper—" Remembering, he corrected himself. "My name is Corporal Liam Campbell, of the Alaska State Troopers, assigned to the Newenham post." He caught Prince's quick, surprised glance at this sudden elevation in rank. Jo's steady eyes didn't waver, but she caught it, too, and he cursed himself for the slip. "My associate is Trooper Diana Prince. This morning we responded to a call from Kulukak, which reported a fishing boat named the *Marybethia*, adrift in Kulukak Bay. It was reported to have been on fire. We went to Kulukak, where the boat was towed. All crew members, seven in number, were dead. We are not releasing the names of the victims pending notification of next of kin. Investigation into the incident is continuing."

Jo waited until it was obvious he was going to say no more and shut off the recorder. "That it?"

"That's it for now."

"Did the fire kill them or not?"

"Cause of death will be determined at time of autopsy."

She pointed the recorder at him. "If you won't say cause, I'm thinking maybe they died from something other than the fire."

He said nothing, arms folded, face expressionless.

She looked at Prince. "Anything to add?"

Prince, face wooden, said, "No, ma'am."

"Look at that," Jo said to Tim. "If you're going to be a re-porter—"

"Over my dead body," Liam said involuntarily.

Tim looked at Liam, at first startled, and then gratified. No one, before Wy, had ever taken enough of an interest in him to be proprietary about his future.

"—then you need to be able to recognize that expression. It's called stonewalling." To Liam, Jo said, "I'll be in touch."

"I'll be around," he said blandly, regaining his composure. "Now if you'll excuse us, I have some business to discuss with my associate."

He saw them to the deck. Tim hopped to the slip, followed by Jo. She paused, looking up at Liam. "Nice legs, by the way," she said, and winked at him before following Tim down the slip to the ramp.

He waited until they were mounting the ramp and safely out of earshot before returning to the cabin. He wouldn't put it past Jo to sneak back and eavesdrop. "You want some coffee?" he said to Prince.

"I could use some," she admitted.

Water boiled rapidly on one of the gas burners, and he poured it through a two-cup cone filter. She picked up the package of coffee. "Tsunami Blend? Never heard of it." She sniffed. "Smells good. Dark roast?"

Nowadays everyone was a coffee snob. "Yeah. Captain's Roast. I order it direct from—"

"Homer, yeah, I've been. In fact, I completed my FTO program there."

"Is that right? Who were your field training officers?"

"Portlock, Wosnesinski and Doroshin."

Liam grimaced. "Talk about dropping you in at the deep end."

"They were all right," she said stoutly, although the undercurrent of surprise that this should be so was unmistakable to Liam's trained ear. "Tough, but fair." She hesitated, and said with a burst of candor, the first totally nonprofessional expression he'd heard from her, "I don't mind saying I was a little nervous going in. At the academy I heard a story about a recruit washing out on report writing because of a personality clash with his FTO."

"I heard that same story," Liam said, turning, mugs in hand. "That's why a recruit has to satisfy three separate officers that he or she is a ready and worthy candidate. That way, if one of the officers has bad chemistry with the recruit, the other two can cancel him — or her — out."

There wasn't enough room for both sets of long legs beneath the tiny galley table, so he sat on the bunk and sipped his coffee.

She shifted her feet out of his way, looking at the imprints her shoes left behind in the carpet. "Uh, sir — you do know that the floor is wet in here?"

"It's Liam in private, Diana, and yes, I do know the floor is wet in here. This boat is sinking."

She blinked at him. "Sinking?" Her voice faltered. "As in, below the surface of the harbor?"

"Slowly." He waved a dismissive hand. "Never mind that. What brings you down here at this time of night?"

Recalled to duty, she sat up straight and made a praiseworthy attempt to forget that the boat she was sitting in was sinking, however slowly. "I flew back out to Kulukak this evening."

He went very still. "I thought I told you to get some rest."

"I wanted to canvass the villagers for information on the Malones, and pick up what information I could on Monday's fishing period."

"I see." Liam sipped his coffee and waited for his irritation to subside. Well, what the hell, she'd already done the deed, he might as well let her tell him what she'd learned. Her air of suppressed excitement clearly indicated that she had discovered something. He lowered the mug and said in a deliberate understated tone, "What did you find out?"

She made a wry mouth. "Well, first off I found that none of the villagers wanted to talk about it."

"I'm not surprised." Her brow furrowed, and he explained. "Most of them were born there, have lived there all their lives. Their first loyalty will be to their neighbors."

"Yes, but—"

"Second, most of them are still pissed at our boss for fighting the Venetie sovereignty case all the way to the Supreme Court."

"John Barton went to court?"

"Our boss the governor."

"Oh." She nodded, still not quite understanding. "I've never paid much attention to politics."

"I'm tempted to say that now would be a good time to start, but I don't know. Maybe the more ignorant you are, the better." He sipped his coffee. "You vote?"

She was insulted. "Of course I vote."

"How do you choose, if you don't pay much attention to politics?"

She hesitated. "Well, actually, I call my father and ask him how he's going to vote."

"You let him tell you how?"

"No," she said, and reached to her collar to loosen her tie. "No, then I vote the exact opposite."

He looked up. She was dead serious. "Oh." Liam decided they didn't know each other well enough for him to pursue that line of inquiry. He wondered how many times he and his father had canceled each other's votes out. He wondered if everyone had a love-hate relationship with his or her father. He wondered how he was going to get through dinner the next evening.

Diana set her mug down, pulled out a notebook and returned to the subject at hand. "Since I couldn't get much from the villagers, I went down to the harbor and went from boat to boat." She paused expectantly.

"And?" Liam said obediently.

"And I found a few fishermen who weren't local who knew the

family. The Malones have lived in Kulukak for fifty years. David Malone's grandfather served in the Aleutians during World War II, and took demobilization in Anchorage after he sent for his family. In 1948, they moved to Kulukak."

"Wonder how he got to Kulukak."

She flipped back a page. "One of the people I talked to—darn it, where is that?—here, a Sam Deener told me that Malone Senior, was looking for a place to get away from it all and raise his family in peace and safety."

His son had found neither, following in his father's footsteps, Liam thought.

Unconscious of irony, Diana plowed on. "He and his wife, Mae, had one son, David. David went away to school, took a fisheries management degree from the University of Oregon and brought Molly home when he graduated. They've lived there ever since. Every five years or so, David buys—bought—a bigger and better boat. They've been adding on to the house at about the same rate."

"Mmm." Liam drank coffee and thought. "How many other white people are there in Kulukak? Year-round residents, I mean?"

She looked puzzled. "I never thought to ask."

"The answer might be interesting." She still looked puzzled, and he relented enough to explain. "A lot of these smaller villages don't tolerate outsiders coming in."

She looked back down at her notebook. "I didn't get a feel for anything like that."

"You wouldn't; you're white, too. There's a lot they won't tell you, or me, for that matter. Not only are we cops, we're white cops."

He could see by her expression that she understood. "They covered that pretty thoroughly in the course on community relations."

"They did in my time, too." And to give the academy credit, the emphasis laid on the responsibility of troopers posted to the Bush to keep everybody's peace, regardless of race, was thorough and decidedly firm. The present colonel was Native, too, which by itself was enough to raise everyone's consciousness a notch.

But, in the end, the troopers worked for the state of Alaska.

They enforced laws passed by the Alaskan legislature. Going into a Bush village, Liam never forgot he was white and an employee of the state, and that of the two, the latter would get him into more trouble than both together. Prince would have an added disadvantage; she was a woman.

"Why doesn't Kulukak have a vipso?" Prince asked. "It's big enough, they could use a local cop."

Liam sighed. The Village Police and Safety Officer Program took rural applicants into the trooper academy in Sitka, trained them in police procedures and then sent them back to keep the peace in their villages. An excellent idea, but it had its drawbacks, one of which was that in any small Bush village, the chances of any local applicant's being related in some way to the rest of the village was very high. "They had one," he said. "About four years ago. Or so I hear tell, as I have been making some calls of my own. He was young, bright, good at his job. Then he quit."

"Just like that?"

"Not quite. He got caught in the sack with a woman of the village. Name of Patty." He met Prince's eyes, and added ruefully, "Patty Larsgaard. When he left town, she went with him."

"Oh," she said. Comprehension dawned. "Oh, I see. Wife?" He nodded. "Young Walter or Old Walter?"

"Young."

"Oh." She thought. "That's interesting."

"How so?"

She hesitated. "Nobody actually said anything . . ."

"Yeah, but?"

"Well, I get the feeling there was something going on between Larsgaard and Molly Malone."

Liam remembered Larsgaard's hesitation in speaking of Molly Malone. "I got that feeling, too, when we were all up at the Malones' house."

"Shall I interrogate him on it?"

"We both will. We're flying back in tomorrow morning."

"Eight, right?"

"Ten," he said firmly, and repressed a chuckle at her expression. "I've got some phone calls to make. The M.E. might have some preliminary findings, and I want to talk to him before we leave." He drained his mug. "That all you got?"

"I haven't been able to track down Max Bayless yet."

"I've got someone working on that for me. Anything else?"

She hesitated. "Well . . ."

"What?" He stretched, yawning. "I'm bushed. It's been a long day. Time to hit the rack."

Her triumphant smile stopped him. "I found a witness, sir. A deckhand on a boat that broke down in Kulukak toward the end of Monday's period."

That caught him in midstretch. "You're kidding."

"No. Chad Donohoe, from —"

His tone was deceptively mild. "And you didn't think this was information important enough to tell me first?"

Her smile slipped. "Well . . ."

He met her eyes. His face didn't change expression but hers did. "Next time? Just run it down in order of importance. Especially at this time of night."

"Yes, sir," she said, subdued. She flipped to the appropriate page in her notebook. "Chad Donohoe, from Mount Vernon, Washington State. He was deckhanding on board the *Snohomish Belle* and she broke down just as the period was ending, about five-thirty. The skipper — Anders Ringstad — had to call in an order to Newenham — Reardon Marine — and have it flown into Kulukak late that night, about ten o'clock." She added parenthetically, "That strip must be rated for after-dark operations. I'll have to check. Of course, if you're not flying passengers, the rules aren't as stringent. Anyway, Ringstad sent Donohoe to Kulukak in the skiff. Where they were fishing is about an hour from the village by skiff. He should have been back by midnight, twelve-thirty at the latest.

"But . . ." Prince looked at Liam over the top of her notebook. "It seems that Donohoe has a girlfriend in Kulukak. Among other places."

"Aha."

"So it was about three a.m. when he got back to the *Snohomish Belle.*"

Liam cut to the chase. "What did he see?"

"He says it was real foggy out, first of all. Worse than it was this morning."

Liam groaned. "Oh great."

"Yeah, that's what I thought, and it was right down on the water, too, he couldn't see but fifty feet off the beam—what's a beam?"

"Beats the hell out of me."

"Anyway, he couldn't see fifty feet off the beam in either direction. But he says a New England dory—what's a dory?"

"A skiff. A big skiff."

"Oh. Donohoe saw this New England dory pass real close off to starboard—that's right—about ten minutes before he got back to the *Belle*. Almost sideswiped him, he said, it was that close. He never would have seen it otherwise. He could hear the engine, of course."

"Why of course?"

"Sound carries in a fog."

Liam thought of the various noises he had heard in and around Kulukak that morning, the rifle shots, the boat engines turning over, the landing plane. "Yes, it does. Did he see the person driving the skiff?"

"He saw a man, he said. He didn't know who he was." Prince looked up, triumph in her eyes. "But his description sounds a lot like Walter Larsgaard."

Liam thought about that for a few moments. Prince waited, her expression indicating a willingness to leap into the Cessna and fly down to Kulukak this minute to make an arrest.

Liam wasn't so sure. He'd seen Molly's picture; all right, maybe she did have a face—and a body—that would launch a thousand dories, maybe even one that might get her husband killed.

But her children? Her brother-in-law? Her husband's deckhands? Herself, ostensibly the object of her lover's affections?

He shook his head. Prince looked disappointed and Liam said, "Just thinking to myself. Here's a little piece of information for you. A fisher named Darrell Jacobson saw a New England dory leave Kulukak harbor at about ten p.m."

"Who was driving it?" she said eagerly.

"He didn't know, he's not from Kulukak, but Jacobson was headed for Togiak, so we can pull him in for an identification if need we need him." He could almost hear Prince's tail thumping the floor and held up a hand, palm out. "Look, we've got a couple of pieces of information, and we'll use them when we need to, but let's not jump the gun. Larsgaard fishes where he lives, I think he's his father's sole support, and he's tribal chair besides. He's not going anywhere. We'll brace him tomorrow, ask him what he was doing out on the Kulukak at that time of night. If it was him, maybe we can surprise an answer out of him." He stood up and put his mug in the sink. "Now I'm hitting the rack, and I suggest you do the same."

Prince handed her mug over without protest. "Sir —"

"It's Liam," he reminded her, taking the mug.

"Is it okay if I bunk here for the night, Liam?"

"No." He wasn't aware that he'd barked the word until he saw her flinch.

She nodded at the bunk opposite. "You've got the room, and as you know, I haven't had time to —"

"No. Well, I mean . . . well, I mean, no."

"But —"

"I mean, no, you can't sleep here. I — it isn't a good idea. I don't — I can't —"

"But Liam —"

He realized, first, that he was babbling, and, second, that his forehead was beaded with sweat. He whipped around and slid the hatch back. "Goodnight, trooper."

She sighed. "Goodnight, Liam."

"Maybe you better call me sir after all."

"All right," she said, submissive. "Goodnight, sir."

He gave her a sharp look. Submissive didn't seem quite in character for Trooper Diana Prince.

"Goodnight," he said, and stood stiffly as she slid past him and up the stairs to the deck. Her hair nearly brushed his nose. It smelled good, some kind of fruity scent. He didn't want to be smelling her hair. He slid the hatch smartly closed behind her, and waited as the boat tilted and righted itself again as she stepped to the slip.

Some sound came to him a few moments later, which might have been that of muffled laughter, but it might also have been the sound of water lapping against the pilings. He went back to bed without trying to figure out which.

FOURTEEN

The next morning dawned early, like all summer mornings in the Bush. The sun would be officially up by six-fifteen, although it had been light out for hours before that. By the end of July they were losing four minutes and twenty-four seconds of daylight every day. You'd never know it by the extended sunrise.

The advantage was that there were very few times of day or night during the summer when you couldn't see your way down the path. It was a steep one, carved into the crumbling side of the bluff, a length of manila line looped between wooden posts the only thing between Wy and disaster. Some of the steps were large rocks, flat sides up, set into the dirt. Others were reinforced with scraps of wood left over from various building projects, one-by-twelves, two-by-fours and one piece of metal grating. On normal days she rather enjoyed testing the limits, seeing how fast she could get down to the beach, but this morning she walked slowly, one hand just touching the rope, tapping each post with her fingertips as she passed it.

The mouth of the Nushagak opened before her, a wide stretch of water gray with glacial silt moving with stately deliberation between banks a mile apart. It formed part of the lifeblood of the Bay, along with the other hundred rivers of the area, providing the way home for salmon returning from the sea. It was, as well, the umbilical cord connecting the interior villages to Newenham. It was to Newenham they came, by boat in summer and by snow machine in winter and by plane year-round, to shop, visit relatives, play basketball, buy duck stamps, apply for moose permits, attend school, stand trial, serve time, take communion. Wy flew the river every day, upstream and down, and its size and power and importance in all their lives never failed to impress her.

In her more fanciful moments, she thought of the river as a woman, old and infinitely wise, loving but stern, never capricious but never quite predictable, either. When she took a life, or lives, when she sucked down a skiff with swift gray intent, or opened a lead in her frozen winter face to swallow a snow machine, she had her reasons, good ones, and if those on shore were left to mourn, why, death was a part of life, after all, and that was the way of the world, and the river, to give and to take with the same hand.

The beach was a wide strip of gravel and sand littered with driftwood bleached white by time and tide. That driftwood made for wonderful fires, and Wy could see the smoke from several here and there. Fishermen out early for the first red of the day.

The closest one was right at the base of her cliff. The last step was a big one, twenty inches to the beach. She jumped it, landing both feet solidly in a patch of gravel that rattled loudly on impact.

The man feeding the fire didn't so much as turn around.

"I already practiced, old man," she said to his back.

"I know," he said. "I saw you on my way down."

"Oh." She hesitated, and then moved forward to sit next to the fire, a little apart from him.

They contemplated the flames in silence. The weight of the river pulled at the banks, tangling in its current here a downed spruce, there an empty skiff that had slipped its mooring. A river otter chittered at her young where a creek flowed into the river. An eagle soared overhead, causing a flock of ducks and half-grown ducklings clustered at the edge of the water to fall silent. The tide was out, revealing the muddy banks of the river and the goose grass growing there. The water was half salt, half fresh, and the marsh on the Delta supported a rich and varied avian lifestyle. The ducks were fattening nicely, and both Moses and the eagle eyed them with approval. When the last salmon had made its run up the river, the ducks and the geese would be next on the menu.

Wy looked at Moses. He wore a dreamy expression, one she

didn't see often, one he did not permit to show through his usual cantankerous crust. His mouth, usually held in a disapproving line, was relaxed, caught in a half-smile. He seemed to be remembering something pleasant. It didn't happen often, and she didn't try to interrupt.

He looked up suddenly and caught her eyes in his. "Are you angry when it rains? Do you blame God?"

"Blame?" she said, puzzled. "Who's to blame? The weather's the weather. It happens."

A light, brief shower of raindrops fell on her hair and she looked up, startled. There were clouds overhead, big, cottony cumulus clouds not heavy enough with moisture to shed any of it. Had they been there when she came down the bank?

"Are we less, then, than the rain?" he said softly, his face turned up into it. A sliver of sun, a deep, rich gold, appeared on the northeastern horizon. "Are we more than the sun?"

She sat very still. Moses was a drunk, but he was also a shaman, and, no matter how thorough her indoctrination had been at the hands of her adoptive parents and at the University of Alaska, Wy remembered enough of the first five years of her life not to reject the presence of what she couldn't see.

Moses opened his eyes and added a piece of driftwood to the fire. The salt crystals caught in the wood flared with color. The wood burned steadily, radiating warmth and light.

"You didn't answer my question," he said.

"I don't have an answer," Wy replied.

"No?" He smiled. "Need some help?"

Wy swallowed. She wanted to say no. "I don't know."

"I say you do," Moses said firmly.

Wy made a show of looking at her watch. "Gee, look at the time, it's past six-thirty. I'm flying in a couple of hours, so—"

"Sit down."

She sat down with a thump, heart beating uncomfortably up high in her throat. "Look, I—"

"You will listen," he said firmly, "and when questioned, you will answer truthfully."

Sez you, Wy thought.

He eyed the mutinous line of her mouth and grinned, a wide,

wise grin as full of charm as it was of guile. "Wy," he said, his voice not ungentle, "what do you want?"

She huffed out an impatient breath. "I want to live my life. I want my business to succeed. I want to fly, and I especially want to fly this morning."

Moses contemplated the fire. "You're in danger."

She was startled again. She looked over her shoulder. No one nearby on the beach, no one on the river. "What do you mean?"

"What do you want?" he repeated.

"Goddamn it!" she shouted. "I want to adopt Tim! I want to live my life!" She leapt to her feet. "I want to be left alone!"

"Sit down," he said again, and she subsided like a puppet who had lost its strings.

He picked up an eagle feather lying next to him in the sand, and used it to cup smoke from the fire over his face, eyes closed, expression meditative. She struggled for composure, and found it in the tuneless humming that emanated from his rusty old man's voice.

He opened his eyes. "Are you so afraid?"

"I'm not afraid of anything," she said, and was immediately ashamed. She sounded exactly like a child whistling past the graveyard. "I'm afraid of everything," she said, as her defenses fell with an almost audible thump. "I'm afraid customers will show up who won't fly with me because I'm a woman. I'm afraid I won't earn enough to make my loan payments. I'm afraid Tim's natural mother will steal him back. I'm afraid—" She stopped.

"Yes?" Still with that unnaturally gentle voice.

"You know what I'm afraid of."

"He's a good man."

"I'm not a bad woman," she snapped. "I'm smart, I'm capable. I don't need rescuing, or redemption."

"How about company?" he snapped back, a momentary backsliding of role, wise shaman to cranky drunk. "He's pretty good company, that guy, even if he is a cop."

"There's nothing wrong with being a cop!" she said indignantly. "They catch the bad guys. They keep the peace. Every day they get their noses rubbed into the worst of human behavior. When someone's shooting off a gun, they have to go take it away. They don't get near enough credit or even half the pay they deserve."

He smiled, a brief, nasty little smile, and she blushed hotly, annoyed at being maneuvered into defending Liam.

"So you don't object to his profession."

"Of course not."

"What is it, then? What stops you from going to him?"

"Maybe," she said through her teeth, "just maybe I don't think there's anybody out there more fun to live with than me." She pushed her jaw out, daring a response.

She got it, a full-throated belly laugh that rocked him backward. "Oh yeah," he said, wiping away a tear, "oh yeah, you are just like your mother, just full of piss and vinegar, self-righteous and pigheaded and so damn sure you're right."

She said sharply, "You knew my mother? My natural mother?" He said nothing. "Moses?"

"Yes," he said finally. His smile faded. "I did. She's dead."

"I know that much. And I know our family came from Icky. What I don't know is her name. Mom and Dad would never tell me." She waited.

He rearranged himself, refolding his legs, and produced a pint of Chivas Regal. Uncapping it, he took a long swallow.

"Moses—"

"Make up your mind, Wy. You either want him or you don't. You don't have much time left. You may have none."

"What? What does that mean?" She rose to her feet as he did, and followed him to the steps. "Moses, you can't say things like that and then retreat into that goddamn druidic silence of yours! Talk to me!"

"Got me a smart woman in a real short skirt," he said, winking at her, "or in this case, a pair of really tight jeans. Time I got back to her." He took another swig from the bottle and headed up the steps.

"Moses?"

Something in her voice halted him halfway up.

"Did you know my father, too?"

There was a long silence, into which crept the sounds of a Bush village waking up: a light plane taking off, the hum of an outboard motor, the start of a truck, bird calls, fish jumping.

"Yes." He began to climb again.

"Moses?"

He halted without turning around.

"Are you my father?"

He stood for a long time on the makeshift stairs, his back to her, and then he continued up and over the edge of the bluff. Moments later, she heard the engine of his truck turn over, heard it grind into gear, heard it leave the clearing and trundle down her lane to the road.

She stood where she was for a long time, listening, watching, waiting for him to come back. He didn't.

Liam donned his only other clean uniform, also tailored, also immaculately pressed, and boxed up yesterday's for mailing to the dry cleaner in Anchorage.

The post office was open, with a new clerk behind the counter, a young, plump-faced man with a sunny smile and a name tag which read Malachi Manuguerra. Malachi sent Liam's uniform priority mail and chatted about his new baby girl, just a week old that day. Liam dutifully admired the picture of the squinched-up, red-faced mite bundled in hospital white, and from the post office went to the Bay View Inn, Newenham's only hotel. It was a two-story building that looked suspiciously modular, sporting neat green siding with brown trim and a corrugated silver roof. It had been kept up, though; siding and trim were freshly painted and the wooden stairs leading up to the front door had recently had some of their steps replaced. The sun shone benignly down on pansies and nasturtiums planted in two homemade rock gardens, and the windows had that just-washed gleam.

The lobby was empty but for a clerk behind a counter. She was reading *The Celestine Prophecy* through little round glasses that had slid down to the very end of her long, thin nose. Her gray hair was cut closely around her face, and she wore a bright yellow cardigan over an even brighter orange shirt and red polyester pants.

It took him a moment to recover from the glare of the primary colors. "Excuse me." Sharp eyes the color of wood smoke looked at him over the silver rims of her glasses and took in his uniform. She moved finally, straightening to reveal a tall frame, lean, long-limbed and supple. Norwegian, Liam thought, or Swedish. Scandinavian, anyway. There was a lot of that going around the Bay.

"You're the new trooper."

"Corporal Liam Campbell." It was getting easier to say.

She extended a hand, square-shaped, callused and confident. "Alta Peterson. You looking for your new trooper?"

So Prince had found the hotel after all. "She spend the night here?"

"Uh-huh. She left early, though. Said she was going out to the lake, service her plane."

"Good."

"She's pretty young for a trooper." She let the remark lie there, with a question mark hanging over it.

He shrugged. "Maybe a little. She's certainly new to the area, just got in yesterday."

She surveyed him. "You haven't been here all that long yourself. How are you liking the posting?"

"I like it a lot." He remembered jumping out of Wy's plane yesterday afternoon, and a sudden grin spread across his face, surprising both of them and making her blink. "Never a dull moment. Alta, is this your hotel?"

She nodded, a positive movement indicative of pride. "My husband and I built it. He was a fisher from Anacortes, came up on his uncle's boat the summer of 1977, and never left. The kids and I came up that fall, and we've been here ever since."

"How many kids and what kind?"

Alta had a wallet full of pictures on the counter before the last word was out of his mouth. He admired the two sons and the one daughter—"All in school at the University of Washington," she mentioned with an elaborate disinterest that fooled neither of them—all three tall, blond, blue-eyed Vikings, all with their mother's firm jawline.

"I suppose the boys went on the boat and the girl helped out around the hotel when they were kids," he suggested.

"You suppose wrong. We were all on the boat at the start," she retorted. "We lost the boat, though, in 1980, coming back from Dutch Harbor. Peri—that was my husband—decided to take the insurance and build this hotel. That was the time of the big runs."

"Yeah," Liam said. Peri, spoken of in the past tense. "I remember reading about them in the newspaper. You could pull in a quarter of a million dollars in reds in one period, you had a big enough boat and an experienced crew."

"Those were the days," she agreed, and they both sighed a little, totally fraudulent expressions of nostalgia for a time gone by. After three summers spent kneeling over the edge of a skiff picking reds out of a net, she was perfectly happy to be permanently shore-based, and after spending three months sleeping on the *Dawn P*, he would have been delirious at the news of an apartment for rent on solid ground.

Liam recovered first. "So this is the only hotel in town, right?"

She nodded. "Yeah. We've heard rumors for years that a Best Western was going to come in, but it hasn't happened yet. Lots of bed and breakfasts, though, since the Wood-Tikchik State Park opened up. And the Togiak Wildlife Refuge," she added, "long as they can afford to hire a float plane."

Liam studied the countertop with absorption, presenting all the appearance of a man deeply embarrassed to ask the next question but forced by profession to do so. "I imagine you have a few, ah, local customers." He risked a look and saw that Alta's unblinking stare was back and fixed unwaveringly on his face.

"If there is something you want to ask me, Corporal Campbell, ask," she said, gathering up her pictures and putting them back in her wallet.

"I'm afraid there is," he said, still more apologetically.

She drummed her fingers on the counter. "Stop tap-dancing. What is it?"

"I suppose you've heard about the *Marybethia*." Beneath lowered lid he watched her reaction.

Her lips tightened, but that was all. "Yes."

"Did you know the Malones?"

"Yes."

"Any one of the Malones in particular? Molly, for example?"

Her smile was frosty around the edges. "If, Liam, you want to know if Molly Malone ever spent the night here with a man not her husband, the answer is yes."

"Ah." His breath expelled on a long sigh. "Who?"

"That I don't know. I never saw him."

His brow creased. "Then how do you know she was with anybody?"

"I make the beds."

"Oh."

"He wasn't with her when she checked in. She must have let him in the back door because he never came through the lobby. But that girl definitely wasn't sleeping alone the nights she spent here."

"Maybe her husband joined her."

"Then how come I never saw him? She was always alone, coming and going."

"How often did she stay here?"

"She came into town on shopping trips on average about once a month."

"For how long?"

"One or two nights, usually. Oh, you mean how long had she been making these trips into town." Alta thought. "I guess about a year. Since before last fishing season, anyway. Last April, maybe, around tax time?" She shrugged. "I can't say for sure."

Liam gave Alta his most winning smile. "Could I see the register?"

She barked a laugh. "We don't have a register." She nodded at the office in back of the counter.

He followed her through the door, and beheld the latest in Dell computers, hooked up to a scanner, a printer, a copy machine and a fax. "Great," he said. "How far back do your records go?"

"Since we bought the place," she said complacently, and sat down. "What do you want?"

"Can you print out a list of all the dates Molly Malone stayed here?"

"Certainly," Alta said with a trace of scorn, and did so forthwith. Liam scanned the piece of paper. "Thanks, Alta, I owe you one."

"I had one of the Malone deckhands in here, too," she said. "Beginning of last season, all pissed off because David Malone had fired him. What the hell was his name . . ."

"Max Bayless?"

She raised her eyebrows. "Why, I believe that was it. Scrawny little guy, nose off a fairy tale witch, big brown eyes like a cow's, mouth that wouldn't stop."

Alta Peterson had a gift for characterization; a vivid picture of Max Bayless materialized before Liam's very eyes. He produced his notebook. "What did he say about the Malones?"

"Said David Malone booted him off the *Marybethia* for no good reason, right in the middle of the season."

"He get paid?"

She nodded. "Oh yes. I made him sign his crew share check over to me before I'd let him register. You can't trust a fisher at settlement. They're liable to drink every dime of their checks the first day they step off the boat, either celebrating a great season or drowning a bad one. I never had that problem with Peri, bless his heart. Anything else you wanted?"

He indicated the computer. "Can you look up the exact date Bayless was here?"

"I don't have to." She smiled, revealing a set of large, yellowing teeth. "He was in on July fourth, out again on the fifth."

"Easy dates to remember. Did he get another job?"

"I'd say about an hour after he flew in," she said, nodding. "I was surprised, since it wasn't that good a year, and it didn't sound to me like he was that good a deckhand. David Malone has—had a good reputation on the Bay. He wouldn't fire someone in the middle of the fishing season for no good reason. It would leave him short-handed, and it would take too much time to find someone to replace him."

"Maybe his kids were coming along," Liam suggested.

"Maybe." Alta didn't sound convinced. "My kids couldn't wait to set foot on dry land, themselves." Humor gleamed in the blue eyes. "There's not a one of them majoring in fisheries management, either."

"What are they majoring in?"

The gleam of humor increased to deepen the crow's feet at the corners of her eyes. "Pre-Columbian art, high-altitude botany, and Eastern religions. Respectively."

Jesus, Liam almost said, but recollected himself in time to snatch the word back. "Well, thank you for all your help, Alta." He pocketed his notebook and turned to leave.

She waited until he was halfway out the door before she said, "You want a list of the dates David Malone stayed here?"

He halted in his tracks. "What?"

Her smile was wicked. "He didn't sleep alone, either."

FIFTEEN

He stopped at NC for coffee and a roll, and headed to the post. Charlene Taylor was waiting for him. She didn't look happy.

Fifty years old, give or take a few, she had a round face topped by a fringe of flyaway brown bangs. Her ample waist was firmly restrained by a thick leather belt, and her epaulets and shoulder pads made her look twice as wide as the Sherman tank she already was. Her eyelashes, long, thick and curling, were disarmingly coquettish until you got past them to the unavoidable brown gaze they screened, a stare that weighed, measured, classified and stamped in one thorough glance. It reminded him a little of Alta's. It reminded him a lot of Bill's.

Liam, a man who had always loved women, was a bit afraid of all three of them. He wondered suddenly what Wy would be like at fifty, and gave an involuntary grin at the thought of what it might be like to live with her then. He'd have to check with Charlene's husband, the D.A. for this district, and see what he said.

"There's nothing funny about it," Charlene said severely, rebuking his grin.

"Nothing funny about what?" Liam said, leading the way into his office.

Charlene planted herself squarely in front of his desk and folded her arms across an impressive chest. "I understand you have Frank Petla under arrest for murder."

Liam, still in the act of pulling off his cap, looked surprised. "He hasn't been charged yet, but, yes, he's in custody."

"He didn't do it."

Liam took his cap the rest of the way off and took a minute hanging it just so from the hat rack on the wall. He went behind his desk, sat down, and took the lid off the coffee. "You want half?" he said, holding out the enormous cinnamon roll.

"He didn't do it, Liam."

"Fine," he said. "More for me." He took a gigantic bite and washed it down with a swallow of satisfyingly strong coffee. "You sound very sure."

"I know him. He's a drunk, but he's not a killer."

"We're all potential killers, given the right circumstances, and you know it, Charlene." He took another bite.

"You weren't," she said pointedly, and he flushed a dark red.

"No, I wasn't." The memory of the man who had killed his wife and child, kneeling in front of him in the rain, on a lonely road fifty miles from anywhere and anyone to see, flashed through his mind. He banished it, the way he always did. His appetite gone, he set the roll down.

"Aw hell," she said, disgusted. "I'm sorry, Liam." She removed her own cap and sat down heavily. "Low blow, totally unwarranted, completely out of line."

"You aren't the first person to have made that observation." A lot of people thought Rick Dyson should have been shot while resisting arrest, many of them within Liam's own command. Liam had felt the weight of their silent contempt every time he walked into headquarters.

Contempt was not manifest in Charlene's glare. "I said I was sorry."

He held up one hand, palm out. "All right. Apology accepted. What makes you so sure Petla didn't do it?"

"Tell me what happened," she said instead.

He told her. She followed the story intently. "How did you catch him when he took off on the four-wheeler? There's no place to land and intercept him around there."

"I brought him back to the dig," Liam said, avoiding a direct answer. "Charlene, he assaulted a trooper."

She looked startled. "You?"

"No, we got ourselves a new trooper, fresh out of the academy, Diana Prince."

"I didn't know that."

"She came in yesterday. Green as she is, I have to say it helped having her here, what with the press of business and all." It was a weak attempt at a joke and didn't earn him a smile. "You hear about the *Marybethia*?" She nodded. "We flew out to Kulukak yesterday morning when the news came in, I sent her back with the bodies. McLynn—you know McLynn?"

"I've heard of him." Her dry tone indicated that she hadn't heard anything good.

"Well, Wy Chouinard's been flying him in and out, and when they flew in yesterday morning they found Nelson's body. Don Nelson," he added parenthetically. "He was McLynn's gofer. McLynn and Wy flew back to town and got hold of Prince. Prince borrowed Wy's Cub and flew out to the dig with McLynn, while Wy picked me up in Kulukak and brought me back." He omitted reference to the brief stop en route. He was getting good at skipping that. "We switched planes and flew out to the dig. When we got there, Prince had been clubbed, McLynn had been shot and Frank Petla was hightailing it over the horizon on a four-wheeler with a thirty-ought-six and a bag of Yupik artifacts from the dig strapped to the handlebars. Which bag of artifacts included the murder weapon, I might add."

"What was the murder weapon?" He told her, and she grimaced. "I knew there was a reason I chose the Fish and Game side of this department. At least people are only murdering moose." She pulled the brim of the cap through her fingers. "Okay." She raised her head. "It looks bad for Frank. Given his presence and his behavior, you didn't have any choice, I see that."

"How do you know him?"

Her mouth pulled down. "He boarded with us for a year when he was a teenager." Her eyes met his, her expression troubled. "You know how it is in the villages, Liam. The elders are trying to hold things together, trying keep the kids off the booze long enough to grow up, but a lot of the time it's just too little, too late. Frank comes from one of the families for which it was too little and too late. His father ran his snow machine into a lead on the river when Frank was ten, and his mother never recovered. She's a great gal when she isn't on the sauce, but it's got her by the scruff of the neck and it's not about to let go. His sister Sarah died when she was thirteen, alcohol abuse. Frank was in trouble in the village, some underage drinking, some disturbing the peace, some small-time B&E—yeah, yeah, I know what this sounds like. Liam, he just never had a chance. The elders called in the troopers when he broke into the school one night and trashed the library, and the trooper brought him before Bill. Jerry and I—well, we don't have any of our own, and we take in a kid now and then, a kid who otherwise will get sent to McLaughlin in Anchorage and get lost in the system. Village kids got no business being sent to McLaughlin, Liam; all that happens there is they get advanced instruction in criminal behavior."

Liam held up one hand. "You're preaching to the choir here, Charlene."

She relaxed a little. "He was real good, the time he spent with us. Stayed sober, did his homework. Even had a girlfriend, Betty Kusma, smart girl, works as a checker at NC. We took both of them to the AFN convention that October, and he signed on with the sobriety movement."

"What happened?"

Her mouth set in an unhappy line. "His mother got an attorney and forced DFYS to give him back to her." She sat back in her chair and closed her eyes. "He was only fifteen. If we could have kept him for just one more year, until he was sixteen and would have had a choice whether to go or stay, he might have made it."

There was silence for a moment. "I'll dot all the *i*'s and cross all the *t*'s, Charlene," Liam said at last. "I won't take anything at face value. But you have to know it looks pretty bad."

"I know." She opened her eyes and stood up. "Thanks, Liam."

"Hold on a minute, would you?" He rose and walked over to the wall map of the Bristol Bay area. He tapped Kulukak. "Can you tell me what part of Kulukak Bay was open for fishing on Sunday?"

"Sure." She came to stand next to him. "All of it."

"For how long?"

She thought. "I'd have to look it up, but I think six a.m. to six p.m."

"Hell."

"What's the problem?"

"It's eight miles across," he said gloomily, "and ten or more north-south. I'm trying to track the whereabouts of forty to fifty different boats on that Bay during a twelve-hour period."

"Because all of it was open, doesn't mean all of it was fished."

He looked at her. "Which means what, exactly?"

"It means that fishermen aren't stupid. They'll wet their nets where it'll do them the most good. In this case . . ." Her forefinger traced a section of the coastline on the northeast corner of Kulukak Bay. "Right about here."

He inspected the bit of coastline. "Why?"

"Because that's where the Kanik River, the biggest creek on the bay, empties into the Kulukak," she said. "You know? Every summer, salmon come in from the ocean to go up the creeks where they were born to spawn their own young? You must have heard something about this, surely."

His ears reddened. "Not a lot of commercial fishing in Glenallen."

"That's no excuse," she said severely. "You've been on the Bay for three months now. Anyway, that's where most of your boats will have been, outside the markers of the Kanik, trying to get in between the fish and fresh water." She pulled her cap on.

"One more thing."

"What?"

"Ivory, walrus ivory."

"The tusks. Sure, what about them?"

"I know only Natives can sell them. Can they sell them as is, or do they have to be carved into something first?"

"The law says it has to be carved on or into something. Walk into any gift shop on Fourth Avenue in Anchorage and look around. You'll see whole heads with the tusk sporting one little carving of a mask or an animal, just to make it legal." Her eyes narrowed. "Why? Is there something you're not telling me, something going on to do with my side of the patch?"

He told her about the suspiciously fresh chunk of ivory tusk he had found in the service tent at the dig. She listened with interest, and when he was done said, "Like I said, it's the law, the pieces have to be finished." She smiled. "But if everyone obeyed the law, we'd both be out of work."

Charlene left the post, and as Liam returned to his desk the phone rang. It was a man, on the ragged edge of losing his self-control, his voice so choked that Liam could barely understand him. "I beg your pardon, sir?"

The man cleared his throat. His voice was shaken but clear. "My name is Donald Nelson, Senior."

Liam closed his eyes for a brief moment, and then sat up straight. "Yes, sir. This is Liam Campbell with the Alaska State Troopers. Are you Don Nelson's father?"

The voice broke again. "Yes."

"I'm very sorry for your loss, Mr. Nelson."

"Thank you." There was the sound of a sob, quickly suppressed, and Liam set his teeth. "Please, can you tell me what happened? I just talked to Don last week, and he was fine. He was fine, he sounded happy, and excited about his work." There was a sound something between a laugh and a sob. "He said Alaska was beautiful and the people were crazy."

"He was right about both, sir," Liam said gently. He would rather respond to a hundred scenes like the *Marybethia* than talk to one grieving parent, but this was part of the job. He had a thought, and sat up. "Mr. Nelson, how did you find out your son was dead?"

"I don't know," Nelson said drearily. "Some woman called."

"When?"

"This morning. Just a little while ago."

"What time?"

"I don't know. About nine o'clock, I think. Mary? When did she call? Yes, about nine."

Eight o'clock Alaska time. Prince? "And you're calling from Seattle?"

"Why, yes," the man said, bewildered all over again. "How did you know?"

"Your son's identification stated his residence. Who called you, Mr. Nelson? Who was it on the phone this morning?"

"I don't know. Mary, where is that piece of paper . . ." Paper rustled in the background, and someone blew his nose. Nelson's voice came back on. "Here it is. Somebody from Anchorage."

Liam relaxed a little. "Someone from the medical examiner's officer, perhaps?"

"That was it. She told us he was dead, and when we asked how, she gave us your name. How did he die, Mr. Campbell? He was fine when we talked to him last week," Nelson repeated. He sounded dazed. "He was—he was fine. Was it an accident?"

"I'm sorry to have to tell you this, Mr. Nelson, but no, your son did not die in an accident." He thought of the hilt of the storyknife protruding from Nelson's mouth and added evenly, "There is evidence of foul play."

"Foul play? Foul play? What the hell does that mean?"

Liam hated the phrase "foul play" himself; it made him think of an Agatha Christie novel. "Mr. Nelson, your son was killed," he said bluntly. "I'm sorry," he added.

"Killed?" Liam had expected the rise of anger in Nelson's voice; it always happened, shock, followed by grief, followed by rage. "Who killed him? Who did it?"

Liam looked at the door, which Charlene had closed firmly behind her. "We don't know yet for sure, Mr. Nelson." He was thinking of Don Nelson's body lying in a sprawl so awkward it could only be death when he added, "But we do have a suspect in custody."

"Who?"

"A local man," Liam said circumspectly.

"How was he killed?"

Even more circumspectly, Liam replied, "Your son's body is at the medical examiner's office in Anchorage, Mr. Nelson. I expect cause of death will be pronounced within a few days. I can give you their phone number, if you like, so that you can make arrangements."

"Make arrangements." That was almost as bad a euphemism as "foul play." Much as we do to sanitize it, Liam thought, everything we do to clean it up for public view, death is messy and painful, and will not be called to order. He thought again of Frost's poem.

"All right," Nelson said, sounding suddenly exhausted. Liam gave him the M.E.'s number. "Thank you."

Before very long Don Nelson, Senior, was going to want answers. Who, what, where, how and, above all, why? It was Liam's job to provide them. "You're welcome. Mr. Nelson, did your son have a particular friend here in Newenham? A girl-friend, maybe?"

"What? No. At least . . . he never said." The tears were coming back. "He would have said, wouldn't he? If he'd met a girl, he would have said. He would have told his mother. He would have. He—"

"So there wasn't anyone?"

"No. Not that we know of. And if it had been serious, we would have known. We were very close."

"I'm glad," Liam said, and said it forcefully. "Did Don have any siblings? Any brothers or sisters that he might have talked to since he talked to you?"

"He had a sister, Betsy. She didn't say he'd called when we talked to her this morning."

"May I have her phone number?"

Liam scribbled it down, and they said their goodbyes, Liam promising to call with any new information. Nelson Senior would call back first, he knew. It would take a day or two for him to filter the information Liam had given him through his grief, but when he did he would be on the phone breathing fire and smoke over the suspect in his son's murder, and if Liam was very unlucky, in less than a week he would be stepping off a plane at Newenham Airport.

The thought brought him to his feet. He donned cap and weapon and headed purposefully for the door. When he opened it, the white, shocked face of Tim Gosuk was on the other side.

"Tim?" Liam said.

"Is it true?" Tim said.

"Is what true?"

"Is it true that Mike Malone is dead?"

"How did you know Michael Malone?"

"I played guard opposite him at regionals last year. Is it true?"

Liam sat down on the top step, and with a gentle hand pulled Tim to sit next to him. "Yes, Tim, it's true."

Tim sat, staring numbly in front of him. At twelve you are immortal and indestructible. This time next year is an aeon away, and the end of your life shrouded in mists you won't penetrate for another forty years. Death just doesn't happen when you're twelve.

It doesn't happen to your friends, either. "I can't believe it. I heard Mom and Jo talking about a boat burning and the crew all dead. I didn't know it was Mike's boat. He was—he was the greatest guy, Liam. Really nice. If you made a good play, he'd slap you on the back and yell, 'Way to go!' Even when you were on the other team. He was a good player, too, always had his hands up, had a great rebound." Tim swallowed hard. Liam pretended not to notice. "He was just a great guy. I learned more playing against him than I did in a year's worth of practice."

There was a rustle of branches overhead, a soft croak. Liam didn't look up. "Did you know the rest of his family?"

A trace of color rose up from Tim's neck. "I met his sister," he said gruffly.

"Kerry?"

He nodded, his head turned away. The tip of his left ear was pink. "She was a cheerleader."

"Pretty?"

Tim nodded again. "Is it true? The whole family is dead?"

"Yes."

Liam's deep, slow voice was its own soporific. Tim's shoulders shuddered with a long sigh and he sat up straight again. "Kerry, too?"

"Kerry, too."

"Damn it," Tim said. "GodDAMN it."

Liam dared to place one hand at the back of Tim's neck and squeeze. To his relief, Tim did not jerk away. "I'm sorry, Tim."

"Me, too," Tim said. "Me, too." He swiveled around. "Mom says they were murdered, that somebody killed them. You gonna find out who did it?"

"Yes."

Again, the deep voice was soothing in its certainty.

Another long, shuddering sigh. "Okay, then." Tim stood up, thin shoulders squared, jaw up in a gesture that looked uncannily similar to the same gesture Liam had seen a hundred times on Wy's face. "Go get 'em."

"All right," Liam said obediently. He wanted to say, How's your mom? but stopped himself in time. It would have been like ninth grade all over again, in love with Mary Kallenberg and trying to discover if she liked him through his best friend, Cal, and her best friend, Melissa.

The raven sitting on the swaying spruce bow beat his wings and gave a raucous croak. Liam's head jerked up. The raven met his eye and croaked again.

"He's around here a lot, isn't he?" Tim said, looking at the raven as he straddled his bike. "I thought they roosted way out of town."

"I just wish they did," Liam said. He looked hard at the raven. It didn't do any good. He looked like every raven Liam had seen since coming to the Bay; big, black, beaky and beady-eyed. You had to perform surgery to tell a female from a male, and you had to catch one and stare down its gullet to tell how old it was. They all looked alike, those damn ravens, which was why he kept thinking he saw the same one over and over again.

He climbed into the Blazer and peeled out of the lot.

SIXTEEN

They landed in Kulukak and taxied the float plane to the dock. The place was still shrouded in what seemed to be its perpetual cloak of mist. No one was there to greet them, but then Liam hadn't called to say they were coming. He had confirmed with Charlene that there was no fishing period scheduled for that day, and so had a faint hope of finding the people he needed to talk to actually in the village. Of course they could be in Togiak buying parts, or on their way to Newenham to get laid, or, for that matter, headed for Dutch to refit for crab fishing.

Liam was an American to the very marrow of his bones—he supported the Constitution, he defended the Bill of Rights and he worked conscientiously to uphold his oath of office—but the distances involved in police work in Bush Alaska were so great that he sometimes secretly longed for the days of the Star Chamber, when you could toss anyone you liked for a crime into a dungeon until you were ready to talk to them. They might be a little rat-bitten when you pulled them out again, but at least they'd be immediately to hand.

They had a third party in the plane with them, an arson investigator from Anchorage who had stepped off the jet that morning with all the air of Stanley heading out into the heart of Africa. He was a short, thin boy with an eager face and a lot of straight, yellow hair shaved at the sides and long enough on top to flop into his eyes. He looked as if he ought to be in Tim's class, but he had the proper credentials, so Liam managed—barely—to refrain from demanding he show his driver's license for proof of age.

The boy, Mark Sandowski by name, redeemed himself by opening the large aluminum suitcase he had brought with him and going immediately to work on the *Marybethia* with various implements and liquids. "We're headed uptown to talk to some people," Liam called through the open hatch. Sandowski, nose an inch from a charred piece of deck, didn't even look up, and Liam's estimation of him rose another notch.

"Who first?" Prince said, heading up the gangplank.

Liam consulted his mental list. "Chad Donohoe, deckhand on the *Snohomish Belle,* said he saw a man answering to the description of Walter Larsgaard in a skiff heading away from the direction of the *Marybethia* at approximately three a.m. on the morning in question, is that correct?"

"That is correct, sir."

"Okay, let's go ask Larsgaard where he was that night."

She was trying hard not to look eager. "It wasn't a positive ID," she reminded him, and herself, warning them both against hoping for too much. "Donohoe isn't a local man, he's from Washington State."

"You said." He held back a grin. He remembered his own rookie days, when every interview was an adventure, every interviewee under suspicion. "Let's go talk to Larsgaard anyway."

Five minutes later they were at Larsgaard's house. They knocked. There was no answer. They knocked again. Another minute passed before the door opened and Walter Larsgaard's father's face peered through the crack. He didn't look pleased to see them. "What you want?" he growled.

"We'd like to talk to your son, Mr. Larsgaard," Liam said. "Is he here?"

"No."

"Could you tell us where he is?"

The old man said something in Yupik that sounded less than complimentary, and the door shut in their faces.

Prince, predictably, wanted to kick it in. "No," Liam said, "we have no probable cause. What's the name of Larsgaard's boat?"

Tight-lipped, Prince consulted her notes. "The *Bay Rover.*"

"Fine. Let's check it out."

They marched back down to the boat harbor, where they ran

into Mike Ekwok, who pointed out the *Bay Rover* without hesitation, a trim little sternpicker about thirty-two feet in length, painted white with blue trim. There was a man at the deck controls, and as they watched, a plume of smoke came from the stack. The rumble of an engine was heard a moment later. "Son of a bitch," Liam said, and hit the gangplank at a run.

"What's the matter?" he heard Ekwok cry over the sound of Prince's footsteps pounding behind him.

Liam almost overshot the other side of the float at the bottom of the gangplank, caught his balance just before he went headfirst into the harbor and continued on toward Larsgaard's boat. He was close enough to see Larsgaard look over his shoulder, a drawn expression on his face, just before the fisherman cast off the stern line. The *Bay Rover* was twelve feet from the slip when Liam skidded to a halt, too far to jump. "Goddamn it!" Liam roared.

"Come on!" Prince yelled, and he turned to see her pounding back to the Cessna. He followed, and by the time he got there she had already cast off and had the prop rotating. The engine caught with a roar. "Get on the float!" she yelled, pointing, and without thinking he stepped to the right float just as it moved away from the slip.

"What the hell are we doing?" he yelled over the noise of the engine.

"If I can beat him to the harbor mouth, we can box him in! If not, I can bring us alongside and you can jump onto the deck!"

Liam clung to the strut with both hands, the sound of the Cessna's engine roaring in his ears, the wind from the prop tugging at his hair, his boots slipping on the wet surface of the floats. He wanted to ask Prince if she was out of her fucking mind, but he was too scared that the physical activity involved in forming the words would jar him off the float. The leading edge of the wings ripped apart the wall of wet, clammy mist, forming droplets of water on the metal surface that with the force of the air coalesced into rain against which he had to narrow his eyes. He could barely see Mike Ekwok running down the slip opposite, waving his arms up and down and shouting something Liam couldn't hear. The front of his uniform was already wet through.

The derelict hulk of the *Marybethia* flashed by, Mark Sandowski's astonished face framed in the hatch.

Prince got the Cessna clear of the slip, moving at a speed that definitely violated the no-wake speed limit inside the boat harbor. Liam blinked his eyes again to clear them, and saw Larsgaard just coming out from between the two sets of floats. The *Bay Rover* heeled over on its right side and the wake foamed up behind the stern. Prince responded by opening up the Cessna's throttle. The rock face of the breakwater loomed dangerously close to the tip of the left wing. "Watch out!" he yelled.

"Get ready!" she yelled back.

The *Bay Rover* speeded up. Forgetting where he was, Liam yelled, "Faster!"

"We're almost up on the step as it is," Prince yelled back. "We go any faster we'll take off, and there's no room!"

Larsgaard looked over his shoulder, saw the Cessna bearing down on his port stern and pointed the bow of the *Bay Rover* toward the entrance of the breakwater. At that moment another boat, a Grayling bowpicker returning to its slip from the fuel dock, crossed the bow of the *Bay Rover*. Its skipper stared at the oncoming boat with the float plane in hot pursuit, mouth open and apparently incapable of thought or action. Larsgaard heeled the *Bay Rover* hard aport and slammed the engine into neutral and then reverse, at the same time Prince cut the throttle on the Cessna, abruptly slowing their forward motion.

That was all it took. Liam's hands lost their grip on the strut and he was catapulted off the float and onto Larsgaard's deck, which was passing inches in front of the Cessna's still-rotating propeller. He retained just enough sense to tuck and roll, and everything would have been fine if his somersault hadn't achieved momentum and rolled him over the opposite gunnel, which caught him painfully in the small of his back but didn't stop him from going over the side.

The cold, dark water of Kulukak's small boat harbor closed over his head, and for a moment all he could think of was what the salt water was going to do to his freshly cleaned and only other uniform. Son of a bitch.

He swallowed water and battled his way to the surface, to find the gunnel of the *Bay Rover* six feet away, engine idling, boxed in by the Grayliner, the Cessna and the breakwater. Two overhand strokes brought him within reach, and he heaved himself up and over the gunnel and onto the deck. He looked up to see Walter Larsgaard standing over him, boat hook raised. He met Larsgaard's eyes and from somewhere found the air to gasp, "Walter Larsgaard, you are under arrest for unlawful flight to avoid prosecution."

Larsgaard stood where he was for a long moment. Liam gulped in more air and continued, "You have the right to remain silent. You have the right . . ."

The boat hook came down, and Larsgaard held it out, in the manner of a soldier surrendering a sword. Liam accepted it automatically.

". . . to have an attorney present during questioning. If you desire to have an attorney and cannot afford one, an attorney will be provided for you."

"What am I being prosecuted for?" Larsgaard said.

Murder, Liam thought, murder times seven, or else why were you running? "I'll think of something," he said. "Do you understand these rights as I've explained them to you?"

"Yes."

"Good." Liam got to his feet, shoes squelching, uniform a soggy memory of its former sartorial splendor. The Newenham posting was hell on uniforms.

"I'd like to take the boat back to the slip," Larsgaard said.

"Fine," Liam said, waving a hand, an expansive gesture ruined when he had to cough water out of his lungs. "Take her on back."

Larsgaard gave him a curious glance, and for a moment Liam thought he might smile. "I can't believe you came after me riding the pontoon of a float plane."

"I can't, either," Liam said wearily.

Although it wasn't like anyone had given him a choice.

It was a silent, soggy flight back to Newenham. Prince flew the plane, Larsgaard stared out the window, Sandowski made one abortive attempt to deliver his report and Liam dripped.

In Newenham they drove straight to the local jail, a compact building consisting of the dispatcher's office and six cells. Lars-gaard went into the one across from Frank Petla, who was suffering from what looked like a monumental hangover. "Frank?" Liam said, standing in front of the barred door.

Frank opened one eye, saw Liam and groaned. "Oh man, leave me alone."

Liam looked at his watch and calculated. It was noon, and he was hungry, not to mention damp. Frank hadn't technically been in custody until about seven the night before. Liam, who knew a sudden and irresistible desire for a greasy cheeseburger and even greasier fries, decided to update Bill on his progress.

He turned to go and saw that one of the opposite three cells was also full. Moccasin Man, he thought. That was his nickname for the tall man with a dark mane of hair that hung halfway down his back, who wore beaded moccasins and a matching beaded belt. Evan Richard Gray, one of Newenham's three dealers, three prior arrests for selling marijuana, no convictions. Probably all the women on the jury were hoping he'd ask them out if they let him off.

Prince shifted behind him and Liam turned and headed into the dispatcher's office. "Mamie, who brought Gray in?"

Mamie, a short, plump, harassed-looking woman with flyaway brown hair, skin still suffering the aftermath of a bad case of teenage acne and eyebrows plucked to a perpetually surprised expression, said, "Roger Raymo brought him in this morning. What?" she said into the phone. "Bobbie, you have to press charges this time, and you have to testify, or pretty soon the guys won't even bother coming out there." She listened. "All right, I'll expect you this afternoon. All right, I'll tell Roger. All right, Bobbie." She hung up the phone. "Bobbie Freedman. Cam keeps beating up on her, and she keeps calling us, and then she won't testify against him after we arrest him." She blew the hair out of her eyes and looked at Prince. "I don't believe we've met?"

"Diana Prince, Mamie Hagemeister. Trooper Prince has been newly assigned to the area. Mamie's the dispatcher we share with the city police."

Prince looked around the office, divided into two halves, one with Mamie's desk and an array of phones and radios, and the other with two more desks and filing cabinets. "Where are they?"

"Out on patrol," Mamie said.

"Or asleep," Liam added. He saw Prince's look. "There are supposed to be six of them. There are only two, Roger Raymo and Cliff Berg."

She nodded, and said, "I'll introduce myself to them as soon as I can."

Good luck, Liam thought. "I'm going to change into some dry clothes and then have lunch at Bill's."

Prince nodded again. "I'll go back to the post and run Petla and Larsgaard through the computer."

They went back to the Blazer. Sandowski was sitting in the back seat, his briefcase on his knees. "Forgot about him for a minute," Liam murmured, and climbed into the driver's seat. He looked up to meet Sandowski's eyes in the rearview mirror. "So, Mark. Anything you can tell me yet?"

Sandowski looked indignant. "I would have told you on the plane, if you—"

"Your report, Mark." Liam smiled.

Sandowski looked down and cleared his throat. "The boat was set on fire first."

"How?"

"Offhand, I'd say the arsonist induced combustion with an inflammatory substance. That is indicated by the high degree of carbonization—"

"English," Liam said.

"Oh." Mark gave a nervous smile. "Somebody poured gas all over the place and lit a match. They started in the galley. That's why the big charred patch in the middle of the floor."

They had to have been dead by then, or at least unconscious. There had been no sign of restraints, and nobody sits still while someone pours gas all over them. "From the fuel tank?"

"The *Marybethia*'s a diesel."

"Oh. Did you find a gas can?"

"No." Mark blinked. "Could have tossed it overboard."

Most likely, Liam thought. There was a hell of a lot of water for it to get lost in. "And then they opened the sea cocks."

"Somebody did," Mark said cautiously. "No way to know if the same person started the fire as pulled the plugs. The fire was started first, though," he added. "You can see where the water level climbed to extinguish the flames."

"You find any bullets?"

Mark stared. "How did you know?" He produced a slug in a Ziploc bag.

Liam took it. It was too flattened for casual identification, but if he had to guess it had come from a rifle, a .30-06, maybe. Easy enough to recognize, since just about everyone in the Bush owned one. More difficult to find out which rifle had fired it.

Mark took the bag back and pocketed it. "I'll turn it over to ballistics when I get back to town. And I'll know more about the fire once I get back to my own lab."

"Okay." Liam started the engine. "There's an Alaska Airlines flight out of here at about two o'clock."

"Drop us both at the post, sir," Prince said. "I'll drive him to the airport in the truck."

His shirt and jacket clung clammily to his skin. "Thanks."

Dry clothes felt good, even though he had to settle for civvies, in the form of a blue plaid shirt and jeans. He had a spare ball cap, though, with the trooper badge on the front, so he felt like he could legitimately strap his backup piece on. His nine-millimeter automatic, which had gone into Kulukak Bay with him, was disassembled and put in an oil bath in a saucepan before he headed out in search of food, by way of the post office. The same clerk was on duty. He eyed Liam's packaged uniform, addressed to the same Anchorage dry cleaner's. Liam held a hand up, palm out. "Don't ask."

"Hey, I just work here. Overnight? Same as this morning?"

Liam sighed and got out his wallet. "Yes." Maybe he should cave and get his uniforms made in some permanent press material, some fabric extruded from the molecule of a petroleum product.

It was one o'clock by the time he got to Bill's, and his stomach was trying to crawl up his throat. Bill took one look at him and yelled, "Cheeseburger and fries, rare!" and went to pour him a Coke.

"Diet," he said. "With lemon."

"Well, lah-di-dah," Bill said testily, dumping out what she'd already poured. "When did you get so refined in your tastes?"

"Regular's too sweet."

"That's generally why people like it," Bill said, setting a napkin on the bar and the glass on the napkin.

Liam squeezed the wedge of lemon into the liquid. "It's why I don't. Even the diet stuff is too sweet. That's why the lemon." He took a swallow, a long one, that resulted in a refill and another wedge of lemon. "Everything's too sweet anymore: pop, Jell-O, canned frosting, sukiyaki, even wine. It's the Pepsi-ization of America. You used to be able to get a decent dry white wine, full-bodied, buttery, you took a swallow, it bit back, you know? Then they sweetened everything up, made it taste like Kool-Aid. That's when I switched to red wine." He drank again. It didn't taste like much, but it was better than Kulukak harbor, which had had the faintest hint of diesel spill for an aftertaste. "Probably only a matter of time before they ruin that, too."

"I thought you only drank Glenmorangie."

"One does not drink Glenmorangie, one worships at its feet."

"My mistake."

Liam's burger and fries arrived and he was not heard from again, or at least not for the next ten minutes. Bill pulled a stool opposite his and sat down with a glass of mineral water and a twist of lime. She had a map of New Orleans spread out on the bar, and was tracing the trolley route to the Garden District. "I've seen pictures of the fence around Anne Rice's house," she said. "Wrought-iron roses. I plan to see that up close and personal when I go. And I hear tell that Jefferson Davis died just down the street, and that there's a memorial. I'd like to see that, too, if only just to spit on it. That old boy did not get half the kicking around he deserved." She turned the map over to look at the advertisements. "The Jazz Festival, when is that, May, June? Jimmy Buffett plays at the festival sometimes. I wonder how hot it is in New Orleans in June."

She wasn't expecting any answers, which was a good thing because Liam's mouth was full. The bar wasn't, maybe a dozen customers all told. One couple was dancing unsteadily cheek to cheek to the strains of "Son of a Son of a Sailor." Four men in a booth loitered over the remains of their beer, paperwork exchanging hands and paragraphs disputed in muted voices. One of them was Jim Earl, Newenham's mayor. The other three were members of the town council. Two booths over four women slapped cards down in a game of Snerts. One man sat at a table, moodily nursing a beer, thinking unpleasant thoughts, if his expression was anything to go by. A table away another man was asleep, head on the tabletop between outstretched arms.

Liam surfaced eventually, his stomach straining pleasantly at his belt. "It occurs to me that I've been eating your cheeseburgers twice a day for three months."

Bill raised her head and gave him a considering stare. "I fail to see the problem here, Liam."

"Come to think of it, so do I," he said, pushing his plate away and finishing his Coke. "I need a couple of arrest warrants, Bill."

She put down the street map she'd been looking at and got up to refill his glass. "I heard," she said, climbing back up on her stool. "You've been busy."

His smile was smug. "Yup."

The door opened behind him and momentarily flooded the dim room with light. A raven cawed raucously, the sound cut off abruptly when the door shut again. "Noisy bastard," Moses muttered, and climbed up to sit beside Liam.

Bill smiled at him, the tender smile she reserved only for him. "Hey."

"Hey, yourself. Gimme a beer."

The smile didn't waver. She got him a beer, a squat brown bottle full, and poured it in his lap.

"Hey!" Moses leapt to his feet. "Goddamn it, woman, what the hell are you doing? Jesus!"

"Teaching you some manners," she replied sweetly. She climbed back up on her stool and said to Liam, "Warrants for whom?"

Liam, struggling to repress a grin and not succeeding very well, said, "One for Frank Petla. I need that one right away, his twenty-four hours are about up."

"What for?"

Moses, still cursing, climbed off his stool and headed for the john.

"Two counts of felony assault, for starters."

She raised a brow. "Not murder?"

"No." The face of Charlene Taylor flashed before his eyes. "Not yet," he said. Not until he'd dotted that last *i* and crossed that last *t.*

Bill grunted. "There's time, I guess. Long as we keep him locked up. Who's the second one for?"

"Walter Larsgaard."

"Old or Young?"

"Young."

"The tribal chief?"

"Yeah."

She winced. "Ouch. That's going to come back and bite us in the ass."

"I know."

Moses emerged from the bathroom, his lap drier than it had been. A cell phone went *brriiiinnnng* somewhere in the bar and his head came up like he was on point. He zeroed in on Jim Earl. Jim Earl saw him coming and tried to get the phone folded up and back in his pocket in time but it was too late; Moses snatched it from his hand. The antenna was still out and it waggled an inch in front of Jim Earl's nose as Moses gave forth.

"I hate these things. I hate anything to do with them. I ain't never getting me one, I ain't never irritating no one by talking on one in a bar, I ain't never disrupting the band when mine goes off, I ain't never trying to talk on one the same time I run into the back of the car in front of me, I ain't never having calls forwarded to one from my home phone—"

"You don't have a home phone, Moses," Jim Earl said, but the interruption was a feeble one and was ignored with the disdain it deserved.

"—I ain't ever gonna have caller ID so I can see who's calling me on one, and"—Moses wound up for a big finish—"if someone ever calls me and I get a beep to tell me someone's waiting to talk to me on another line, I'm letting them fucking WAIT!"

He marched to the door, opened it, went into a pitcher's windup and launched the cell phone into low earth orbit. "FUCK the twenty-first century!"

There was a startled squawk and a flurry of indignant croaks and clicks before the door shut. Moses dusted his hands and climbed back up on his stool. "May I have a beer, please?"

Bill's smile was radiant. "Certainly." She got him a beer. This time it made to Moses in the bottle. He drank it down in one long swallow. "May I have a refill, please?"

Bill had been waiting to do just that. "Certainly." She brought another bottle to him. Moses showed no inclination to drink this one dry right away, too, so she sat down again.

The door opened and Moses looked over his shoulder. "Oh, shit." He raised his voice. "I told you, not today!"

Malcolm Dorris came up behind him, his hat in his hands. His expression was apologetic but determined. "Uncle, I need to know now. Please."

Moses buried his nose in his beer and didn't reply. Nobody said anything for a minute or two. Malcolm waited. He was a stocky young man, maybe eighteen, maybe nineteen, with clear skin and neat black hair. He'd laid on the aftershave a little heavy that morning, and the strong smell of English Leather interfered with the far more seductive aroma of deep-fried grease.

Liam frowned and nudged Moses with his elbow. "What's he want?"

Moses rolled his eyes and held his bottle out to Bill. "The answer."

"What was the question?"

Moses huffed out an impatient breath. "His father wants him to stay home and fish and hunt and keep to the old ways. Malcolm wants to go away to school."

"And the question?"

Moses drank from his new beer. "Should he go?"

"Oh." Bill pored over her map. Malcolm waited. Moses drank beer. The smell of English Leather got stronger. "Well? Should he?"

Moses slammed down his glass. "How the hell should I know?"

"Because you always do, uncle," Malcolm said.

"Go," said Bill, not looking up from her map. "It doesn't take the resident shaman to figure that out. Go to school. Learn a trade for when the runs are bad. Like last summer. Like this summer. Maybe like next summer."

Malcolm hesitated. "It's tough, uncle. I'm a Yupik in a white world."

Moses said nothing.

"I'm a woman in a man's world," Bill said. This time she looked up, her stare so piercing Liam saw the boy flinch away from it. "I need all the edges I can get. You're Yupik in a white man's world. You need all the edges you can get, too. Go to school."

"Oh for crissake, go to fucking school," Moses shouted.

It was enough. "Thank you, uncle," Malcolm murmured, and backed out of the building.

"Don't ever be a Native," Moses told them. "Have you ever wanted to be a Native?" he demanded of Bill.

"God, no," Bill said.

"Why not?" Liam said.

Bill took her time replying, polishing a couple of glasses with a bar rag and lining them up at attention. "I'm the laziest person on earth. I don't want to have to work that hard to get up to go."

Moses gave a short bark of laughter.

"Somebody explain," Liam said.

Bill picked up a glass that didn't need it and started polishing. "What do you see when you look at me, Liam?"

A brief but mighty struggle kept Liam's eyes from dropping to her breasts, today enfolded in the loving embrace of a T-shirt touting Jimmy Buffett's *Banana Wind* tour.

Moses growled. Liam felt the heat rising up the back of his neck.

"After that," Bill said dryly.

"Magistrate," Liam said. "Barkeep."

"No," she said. "First off, before everything else, I'm white. I'm as white as you can get without bleach. Before I'm a woman, before I'm a bartender, before I'm a magistrate, before I'm a goddamn Alaskan, I'm white. And because I'm white, I was *born* at go. I don't have to work my ass off just to get that far."

"And Malcolm does," Liam said to Moses.

Moses raised his glass in a toast. "I may have to change my estimation of your intelligence, boy."

"Gee, thanks."

Bill wasn't done. "People look at boys like Malcolm, they see

Native and think Fourth Avenue. Outside, they'd look at you and see a nigger. In South Africa they'd see a kaffer; in India, a Muslim; in Pakistan, a Hindu. The color of your skin isn't an asset, it's something you have to overcome." She gave the glass a final rub and held it up to admire the sparkle. "Whereas I, because my ancestors were so kind as to spend the last two thousand years terrorizing the people of color of this world into submission and servitude and too often downright slavery . . ." She shrugged, and repeated, "I was born at go." She set the glass down and looked at Moses. "Only place in the world for a lazy person."

She looked at Liam. "What's the charge on Larsgaard?"

"Who? Oh. Flight to avoid prosecution," Liam said.

"Prosecution for what?"

"Mass murder," Liam said, and Moses erupted again.

"Goddamn it, you are the worst I ever saw for jumping to conclusions! A son owes his father, goddamn it!"

Which reminded Liam that he had to get back to the post and call his father's office in Florida.

Moses stared at him. "He's no different that any other stick-up-his-ass officer I ever ran across in the service, and I wasn't talking about your father, anyway."

In spite of himself, Liam felt his dander rise, enough to blot out Moses' last words. "He's a career officer," he said, careful to keep any hint of defense out of his tone. "They are very . . ."

"Proper," Bill suggested, and he gave a grateful nod.

Moses snorted. " 'Proper.' Yeah, right. If you can't stick to the point, boy, you've gone as far as you'll go in your service."

Liam stood up. "Moses, I never know what the hell the point is when I'm around you, and I'm not sure I want to go anywhere in my service anymore." He tossed some bills on the bar. "Thanks for lunch, Bill. I'll be back in for dinner this evening, with my stick-up-his-ass dad."

"See you then," she said, unperturbed.

He walked toward the door, and behind him Moses said to Bill, "Malcolm won't ever come home, you know.

"He goes to school, he's gone for good."

SEVENTEEN

"Doctors are lousy pilots," Wy said. "Pisspoor, actually. They don't listen worth shit. You can't tell them anything, they're used to doing the telling. Guy says he's a doctor, he's not driving my plane and I ain't riding in his."

Tim committed this to memory, and handed her a socket wrench.

"Thanks." Wy tightened down the nut, wiped her hands on the legs of her overalls and closed the cowling before descending the stepladder perched at the nose of the Cub.

"How about troopers?" Tim said.

Wy looked at him, and he grinned. "Yeah, okay, smarty," she said, "it was fine, she didn't hurt our baby any."

"She better not've." Tim sounded cocky and threatening and very proprietary as he put the wrench back in the red upright toolbox.

Wy eyed his back for a moment. "You want to learn?"

He looked around. "Learn what?"

She hooked a thumb at the plane. "You want to learn to fly?"

He stood straight up, the toolbox drawer left open. "Learn to fly?" His voice scaled up and ended on a squeak of disbelief.

"Yeah."

He stared from her to the plane and back again. He looked dazzled. "You'd teach me?"

"Yeah."

"To fly?"

She grinned. "Hey. It's what I do."

A warm wave of color washed up over his face. "You're just kidding," he said gruffly. "Aren't you? I'm too young. Aren't I?"

"Younger than me when I started," she agreed. "But then I started awful late. I was practically an old lady."

"How old?" he demanded.

"Sixteen."

"Do you mean it?" he said again.

He threw the question down like a gauntlet, a challenge to her to take it up. Promises had been made to him before, many promises over the twelve long years of his young life, promises made and promises broken. "Yes," she said soberly. "I mean it."

He still didn't quite believe her, she could see it in his eyes. "Next Sunday morning," she said, turning back to the plane. "I don't have anything booked until four that afternoon. We'll take the Cessna up. She's got dual controls." She thought about mentioning ground school, and left it for later. If she could get him hooked on flying, he wouldn't have a choice.

After a moment or two, she heard him wheel the toolbox back into the shed.

There was a shed just like it in back of every one of the light planes drawn up at the edge of the tarmac at Newenham General Airport, but theirs was the only one currently in use. The open door revealed shelves packed with tools and parts, as well as camping and fishing gear. A fifty-five-gallon Chevron fuel drum, cut in half, sat in one corner, filled to the brim with Japanese fishing floats made of green glass. Wy picked them up whenever she made a beach landing and sold them to tourists for as much as the traffic would bear.

"Wy?"

"Yeah?" Wy was in the shed, smearing Goop on her hands, trying and failing to get the oil that invariably migrated beneath her fingernails.

The possibility of slipping the surly bonds of earth had faded from his face. "You remember the Malones?"

Her hands stilled, and she looked over her shoulder. Tim had one hand on the Cub's right strut, watching an Alaska Airlines 737 bank left out over the river in preparation for landing. "You mean the people who were killed on the boat in Kulukak?"

"Yeah."

Wy reached for a rag and went out to stand next to him. "I didn't know them, Tim. I don't think I ever met them. I don't think I ever flew them anywhere."

The 737 lined up on final.

"I knew the boy. Mike."

"Did you?"

"He played basketball."

"What position?"

"Guard."

"Like you."

"Yeah. I had to guard him last time the Kulukak team was in town. Our last game of the season."

"When was that, March?"

"Yeah."

Wy thought back, in her mind trying to distinguish one adolescent from another on a court that seemed remarkably full of them. "Number twenty-two, right? Hands like catcher's mitts, arms that stretched from here to Icky, and a good sport?"

"Yeah."

Mike Malone had guarded Tim like Tim was Bastogne and Mike was the entire 501st Airborne. "You played really well against him."

Tim's shoulders rose in a faint shrug. "Have to, against a guy like that."

"Did you meet his sister, too?"

"Yeah. He introduced me once." A pause. "She was a cheerleader, traveled with the team."

"Pretty?"

"Yeah."

The 737 touched down just inside the markers in a runway paint job, the engines roaring immediately into reverse so they wouldn't miss the first taxiway. Hot dog, Wy thought. Definitely the sound of someone not flying their own plane.

"Liam says they're dead." He looked at her.

Wy finished with the rag and turned to pitch it, accurately, in the wastebasket just inside the door of the shed. "Yeah." She turned back. "When did you talk to Liam?"

"This morning. I went over to the post. When you left to take the mail to Manokotak."

Bless the U.S. Postal Service, Wy thought automatically. A mail contract was the difference between red and black on the bottom line to a Bush air taxi. "Oh."

"You didn't say I couldn't."

"No," she agreed. Did he ask about me? she wanted to say, but managed to refrain from anything that sophomoric.

"So they're dead," he repeated.

"Yeah." Her hand settled on his shoulder and squeezed, as the 737 popped its hatch and let down its rear air stair.

"It's—it's—it *stinks*," he said, and his eyes when he raised them were dark and wounded.

"It stinks to high heaven," Wy agreed. "Tim. Did you ever meet the rest of Mike's family? His mom? His dad?"

Tim shook his head. "No. Just Mike." He hesitated.

"What?"

He colored, and looked at his shoes. "One time, it was like the first time we played the Wolverines, I remember Mike got benched for fighting."

"What about?"

His color deepened and he wouldn't look up. "Somebody'd said something about his mother."

"What?"

He said gruffly, "Said she slept around on Mike's dad. Called her a whore. So Mike beat him up, and the coach benched him." He added wistfully, "That was the only time all year we beat them."

"Who said that? Who did Mike beat up?"

"Arne. Arne Swensen. He plays guard, too. He's a senior this year, so he'll probably start even if he doesn't deserve to." He looked up. "That stinks, too."

Wy smiled and ran a hand through his hair. "Yeah."

He pulled back and anxiously patted his glossy black locks back into their previous perfect order. The last person off the 737 was a big, bulky man wearing a parka and mukluks. In July. "Tourist," he said.

"And how."

"Mom?"

He'd called her Mom from the first day she brought him home from the hospital, a direct and determined repudiation of his birth mother. Now that he felt more secure, he used Mom and Wy interchangeably. She did notice that when he was particularly bothered about something, he usually called her Mom. She steeled herself. "What?"

He fidgeted. "They weren't—they didn't—Kerry and Mike . . . nobody, well, hurt them, did they?"

It only took Wy a second to understand. Tim had grown up among a succession of people who had regarded his body as their personal punching bag. "No," Wy said.

"Are you sure?"

"Yes," Wy said. "I'm sure."

She wasn't, of course, she knew nothing about the condition in which the bodies had been found, but she was willing to lie herself blue in the face before she contributed one more scene to Tim's recurring nightmares. Imagining how Mike, a boy he'd admired, and Kerry, a girl he might have had a secret crush on, had been tortured before being killed was not going to lessen their frequency or ease their intensity.

The 737 started loading passengers for the return trip to Anchorage. First on board was a skinny little blond kid in a blue nylon jacket, jeans and sneakers, clutching a silver briefcase almost as big as he was. He looked purposeful, on a mission. Wy wondered what was in the suitcase.

A shout distracted her attention, and she looked around to see Professor Desmond X. McLynn bearing down on them. "I'm outta here," Tim muttered, and he grabbed his bike and shot off. Wy didn't blame him.

"What can I do for you, Mr. McLynn?" Wy said as the professor came trotting up.

"Do? You can fly me out to my dig, is what you can do. Where have you been all day? I was here at nine o'clock and you were gone! You've contracted to be my air support for the summer, and then you disappear when I need to fly! Give me one good reason why I shouldn't hire another pilot!"

Wy, one of the more reliable pilots on the Bay, bit back an invitation for Professor Desmond X. McLynn to do just that, didn't say that she'd contracted to fly him in and out once a week, not twice, and plastered a smile on her face. "I do have other contracts to fulfill besides yours, Professor McLynn, but"—she overrode his protest—"I'm here now. We can be in the air in ten minutes."

McLynn blustered for a few moments before giving in. They were in the air in the promised ten minutes. It was their fastest flight to the dig yet. "Are we back on a normal schedule?" Wy said, when she had him and his gear on the ground.

"What? Yes, yes, pick me up Friday evening."

"Certainly, sir," Wy said to his retreating back. She was in the air before he reached the work tent. She left his gear where it was.

Some jobs didn't pay enough. Some jobs wouldn't pay enough if you were making a thousand dollars an hour. Still, a job was a job, a paycheck was a paycheck and a lawyer's fee was most definitely a lawyer's fee. Wy brought the Cub around and headed back to Newenham.

Liam went back to the post to find Prince had left a note, saying she'd gone to lunch and that she'd be back in time to sit in on the interrogations. So they were interrogating suspects this afternoon, were they? Liam picked up the phone and dialed his father's number in Florida. It rang five times and he was just about to give up when someone picked up. It was a woman's voice, very young and breathy, which made "Hurlburt Field Strategic Operations School" sound like phone sex. "Hi, I'm Liam Campbell, Colonel Campbell's son," he said. "Is my father in?"

There was a brief silence, and the voice said brightly, "I'm sorry, Mr. Campbell, but Colonel Campbell has been reassigned."

Has he indeed? Liam thought. "Could you tell me where?"

"I'm sorry, sir, I'm not allowed to give out that information."

"Oh." Liam waited for a moment, letting the silence gather. "I really need to talk to him about some family business—what was your name again? Valerie? That's a pretty name. Are you single, Valerie?"

Valerie giggled. "You're not very subtle, are you, Mr. Campbell?"

"I don't play hard to get," he purred, shamelessly dropping his voice down into its best lower register, sexy-guy-picking-you-up-in-a-bar accents.

She giggled again, sounding very young. "I don't know . . ."

"I'm his only son, Valerie, and it really is important that I reach him soon. Kind of a family emergency. Just a phone number. I won't even say I got it from you."

He hung up a minute or two later. Definitely a threat to national security there, he thought, dialing the number he'd scribbled on his desk calendar. This time he was unlucky; an answering machine picked up. The message on it was illuminating, though.

At three o'clock he was back at the jail. He showed Mamie the warrants Bill had sworn out, and she copied them and filed them away. "There's an interview room in the back," she told them.

There was: four walls, a barred window, a table and four chairs, so tiny there was barely enough room to inhale. Liam reached through the bars and opened the window. A raven's croak was the first sound he heard, and he craned his head for a look. Nothing. Big black bastard ought to mind his own business.

He caught himself. There was a word for that, anthropomorphizing, the assigning of human feelings to plants, animals and inanimate objects. Like giving your car a name and begging it not to stall out at a red light in February. Like telling the Chugach Mountains they looked beautiful all dressed up in alpenglow. Like talking back to a raven.

Newenham wasn't just hard on his uniforms, it was hard on his sanity. There was a reason the inhabitants referred to it as Disneyham, strictly among themselves, of course.

He turned and sat at the table, Prince on his right with a lined pad and a pencil, Frank Petla across from him. Frank was sucking on a Dr Pepper. "Can't you guys get me a cigarette, man? I mean, one lousy smoke?"

"Secondary smoke, it's a killer, Frank," Liam said, and started the handheld recorder. He gave the date, the time, said who was in the room and then set the recorder to one side. Frank Petla looked at it with the eyes of a rabbit caught in the headlights of an oncoming car. "You've waived your right to an attorney, Frank, is that right?"

Frank nodded.

"Say so for the recorder, please."

"Yeah."

"You're sure about this? Yesterday afternoon you said you wanted a lawyer."

"I'm sure. Don't need no damn lawyer."

"All right. You want to tell us what happened out at the dig yesterday?"

What had happened out at the dig yesterday was that Frank Petla, a completely innocent man, had been out for a peaceful ride on his four-wheeler on a sunny summer day, when he had accidentally driven his four-wheeler into this hole in the ground. In the hole in the ground were a bunch of things that Frank, a completely innocent man and an Alaska Native, instantly recognized as family heirlooms. He had collected them in a bag, as any completely innocent man, Alaska Native and traditional tribal member would do, to return them to their rightful owners, his village elders.

"That's what you were going to do, Frank?" Liam said. "Return them to your village?"

Frank had been, and he was indignant at the suggestion that he might have been going to sell them. He strenuously denied ever having been to the dig prior to yesterday, and when commanded to look at Prince and try to remember the last time he, Frank, had seen her, hazarded a guess that it might have been last October at AFN. "Didn't we dance at the Snow Ball?" He hadn't hit anybody, he hadn't shot anybody and he most certainly hadn't stabbed anybody with anything, least of all with something that he, a completely innocent man, an Alaska Native, a traditional tribal member and a signatory to the AFN Sobriety Movement, recognized as a storyknife. "It's a girl thing, that storyknife," he said confidentially, as if it were a secret. "Only girls could play with them. They would take it down to the riverbank and draw pictures in the mud and tell stories to their brothers and sisters."

He was silent for a moment. Liam, watching him, saw a shadow pass over his face. "My sister storyknifed." He said a word in Yupik that sounded like 'yawning ruin.' "That's Yupik for storyknife, did you know that?"

"No," Liam said. "I didn't know that."

"She was beautiful, my sister," Frank Petla said, no bombast or bluster or wounded innocence now. "She had the longest hair that she would braid with beads. When she danced, she would toss it around like a cape. All the boys loved her."

"What happened to her?"

"She died," Frank said, still in that quiet voice. "She drank too much, and she died."

There was a brief silence. In a gentle, unthreatening voice, Liam said, "Where were you this weekend, Frank?"

It was a while before Frank came back from wherever he'd gone. "This weekend?"

"The two days before yesterday," Prince said, and subsided when Liam touched her arm.

"Don Nelson was killed sometime between Friday night and Saturday night. If you didn't stab him," Liam said, the voice of sweet reason, "you obviously weren't at the dig. So where were you?"

Frank stared at him in stupefied silence for a good minute and a half. "I don't . . . Fishing?"

"Fishing where?"

"On my boat."

"You have a boat?"

"Yes. The *Sarah P.*"

"Is it down at the harbor?" Frank nodded. "What's the slip number?" Frank told him. "Where were you fishing, Frank?"

Frank thought. "On the river. Drifting. Off a creek."

The Nushagak River was hundreds of miles long, with on average one creek per ten feet. "Which creek?"

"I dunno." Frank looked helpless.

"Was anyone fishing with you?"

"No."

"Did you see any other boats?"

"No." Frank's eyes slid sideways.

Aha, Liam thought. "Was this creek open to fishing, Frank?"

Frank was indignant. "Of course! They could take my boat if I got caught fishing in a closed area!"

They certainly could, Liam thought. He could ask Charlene which areas on the Nushagak had been open to fishing on Monday, but there might be an easier way. "Who did you deliver to, Frank?"

"A fish buyer," Frank said promptly. "He was buying off the dock."

"Did you get a fish ticket?"

Frank shook his head. "He bought with cash."

They left him in the interview room for a moment.

"Convenient how no one can confirm his story," Prince said, eyes bright. She smelled a conviction.

"Yeah, but he was drunk as a skunk when he ran into you."

"So?"

"So, how did he pay for his booze?"

"He bummed some off a friend, I don't know. Why do we care?"

We don't, Liam thought, but Charlene will.

When they went back in, they found Frank trying to squeeze through the bars on the window. His head was too big, and he'd gotten stuck. They extricated him and returned him to his cell.

Walter Larsgaard was up next, and he was in the mood to talk. He sat down, folded his arms and waited until Liam started the recorder. He declined representation and said simply, "I killed them. I killed them all."

"You killed David Malone, Molly Malone, Jonathan Malone, Michael Malone, Kerry Malone, Jason Knudson and Wayne Cullen?"

"Yes?"

"How did you kill them?"

He'd killed them, he said in a monotone, with a rifle, a thirty-ought-six.

"Where is that rifle now, Walter?"

"Over the side."

"And then what?"

"And then I set the boat on fire."

"What with?"

"Gasoline."

"Where did you get it?"

"I keep a spare tank on my dory."

"Where is that tank now?"

"Still on my dory. I knew you could trace the rifle, but no sense in wasting a good gas tank."

"What did you do with the gas?"

"Splashed it around. Lit a match."

"Where did you splash it around first?"

"The galley."

"On the bodies?"

"Yes."

"You'd already killed them, why burn them?"

"I was hoping to get away with it."

"Cover up your crime?"

"Yes."

"Why didn't you just sink her?"

"I tried. I pulled the plugs."

Liam looked at the still, remote face across from him. Larsgaard had his hands linked behind his head, had leaned back so that his chair was balanced on its rear legs. "Why did you do it, Walter?"

There was a pause. "She broke it off." He said the words slowly and carefully, as if it were an effort to get them out.

"Who? Molly?"

"Yes."

"You were seeing her?"

"Yes."

"Sleeping with her?"

"Yes?"

"At the Bay View Inn?"

Larsgaard met his eyes briefly. "So you already know about it, do you?" He shook his head. "There are no secrets in small towns. I told her and told her, I . . ."

Liam waited, but Larsgaard didn't finish. "So you shot her because she broke off your relationship."

"Yes."

Liam kept his tone mild and inoffensive. "Why did you shoot her husband?"

"He had her. I didn't."

"Her brother-in-law?"

"He was there."

"That why you killed the deckhands? They were there, too?"

A shrug.

"And the kids? Michael and Kerry. Teenagers. They had to die because they were there, too?"

"That's about it."

The muscles in Liam's shoulders were so tight he thought they might pop out of their sleeves. He saw Prince look at him, and willed himself to relax with only moderate success. "When did all this happen?"

"What, the affair?"

"When did you kill them?" Liam said coldly.

"Sunday night."

"What time?"

For the first time, Larsgaard hesitated. "I don't know. Midnight, maybe one o'clock. It was dark, or almost, so it had to have been late. Hard to tell because of the fog."

"How did you know where they were?"

"I saw them during the fishing period."

"The fishing period was over."

"They'd had some engine trouble. Dave anchored up offshore to work on it, and I figured he'd still be there after the fog rolled in. He was."

Liam sat back in his chair. "So you fished next to them on Sunday afternoon, saw them anchor up offshore with engine trouble, marked the spot, went back into town, waited until dark, got in your dory, went back to Kulukak Bay, shot Molly Malone because she wanted to end your affair, shot the rest of them because they were there, tried to burn the boat to cover up your crime and when that didn't work tried to sink her."

"Yes."

They stared at each other for a long moment. Liam looked at his watch, said the time for the tape and terminated the interview.

They put Larsgaard back in his cell. Frank Petla still wanted a smoke, and Moccasin Man was still playing solitaire.

It was five o'clock, and the sun had just barely begun its descent into the west. "I want a witness that puts Larsgaard and Malone in the Bay View Inn together. I've already talked to the owner, Alta— Alta Peterson. She made the beds when Molly Malone stayed there and Alta knew Molly wasn't sleeping alone, but she never saw who she was sleeping with. Find someone who saw them together."

"Yes, sir. What about Frank Petla's alibi?"

"I'll work on that." He thought again about Charlene Taylor. He'd have to ask her what areas of the Nushagak had been open for fishing on Monday. "I'm going to go down to the harbor and look at his boat."

"If it's there."

It was there, a tiny little bowpicker barely big enough to sport a one-bunk cabin on the stern, a reel in the bow and an open deck in between. Liam poked his head in the cabin. Except for the empty bottle of Windsor Canadian rolling around on the deck and the rumpled state of the bunk, the little cabin was surprisingly neat. He opened a few cupboards, looked under the miniature sink, tested the two-burner propane stove. The dishes were clean, the clothes folded neatly, the canned goods ordered and stacked. There was a picture in a green wooden frame nailed to the wall over the bunk. It was of a young girl with thick dark hair past her waist, standing next to Frank Petla. They were both looking at the camera, both with big, bright smiles and an Alaska Federation of Natives' Sobriety Movement poster on the wall in back of them. There was another picture, this one in a blue wooden frame, of Frank standing between Charlene Taylor and her husband the D.A., a short, skinny guy with bushy red hair, freckled white skin and a wide, wry grin. All three of them looked real proud of something.

The deck had been hosed down but there was evidence that fish had been there, in the form of scales. Liam wet a forefinger and touched one. It felt dry. No telling how long it had been there. The net was dry on top. Liam managed to wedge a hand in a layer or two and thought he felt dampness, but that probably didn't mean anything, either; rolled on a reel, it would take a long time for a net to dry out. The dampness he thought he felt could have been from a period last week, or one in June, for that matter.

He canvassed a few boats. Most were already out in the Bay, hauling in as much fish as they could find. Bad summer or not, missed forecasts or not, they still had to try. They had mortgages, insurance, grocery bills, college tuition to pay.

They had Windsor Canadian to buy. Liam stood on the slip next to a big seiner and yelled, "Hello the *Deirdre F*!" There was a thud and a curse and someone stuck his head out the door. "What?"

"Liam Campbell, Alaska state trooper, I'm wondering if you saw the *Sarah P* come into the harbor."

"The *Sarah P*?" The man squinted, looking as if this were the first time he'd seen daylight in weeks. "I don't even know which boat that is."

"The little one, right over there." Liam pointed.

"I don't know, I—wait, what day?"

"Anytime this weekend."

"I didn't get in until yesterday afternoon. Blew the goddamn drive shaft. And I'd like to get back to it, okay?" he added pointedly.

"Okay."

Further inquiries proved equally fruitless. Liam plodded on up the gangplank. It was getting close to six o'clock. Time for dinner with Dad. Oh joy.

EIGHTEEN

Force of habit made him check his uniform before he went inside, except he wasn't wearing his, which had him at an automatic disadvantage. No help for it. He squared his shoulders and pulled open the door.

Charles was already there. Seated across from him was Diana Prince, who had changed into civilian clothes herself. She looked very nice in a dark red sweater and a string of pearls. Her hair had been ruffled up from its neat, restrained daytime style in that way women do that indicates they are off duty and on the hunt.

"Yeah, well, being found not guilty of driving an oil tanker onto Bligh Reef while drunk is not necessarily the same thing as being innocent of doing the same thing," Charles was saying as Liam came up.

Liam winced. The investigation of the grounding of the *Exxon Valdez*, like the deaths in Denali the previous winter, was one of those cases troopers didn't like to brag about.

It apparently wasn't bothering Prince, who laughed. Before her time.

"Liam," Charles said, looking up. "I've invited Diana to join us. I hope you don't mind."

"Not at all," Liam lied courteously, and, choosing the lesser of two evils, sat down next to Prince.

"You've had a busy day," Charles said genially, signaling Bill, who sent Maria, the server who had taken Laura Nanalook's place, over to take orders. Maria was in her mid-twenties and looked like she practiced bulimia as a religion. Her clavicles held up her T-shirt like a hanger, and her blond hair was so fine you could see her pink scalp between strands. Her lips didn't have enough flesh to stretch over her teeth in a smile, but she took Liam's order, whirled to the bar and was back in two minutes flat.

Liam, who had the feeling he was going to require backup, had ordered a Glenmorangie, a double. Charles raised his eyebrows. Liam had always hated those eyebrows. "Bill keeps it in stock for me."

Prince was nursing a glass of white wine, Charles a beer. "What did you find out?" Prince said.

"Not now," Liam said, more curtly than he'd intended. He opened his mouth to apologize, and felt someone standing next to him. He looked up. It was Wy.

For the first time since he'd seen her again in May, her hair was loose, the same tumbled mass of bronzed blond curls he remembered from those days in Anchorage. She was wearing a teal-blue T-shirt tucked into her jeans and wide gold nugget hoops in her ears. His eyes lingered on the hoops for a moment.

Her glance, when she met his, was direct and somehow questioning. Liam was burningly aware of two things: his memory of their in-flight stopover on the gravel airstrip the day before, and that his hip was touching Prince's. Carefully, he edged away.

"Well, hello—Wy, isn't it?" Charles said. He looked from Wy to Liam and back again. "Are you meeting someone?" Wy shook her head. "Then why don't you join us?" He moved over and patted the bench next to him.

Still without speaking, Wy slid in next to him. Her knees brushed Liam's. They both jumped.

An awkward silence developed, broken when Maria appeared. "Uh . . . wine," Wy said. "Red."

"Cabernet or merlot?"

"Cabernet." In an obvious move to make conversation, she said to the others, "Merlots are sometimes too sweet. Same reason I don't drink white."

Prince looked down at her glass. "I guess I like sweet."

Wy shrugged. "To each her own."

Liam drained his glass in one gulp. Everyone reordered. Silence until the new drinks came.

Charles said, "What about—"

Prince said, "Charles, why are you—"

Wy said, "How is the—"

Liam said, "When are you leaving, Dad?"

A brief silence. "I don't know, Liam," Charles said. "I'll be around for at least another week, I think." There was a clear invitation in his smile when he looked at Prince, and a corresponding sparkle in Prince's eyes.

"What are you doing here, precisely?" Prince said. "You haven't said. Where are you stationed?"

"Florida," Charles said easily. "Hurlburt Field."

Really, Liam thought. Somebody tell Hurlburt.

"And I'm here to see what the Air Force can do about turning over some of our disused buildings to the local communities." He ran the same spiel by them he had run by Liam the day before, and, as they were supposed to, Wy and Prince looked politely impressed by the Air Force's commitment to public service.

Another hiatus in the conversation. Liam was trying hard not to stare across the table at Wy, was trying even harder to pretend he wasn't sitting next to Prince, although Charles had made his interest clear. For the first time in his life Liam was grateful for Charles's invariable habit of chasing the best-looking woman in every town he visited. Liam abandoned any concern for Prince's tender feelings; Charles was right, she was a grown woman, and besides, Liam was not about to appear protective of another woman in front of Wy.

His legs, too long for the booth, cramped, and he stretched a little, bumping again into Wy's. Their eyes met. Hers widened. His mouth went dry. He alleviated the problem with single-malt scotch, but refused a refill when Maria reappeared to take their orders for dinner. Since the only thing on the menu was beef, and since the choices were New York strip, rib eye or T-bone, they all had steak. Liam and Wy chose New York and rare, Charles and Prince T-bone and well done.

Until their salads came, Charles entertained them with an account of his tour in the Gulf, with an emphasis on sand. "It got into everything, your hair, your eyes, your mouth, your shorts, you name it. Not to mention the engines. You haven't lived until you've tried to change out the engine on an F-15 in the desert."

Prince listened, rapt, Wy said something noncommittal about engine maintenance and Liam contributed an occasional grunt and tried to remember when he'd last seen a bird colonel in the Air Force change out his own engine. He greeted his salad with relief and kept his mouth full. It seemed like a strategic decision worthy of Alexander.

He felt a foot press against his, and he looked up sharply. The last time he'd felt her foot, it had been hard against his shin, right before she slugged him. This time, she winked at him. His fork remained suspended in midair as Maria arrived with the main course. She whisked away the salad plates and replaced them with metal plates in wooden frames loaded with red meat. Wy dropped her eyes, Liam dropped his fork and Maria, nothing loath, fetched him a new one.

In the meantime, Charles had shifted the subject to Alaska and his experiences in the air over Elmendorf. He missed the Cold War, it seemed. He told of the time he'd taken a rubber mask in the shape of Ronald Reagan and worn it on patrol.

"Could the pilots in the Russian planes see you?" Prince asked, grinning.

"Hell, yes, or what was the point?" Charles laughed. "Next time we went up, one of theirs was wearing a Brezhnev mask."

Prince laughed, obviously enchanted. Charles wasn't sleeping alone tonight. Unlike himself, Liam thought mournfully, and looked at Wy, who was listening with every appearance of interest to Charles and Prince's conversation. Eventually Prince realized that they hadn't heard from the other two guests. "How long have you been a pilot, Wy?"

"Since I was sixteen."

"When did you start your business?"

Wy glanced at Liam and back at Prince. "The one I have now? Three years ago. I moved to Newenham and bought out an air taxi service."

"Do you like it?"

Wy smiled and said, "The worst day flying beats the best day off. To coin a phrase."

No one doubted the calm conviction that underlined her words. "You make any money at it?" Charles said.

"I do all right."

"Ever want to fly jets?"

"Who hasn't?"

Charles smiled, pleased.

"Why did you become a trooper, sir?" Prince said, who seemed to have taken on the duty of hostess.

"Too much *Hawaii Five-O*," his father said.

"I like order," Liam said firmly, if a bit pompously. "I like rules. We're a pretty unruly race, when you think about it. The law, imperfect as it is, is the only thing that keeps us a step ahead of the apes."

Prince looked at him, waiting.

"Oh all right," Liam said. "And I like the action. I get a charge out of bringing down the bad guys." He looked at her. "You're going to be a good trooper."

She grinned and dimples flashed. "I already am."

"Hold that thought."

"So why? Really. Why?"

It wasn't something he talked about, so it was hard to put it into words. "The first case I rolled on after my probationary period was a guy beating up on his wife."

"Ugh." Prince shuddered. "Domestic disputes. Hate 'em."

"Don't we all. This was a bad one: her eyes were swollen shut, her right arm was broken in two places, he'd strangled her so she couldn't talk."

"Repeat?"

"My trainer said it was the sixth time in two months he'd had a call to their house."

She looked sympathetic, or as sympathetic as someone can look with a mouthful of T-bone steak.

"Yeah," Liam said, "I know. This time, he went away, seven years and change. I saw her two years later, and I didn't recognize her. She was healthy, and happy, she had a job, she was the manager of the produce section of the local Eagle store. She recognized me immediately, and came right up to thank me. I knew somebody at a shelter, and had given her the number that night. It changed her life, she said. I'd changed her life. I tried to tell her that all I'd done was give her a number, she was the one who had made the call. No, she said, it was me. I'd rescued her, and I'd have to live with it." Liam grinned. "And then she tried to give me five pounds of nectarines."

"Which you of course refused."

"Hell, yes, there must have been fifty people in the store. Didn't want anybody to see me taking a bribe." He ate a bite of steak, and added, "I told her to put 'em in the car."

Charles laughed. After a moment, Prince did, too, although Liam could see she was trying to decide if Liam was joking or not about the nectarines. "How about you?" he asked her.

She shrugged and grinned at Charles. "I always wanted my own uniform, and the Girl Scouts don't issue guns with theirs."

Maria bustled by, her size two jeans all but slipping off her behind, and inquired as to their needs. She brought back another glass of wine for Prince and another beer for Charles.

"How is the case coming?" Wy said to Liam, under cover of Charles's voice.

"Which one?"

She shrugged. "Either. Both."

Liam cut a piece of steak. It was perfect, the best cut of meat this side of the Club Paris in Anchorage, the perfect ratio of exterior char to bloody interior. "Well, I've got one confession."

"Which?"

"The *Marybethia*."

"Who?"

"Walter Larsgaard. Do you know him?"

She frowned. "Isn't he the mayor of Kulukak?"

"Tribal chief."

"Same difference." Her brow creased. "He killed them? All of them?"

"So he says."

She put down her knife and fork. "Seven people? Did he say why?"

"He was sleeping with Molly Malone. She wanted to break off the relationship. So he killed her."

"Why did he kill the rest of them?"

"Her husband, because her husband had her and Larsgaard didn't. The rest of them, mainly because they were there."

Wy thought about this. "You should pardon the expression, it sounds a little like overkill."

"It doesn't sound like it, it was," Liam said.

She shifted and her foot bumped his again. She didn't move it away this time. Their eyes met, and she smiled. Bewildered at this sea change—maybe he wouldn't be sleeping alone tonight after all, he couldn't help thinking—he smiled back.

"I was talking to Tim today," she said.

He raised an eyebrow. "Me, too."

"Yeah. He told me." She toyed with one of the crisp, golden fries, what Bill deemed appropriate for a steak side. "He said he knew Mike Malone."

"He told me that, too. Played guard opposite him, he said."

"Did he tell you that Mike Malone got benched for one game for fighting with some boy who called his mother a whore?"

"No. Did Tim know who it was? Who Molly was sleeping with?"

"No."

"Walter Larsgaard says it was him. Alta Peterson down at the hotel says Molly used to stay there once a month, and that she didn't sleep alone, but that Alta never saw who it was." He stared down at his plate. "I'm thinking it's an awful long boat ride from Kulukak to Newenham. Even if it's only once a month."

Wy shrugged. "I didn't fly him in, but then I'm not the only air taxi around. Unless . . . does Walter Larsgaard fly?"

"I don't know." He turned to Prince, who was giggling like a fifteen-year-old—or so it seemed to Liam—at some joke Charles was telling. "Did you run Larsgaard through the system?"

In midgiggle she shifted from lovestruck girl to officer of the law. "Yes, sir."

"Does Larsgaard have a pilot's license?"

"No, sir."

Liam turned back to Wy, and raised his shoulders.

Maria came to clear away their plates and tempt them with dessert, Alaska Silk Pie, one of which Bill air-expressed in from Anchorage on Alaska Airlines every day she was open. She charged about a third of what the entire pie cost per slice, so it was worth it, and there was never anything left when the bar closed at night.

Liam was full of steak and Glenmorangie and the hopeful promise of Wy's foot pressed warmly to his when he became aware of Prince speaking. "You should have seen him. Dropping his coffee mug, stumbling into things, banging his head against the overhead, all the time hopping around on one leg trying to get into his pants. He acted like he thought he was about to be raped."

Charles laughed, and Prince was encouraged to elaborate. "It was everything I could do not to start unbuttoning my uniform shirt. I think he might have gone right over the side." She put her cup down and smiled at the man across the table, unaware that the man next to her was stiffening in outrage, not to mention fear. "In the end, I decided against it. He is the senior officer on the post, after all. It might have made working together in the future, well, difficult."

Charles laughed out loud, looking at Liam to share the joke. Prince looked, too, and for the first time became aware that she might have overstepped the bounds of propriety. She flushed and frowned down at her wine glass as if it were all its fault.

Wy, watching him, saw the irritation and the fear. Both delighted her. She knew they shouldn't have, she knew only a lesser person than she was practicing to be would rejoice in the discomfort of someone else, but there it was. She put down her coffee mug and said, "Well, I'd better be going."

"Me, too," Liam said instantly, rising to his feet. "I—ah, I need to get back to the post."

Scared sober, Prince started to get up, too. Liam waved her back with a frigid, "As you were. I'll see you in the morning. We'll start putting the case paperwork together then."

"Sir—"

"Goodnight, Dad," Liam said, directing a nod in his father's direction. Charles's gaze was full of knowing mockery. Liam directed his eyes to somewhere over his father's left shoulder. "Will I be seeing you again before you leave?"

"Certainly," Charles said jovially, and smiled at Prince. "I'll be here awhile yet. No, it's on me," he said when Liam and Wy reached for their wallets. "My pleasure."

He watched them walk to the door, a careful foot of distance between them. "They got something going?"

Prince was watching them, too. "It looks like it."

"I think so, too." Satisfied, he turned his attention back to her. "Now, where were we?"

She fluttered her eyelashes. "You were just trying to talk me into a dance."

"I was?" Charles looked around and saw a half-filled dance floor swaying to the strains of "That's What Living Is to Me." "I guess I was," he said, and led her out onto the floor.

"Cocky bastard," Liam muttered in the parking lot.

"He's a pilot, Liam," Wy said. "We invented cock."

"That's not what it's about, Wy. Ever since my mother ran off, he's been screwing everything in skirts just to prove to himself and everybody else how fucking irresistible he is."

"Oh." She was silent for a moment. "Do you remember her at all?"

"No. She left before I was six months old."

Wy winced. "Ouch."

"Yeah. I always figured he was probably screwing around before she left and that was why she did." He shrugged awkwardly. "Anyway. Well, goodnight, I guess."

Just as awkward, Wy said, "Yeah."

The door to the bar banged opened and a couple staggered down the stairs. They weren't drunk, really, just flushed with laughter and good food and good times. They paused at the foot of the stairs for a passionate embrace. When they pulled apart the man whispered something and the woman, trying to be haughty, said, "What makes you so sure?" The man snatched her up into another kiss, and when he put her down again they raced each other to see who'd make it to their truck first. Liam was fairly certain he could have followed them home and enriched the state's coffers with a hefty fine for speeding.

"The state's got enough money," he said out loud, and turned to find that Wy had gone.

He drove to the post in no very good temper, slammed into the office and punched out a number on the phone in the manner of someone wielding an ax. When the voice at the other end protested his request, he said, "Just do it, okay? Leave a note for the M.E., asking him to take a tissue sample, run a test and get back to me. How long could it take and how hard could it be?" He hung up without waiting for an answer and dialed another number. A voice answered, yawning. "Yeah."

"Jim?"

"Yeah?"

"It's Liam."

"Liam." Another yawn. "Jesus Christ, man, it's not even ten o'clock."

Once upon a time, Jim Wiley and Liam Campbell had been college roommates, Liam majoring in criminal justice with a minor in sociology, and Jim majoring in girls and Rainier beer with a minor in computer science. Upon graduation, Liam magna cum laude and Jim with the exact amount of credits and grade-point average required and no more, Liam had gone on to study for a master's degree and Jim had moved into a house in Muldoon, in Anchorage, and gone into business selling information. He had acquired, legally or otherwise, the names, addresses and Social Security numbers of every single citizen of the state of Alaska. He knew where they worked, how much they made, where they lived, if they voted and where, their phone numbers, listed or not. He knew if they had a license to hunt, to fish, to shoot ducks, to dig clams, to fly a plane, to drive a car, a taxi, a bus or a semi. He knew if they had parking spots at Lake Hood and how much they paid for them each year—"I'd sure like the concession on that racket," he told Liam—and if they were rated to fly floats. He knew if they owned a car, a plane, a boat, an RV, a snow machine, a four-wheeler, a dog or a cat, and he knew all the numbers, from the tags on their cars to the tags on their cats. He knew how much they spent at Nordstrom, how much they owed Visa, how often they flew Outside to visit their parents, he knew what cable channels they subscribed to, he knew where they ate out and once theaters started accepting credit cards he'd know what movies they preferred.

He organized all this information into tidy little packets; everyone who lived on Hillside, say, with homes worth more than $350,000, a combined income of six figures, two children, three dogs and a bow-hunting permit. He would turn around and sell their names and addresses to a real estate agency looking to market property in the area, or to the state senator from their voting district who was soliciting funds for his next reelection campaign, or to the gourmet pizza parlor that had just opened at the corner of O'Malley and Old Seward. It made him a very good living, which he spent immediately, having moved into his own graduate program, from girls to women and from Rainier beer to French champagne.

Wiley Jim could get to more information quicker than any state computer Liam had ever turned on. Prince had run Larsgaard and Petla through the trooper database; now they would face a real search. "I need you to run a couple of names."

Another yawn. A voice murmured in the background, something feminine and seductive. "If you've got time," Liam added.

"Gosh, we sound like we're in a good mood tonight," Jim observed. "Who?"

"Walter Larsgaard, Junior. Frank Petla."

"Spell them." Liam did. "Hang on a minute. Honey?" This apparently not to Liam. "Could you get another bottle out of the fridge?" Rustling sounds, followed by nuzzling sounds, followed by kissing sounds. "Thanks." Another murmur, followed by low laughter.

"Should I call back later?" Liam said, with awful politeness.

"Jesus, Liam, go get laid."

"I'm trying," he said before he could stop himself.

A brief silence. "Really? Anybody I know?"

Liam said nothing.

"Is it Wy?"

Jim was the only person he'd told about Wy. "Yes."

Liam heard the sound of keys clicking on a keyboard. "It's about time."

"She's resisting."

"She's scared. You hurt her."

"She hurt me."

"Yeah, but you had your family to go back to. She slept alone."

Liam thought about that until Jim's voice said, "Okay, Larsgaard. Forty-two, born in Newenham, resident of Kulukak. Not registered to vote. Hey, no credit cards, not one. Checking account has fourteen thousand and change. Owns a boat, has a Bristol Bay drift permit. Doesn't own his own home, but I don't see any regular payments that might be rent—"

"He lives with his father."

"Ah. Well, he pays his bills on time. No missed payments on the boat. He had to split up an insurance payment in 1993 but he cleared it with the company first. Taxes paid in full on April 15 every year."

"Anything in my area?"

"Not so much as a parking ticket. He's got a truck, but it's twenty, no, twenty-two years old. Hasn't had an emissions check, but then he's not required to have one out in the Bush. Pays the minimum in property tax on it, on time."

"A pilot's license?" Liam trusted Wiley Jim more than he did the State computer.

"Nope."

"How about Frank Petla?"

Jim's voice brightened. "Joseph Aaron Petla; now, there is someone I can sink my electronic teeth into. The state's been renting him rooms since he was eleven—"

"I thought juvenile records were sealed."

Jim made a scoffing noise. "Renting him rooms since he was eleven, when he and two friends were taken into custody for robbing a house. The record refers to him as a repeat offender, so they shipped him off to McLaughlin."

Liam thought of Charlene Taylor's words— "Liam, he just never had a chance"—and pinched the bridge of his nose between thumb and forefinger.

"It was the first of many visits, up until he was fifteen." There was the sound of keys being hit. "Darn it, there should be some record of his transfer to an adult institution—"

"He was fostered out the year he was fifteen," Liam said.

"Oh. Okay, that explains it. It was a year before his next offense."

"Anything major?"

"A lot of drunk and disorderly, a couple of assaults, four B&Es, only one of which stuck."

"He ever shoot anybody?"

"No."

"Stab anybody?"

"No."

"Kill anybody?"

"No."

"Assault anybody?"

"Not on record."

"How's his income?"

"Shows a little bump in the summer. He's been on unemployment every winter but one for the last five years. He owns a boat." Jim sounded surprised. "It's mortgaged to the hilt, and he misses about one payment a year, around April, but he makes it up, usually in July or August."

"Does he own any vehicles?"

"Nnnnnope."

"Not even a four-wheeler?"

"Let me check the tax records." Click, click, click. "Nope. Although in the Bush, as you well know, it's a lot easier to hide real property from the tax assessor."

"I know. I've got a vehicle number for you." Liam read it off. "Can you tell me who it belongs to?"

"Hang on." The feminine voice was back, breathing sweet nothings into Jim's and Liam's ears. That they were sweet nothings, Liam could tell only by intonation, as the words were in a tongue foreign to him.

Jim laughed. "In a minute, honey. Okay, Liam, got it. The owner's name is Dick Ford. Ah, lives in Newenham. Only have a P.O. box for an address." Jim sounded sad that this was so.

"Thanks," Liam couldn't resist saying, "I can get his street address from my local data bank." Jim bristled at the idea that someone, anyone would have more information available than he did, and Liam was pleased to have gotten a rise out of him. "Thanks for the help, Jim. Who's the babe?"

"Who, Varinka?" More disgusting kissing sounds. "Varinka's visiting from Magadan. I met her on a wide-band frequency a year ago and invited her over."

"Yeah, well, give her my best."

Jim's voice dropped to a good-naturedly lecherous purr. "I'll give her mine."

Jim was an avid ham operator, although Liam had once accused him of getting his license just so he could pick up girls in Kalgoorlie. Jim had looked wounded, but it was a fact that he dated globally, women parading into Alaska from as far away as Helsinki, lured on by Jim's siren song. On one halcyon occasion, Liam had been present when a beauty who said she was from Graaff Reinet, South Africa, showed up with a sister who was only marginally less stunning than she. Unfortunately, Liam had been married at the time.

Not that that had stopped him when he met Wy.

"Stop it," he said out loud.

"Stop what?" said a voice from the doorway.

He looked up and saw Wy.

She let the door swing closed behind her and said again, "Stop what?"

"Nothing," he said automatically, and then thought, the hell with it. "Stop feeling guilty about sleeping with you when I was married to Jenny."

"Oh." She pushed her hair behind her ears and then shook it forward again, a habit she had when she was nervous. "Do you think about it a lot?"

"Every day."

She bit her lip. "Me, too."

He turned off the computer and sat back. "What are you doing here, Wy?"

She took a deep breath. "I didn't—I . . . hell." She squared her shoulders and looked him right in the eye. "Jo said something to me last night."

"Oh great," he said, remembering the last time he'd seen Jo, or rather she'd seen him, dancing around with his pants half off, in company with Diana Prince. "My new best friend, I'll bet."

"She called me a martyr."

"A what?" he said, startled. It wasn't what he'd been expecting.

"She said that three years ago I sacrificed my happiness for yours. She says it's become a habit, and that I'm afraid that a relationship with you wouldn't measure up to our affair, and that's why I won't . . . why I won't . . ." She made a vague gesture and lapsed into silence.

Liam digested this for a moment. "Is it true?" he said finally.

She blew out a breath. "I've been asking myself that over and over again. I don't know."

He got up and came around the desk. "I can only speak for myself, Wy, but it's there, everything I ever felt for you. It's still there."

She regarded the buttons of his shirt. "There's a lot you don't know about me, Liam. A lot I never told you. Some of it . . ." She hesitated. "Some of it could be hard for you to take."

"I can hear it all. I want to hear it all."

"You say that now. No, wait. Liam, I learned about catastrophe at an early age, and I've lived my life preparing for it to happen again." She looked up at him. "I looked at you and I saw another catastrophe coming at me like a freight train. Maybe that's why I couldn't say the words you needed to hear. And maybe that's why you couldn't make the commitment I needed you to make." She took a deep breath, met his gaze, held it. "Do you know what I wish?"

"What?"

"I wish that just one time I could kiss you on purpose. No, Liam, you know what I mean."

Liam, in the act of reaching out, halted. "No. I don't."

She made a frustrated sound. "Every time, it's like we jump on each other, a surprise attack, quick and dirty and then we're gone. Just once I'd like to kiss you and have started out meaning to kiss you." She took a step forward. "Bend down a little. Put your hands on my waist."

He obeyed. She was trembling, visibly, but she stood on tiptoe and brushed her cheek against his. He quivered at the feel of skin on skin but didn't make any moves. Her nose nuzzled his, she ran her chin along his jaw, her brow against his neck. Her lips came to rest against the pulse in his throat, which instantly accelerated. She raised her head and slid a hand behind his to urge it down. Her lips were full and soft, her breath light and warm. Her lips parted, her tongue flirted with his, her teeth nipped at his lower lip.

She pulled back and stood in the circle of his arms, staring up at him. It was late, and dim in the little office, but he could see her features clearly, her enlarged irises, the lovely flush of color in her cheeks, the quick rise and fall of her breast. "Like that," she whispered.

He understood. They'd gone at each other like they were starving, like they could never eat enough to fill themselves up. He sat down on the small couch behind the door and pulled her into his lap. "We never had time to play," he whispered back.

She put her head on his shoulder. "No." His heart beat steadily, reassuringly beneath her cheek. He ran his hand slowly, lazily up and down her spine, such a fine, firm arc of flesh and bone, supple, strong, sexy. He was convinced he could recognize it out of a thousand different spines by touch alone.

She raised her head and smiled at him. "I'd better get home."

"Me, too, damn it. I've got to get some sleep. Tomorrow's going to be a long day."

"I know." She lifted her face and kissed him again and he lost himself in it and in her.

He cupped her cheek in his hand. "Is it okay that I want more?"

She smiled, the smile of every temptress since Eve. "It's more than okay."

They stood up and paused, both of them reluctant to say good-night. "What next?" he said.

She looked thoughtful. "I could say, we start dating."

"In principle," Liam said, "I like the idea. In practice, though . . ."

She smiled. "I know. There really isn't anyplace to go on a date in Newenham."

"We could drive out to the dump and watch the bears," he offered.

She pretended to consider, and shook her head. "Too early in the season. There's still salmon in the streams."

"Well, then, I could take you to dinner at Bill's."

"We just did that."

"Right, right."

"I could take you on a flightseeing trip to Round Island," she said.

"Round Island? Where's that?"

"It's a state game sanctuary fifty-plus miles south of Kulukak Bay. Walrus haul out there in big herds. It's quite a sight." Her nose wrinkled. "And smell."

Liam remembered the walrus head on Walter Larsgaard's kitchen wall. "Walrus, huh? And since it's a sanctuary, I suppose you can't hunt them there."

Since he seemed interested, she obliged. "Not until recently. Around 1960 the state government declared the area off limits to everyone, Native or non. Pissed off a lot of people, because it was sort of a ukase from the czar, they did it without any hearings held in the area. It was pretty drastic, but there was some justification."

"Why? The walrus go the way of the otter?"

"Pretty much. It had been hunted nearly to extinction, not by Natives but by Yankee whalers in the 1800s, and not for their meat or hides but for their ivory."

Liam thought again of the walrus head, the long, curving tusks of smooth, glowing ivory. A tempting target, all right.

"The population has come back since then; you can see thousands of walrus hauled out on this one particular beach alone."

Liam thought of what Ekwok had told him about Larsgaard Senior. "So the state was forced to reopen the area to hunting."

"Depends on how you define hunting." Wy's voice was very dry. "Native hunters only, of course, and no hunting at all until a ten-page agreement had been drawn up and signed between state and villagers, detailing where the boats could go ashore, how the animals could be shot and allowing for tissue samples to be collected from each kill. Observers from both federal and state governments were on hand to witness the event, hand out permits and videotape the results."

With a smile, Liam said, "You flew some of them in."

She nodded. "A whole plane full of observers and equipment. So. You want to go?"

"No first dates that involve flying," Liam said firmly. "I'm better at making my moves when I'm not airsick. How about you cook me dinner tomorrow night? I'll bring a movie to watch after."

"Tim will be there."

"I know."

She smiled, this time a sweet smile full of promise. "It's a date."

NINETEEN

Liam rose early, stood post and practiced all sixty-four movements of the form with what he was sure was exquisite grace and superb style, showered briskly and was at his desk, whistling while he worked, by seven-fifty-nine. He called the medical examiner's office in Anchorage and left a message on the machine for Brillo Pad to call him. He went through the evidence he'd collected from the archaeological dig at Tulukaruk. Don Nelson's journal made very interesting reading, but there was nothing in it that Liam identified as pertinent to his murder. He reviewed his notes on the interview with Alta. Molly and Larsgaard's last meeting had been the previous Monday. One week alive and loving, the next dead and buried. Sounded like a line from a country-and-western song.

He got Bill out of bed at eight-thirty, and heard an irritated Moses complaining in the background. Everybody got some last night but him, but the thought did not depress him as much as it might have.

"Dick Ford?" she said. "Nice guy. Good fisherman, too, but he's such a soft touch that he never hangs on to any money. A four-wheeler? I don't know, Liam, he's never driven it into the bar."

He called Dick Ford's phone number. No answer. He saddled up the Blazer and galloped purposefully down to the harbor, pulling up in front of the office door for Seafood North. Tanya paled when he walked in the door, and then looked relieved when he said, "Is Dick Ford a fisherman of yours?"

"Yes."

"What's the name of his boat, and do you know its slip number?"

Of course she did. She even accompanied him out to the dock to point out the boat. "Right there, the *Selina Noel*, slip number one-eighty-seven. Pretty name, isn't it?"

"Thanks." He waited until she had turned to go and said, "Oh, one more thing."

Her back was almost as nice as Wy's, slender, straight and at the moment vibrating with tension. "Yes?" she said, looking over her shoulder and narrowing her eyes against the still-rising sun.

"You were meeting David Malone at the Bay View Inn, weren't you, Tanya." He made it a statement, rather than a question.

For a moment, one very brief moment, her shoulders slumped. She turned to face him fully, looking naked and defenseless in the bright morning light. "Yes."

"Once every couple of weeks for the past three months."

"And last summer. Yes."

She offered no apologies and no explanations, and he admired her for it. "You don't have to worry, I'm not going to tell anyone, and if Alta Peterson down at the hotel hasn't by now, she won't be, either. The fact that you were having an affair with David Malone had nothing to do with his or his family's death, and it doesn't matter to the investigation."

"It matters to me," she whispered.

She looked very young and very defenseless, and he had a sudden vivid memory of Wy's face the day she'd walked away from him in Anchorage. Pain, loss, guilt, shame, more than he could put a name to, all of it reflected in the young face before him now. "Move on," he said.

"I can't," she said.

"You can't do anything else," he said, and went down the gangway, leaving her standing on the end of the dock, staring out at the Bay.

Dick Ford wasn't on board the *Selina Noel*. Well, shit. Well, then, how about Max Bayless? He knew what Prince would say, that he was tracking down useless leads, that they already had a confession in one case and an alibi with holes big enough to drive a truck through in the other. He should be in the office, doing paperwork, wrapping things up.

Instead he went to the only other bar in town, the Breeze Inn, which sat on the exact opposite edge of town from Bill's Bar and Grill. It was half the size of the other bar and twice as noisy, mostly because there was a television hanging from every corner of the room and two over the bar, all of them on at once. The bartender was a fat man with three strands of black hair stretched carefully across his otherwise bare scalp. He didn't say much. He shook his head when Liam asked him if he'd seen Max Bayless. He shook his head again when Liam asked him if he knew Max Bayless. The two guys nursing Bloody Marys while they watched ESPN didn't know Max Bayless and hadn't met him lately, either. Nobody'd seen Max Bayless, not Tanya, not Bill, not anyone; Max Bayless was the original invisible man.

He went back to the office and dialed Wiley Jim's number. It rang eleven times before Jim picked up. "I don't know who this is and I don't care, if you want to live you'll let me go back to sleep."

"One more name, Jim," Liam said. "I'll fix your next ticket."

Jim drove a white Desert Rat Porsche convertible around Anchorage, even in winter, at no known and certainly no legal speed limit. A feminine complaint could be heard in the background but it didn't grate as much on Liam as it had the night before, and he grinned at the opposite wall. "Max Bayless. Come on, Wiley, I know you never turn that computer off. Just stagger into the office and type in the letters. M-A-X—"

"I got it, I got it," Jim said, "and fuck you."

"Thanks, Jim, I knew I could count on you."

He waited. Five minutes later Jim said, "He's in jail. Cook Inlet Pre-Trial."

"What for?"

"Selling cocaine."

"Where was he arrested?"

"Anchorage. Wait a minute." Click, click, click. "Fourth Avenue, the Hub, if you can believe it."

"How long's he been in custody?"

"Eleven days. Can I go back to bed now?"

"With my blessing."

"One ticket?"

"One."

"Oughtta be three."

"One," Liam said firmly. "Say goodnight, Jim."

So, Dick Ford owned the four-wheeler Frank Petla had been riding on, and was presently nowhere to be found. Max Bayless had threatened to kill David Malone, but he'd been in jail too long to have actually done it, and it was a year-old threat, anyway.

The phone rang and he snatched it up. "Brillo Pad, is that you, you old bastard, what took you so long?"

"You watch your mouth, mister, or I'll come over there and wash it out with soap," Mamie Hagemeister said primly.

Liam sat up. "I'm sorry. I thought you were someone else. Mamie?"

"Yes."

"There's nothing wrong with the prisoners, is there?"

"No, but one of them wants to talk to you."

"Which one, Petla or Larsgaard?"

"Neither. Mr. Gray has asked me to ask you to stop by when you have a moment."

"Gray? Who—oh. What does he want?"

"He says he has some information for you." She gave a discreet cough, and added in an even primmer voice, "There was some mention of a deal."

"It wasn't even half a lid," Moccasin Man said.

"Tough luck. Unless you've got a medical prescription to smoke dope, possession is still illegal in Alaska, and punishable upon conviction by time in jail."

"That's such crap."

"Hey, you're preaching to the choir," Liam said, spreading his hands. "If I had my way, all drugs would be legalized and taxed. If I had my way, we'd buy all the coke, opium, heroin and crack there is and pile it up on street corners, free for anybody who wanted it. Next morning I'd go around with a front-end loader and haul the bodies off to the dump, a gain not only to the state but to the gene pool. Not to mention which it'd cut down on my overtime something considerable." Liam leaned back in his chair and laced his fingers behind his head. "But I don't have my way. It's still illegal to be in possession of marijuana in the state of Alaska, which substance you were caught with by a sworn officer of the law." Liam leaned forward and flipped open the file in front of him. "Officer Roger Raymo, in fact, on Saturday night. Seems he saw your truck pulled off the side of the road about halfway to Icky."

"The dope wasn't mine."

Liam smiled and closed the file.

"It wasn't, goddamn it," Gray muttered. "It was hers."

"Who is 'her'?"

"May Hitchcock. The broad who was with me."

Liam opened up the file again and perused it slowly, to Gray's increasing impatience. "She had it on her. She must have dropped it on the floor and kicked it under the seat when that dick Raymo pulled up behind us in his dickmobile."

Liam clicked his tongue. "Now, now, Evan, you're not going to get anywhere with me by bad-mouthing a fellow officer. So, you say the dope was May's. She buy it from you in the first place?"

Gray met his eyes full on and lied like . . . well, like a trooper. "No."

"Of course not." Liam closed the file again. "Tell me, Evan, how do you make your living?"

"A little of this, a little of that."

"Uh-huh."

"Look, it doesn't matter how I make my living, this charge is bogus. Get May in here and I'll prove it."

"Officer Raymo let May go, did he?"

Gray snorted. "It was an answer to his favorite wet dream, catching me holding."

"What do you want, Evan?"

"I want out of here. I want the charge against me dropped." His grin was cocky, as cocky as Charles's had been the night before. "I want a hot shower and my own bed and a good-looking woman in it, in that order."

All trace of humor had vanished from Liam's face. His eyes

were cold and steady, his hands flat on the table, muscles in his arms taut as if he were about ready to get up and go. "What have you got to trade?"

Liam sent Gray back to his cell and brought Larsgaard into the interview room. He got him a cup of coffee, heavy on the cream and sugar. Larsgaard took the first sip and looked surprised that Liam had gotten it right. "I watched how you fixed it at your house," Liam said. He blew on his own coffee and sipped.

The window was open and that damn raven was sitting on the branch of a mountain ash right outside the window, looking as if he had been carved from a single piece of the darkest obsidian. Liam didn't really know anything about obsidian except that it was a rock of some kind that was black and shiny, but he liked the sound of the word and it was what that black bastard looked like he was made of, from his enormous curved beak to his black beady eyes to his fat black tailfeathers. Although he didn't look so black this close up, more a mixture of green and blue and dark brown. Sort of like snow and how it wasn't really white.

Larsgaard followed his glance. "Raven," he said. "My favorite bird."

"Really?" Liam gave the raven an unfriendly glance. "Why?"

"They're smart."

"If they're so smart, why don't they fly south for the winter?"

"And they're loyal."

Liam raised his brows. "Loyal?"

"Sure." Larsgaard gestured with his mug. "When one of them finds something to eat, say a moose or a caribou or a bear, anything, they wait and watch it, sometimes hours, sometimes even days to make sure it's dead, and then they call in their friends and relatives for a feast. They're like wolves with wings." He paused. "The elders say that a raven will lead you to your moose, because he knows when you're done butchering out, there will be some left over for him." He saw Liam's skepticism and said, "It's true. Have you heard them talk?"

Liam thought of all the various sounds he had heard from either the one raven following him around or the hundreds of ravens living around the Bay, one of which he seemed to see

everywhere he went. Each raven utterance was a different sequence of clicks and croaks and caws, each sequence in a different series of tones. "Yeah, I've heard them talk."

"They have different kinds of calls, and each call has a different meaning. Why shouldn't 'Supper's on the table, come and get
it' be one of them?" Larsgaard shrugged and drank coffee.
"Wolves have a language. Whales. Why not ravens?"

Why not ravens? Liam thought. "Walter, I want you to take
me through it again, step by step this time."

Larsgaard sighed and turned around to face Liam. "Why? I've
already told you once. You already have it on tape. I'll tell Bill I'm
guilty."

"A magistrate doesn't sit on felony cases." Or she doesn't if I
get the felon on a plane to Anchorage first.

Larsgaard shrugged. He didn't look much the worse for wear
for his night in prison. His hair had been combed and his eyes were
calm, a marked contrast to the panicked expression on Frank
Petla's face every time he saw Liam. "Whatever. I read about
Spring Creek in the paper. I expect that's where I'll wind up?"

Spring Creek was the state's maximum security facility in Se-
ward. "If there's room."

"And if there isn't?"

"A prison Outside until there is."

For the first time Larsgaard looked anxious. "I'd rather stay in
the state, if I could. Close to my father. You understand."

Again Liam thought of Charles, whom Liam couldn't wait to
put on the first plane south, but he said yes to avoid an explanation that would only get them off track. "Humor me, Walter. Run
through it again. One step at a time. When was the first time you
slept with Molly Malone?"

Larsgaard flushed. "None of your business."

"Okay, then tell me when you decided to kill her."

"I told you," Larsgaard said, his voice rising. "On Sunday."

"When did she break things off between you?"

"Last week."

"What day?"

"I don't remember. I—I was pretty broken up about it. I don't
remember much."

A bad memory, always a convenient tool in the suspect's cache. "The twentieth?"

"I told you, I don't remember."

"The seventeenth? Maybe the twenty-first? How about the fourth of July?"

Larsgaard drew his hands back from the mug and sat upright. He'd regained his composure, and his eyes became distant, his manner remote. "I told you. I don't remember. I'd like to go back to my cell now."

Liam stood up, his six-foot-three frame filling up the little room. "Well, then, let's try something easier. Do you remember what you said to Evan Gray last night?"

"What?" Larsgaard's eyes snapped back into focus, staring up at Liam, startled out of whatever inner hiding place he'd run to.

"Last night did you tell Evan Gray that you didn't kill Molly Malone, that you loved her, that you could never have killed her?"

Liam watched the color drain from Larsgaard's face, and tried like hell to read the expression there. The closest he could come to was fear, which made no sense. Why would Larsgaard be afraid? Of what? He'd already confessed to seven murders, he would only ever see the sun again from behind a barbed-wire electric fence; what could he possibly fear now?

There was a brisk knock on the door, and Liam cursed under his breath. "It's open!"

Prince opened the door and gave an apologetic cough. "Sorry, sir, but it's almost ten o'clock. We need to get in the air if we're going to get back in time for the arraignment this afternoon."

"You're going back to Kulukak?" The words forced themselves from Larsgaard's throat.

They looked at him, curious. "Yes," Liam said.

"Why? What for?" He saw their expression and with the same visible effort at control Liam had seen before he pulled himself together. "I said I did it. You've got the bodies. You don't need to go back there for anything."

Liam stared at him. "I'm beginning to think I do, Walter."

"I don't understand," Prince said as she followed him the door. "We've got a suspect in custody, we've got his confession, he had means, motive and opportunity, we've even got a witness. What else are you digging for?"

The phone rang, saving him from trying to come up with an answer. "Brillo Pad. About time. What have you got?"

"It's Brilleaux," the voice said, made husky by the three-pack-a-day and two-martini lunch habits he refused to quit no matter how much his wife and his doctor nagged him. "Bril-LEAUX, how many times do I have to tell you?" He coughed heavily, and Liam involuntarily held the phone away from his ear.

"This isn't official, okay?"

"Okay."

"They were shot about two hours before they were burned. Maybe a little more, maybe a little less. Seawater fucks up all the time-to-decay stats, and the water's been colder than normal down there this year."

"Who says?"

"Jesus, the weather fairy, who do you think? I called Jim over to the National Weather Service. Oh, and one other thing."

"What?"

"Molly Malone was pregnant."

Dr. Hans Brilleaux, having delivered his message and having no further use for the telephone in his hand, hung up.

Liam put down the phone and looked at Prince. "Molly Malone was pregnant."

She stared at him. "With whose baby, I wonder?"

"So do I. Tell me something, Prince, if you shot seven people and you wanted to cover it up, would you wait two hours before you tried?"

He could tell Prince was making an effort to maintain her professional calm. "I wouldn't shoot seven people, sir," she said carefully. "Do you—sir, you don't think he didn't do it, do you?"

"No, I think he did it, all right, but he's not telling us the truth about why or how, and I don't want this case to unravel in court."

"It couldn't," she said, shocked.

"I have two words for you," he said. "O. J. Simpson." One word and two letters, actually, but what the hell.

"But—"

"Prince, we're not talking burden of proof or rule of law or even simple logic, here. We're talking juries, twelve individual people, each with their own boatload of biases and prejudices, and each as susceptible to the suggestions of the defense as they are to the evidence we hand off to the prosecutor. More so, if the judge comes down hard on reasonable doubt during instruction. I don't like leaving juries with any wriggle room." He grabbed his cap and headed for the door. "I want all the evidence there is to get before we turn this case over to the D.A. We need a signed statement from Chad Donohoe, too, and I don't think he's going to leave in the middle of fishing season to come into town and give us one."

He paused, one hand on the open door. "Besides, Larsgaard doesn't want us to go back to Kulukak. I want to know why."

TWENTY

"I need a ride," Jo said.

Steam was rising from their coffee cups as they sat around the kitchen table, watching the sun rise up over the mouth of the Nushagak and the Bay beyond. The kitchen of Wy's house was flooded in golden light, and Wy didn't have any flights scheduled to anywhere until that afternoon. She put her feet up on a chair and said lazily, "You buying?"

"The paper is."

"Where to?"

Jo added half and half to her coffee and stirred in another teaspoon of sugar. "I came out here on a story."

"I know, you told me, but you wouldn't tell me what it was."

"Yeah. The guy who contacted me about it didn't want me to spread it around."

"Who was it?"

"Don Nelson."

Wy sat up with a bump. "The guy killed out at the dig?"

"Yeah."

"You know I found him? Well, me and McLynn."

"Yeah. I mean, not right away, I went in to say hi to Bill last night and she told me. Saw you at dinner, by the way." Jo's green eyes watched her over the rim of her mug.

"Oh," Wy said. She could feel the color rising up into her cheeks. "Yeah, well. We had dinner."

"So I saw."

"It was just . . . it was dinner, okay? His father was there, the new trooper, it was just dinner. The ingestion of food in return for a caloric warming of cell tissue."

"Uh-huh. With a little footsie on the side."

Wy drank coffee. "I went to see him at the post afterward."

"Did you?"

Wy glared. "Oh, stop being so fucking smug, Dunaway."

"Then stop being so fucking evasive, Chouinard. Jesus, you're worse than Bill Clinton when it comes to talking about your sex life. It's true what they say, denial is not just a river in Egypt."

"It's not sex."

"Not yet."

"Do you want to hear this or not?"

Jo's smile was wide and salacious. "I want to, I want to."

Wy fiddled with the sugar spoon, raising spoonsful of sugar and letting it fall back into the bowl. "Maybe you weren't wrong, some of those things you said the other night."

For once, Jo maintained a prudent silence.

"I told Liam what you said. Some of it, anyway."

"What'd he say?"

"Not much." Wy let the spoon fall. "He just wants me, Jo. Just flat out wants me, all of me, marriage, kids, for better or worse, so long as we both shall live, until death us do part, everything, the whole nine yards."

"Kids?"

Their eyes met. "I haven't told him."

"You'll have to."

"Not yet," Wy said, a plea in her voice.

"I'm not your mother, Wy, or your conscience." Jo drained her mug. "I don't have to be, you've got enough conscience for any ten people I know. You want to be happy with him for a little while before you lower the next boom, okay, I get that. But not telling him now means you don't trust him enough to understand and accept. He won't like that. And it is a lousy way to start any relationship, let alone this one." She stood up. "In the meantime, I want to take a look at that archaeological dig—what did you call it?"

"Tulukaruk."

"Everything around here starts or ends with a k, or both," Jo said, grumbling. "Tulukaruk, Kulukak, Manokotak, Stoyahuk, Koliganek, Egegik. Anyway, I want to see the place with the *k*'s where Nelson died."

"What did he write to you about?"

Jo hesitated. "He said he'd found something that would make a great story. It had to do with a government cover-up."

"Government?" Their eyes met. They both knew what kind of government institution was closest to Tulukaruk.

Wy was silent until they got to the airport. As they were strapping into the Cub, she said, "When did Nelson first contact you?"

"I got his letter four days ago."

She pulled the throttle, adjusted the mixture and started the prop. The headsets crackled into life. Wy got clearance to taxi and the Cub rolled off the apron and down the runway. Just before they took off, she looked around at Jo. "Colonel Campbell has been here almost a week."

"I know," Jo said.

The flight to Kulukak was uneventful, not so much as a bump of clear-air turbulence to mar the journey. As usual, Kulukak was fogged in and, as usual, not enough to abort an approach and a landing. Liam noticed that Prince didn't take the care that Wy did in a landing; they came down hard, smack, so that the plane shuddered and water washed over the floats. She didn't let up on the throttle, either, taxiing flat out to the float slip and running the plane well up onto the boards.

"Thought you were going to take us right up the gangway and into town," Liam said, dry mouth forming the words with difficulty.

"Just get her down," Prince said, switching off the mag and opening the door in the same motion. "Just get her down in one piece, and in good enough shape to get her back in the air again, that's all that's important."

Liam wondered what the maintenance bills were like for the Cessna, and decided it was something he didn't need to know. That was the difference between flying your own plane and someone else's. Sort of like driving a rental car. A rental car three thousand feet up.

It was the twenty-forth, a Thursday, and judging by the number of boats idle in the harbor, the Fish and Game had not counted enough salmon going up the various rivers and streams. Men were hanging and mending gear, scrubbing down decks, working on engines, readying themselves and their craft for when the Fish and Game renewed their contact lens prescriptions and could see well enough to count fish. It was probably Liam's imagination but it seemed like a silence fell as they approached, and gathered in strength behind them as they passed. Prince put it into words. "I feel like I've got a bull's-eye painted on my back."

"Larsgaard is the tribal chief," Liam said. "He is probably a popular man, and even if he wasn't, he is still an important one." Liam cast a look over his shoulder. Action, momentarily suspended, resumed with immense vigor. "And he is a local boy. No matter what he has done, a local boy is still a local boy first and foremost, especially in a Bush village. We work for the state government, remember."

"I think I remember you saying that about five or six times in the past twenty-four hours, yes."

They reached the foot of the gangway. "Okay," Liam said, "you track down Chad Donohoe and get his statement. What's his boat again?"

"*Snohomish Belle.*" Prince pointed. "Right over there."

Liam squinted at the trim forty-footer moored near the mouth of the breakwater. "Okay. I'll head up to Larsgaard's, talk to his father."

"How you going to make him let you in?"

"Innate charm," Liam said.

The tide was low and the gangway at a steep angle. Liam hoofed it to the top in long strides. A man stood at the dock, blocking the way. "Excuse me," said Liam, who like any other man had an excess of pride in his physical abilities and was trying not to puff too heavily.

The man moved a half step back. "You're the trooper, aren't you?"

Liam stopped and took a long, he hoped subtle breath. "Yes. Corporal Liam Campbell, Newenham post."

The man looked at his plaid shirt and jeans with a puzzled expression, then seemed reassured when he saw the trooper badge on Liam's ball cap. He was a thin, wizened man with bandy legs that looked like they'd just stepped down from a mustang. He took two quick steps for every one of Liam's strides. "Name's Greasy Rust. I'm the oil man."

"I beg your pardon."

Greasy waved a greasy thumb in the direction of the small tank farm on the hill. "I work for Standard Oil. I sell fuel to the boats."

"Yeah." Liam's stride didn't slow. "Nice to meet you, Greasy, but I've got to talk to somebody, and I'm in kind of a hurry, so if you'll excuse me—"

"You really think Walter killed those folks?"

"The case is still under investigation," Liam replied with exactitude.

"Yeah, but you've got him in jail in Newenham, right?"

Liam paused at the end of the dock to get his bearings. Larsgaard's house was up the hill on the right, as he remembered. "Mr. Larsgaard is helping us with our inquiries, yes."

"I can't believe I sold him the gas to go out there," Greasy said.

Liam looked down at Greasy, the top of whose balding head came barely to his shoulder. "You sold Walter Larsgaard gas last Sunday?"

Greasy had inquisitive brown eyes veined with red like a map of downtown Los Angeles. He preened a little now that he had Liam's full attention. "Yeah. Well, I fueled them all up, you know."

"No, I don't know, Greasy. Tell me."

"When the fleet came in from fishing the period. Even if they haven't pulled that many fish, everybody always tops off the tanks afterward, just in case the Fish-and-goddamn-Game pulls their thumb out in time for another period the next day. You don't want to be caught at the dock with an empty tank if that happens, believe me. I remember old Mick Kashatok got caught that way one day a couple of years back, missed the biggest run of reds Kulukak has seen in the last ten years because he'd come in from the previous period running on fumes. By the time he'd fueled up, the fleet was an hour ahead of him, and by the time he'd gotten to the fishing grounds, everybody had their nets in prime water and no room left for him. He tried to cork Nappy Napagiak and of course old Nappy don't put up with that for a New York minute and he run his prop right over Mick's gear. Cut Mick's corkline. Course it fouled Nappy's prop and neither of them got much fish that period. Bob Halstensen said he'd never seen such a Chinese fire drill in his life, and then he got into it because both boats were without power and they drifted across the markers and the Fish-and-goddamn-Game got into it — "

Liam, fascinated though he was with this flow of reminiscence, had to break in. "That's all very interesting, Greasy, but you say you refueled everyone, the whole, er, fleet on Sunday afternoon?"

"Yeah." Greasy shifted a lump from one cheek to another and spat a wad of tobacco juice, accurately hitting the area where the upright on the dock railing intersected with the crossing two-by-four. "Everyone who'd been out fishing that day. Which was pretty much everyone, including a bunch of jerry cans for outboards. Except maybe Alan Seager. Seeing as how the *Cheyenne* sunk at the dock the week before. It was my busiest day this month."

"So it wasn't out of the ordinary for you to refuel Walter Larsgaard, too."

Greasy's brow creased. "Well, no. I guess not."

"Okay, Greasy. Thanks for the information, we can use all the help we can get." It was wise for Liam to build relationships with as many members of the local populations of the villages in his district as he could, and the fuel man in a marine community would see more of the populace more of the time than most. After all, he never knew when he might be back in Kulukak on another case.

"You're welcome," Greasy said, wiping his palm carefully down his pants leg before accepting Liam's hand. "Always glad to help out."

"Good to know," Liam said. He smiled and eased his hand free. "Be seeing you."

"Anything you need to know, you ask," Greasy called after him. "I been here forever, and I ain't going nowhere."

Five minutes later Liam was knocking on Larsgaard's door. There was no answer. He knocked again. Still no answer. He tried the knob. It turned and he stuck his head in the door. "Mr.

Larsgaard? Sir? It's Liam Campbell, the trooper from Newenham. I need to ask you a few questions."

He pushed the door open and stepped inside, and something came down on his head like a sledgehammer, knocking the legs right out from under him. He fell backward, landing with his back half supported against the wall, and the last thing he saw before the lights went all the way out was the walrus head on the opposite wall, the ivory tusks rising in what seemed like a knowing leer.

The same sledgehammer hit him again and a wave of blackness overwhelmed his vision and he stopped thinking at all.

The ride to the dig was uneventful, not so much as a bump on the way. They touched down smoothly and rolled to a stop. As Wy pushed up the door, McLynn stuck his head out of the work tent. He had a peevish expression on his face. Looking at him, Jo said, "You didn't tell me what an attractive man Professor McLynn was, Wy."

Wy looked at her. "Oh god, are we doing the come-on thing again? I hate it when you do that, Jo."

She climbed out of the plane, Jo right behind her. Jo smoothed her T-shirt, patted her hair and walked toward McLynn, giving her hips that extra roll the oil executive could have recognized and would have advised Professor Desmond X. McLynn to run from, as fast as his little legs could carry him.

But the oil company executive was still in jail, and Professor McLynn was only human. He tore his eyes from the way Jo was walking to the way Jo was smiling, smoothed his hair, sucked in his gut and advanced to meet her. By the time Wy reached them, Jo was listening, round-eyed with rapture, to an account of Professor McLynn's personal discovery of the abandoned settlement of Tulukaruk. "Really?" Wy heard Jo say. "Why, Professor McLynn, how positively prescient of you!"

Wy made an abrupt ninety-degree turn and veered toward the edge of the bluff. She thought about jumping off, and then thought better of it, sitting down instead to hang her legs over the edge.

Tim was helping Moses mend his gear. In a couple of days

they'd head upriver to Moses' fish camp, to pull in their share of the season's silvers. Wy wouldn't see Tim again for two weeks, maybe three. The one condition she'd laid down to Moses was that Tim had to be back in time for the first day of school. Moses had bitched and whined and in the end made her promise to practice her form twice a day, instead of just once, before reluctantly acquiescing. There had been a gleam in his eyes that made her wonder if he hadn't been driving her in that direction all along.

Neither of them referred to her question of the day before. She hadn't forgotten asking it. She could wait for her answer, though, so long as she got one. The Yupik in her, she thought, willing me to patience. What if he is? What if he isn't? What does it matter either way?

Three years before, she'd moved to Newenham, bought out an air taxi business, had rescued an abused child and acquired a son in the process and had begun—had been dragooned into, was more like it—learning tai chi. She had come to Newenham to start a new life, and all Moses could say was that she was escaping from her old one. He knew things, that old man, and he was always around to prophesy—or pontificate.

And now here he was telling her that he'd known her mother. Martha and Ed Lewis had been BIA teachers all over southwestern Alaska, a year in Ouzinkie, two in Old Harbor, one in Egegik, four in Togiak, five in Manokotak, two in Icky, nine in Newenham. They retired two years before Wy graduated from high school and moved to Anchorage, to a home in Spenard they had bought years before. At West High she made her first real friend, Joan Dunaway, and in spite of the trauma of being yanked out of high school and moved from a Bush community into the big city, she had never resented it.

Martha and Ed had demanded A's on her report cards but had not punished her for her occasional lapse into the nether world of the C student, made her go to mass when Father Mike flew in but had deferred baptism into the church until she came of age and hadn't objected when she'd decided against it, hadn't let her date until she was sixteen but thereafter had set her curfew at midnight and had trusted her enough not to stay up to see that she kept it. They'd loved her, she was sure they still did, but she often wondered if it was a love that had grown more out of duty than any real affection.

She worried that she was doing the same thing to Tim; if what she felt for him was obligation, if she had acted out of compassion and pity, or maybe because she felt she had to pass it on. That was their mantra, Martha and Ed: Pass It On. If someone did something for you, don't pay it back, Pass It On. Was she doing the Pass It On thing with Tim?

Martha and Ed Lewis had removed Wy from the cycle of alcoholism and abuse embraced by her birth family before it had had a chance to take hold of her, the way it had Frank Petla and so many others. She would always be grateful, she would forever honor them, but try as she would, she could not remember a time when one of her adoptive parents had hugged her. Jo's father had hugged her the first time she went home with Jo at Thanksgiving. He hugged everybody, big bear hugs strong enough to lift you right off your feet. So did his wife, so did Jo's sisters and especially her brother—her mind veered away from that memory. It was the first real affection she had ever felt, and the Dunaways heaped it on her lavishly, without question. She was Jo's best friend, therefore she was family. She hadn't known families could be like that. It was what she wanted for Tim.

And Liam? How did Liam fit into the picture? She didn't know yet. She wanted him physically, but then she always had; that was nothing new. She respected the work he did, and that was very important; she could never commit to someone who was not good at his job. It didn't matter if he dug ditches or programmed computers or cleaned teeth or was a state trooper; a man had to be good at what he chose to do with his life or Wy wouldn't look at him twice. Gary, Jo's brother, had been the first in his class of petroleum engineering. He worked for British Petroleum now, from the North Sea to China to Siberia. If they hadn't— No. She wouldn't go there. That was then, this was now, and now she had a business, a son and, on the horizon, a relationship forming with a man she wasn't sure she either trusted or respected, at least in a personal, emotional sense. They were dating, that was all she knew for certain. If it was possible to date in Newenham.

Her thoughts hounded her up and back to camp. The deck chairs had vanished and she heard the murmur of conversation coming from the work tent. She made a seat back out of a Blazo box and sat down on the ground, stretching in the sun. So much of an air taxi's business was hurry up and wait. Hurry up and wait on the customers, hurry up and wait on the fish, hurry up and wait on the caribou, hurry up and wait on the weather. Especially the latter. She thought of the omnipresent fog in Kulukak and was grateful it was keeping to that side of the Bay for the moment, unusual for this time of year, when the normal weather pattern called for blankets of fog and mist miles in diameter to come sweeping up the Nushagak and envelop all of the coastal communities in a dank, damp shroud.

She closed her eyes and was dozing off when she heard Jo say firmly, "He wrote to me several times, Desmond."

"Did he?" There was a rustle of movement. "What did he say?"

McLynn's voice sounded stern, even harsh, as if he were calling Jo to account for something. Wy got up and maneuvered around a Blazo box full of what to her untrained eye looked like clods of dirt, and waited outside the tent flap, listening.

Jo didn't seem concerned. "He said he'd discovered something at the dig that I would be interested in seeing."

"Really? What was that?"

"He wanted me to come out so he could show me in person."

"I see." More rustling. "You see this, Jo?"

"Yes."

"Do you know what it is?"

Jo, voice puzzled, said, "It looks like a manuscript."

"It is. It's mine. It's the product of twenty years of study and work and making aerial maps and grubbing around in the dirt and no summers off."

Jo oozed respect and deference for the sacrifice involved. "A long-term project."

"Very long. My wife left me over it," he added abruptly.

"Oh." Jo sounded startled, then rallied. "I'm sorry to hear that."

"Her name was Noreen."

"Oh," Jo said again, adding lamely, "It's a beautiful name."

Wy grinned.

"Yes. She was a good worker. There wasn't anything she couldn't turn her hand to: cooking, cleaning, bookkeeping, mending. She'd even take a hand in the dig—under strict supervision, of course."

"Oh, of course."

Jo's irony was lost on McLynn, who was lost in reminiscence. "It halved the work, having her here."

"I imagine it did. How long was she here?"

"One summer."

Another tiny pause. "One summer out of the last twenty?"

"Yes. She walked away from me at Anchorage International Airport, when we were on our way back to campus for the fall semester. She said she was going to the ladies' room. I never saw her again."

"I see. What did you do?"

"What could I do? I went back to school, and I taught my fall and spring semester classes, and then the next summer, I came back here. It was all I had left."

"I see." Jo was noncommittal, but Wy could hear her thoughts as if she'd spoken them out loud. If McLynn hadn't treated his wife like his own personal serf, he might not have run her off.

Wy was more charitable. McLynn had loved, and lost, and nineteen years later, he was still grieving. It explained a lot of his behavior, if it didn't excuse it.

McLynn's voice rose a little. "Twenty years I've been coming here, most of the time alone, sometimes with an assistant. None of them ever had the commitment to the project that I did."

Jo was soothing. "I'm sure they didn't."

"Not one of them ever believed in my thesis, that the Bristol Bay Yupik was an entirely different people from the Yukon-Kuskokwim Delta tribes. Have you ever looked at a map of Alaska?" He rushed on without waiting for a reply, which was probably just as well. "There's a mountain range that divides the Delta from the Bay. That's one thing. Another is that the Yupik used to paddle regularly across the Bering Sea from Siberia to the Aleutians, first to make war and then to visit relatives."

"It's almost a thousand miles, continent to continent, in some places." Jo was noncommittal, reserving judgment.

McLynn's voice went up again, a specialist mounted securely on his own personal hobbyhorse. "There are family names in common between the Siberian Yupik and the Aleutian Yupik, did you know that? Right down to the present day. There are some very fine examples of woven armor, too, and waterproof boatwear made from seal gut. The art is very similar—since the Wall came down I've been to Korjakskoe, I've seen some of the villages there." He was excited now, skipping from subject to subject, eager to bolster his thesis. "There is one small village—I won't tell you the name, I'm saving that for publication but I'll give you an exclusive—where I found items in use by the people who live there this"—a thump of a fist—"very"—another thump—"day"—a third thump—"that are so similar to thousand-year-old artifacts which I have excavated from this"—thump—"very"—thump—"site"—very loud thump—"that the items could be exchanged and put into use with little or no familiarization on the part of the user." A triumphant pause.

"Well." Jo seemed at a loss as to what to say next. "I—it does seem to support your premise, sir."

"It proves it!" Thump!

Jo maintained her respectful silence, and again Wy could almost hear her thinking. Jo didn't know anything about archaeology or anthropology, Alaskan or otherwise, but she knew enough about fanatics to realize that any opposition to pet theories could get one killed. Wy smothered a chuckle and waited to see how Jo would divert McLynn back to the topic she was investigating.

Surprising them both, he returned to it voluntarily. "And after all this, after twenty years' hard labor, the ridicule of my colleagues, the funding reduced and then taken away, the days spent fighting mosquitoes in Alaska and the nights spent fighting Stalin's revenge in Korjakskoe, do you know what that ignorant little brat was going to do?"

"You mean Nelson?"

"He was going to ruin it! Ruin it all! Destroy my thesis, negate twenty years of work, besmirch my standing in the academic community, all for what? All because he'd found a storyknife and decided that all by itself that proved that the Yupik of Kulukak were an offshoot of the lower Yukon tribes, instead of a migratory band of Chuckchi from Siberia!"

Wy's smile faded.

"What nonsense! Anyone with half a brain would review the evidence, the artifacts, and know the truth for what it was! Look at this! A stone lamp with a bear fetish, a classic Siberian Yupik design! Look at this!"

"What is it?"

"Can't you tell? It's a fragment of an armored vest! Look at the weaving! That pattern never originated on this side of the Bering Sea!"

"If you say so." Jo was doing her best to be soothing.

At first, McLynn seemed to calm. "I told Nelson there was nothing in it, that it had been left behind by a much later group passing through."

"Certainly seems like a viable possibility. Desmond, what I really wanted to ask you was—"

"You see my whole thesis is predicated on the movement of peoples between the Siberian Chuckchi region and the subarctic region of western Alaska."

"Er, yes," Jo said. "The Aleuts used to row their kayaks—"

"Baidarkas."

"—whatever, across eight hundred miles of open sea to get from one continent to the other. I remember learning that in Alaska history in high school. Very, ah, daring. Gutsy. Admirable, even. But what I—"

"And they settled here," McLynn said firmly.

A barely repressed sigh. "Yes."

"No matter what Don Nelson said." A contemptuous sniff. "A grad student. Really. What could he know?"

"Less than the dust beneath your chariot wheels," Jo agreed, "but what about—"

"He had to be stopped."

"—what he says here, where— What?"

"Nelson had to be stopped."

Silence.

"I couldn't let him do it. Years of fieldwork, excavation after excavation, most of the time pulling up nothing but potsherds. The semesters teaching undergrads with minds like sieves the ABCs of anthropology. All for nothing, if I let Don Nelson tell his theory of the storyknife. I couldn't let him. I had to stop him. Now I have to stop you."

Before Wy could yank back the flap, she heard the sound of a dull, metallic thunk. When she finally got the canvas out of the way, she found Jo in the act of rolling into one section of the excavation, her eyes closed and blood draining from her temple.

There was a movement to her right and her gaze shifted just in time to see McLynn, a determined frown on his face and a number two spade in his hands. The spade was already on the downswing and Wy instinctively stepped back, tripped over the Blazo box and went sprawling.

TWENTY-ONE

"Sir! Sir!" An ungentle hand shook his shoulder. "Sir, wake up!"

Liam swam up from a great depth. The light was dim and distant at first, steadily increasing in wattage, until it became so bright it hurt his eyes. The light resolved into a long, rectangular fixture on a ceiling somewhere. The two fluorescent bulbs behind the white plastic cover seemed to burn right through his retina, and he closed his eyes. Somebody groaned.

"Sir! Are you okay?"

His head hurt. No, that wasn't right, his head was thumping, pounding, hammering with pain. He felt his gorge rising. He opened his eyes again and this time saw Prince, her expression anxious. "Help me up."

"What?"

"Help me up."

Prince helped him sit up, and he staggered to the sink and vomited. The water ran cold and clean from the faucet and he held his head under it. The water swirling in the bottom of the sink turned pink. He kept his head under the faucet until it ran clear again. She was waiting with a tea towel when he stood up.

"Help me to a chair."

He propped his head in his hands. "How long have I been out?"

"Over an hour, if you got clobbered right after we split up."

He explored his scalp with tentative fingers; there was an enormous lump over his right ear and his right eye felt puffy. "Am I going to have a shiner?"

Prince regarded him gravely. "It looks like it. Who hit you?"

"I didn't see him. Where's my cap?"

Prince found it where it had rolled beneath the table. It no longer fit around his head. He adjusted the band to its widest extension. It perched on top of his lump at a precarious angle.

"Who do you think hit you?"

"I don't have a clue," Liam said. "How about you?"

Head trauma often resulted in short-term memory loss. Prince pulled out a chair and sat down. "I got Chad Donohoe's statement."

"Good."

"He saw the skiff pass him that night, he thinks around three a.m. Monday morning."

"You told me that two days ago."

"He signed his statement."

"Good."

"So did Fred Wassillie."

Liam squinted at her through his one good eye. "You didn't say Donohoe had somebody with him."

"He didn't."

Liam sighed and shifted carefully in a tentative attempt to sit upright. His head didn't fall off, so he was more patient than he might have been. "Look, Prince, you've obviously discovered some new evidence that you think is important, and any other time I'd be willing to let you lead me to it a piece at a time, but I've just been sucker-punched by an unknown assailant, I'm sitting here with a lump on my head the size of Denali, I've just lost my breakfast and most of last night's dinner, I can only see out of one eye and NOW IS NOT THE TIME TO GET CUTE!" Yelling hurt. He dropped his voice. "Talk. And keep it short and to the point. Who's Fred Wassillie, and what'd he say?"

Prince looked hurt. "He saw the skiff coming out of Kulukak Bay, too," she said stiffly.

"So we've got two witnesses. All the better."

"He saw it three hours earlier."

A short, charged silence. Liam wanted to lay his head—carefully—in his arms and close his eyes for the next month. "At midnight."

"Right around."

"He's sure of the time?"

Prince cleared her throat. "He was—ah—trysting with Edith Pomeroy on the deck of his boat at the time."

"And—ah—trysting with Ms. Pomeroy was such a memorable event that he was looking at his watch?"

"Mrs. Mrs. Edith Pomeroy. Ralph Pomeroy's wife. Ralph is a local fisher."

Liam looked at Prince, who was looking prim as a Victorian spinster. Maybe his father had slept alone the night before after all.

His father . . . Something nagged at the back of his mind. What was it, his father and—his father and . . . he couldn't remember. The walrus head on the opposite wall seemed to be laughing, head raised, ivory tusks ready to strike. "And he was persuaded to share this information—how, exactly?"

"I—ah—overheard him telling a couple of his friends about it. On my way back to the *Snohomish Belle*. About seven friends, actually. It seems Mrs. Pomeroy had been pretty elusive, and Mr. Wassillie was—er—collecting debts now owed him."

"I'm surprised he noticed the skiff."

"Apparently Mr. Wassillie thought it might be Mr. Pomeroy in search of his wife."

In spite of the throbbing of his skull, Liam had to smile. "You know, there sure were a hell of a lot of boats wandering around out there in the fog that night."

"It moves in, it moves out." Prince shrugged. "We keep finding holes to land through."

Liam repressed a shiver. "Don't remind me. Who was it? In the skiff? Who did Wassillie see?"

"He described a skiff—a dory, excuse me, a New England dory, a big skiff about twenty feet long. If not the twin, then very similar to the one Donohoe saw."

"Did he see who was in it?"

Prince didn't even try to hide her triumphant smile. "A man very similar to the one Donohoe saw."

They sat in silence for a moment, digesting this. "So he went out twice?"

"It would explain the two hours between the shootings and the fire."

"Yes, but why? Why go out twice?"

With some asperity, Prince said, "This is a man who can kill one woman for leaving him, one man for having her and three men and two kids for being there when it happened. I don't think we can expect rational thought from someone like that. I don't think we have to."

Mike Ekwok skidded in the door. "Sheriff!" he cried.

"It's Trooper," Liam said tiredly.

Ekwok saw Liam's shiner and the lump that was giving his cap a rakish tilt and his eyes widened. "What happened, Sheriff?"

Liam gave in. "Somebody coldcocked me when my deputy wasn't watching my back."

Prince looked offended, but Mike Ekwok's round face hardened into determined lines. "I'll back you up, Sheriff."

"Thanks, Deputy." Liam got to his feet, carefully avoiding Prince's gaze. "Are Wassillie and Donohoe somewhere around?"

"They're waiting on board the *Cheyenne*."

Liam spoke more sharply than he intended. "They're not in the same room, are they?"

"There's an old guy watching them. I snagged him off the dock and told him to stand guard, not let them talk."

The walrus leered at him from the wall. "The old man," Liam said suddenly. That's what he'd been trying to remember. "Walter Larsgaard's father. Is he here? In the house?"

"I . . . don't know. I didn't look."

"Well, look. Mike, help her."

Ekwok sprang into action. Five minutes later they were back. "House is empty, Sheriff."

"Did you check everywhere? Closets, basement, attic?"

"It's a crawl space, not a basement, and there is no attic." Prince's expression was quizzical. "Why?"

"I don't know, I . . ." Again Liam thought of his father. "Damn it, there's something I'm missing—wait a minute."

"What—"

Liam silenced Prince with a wave of his hand. His father. Don Nelson's father. Frank Petla's ancestral fathers, tribal fathers, his real father, his adopted father. Walter Larsgaard's father. Fathers and sons. Sons and their fathers, and what they did to each other, and what they did for each other. He remembered something he'd read in Don Nelson's journal, and his own reaction to it, and suddenly he understood. "Mike?"

"Yessir?"

"Are you a good friend of Walter Larsgaard, Senior?"

Mike's face showed his bewilderment. "I guess so. I've known Old Walter since we were kids."

"That's not what I asked. Were you friends?"

"We've lived in the same village all our lives."

Liam sighed. "Never mind. Did he drink?"

Ekwok shuffled his feet and looked at the floor.

"Mike—Deputy," Liam said sternly, "this is important. Was Old Walter a drinker?"

Ekwok shuffled some more and looked everywhere but at Liam. "I guess he'd been known to knock back a few Olys," he muttered finally.

"He do it often?"

"No more than anybody else."

"Does he or his son own a big skiff? A New England dory, a twenty-footer?"

Relieved to be off the hook, Ekwok gave an eager nod. "Sure. Nice big dory, new last summer. Twenty-one feet long. You could get to Togiak in it if you had to."

"Is it in the harbor?"

"I guess."

"Did you know Walter Junior was sleeping with Molly Malone?"

Mike Ekwok's face showed first surprise, and then envy. "No kidding? That lucky—" He turned whatever he'd been about to say into a cough. "No, Sheriff, I didn't know that."

"How would Walter Senior have felt about that?"

"I—hell, I don't know. He didn't poke his nose into much, Old Walter. He minded his own business, and he let people mind theirs. He was a good neighbor." Mike Ekwok sounded as if he had only just learned this fact, and was surprised that it was so.

"Sir—" Prince said.

"Did Wassillie say if the guy was rowing the dory, or if he had the outboard going?"

Prince consulted her notes. "Rowing."

"That matches the Jacobsons' statements. But Donohoe said the dory he saw had the kicker running."

Comprehension dawned. "Two different boats."

Liam shook his head. "The same boat. Two different men." He leaned his aching head on one hand. "I'm in his house," he muttered, staring at the walrus head. It wasn't leering now. "Who else would hit me?"

"Who do you think did?" Prince said, but she knew. So did Ekwok if his open mouth and staring eyes were any indication.

"Old Walter, that's who. He was in the first skiff, the one Jacobson saw going out, the one Wassillie saw coming in. He shot the crew of the *Marybethia*, and then he came home and either told his son what he'd done or his son guessed. Young Walter went out to destroy the evidence, and that's who Donohoe saw."

Prince stared at him, mouth slightly open.

"Young Walter must have been frantic to get rid of the evidence. He set fire to the boat, but it wouldn't burn, so then he tried to sink her. He must have been pretty sure he'd succeeded because he left to go back into town."

They left Ekwok behind in their run for the boat harbor. In spite of his aching head and the accompanying slight sense of disorientation, Liam was first down the gangway when they arrived, and first to step on board the *Cheyenne*. So it followed that he was the first to see the bodies.

"Son of a bitch!" Prince's voice rang out across the harbor. She leapt first to one downed man, then the other. "Mother-fucking son of a BITCH!"

"Donohoe and Wassillie?" Liam said.

Prince's face was red with rage. "Yes," she said tightly, regaining her poise. Mike Ekwok, looking scared, edged away from her. She knelt, felt for pulses. "Both dead. Looks like shot."

"Tell me this, Prince," Liam said. "Did the little old guy you set to guard them look anything like Walter Larsgaard?"

She stared at him, confused. "I don't know, I—he was Native," she said. "He was short, and he had black hair, and dark skin with wrinkles, and—"

"And besides, they all look alike," Liam said.

She flushed.

"They better stop all looking alike if you want to get ahead in this job," he told her. "I don't suppose you noticed if he had a rifle?"

"He was wearing a big coat," she said. She looked down at the sprawling forms of the two fishermen. There is no attitude as awkward as death. It didn't matter if you were a ballet dancer; death took pride in the ungraceful splay of limbs, the disjointed twist of the neck, the ungainly looseness of hands and feet. To look at death and know some carelessness of your own had caused it was not pleasant.

"Where's the . . . what was his boat's name?" Liam asked Prince. She looked at him, mute. "Young Larsgaard. Where is his boat?" She remained silent. "Prince, snap out of it! Where's Larsgaard's boat?"

He felt a timid touch on his elbow. "I know where it is, Sheriff." But of course by then the *Bay Rover* was long gone.

The shovel came whistling down. Wy rolled. It smacked into the dirt next to her head and she scrambled to her feet just in time to catch the business edge of the shovel against her shoulder. She looked down for a stunned moment to see blood welling from the cut. The shovel was coming at her again, McLynn amazingly calm, still with that determined frown on his face, as if he were in the process of deciding where the shovel would do the most good and estimating range and trajectory to target. Time seemed to slow down, as if she were in a dream. Only the blood was real.

The blood was in fact very real, staining the sleeve of her shirt, and the sight propelled her to her feet, just in time to catch the shovel on her shoulder. She turned, managing to deflect its edge, but the force of the blow sent her staggering into the other tent. The wall collapsed. The rest of the tent, unaccustomed to this kind of abuse, collapsed with it, and canvas engulfed her.

For a panicky moment she thought she couldn't breathe. Blows came at her from every direction, one catching her foot, another her thigh, a third her elbow, as she rolled and twisted and fought, the canvas as much as McLynn. She rolled into an object that fell over with a crash, probably one of the tables on the inside of the tent. Other crashes followed as she blundered through the folds of canvas. She had a gun in her plane, part of the survival gear required by law of any Bush pilot. If she could just get to the Cub and get the gun . . . Another blow caught her squarely between the shoulder blades.

"Goddamn it!" Suddenly, gloriously, she was angry. The hell with the gun, she was going to clean this little bastard's clock right here and right now with her bare hands. She caught a glimpse of daylight and dove for it, squirming out into the fresh air, a half step ahead of the maniac with the shovel. The shovel hit the opening in the fold of canvas a second after she had exited it, and she reached down to grab the canvas and yank it as hard as she could, pulling it out from under his feet. McLynn lost his balance and fell heavily. He was back on his feet almost at once, never dropping the shovel. All those years digging ditches in old graveyards had toughened him up.

The shovel came up again, and this time something happened, something deep inside her. Her feet were parallel, a shoulder's width apart, and without volition her hands and arms moved into Ward Off Left, right hand cupped and down, left hand cupped and up, most of her weight forward on her left knee. Of its own will her left hand shifted so that her forearm caught most of the blow, yielding but not giving way before it. Her right foot stepped forward and her right arm came around and up into Right Push Upward, her right hand grasping the shovel handle. She went into Pull Back and McLynn was jerked off balance and he lost his grip on the shovel and then lost the shovel.

Wy didn't know who was more surprised, herself or McLynn. "It works!" she said involuntarily. "You cranky old bastard, it actually works!" She looked at McLynn, who still couldn't figure out how he'd lost his weapon, and smiled at him. He fell back a step at the sight of that smile, and it widened. "God, I wish Moses could have seen that."

"It's okay," a weak voice said from the door of the one tent left standing. "I did."

Wy looked over to see Jo, bloody and maybe a little bowed, but otherwise conscious and back in the world.

It took them an hour of making wider and wider circles in the air before they found him, and that only after they'd spotted two other boats and come down to find they were the wrong ones. The *Bay Rover* was on a south-southwesterly heading, throttles all the way out. "How are we for gas?" Liam said.

Prince's voice was grim over the headset. "There is no av gas in Kulukak, so our nearest refueling is Togiak or Newenham." Her eyes narrowed as she checked the dials. One readout didn't please her, so she flicked the plastic cover with her finger. That must have helped because her brow cleared. "Depends on where he's going, sir," she said. "We're good for another hour or so."

Liam didn't inquire into the "or so." He'd always found ignorance an enormous comfort in the air, and he saw no reason to change that now.

"What do you want me to do?" she said.

"We might as well tell him we're here."

She looked apprehensive. "You're not going to jump out of this plane, are you, sir?"

"You're not going to make me jump off the float again, are you, Prince?" he replied. "Just lose some altitude, make a couple of passes, let him know he's not alone."

"He's got a rifle, sir."

He couldn't believe he'd forgotten that little detail. He blamed it on his headache, a repetitious thud that seemed to harmonize with the noise of the engine. "Okay, one quick pass, close enough for him to see us, and then climb to a safe distance." What was a safe distance? Liam wondered. Depended on the kind of gun Larsgaard had, he supposed. Ah well, anything for the cause of justice.

In a steep dive the Cessna fell from a thousand feet to one hundred. The engine roared, and the pain in Liam's head increased. The bow of the boat flashed by and they were climbing again, the engine flat out and Liam's aches and pains with it.

"It looks like he's headed there," Prince said, pointing.

Liam squinted against the sun. As usual, the fog had been left behind in Kulukak, clearing to blue skies as soon as they were out of the little bay. It was noon straight up, and the rays of the sun threw everything into bold relief against the darker blue of the water. There were half a dozen main islands in the Walrus Islands group, High, Round, Crooked, the Twins, Black Rock and even Summit, although Summit was a lot closer to the mainland. It looked as if Larsgaard was heading for one of the smaller ones. "This is a game sanctuary," he told Prince. "Off limits to just about everyone."

"Why the hell would he come here? He has to know he can't get away."

"Did you see that walrus head on the wall of Larsgaard's kitchen?"

"Yes."

"One of his friends told me that he's been hunting since he was a boy. He's been here before, knows the territory, which we don't." Liam tried to remember past the thumping in his head; someone had been talking to him about the Walrus Islands just recently. The plane hit an air pocket and his head bobbed forward and for a moment it felt as if the dense matter behind his forehead was going to detonate. Wy. Her smart-ass suggestion for their first date. "There's a big, wide beach where all the walrus haul out. That's where the hunters go for harvest. That's where he'll be. Can you land?"

"Easily," she said. "It's like glass."

"We got enough fuel to get back with all three of us on board?"

She flicked one of the dials again. "Yes."

They kept their distance, close enough to be in visual range but far enough to be out of gunshot. Sure enough, the *Bay Rover* dropped anchor off a dark-sand beach sandwiched between sheer vertical cliffs of rock the same color. One side of the beach, the one with the most sun, was strewn with big brown bags.

"What are those—" Liam started to say, and then he realized. They were walruses, hundreds of them, packed tightly one against the other across the sand, asleep in the sun, their ivory tusks gleaming white, their taut hides a golden brown. "Jesus."

"I hear they can weigh up to a ton and a half each," Prince said.

They looked bigger than that to Liam, but he had no more time to marvel. "He's launching a small boat!" Prince shouted, and pointed.

The tiny figure of a man jumped nimbly from deck to rubber raft. He was carrying something that could have been a rifle, but the raft didn't have a kicker, so he was going to have to row, which wouldn't leave any hands free for shooting. "Put her down," Liam said. "Can you taxi into the beach?"

Prince put the Cessna into a sharp left turn, banking so she could inspect the water close to the beach for any hidden rocks and reefs. Liam's head hurt too much for him to be afraid, but his ears did pop in protest. "Yeah, I think so. Here we go." She brought the Cessna around and set her down in a soft kiss of a landing. She taxied straight into the beach, but wasn't quick enough to beat Larsgaard, whose raft was already sitting at the edge of the tide, empty.

Liam stepped out on the float, drew his weapon and walked forward to hop onto the beach. Footsteps in the sand led from the beached raft directly toward the herd of walrus. They looked like they were sleeping, the whole bunch of them, soaking up rays. There was some twitching and grunting but for the most part they seemed dead to the world. He approached them cautiously, his headache forgotten. They were enormous creatures, all fat and fur and tusk.

A breeze came up. Liam was downwind. "Jesus!" he said again, this time for a different reason. The smell of ammonia was overpowering. They were sleeping in their own piss; a lot of it, judging by the smell. A three-thousand-pound beast would generate a lot of waste. Instantly his eyes began to water and he blinked them furiously, trying to see.

He heard someone say something that sounded like, "Tookalook."

Through a blur he thought he saw a small figure slip between two enormous ones and he started forward involuntarily.

"Asveq!" someone yelled, and Liam threw himself to the sand when a rifle went off. He rolled sideways and of course now his face was right in the sandy residue of urine and feces, and his eyes were tearing so badly he couldn't see at all. He couldn't seem to catch his breath, either, and it didn't help that the sound of the rifle shot had woken up the walrus. All of them.

A roar sounded right over his head and he looked up, blinking the tears away to see a bull rear up, tusks that must have been two feet long at present arms. Down they came, straight toward him, in a slashing move that would have splattered him all over the beach if he hadn't pushed himself away, scuttling backward on hands and feet like a crab. At the same time something swept down on ebony wings, straight into the face of the walrus.

The whole herd was up now. Their grunting roars of protest were deafening. On his feet, Liam was dazed and disoriented. He still had his weapon but what good would a little popgun like this be? The bullets would be lost in all that blubber. He wiped his arm on his sleeve in time to see a walrus lumber toward him, probably the same one, tusks raised again. No, this one had a tusk broken off halfway up, leaving a jagged point that looked even more threatening than a whole one. He thought Prince yelled something but he couldn't hear what. He saw what he thought was Old Walter in the middle of the herd, standing still, watching him. Down the tusks flashed; again he avoided them by the merest inch. He thought he saw the dark-winged shadow diving at the walrus for the second time, and the walrus dodging out of the way of its wickedly curved beak.

Prince yelled again, and Liam blundered backward until he ran into her. They both sat down heavily in the sand, and watched as the river of brown fur poured into the water, yipping and barking and growling and roaring defiance. A moment later there was nothing left but roiled sand and glassy water and blue, blue sky.

"He's gone."

"He must have been flattened by the herd."

"I don't see anything, do you?"

"No." She swept the beach with the glasses. When no walrus popped up from behind a rock, she ventured forward to explore the beach where Larsgaard and the walrus had been. When she came back she said, "Okay, this isn't weird or anything."

"No sign of him?"

"None." She paused, and said doubtfully, "You don't think they ate him, do you?"

"I think they mainly eat fish and shellfish."

"Oh." Nobody said anything for a while. "Well, he's gone."

"He's gone," Liam said. He got to his feet. "And so are we. Let's head for home."

TWENTY-TWO

Their dinner date had been postponed a week and changed to a picnic on the beach. They were one short, as Tim was long gone up the river with Moses, but as Wy was guiltily aware, they didn't even miss him.

"I was so smug," Liam said, regarding the hot dog he held suspended over the flame with a critical eye. The raven croaked agreement from a convenient spruce branch on the cliff. "I had them both, both perps, locked up in the local jail. Petla was as good as convicted, and I didn't think twice about walking into Larsgaard's house. I didn't think for a moment Larsgaard Junior didn't do it. Sure, there were things wrong with his story, but hell, he had means, motive, opportunity."

"So did I, in May." Her smile was tentative, as if she wasn't sure it was permissible to joke about that yet.

He grinned at her. "Yeah, but you I'm hoping to get back into the sack at some point. I couldn't put you in jail."

She laughed.

"Besides, Larsgaard had even confessed, for crissake."

"True."

"And then there's Frank Petla." He looked at where the bandage showed beneath the arm of her T-shirt. "He was there, he had a gun, he was in possession of goods stolen from the scene, including the murder weapon, he'd assaulted two people in fleeing said scene, what more could I want?"

"Yeah, well, Frank kind of set himself up for that."

"Still," Liam pulled his hot dog out of the fire, decided it didn't pass and put it back. "So after we got back to town and find Don Nelson's real killer in your custody, I went after Dick Ford again. I found him this time, up in Icky helping Aneska Ugashik fillet her salmon so she could hang it. He tells me he loaned his four-wheeler to Frank Monday morning, and then he tells me that he was fishing the same section of river Frank was over the weekend, Cache Creek, and Frank was out there all day both days, and Charlene was right, he didn't kill Don Nelson."

"He shot McLynn. He hit Diana."

"He was drunk."

"Don't make excuses for him, Liam. He's already made enough of them for himself."

"You know who I think of when I think of Frank Petla?"

"Who?"

"Tim."

"Tim?" Wy ruffled up. "He's nothing like Tim, he—"

"I didn't mean it like that. I meant, Tim gets a chance. You gave him a chance."

"Charlene and Peter gave Frank a chance."

"Yeah. Well. Maybe if they'd gotten to him sooner. Or for longer."

"Maybe." She didn't sound convinced. She'd taken a liking to Diana Prince, and she didn't take kindly to Frank shooting her. "Are things back to normal now?"

He thought about the nine funerals in Kulukak, the plain coffin shipped home to Seattle. "It is for us. Not for others. But yeah, for us, I think so."

"Is your father gone?"

"Oh yeah."

The raven let loose with a series of calls that sounded like one big, continuous belly laugh.

"Why do you say it like that?"

Liam thought back to two days before, two weeks after Don Nelson had been found dead on the site of the old dugout. "So you had the wrong man," Charles had said.

"The wrong men," Liam had said equably.

Charles shook his head. "Sloppy."

"Fairly," Liam agreed. "Must be hereditary."

"I beg your pardon?" There was frost on Charles's vowels.

"I called your office. At Hurlburt Field."

"Really?" Charles examined the contents of his glass with interest. "Why, when I'm right here?"

"You are no longer assigned to Hurlburt. You up for promotion, Dad?"

Charles laughed it off. "I'm always up for promotion."

Liam had heard that kind of laughter before, the laughter of military officers trained to support one another in life-and-death situations and yet oh so aware that a misstep here, a missed salute there and you were retiring at your present rank. It was sharply edged, competitive laughter that gave no quarter and had nothing to do with humor. "Sure you are. You've been a colonel now, what, five, six years? About time to move up, isn't it? What's next? Major general?"

"Brigadier," Charles said involuntarily. His mouth snapped shut and formed a thin line.

"That's right, brigadier," said Liam, who had remembered that perfectly well but had wanted to see if Charles would jump at the bait. "Means you're off active flight duty, right, your next promotion?"

He waited with every outward sign of being willing to wait until this time next year for Charles's answer, until his father said reluctantly, "Not necessarily."

"Yeah, but you'll be flying a desk sooner or later, so it makes sense that you'd already be looking for a job that suited you. So then I called your new office."

Charles frowned down at his plate, disconcerted by Liam's sudden change of subject. "How did you get the number?"

"Innate charm," Liam replied. "Also hereditary. You're working on some kind of Superfund cleanup task force, aren't you, Dad? In fact that's the real reason why you're here. Not to facilitate turning redundant Air Force buildings over to the local community, but to hide a toxic waste site."

"I don't know what you're talking about. I've got to get back, anyway." Charles pushed his plate away and half rose to his feet.

"Sit down, Dad." Charles had sat down, had glared at Liam from the other side of one of Bill's booths where they were having a meal before Charles shipped out. "Don Nelson had it all down in his journal. He found your dump site. He went down to the river below the dump site and smelled fumes, so he figured it was leaking. He wrote to a reporter for the *News*." A good one who could be your worst nightmare, Liam thought, and wondered why he hadn't said it out loud.

"I had a friend do some searching on the Net for me. Fuel spills into fresh water are less publicized than ocean spills, although spills into fresh water are way more destructive. Freshwater is more sensitive to a spill than salt water, plus people and other mammals drink fresh water, and birds nest in it, fish lay eggs in it, mosquitoes give birth in it, like that. And of course the fish eat the larvae and the birds eat the fish and the people eat the birds and pretty soon you've got toxic poisoning of human beings, never mind the environment. Did you know," he added parenthetically, "that human beings are inedible? It's a fact. We sprayed DDT all over the place for years and it got into the food chain and now we're inedible. I ought to find that comforting, but I don't somehow."

Maria stopped by with another round of drinks. Charles flashed his automatic smile. Maria wilted a little, rallied and moved on to the next table.

"You get the idea, Dad," Liam said. "You spill petroleum or petroleum by-products into fresh water and it gets into everything from the algae up." He took a bite of cheeseburger. "You want to know the worst kind of fuel spill there is?"

Charles, busy with his own burger, didn't reply.

"I'll tell you," Liam said. "Light refined products. Kerosene. Gasoline. Jet fuel. It spreads like that"—he snapped his fingers—"and it soaks right into the ground. No surface tension to speak of, like crude oil has. Specific gravity is way lighter than crude, and viscosity . . . well, hell, jet fuel hasn't much more than lighter fluid. The fumes evaporate, there isn't any residue, you'd hardly know it was there." Liam dug into his fries. "Until it starts showing up in your drinking water as benzene. A known carcinogen. Cancer-causing substance," he added helpfully.

"I know what carcinogen means," Charles snapped.

Liam wiped his mouth with a napkin and leaned forward,

speaking in a low voice. "Good. Because I want you to know just what it is YOU'VE BEEN DOING OUT ON THAT FUCK-ING BASE!"

There was a reasonable lunch crowd at Bill's that day, and conversation stilled for a moment when Liam's roar echoed around the room. But people were eating and drinking and talking and laughing, and Jimmy was singing about fruitcakes strutting naked through the crosswalk in the middle of the week, so it was only a momentary lull. Bill eyed Liam narrowly before deciding to let it ride and returning to her New Orleans guidebook. It was open to the section on graveyards, which in New Orleans, she had informed everyone the previous day, were a tourist attraction.

For his part, Liam felt another root send out tentative tendrils into Newenham ground. He wouldn't have put it in quite those words, but he was rallying to the defense of his new home. He was telling his father, Air Force Major Charles Bradley Campbell, You may not shit in my nest. He let his voice drop back to a normal tone. "You've been burying fifty-five-gallon drums of byproducts, haven't you? I saw all the heavy equipment at the base. Thought it was mostly there for snow removal, and it probably was, to begin with." Liam ate a fry with more relish than he was feeling. "Why, Dad? Do you make general quicker if you don't go to all the time and expense of disposing of toxic waste in an environmentally acceptable manner?"

Charles wiped his hands on his napkin and folded it precisely in fours. "You said there was a journal?"

"Yeah, there's a journal."

"What are you going to do with it?"

Liam looked at the last of his cheeseburger with regret, and savored it as it went down. "I had the M.E. test a sample of Nelson's tissue. He and McLynn had been getting their drinking water out of the Snake River. They'd been filtering it, of course, for beaver fever. But Nelson had traces of benzene in his body."

"I repeat," Charles said, very controlled, "what are you going to do with the journal?"

"I don't know," Liam said. His brow creased in deep thought. "Wy's a friend of that reporter Nelson wrote to," he offered. "Do you think she'd be interested?"

Charles's mouth set in a thin line. "Cut the crap, Liam. What do you want?"

"I want you to dig up that dump east of the archaeological dig," Liam said promptly.

"Do you know how much that would cost?"

"Nope," Liam said. "Don't care, either. Dig it up and dispose of it properly. And I'll be checking, Dad. Wy and I will be doing fly-bys on a regular basis. Dig it up, move it out, dispose of it, and I don't mean drop it in the Nushagak. I'll find out if you do, and I'll resurrect that journal and the results of that tissue sample. I'm pretty sure this was all your own idea, so I don't imagine the Air Force would be pleased to hear officially about it." He smiled. "One thing for sure after that: you wouldn't have to sweat out any more promotion reviews."

"You're blackmailing me," Charles said.

"Oh, you noticed," Liam said. "It's my first attempt, I was afraid it wouldn't go over. Yeah, I'm blackmailing you, and it's a damn sorry thing to have to do to your own father." He wiped his hands and tossed his napkin down. "You raised me better than that, Dad."

Thinking back on it now, on this lazy evening on the beach, he looked down at the powerful flow of the Nushagak and wondered what an analysis of its waters would produce. Maybe that was one of those things he was better off not knowing.

He wouldn't give Nelson's journal to Jo. He never would have, no matter what he'd said to his father. Jo was going to have to leave without her story. He hadn't even told Wy about what Nelson had written.

For better or worse, Charles was Liam's father, and if you were any kind of a human being, you looked out for your own. He hadn't told Charles that, of course. He wasn't sure he ever would. But he had used Nelson's journal to start the fire which was cooking their dinner.

For now, he had a hot dog so burned it was about ready to drop off the stick onto the fire, just the way he liked them, and a bun prepared with mustard, onions, relish, shredded cheese and jalapeño peppers, just the way he liked them. He was sitting next to the woman of his choice, that goddamn raven was keeping his distance, and . . . "Wy?"

She was absorbed with putting the finishing touches on her own hot dog. "What?"

"I know you were really young when you left the village and moved to Newenham, but do you remember any Yupik?"

She looked up from the bun upon which she was lavishing mustard. "Some. A few words. Like the word for storyknife." She said it, and it still sounded like "yawning ruin" to him, just like it had when Frank Petla said it.

"What about 'tookalook'?"

"What?"

" 'Tookalook,' " he said. "I heard it for the first time this week, and I was wondering what it meant."

"Tookaluk. Tookalook. Um, maybe *tulukaruk*?"

"Oh," he said, disappointed. "That's just the name of the dig."

"Yeah," she said, heaping chopped onions on the bun. "And raven."

Overhead, the raven clicked, *k-k-k-k-k-krACK*. "Tulukaruk means raven?"

"Uh-huh."

Liam thought about that afternoon on the island beach, with the hundreds of walrus between him and Old Walter. The old man had said two words. "Tulukaruk. Asveq." Raven. Walrus. Had he seen a raven, there on the beach that afternoon? He said, "How long did you say Tim was going to be gone?"

"You didn't answer my question," she said severely. "Why did you say, 'Oh yeah,' like that when I asked you if your father was gone?"

He fell in love all over again with her reproving frown and abandoned the hot dog to the fire to pull her into his arms. She came willingly and they tumbled down next to the big driftwood log they'd been leaning against. "God, you feel good." He looked down into her face, at her eyes, her skin, her mouth, her hair. Maybe another man wouldn't see what he saw, maybe another man wouldn't see the beauty and the intelligence and above all the strength, but then maybe that was what made her the only woman for him. "You could live without me, couldn't you?" he said suddenly.

"I have," she said simply, and smiled. "But I'd much rather not. If I have a choice."

"You don't," he said, and kissed her. He had her shirt up and her bra open and then he was cupping her breasts, biting her nipples so that she whimpered and arched her back, instantly ready. "That's what I love most about making love with you," he murmured. "The way you respond. You go off like a rocket when I barely touch you, don't you?" He laved the nipple he'd bitten with his tongue. She moaned, her breath coming faster, and he felt like the king of the world. He slipped the snap of her jeans and slid a hand between her legs. "You're wet, ready and waiting for me. Only for me, Wy."

"Please," she said, "hurry."

"I don't want to hurry," he said. "I like you needy." He rolled her to her back and captured her hands to hold them over her head.

"Liam."

His free hand wandered, down, up, in. Her breath caught and her hips moved against his hand. He sought out another spot with his thumb and rubbed, oh so gently. Her eyes squeezed shut and she arched and cried out, and he watched with immense pleasure as a deep, dark flush rushed up over her breasts and throat and face. "You are so easy, Chouinard. How many times can I make you come?"

She opened her eyes to meet his. "That was one," she whispered, and he was on her and in her before the last word was out of her mouth.

It was almost dark, or as dark as it gets in August in Alaska, and the fire had burned down to a steady bed of dark red embers. They lay breast to breast, and Liam could feel the slow thud of her heart next to his, the skin of her back warm against his palm. Jimmy's right, he thought through a haze of contentment. Maybe twenty-four hours, maybe sixty good years, it's not that long a stay. This was what made the sixty years good.

She stirred. "So Walter's home now?"

"Yeah." He shifted and pulled her closer. "I could have charged him with obstruction of justice and accessory after the fact, but hell, he's just lost his lover, their child and his father. Going home to an empty house that is going to stay empty for the rest of his life is punishment enough."

"Why did he do it? Old Walter? Why did he kill her, all of them?"

"He had a problem with booze. He used to live in Anchorage but he spent most of his time between Fourth Avenue and Cook Inlet Pre-Trial. The last time, about four years ago, right after Walter's wife ran off with the vipso, Young Walter flew to Anchorage and brought his father home. Kulukak's a dry town, but Newenham's only a plane ride away. I finally got Mike Ekwok to tell me that Old Walter was in the bag more often than not. I'm figuring he was fairly well oiled that Sunday night."

"But why, Liam?"

"Molly Malone was pregnant."

Wy raised her head. "I don't see why —"

"It was her husband's baby, or so she told Young Walter. It was David's baby, and she was going to have it and be a good mother and a good wife and that was why they had to break things off. Young Walter didn't believe her. He made the mistake of telling his dad so."

"Still, why —"

"Wy, never try to understand a drunk. Young Walter says that when he came home that night, Old Walter told him his son's son was free of his *gussuk* mother, that his spirit had been released to return when Young Walter took another wife, a proper daughter of the walrus this time."

"A 'daughter of the walrus'?"

Liam thought of the walrus head mounted on the wall of the Larsgaard kitchen, of the lack of remains of Old Walter on that gray sand beach. "Apparently Old Walter had something of a fetish for walruses."

"Oh."

"Like I said, don't try to make a drunk make sense. It'll drive you crazier than he already is."

"Still . . ." She pressed against him, seeking comfort. "To shoot seven people —"

"Eight, if you count the baby."

"Eight — I — Liam, I can't imagine ever getting that drunk."

"Not many people can, and we should be grateful." He ran his hand down Wy's spine. A boat went by, but it was far enough offshore and the driftwood log they were lying behind was high enough that they were hidden from view. He noticed Wy hadn't bothered to check, and smiled to himself. "Max Bayless saw Molly Malone and young Walter together last summer. I talked to him on the phone last week. Bayless won't come right out and admit it, but young Walter says he tried to blackmail him. He told Bayless to shove it. I think he was hoping that Bayless would tell David, that it would force a situation so Molly would leave David for him. Well, Bayless told him, all right, but all David did was fire him."

And start an affair with Tanya Bernard, he thought. The dates were about right, and she was ripe for the picking. Poor little Tanya.

"Luckiest thing that ever happened to Max Bayless," Wy said. "If he'd still been David Malone's deckhand, he'd be dead today. What about Frank? What's going to happen to him?"

"Frank is another matter. He assaulted a state trooper. Frank's going away for a while."

"And McLynn?"

"McLynn will never take another free step in his life, not so long as I have breath in my body." Liam's hand strayed to rub lightly at the bandage on her arm. "I'm sorry for this, Wy."

She raised her head. "What? Why? You had nothing to do with it."

"Yes, I did," he said. "Yes, I did. I should have taken McLynn's personality into account. Every sentence he started began with 'I' or 'My.' 'Artifacts I have excavated over the summer,' remember? 'I was going to stop him.' Nelson didn't help him on the dig, Prince wasn't with him when he tried to stop Frank. A guy who can see only himself in any picture is someone you don't turn your back on. And I should have listened to you."

"Me?"

"Yes, you. You're very observant, Wy. You'd have made a good cop."

"Thanks, I'll stick to flying."

"You told me exactly what McLynn did when you landed at the dig. Something about that bothered me, but I was paying more attention to you than I was to the case. As the calypso poet says, I've got to learn to play all of my hunches. McLynn went to the camp tent first, not the dig tent like he usually did, you said."

She sat up. "I didn't even think — he meant me to find Nelson's body, didn't he?"

"Let's say he didn't want to be the one who did find Nelson's body. And the dig tent flap was tied, wasn't it?"

"From the outside!" She was indignant. "That prick!" She looked down at him. "Did I tell you how I got the shovel away from him?"

His chest shook with a laugh. "About fourteen times."

"Oh." Silence. "I was standing facing him, see, and I went into Horse Stance, hands at —"

She squealed when he rolled over on her and started tickling her.

The voice came to them from the top of the bluff. "Wy! Wy?"

"It's Jo, Liam, let me up."

"Jo and me have got to talk," he mumbled, disgruntled.

"Jo?" Wy called. "What do you want?"

"There's somebody here who wants to talk to you. He's coming down."

"Wait a minute!"

"Too late, he's coming down."

"Shit!" Wy said, scrambling for her clothes. She got one leg into a pair of jeans, realized they were Liam's and threw them at him. "Get dressed!"

Getting naked with Wy Chouinard had been a cherished goal for a very long time and Liam wasn't ready to get dressed. Grumbling, he did so, because he didn't know who this visitor was, and there wasn't anyone besides Wy he wanted to be naked with anyway. "Who is it?"

A log shifted on the fire and the flames blazed up as the man took the last step down in one big jump and landed with a thump in the sand. He was of medium height, with well-defined shoulders, a thick pelt of dark blond curls and a pair laughing green eyes.

"Oh my god," Wy said.

Liam squinted at the man coming up the beach. "Who's that?"

Wy got to her feet. "Gary? Gary, is that you?"

The man saw her and broke into a grin. "Wy!" He sprinted forward, kicking sand up behind him, and grabbed Wy in his arms to swing her around in a circle. "Wy!" He kissed her, an exuberant and enthusiastic smack you could have heard on the other side of the river.

Liam stood up, at first astonished and then annoyed. He was afraid that anything that came out of his mouth would make him sound like a jealous fool, so he contented himself with brushing the sand off of his jeans, which he was suddenly very glad he had on.

After what seemed an inordinately long time Gary put Wy down and looked at Liam over her shoulder. "Gary Dunaway," he said, and stuck out a hand.

Liam accepted it with reluctance and a nameless, nagging fear. "Liam Campbell." Dunaway's handshake was firm and dry. Liam hated it.

"I figured. My sister told me about you."

"Jo Dunaway? Jo's your sister?"

Gary nodded, grinning. It wasn't a humorous grin, Liam noted that right off, it was hard-edged and challenging and not very friendly at all. "Yeah, my sister the muckraker. Lincoln Steffens lives."

Wy chuckled. She was flushed and smiling, Liam noted. "I always knew she was possessed by someone."

"So that's how you know Gary," Liam said to Wy, determined to relegate this guy into a safe, brotherly role.

Her smile faded. "Sort of. I went home with Jo for Thanksgiving, the first year we were in Anchorage. That's where we met."

"And I followed her all the way to college," Gary said, still grinning, still with that edge, still with that challenge.

Wy's laugh was weak and unconvincing.

Liam felt himself bristle, and told himself to knock it off. It wasn't like there weren't any women out there before Jenny.

Gary's grin widened.

In an instinct that went back to the caves, Liam stepped next to Wy and settled his hand at the base of her neck. He could feel the muscles tense beneath his palm, and he waited with a curious kind of fatalism for her to shrug him off.

She didn't. She looked Gary straight in the eye and said, every inch the polite hostess, "It's great to see you again, Gary. How have you been?"

Overhead, the raven stretched out his neck and gave a long, mocking croak.